NOT FOR SALE

"S-speak up. We haven't got all night."

"Would that we did, my love," he teased. As she would have protested, he raised a hand. "Very well. Once again, I've come to tell you I'm prepared to offer you full price."

Viveca's pulse dove straight into her belly at his provocative statement. "For what?" she rasped.

His gaze gleamed with devilment. "Should I say for you?"

"Say it and die."

He grinned. "For this house, of course."

She blinked angrily. "Mr. Beecher, I'm beginning to question your sanity—or rather, the lack thereof. As you're more than aware, this property is *not* for sale. And you've wasted yet another trip over here."

His gaze slid insolently up and down her body. "Oh, I wouldn't call it wasted."

The Phantom Of The Bathtub

Eugenia Riley

LOVE SPELL   NEW YORK CITY

LOVE SPELL®

August 2006

Published by

Dorchester Publishing Co., Inc.
200 Madison Avenue
New York, NY 10016

ISBN 0-505-52652-2

The name "Love Spell" and its logo are trademarks of Dorchester Publishing Co., Inc.

Printed in the United States of America.

Visit us on the web at www.dorchesterpub.com.

This book is dedicated,
with love always,
to Mary Elizabeth Lundblad
1910–2004.
Adored aunt, cherished friend,
family matriarch, flower of the South.
We'd all love to have you haunt us,
but only heaven can own you now.

Chapter One

Savannah, Georgia, 1896

Viveca Stanhope's first glimpse of Hangman's Square was a fright.

She heard her man, Emmett, utter a gasp as he turned their rented buggy onto moss-draped Lost Lane, which fronted the square. Lost Lane, indeed! Although the canopy of green shading their path was lovely, ruts and weeds marked the road, a peculiar smoky haze hung about the landscape, and there was a stagnant smell in the air. And although the red brick Georgian mansion in the foreground appeared respectable enough with its neat hedgerows and shiny shutters—the gazebo next to it quite charming—the house looming beyond, which she recognized from the photograph Agent Cornelius had sent her as *her* house—looked even more ghastly than it had in the tintype, if that was possible.

The aging Greek Revival monstrosity sported peeling Tuscan columns and wraparound verandas with missing porch railings. Several loosely attached shutters rattled in the breeze, and on the tarnished slate roof, a crow cackled from his ominous perch on a bent lightning rod. On the graying front gallery, a porch rocker creaked to and fro, as if a ghost were sitting there whiling away the afternoon.

Only two other houses faced the square—an even more ramshackle Gothic Revival house to the east, and a neat, shuttered, stone Victorian mansion to the south. On the square separating her from her other neighbors, a few benches had been placed about a massive, centuries-old oak that snaked its gnarled branches through the haze. Usually, the site of such a tree was awe-inspiring for Viveca, but this tree somehow elicited a shudder instead. Perhaps it was the cemetery extension that loomed behind them to the west.

Viveca hadn't expected her first glimpse of her new home to rouse such a sense of menace. Indeed, ever since she and Emmett had arrived in Savannah on the Central Railroad from Macon, her initial glimpses of the Southern port city had been inspiring ones: the splendor of the Factor's Walk and the Cotton Exchange; the majesty of the tall clipper ships docked in the Savannah River; the glory of Old Town with its gracious, shaded antebellum homes surrounding verdant squares; the quaintness of the trolleys, so reminiscent of her San Francisco days; the glorious blooming of azaleas, dogwood and magnolia; the citizens in their finery, strolling about their daily routines in shops, offices, parks and eateries.

Then Emmett had driven them past headstone-studded Colonial Cemetery . . . and now, it seemed, they had turned a corner smack into hell. Disquieted, Viveca cooled her face with her ivory-slatted fan and wiped a thin layer of sweat from her brow with a gloved hand. She batted at a mosquito buzzing at her face. Although she hardly missed the cold, damp air of San Francisco, if this was May in Savannah, she already dreaded July!

With the large dun-colored horse plodding closer to Viveca's new abode, Emmett turned his graying head toward his mistress and pointed a brown finger toward the stacks of debris piled in the weed-choked front yard. "That be our new home, Miss Viveca?"

Viveca heard the disapproval hardening his voice. She stiffened her spine and smoothed down a red curl that had broken free from her tight chignon. "Emmett, you're well aware that this house is all I can afford. There wasn't much left of Father's estate once I settled his debts."

"Why do you want to go across country like some gypsy with a bandwagon anyhow, miss?" he asked for surely the hundredth time since they'd embarked on their journey together. "You was doing right fine there in San Francisco. You had your daddy's house on Nob Hill—"

"Along with a mortgage and unpaid taxes that would have sent us both to the poorhouse in short order," she finished sharply.

Emmett harrumphed.

"Accordingly, as I remembered Father's dear friend Mr. Cornelius in Savannah, it seemed only logical that we should move here where I can afford suitable lodgings—"

"I seen chicken coops more fittin' than this," Emmett grumbled. "You're just running away like a scar't kitten after Mr. Erskine made a fool of you, when it was him that done you wrong—"

"Emmett, please!" Viveca implored, lowering her voice. "You are meddling in matters that are none of your concern."

"*You* my concern, Miss Viveca."

That admonition brought an unwitting smile to Viveca's lips. She had, indeed, been Emmett's concern for all of her twenty-three years, and she loved him dearly, even if his scolding did vex her at times. "Nevertheless, I've told you repeatedly that we must pretend Mr. Erskine . . . well, never even existed."

"Him and old Lucifer too, eh? Well, it just ain't fittin' how you stole out of town like some tainted lily . . ."

As he continued his lecture, Viveca sighed, realizing her pleas were futile. Emmett had been a family institution for over fifty years and doubtless there was no changing him now. For that matter, she tended to be rather outspoken herself.

When at last he'd exhausted his indignation, she stated

calmly, "Emmett, my point is, no one in this town is aware that I fled San Francisco like some 'soiled dove,' and we must keep things that way. We'll have a new beginning here."

"Yeah, right here in shantytown," he drawled back, pulling on the reins.

Viveca was prepared to issue a sharp rejoinder, but her outrage melted as she watched her manservant hitch himself down out of the buggy with slow, pained awkwardness. She noted how frail his back was, how heavily lined his face. Bless his soul, he was getting quite old. Nonetheless, fully aware of his stubborn pride, she accepted his assistance out of the conveyance, grimacing as the horse snorted and swung his smelly tail too close to her nose. She smoothed down the lines of her navy blue traveling suit and adjusted the plume on her matching, round-brimmed hat. With a brave nod toward the commons, she remarked, "At least the square is green and shady."

Emmett jerked his thumb toward the small area. "Guess that be the Hanging Oak."

"Oh," Viveca muttered, glancing balefully at the serpentine tree. No doubt Emmett was right, and no wonder the oak seemed so creepy. When Mr. Cornelius had mentioned in one of his letters that her new home was on "Hangman's Square," Viveca had found the term quaint. It hadn't occurred to her to ask whether folks had actually been hanged here . . . doubtless, it should have!

Nonetheless, she straightened her spine and marched toward the rusty gate. "I see no sign of Mr. Cornelius."

"Yep, he hiding out like a rat in a hole after he snookered you on this place."

"Emmett, enough!"

As they walked into the yard, Viveca turned toward the Georgian mansion next door just in time to watch a tall, handsome gentleman emerge through French doors onto his side veranda. Broad-shouldered, hatless, he wore his thick dark hair rakishly down to his collar, and was dressed in a black morning coat and striped dark trousers. Puffing away on a cigar, he presented an image of debonair disdain—and he seemed to be scowling at her.

Why ever for? "That must be the neighbor Mr. Cornelius spoke of," she muttered. "I must say he appears quite unpleasant."

"Think he be wishing for a bolt of lightning to set this place afire."

Casting Emmett a forbearing look, Viveca continued through the yard, wrinkling her nose at a pungent, rotting odor, grimacing at the sight of rickety rattan furniture strewn about, rusty food tins and broken mason jars, splintered wood and discarded fixtures. Given Emmett's foul temper, she dared not state the obvious, that this place *was* a junkyard and would need a great deal of work.

Suddenly she turned, distracted, at the sound of hoofbeats, and watched a portly man in a white Panama suit and broad-brimmed hat gallop up on a large gray horse. Sliding to the ground, the newcomer huffed and puffed his way into the yard, red-faced and beaming. "Miss Viveca! Is that you, Miss Viveca?" he called in a pronounced Georgia drawl.

"Mr. Cornelius?"

Arriving before her in a cloud of mingled sweat and pomade, he extended a plump hand. "Welcome to Savannah, Miss Viveca."

She briefly shook his damp, fleshy hand and found herself staring into a round face with a thin black mustache and unusually dark eyes. Although disquieted, she murmured back, "Thank you, Mr. Cornelius."

He mopped his brow with a handkerchief. "I regret my tardiness, but unhappily, dear Mother had another sinking spell."

"Oh, I'm sorry to hear of it." Viveca inclined her head toward Emmett. "My man, Emmett Taylor."

With a cursory nod toward Emmett, Cornelius inquired, "Have you met your neighbor, Maxwell Beecher, as yet?"

Viveca glanced toward the west, where their brooding neighbor still stood watching them. "Oh, you mean the scowling man on the veranda? No, we only just arrived."

Cornelius chuckled. "Well, I don't doubt Max is a bit peeved at the moment, as he wanted to buy this place himself."

"Indeed?" Viveca smiled triumphantly at Emmett.

Cornelius grimly shook his head. "Yes, Max wanted to steal it out from under me for a pittance, then raze the entire property. Can you imagine?"

Emmett raised an eyebrow at his mistress.

"Why, he even had the gall to call the house a damnable eyesore," Cornelius continued.

Viveca watched a frayed curtain flap at a broken windowpane. "Did he? Why ever would he say that?"

At Viveca's acerbic tone, Cornelius quickly stumbled on. "At—er—any rate, I knew old Miss Grace wouldn't want me to sell Hangman's House to just anyone—but to a lovely lady such as yourself who will better appreciate this property's undeniable virtues."

"Hangman's House?" Viveca repeated, wide-eyed. "You never told me my home is called *Hangman's House*. Did a hangman live here?"

"Only briefly," he assured her. "I believe there used to be an old jail annex at the back of your property."

"A jail, as well?"

"Actually, more like a death house."

"*What*?"

"You know, where the condemned await their fate."

Viveca's mouth fell open.

Visibly discomfited, Cornelius cupped a hand around his mouth and pivoted toward the house next door. "Oh, Maxwell!" he bellowed. "Care to come meet your new neighbor?"

Maxwell Beecher stared a moment longer, then turned and reentered his house, slamming the French doors.

"Why, I never!" Viveca gasped. "What a rude man."

Cornelius sighed. "Max is quite proud, but then, he hails from noble lineage. The Beecher Shipping Agency is quite an institution in Savannah, not to mention the half dozen or so banks Max's family owns here in the Low Country. Max's forebears built one of our original warehouses along Factor's Walk. Actually, as the sole heir to an impressive business empire, he's considered quite a catch," he added meaningfully.

"Well, I wouldn't catch him in a snake trap," Viveca asserted.

Emmett grinned, and Cornelius guffawed nervously. "At any rate, Max cannot stand being bested, and you definitely beat the pants off him with this deal, miss."

"I beg your pardon?" Viveca said archly.

Cornelius flushed deeply at his faux pas. "Figuratively speaking, of course."

"Well, I should hope so," replied Viveca primly.

"Besides, your offer was so much better than his."

Viveca glared.

"You mean you fleeced Miss Viveca like a lamb to the slaughter," Emmett drawled.

Cornelius sucked in an outraged breath. "I must say, miss, that your manservant here doesn't seem to know his place. Such an uppity attitude won't go over well in this town."

Now Viveca stared daggers at Cornelius. "Yes, Emmett doesn't know his place—and that's precisely how I like him. As for the community, I'm quite confident the backwater of Savannah will adjust."

Clearly chastised, Cornelius cleared his throat. "Well, isn't she a beaut?" he asked with a sweeping gesture toward the house.

"I suppose beauty is in the eye of the beholder."

Cornelius kicked a discarded tin can out of their pathway. "Shall we have a look?"

Viveca dreaded taking her next step. Indeed, she moved forward only to cringe at the sight of a scrawny black cat scurrying out of a basement window and skittering across their path, surely a less-than-fortuitous portent of their future here. "Heavenly days!" she declared, her hand flying to her breast.

Emmett crossed himself.

"You aren't superstitious, are you?" Cornelius inquired.

"Certainly not!"

"Well, Miss Fulton, the previous owner, was. Some even claim Grace died of fright."

Viveca's hand crept to the tight, high collar of her blouse. "You don't mean the house is—"

"Haunted? Just silly rumors, of course."

"Oh, yes, of course, why ever would the house be haunted?" Viveca mocked back. "Only a hangman's house, next to the Hanging Oak on Hangman's Square, with an enormous cemetery and the specter of an old jail both conveniently adjacent. No reason to shudder in the least."

Cornelius stared at Viveca as if she'd lost her mind.

"All we need now are a few black spiders and cobwebs," she muttered.

Indeed, Viveca batted at those pesky cobwebs as they climbed the squeaky steps to the main story. Staring at the front door with its chipped paint and crazed, oval glass panel, the rocker with its seemingly perpetual motion, she felt even more uneasy, as if some unbidden force were warning her not to proceed.

Unbidden? Hadn't she just seen a black cat?

Nonetheless, Viveca bucked up her courage and marched forward. Next to the door, she firmly stilled the creaking porch rocker with the tip of her leather slipper. But the instant she let up, the rocker began to rock to and fro again . . .

"My kingdom," Viveca managed.

Standing on a moth-eaten Persian runner in the wide, dilapidated central hallway of her new home, she glanced from the parlor on her left, with its frayed furniture and tattered wallpaper, to the dining room on her right, with its scarred Queen Anne table and rickety side chairs. The pungent odors of rot and mildew permeated the air, and dust motes hung in slanted beams of sunshine.

Cornelius cleared his throat. "The place could use a bit of spit and polish, eh, Miss Stanhope?"

"Spit and polish?" she repeated in amazement.

"Looks like you could spit it down in a good breeze," Emmett added drolly.

Cornelius glowered at Emmett. "The house does come fully furnished, including linens."

"How lovely." Near the front door, Viveca examined a length of moth-eaten lace curtain, sending a spiral of dust showering down upon herself. "Just lovely," she repeated, between violent sneezes.

Cornelius squirmed from foot to foot, then turned as a skinny black woman, dressed in a blue cottonade blouse and matching skirt, appeared in the hallway. Of medium height, with her fuzzy hair bound with a red silk bandu, she appeared to be about thirty years old. She grinned at Viveca with a flash of a gold front tooth.

"Mistress Stanhope?" she asked excitedly in a Jamaican accent. "You be Mistress Stanhope? I be Winnie, your housekeeper."

At first Viveca was too astounded to reply, staring at the woman's sharp features, strongly arched brows, and gleaming eyes. Thankfully, Emmett intervened, saying stoutly, "Miss Stanhope already has a man, thank you."

She waved off Emmett with a cackle. "Ah, what good is a mon, eh, mistress? Dey just gobbles food, drink rum and smoke ganja. You need a female to attend you, nuh true?"

Perturbed by the woman's presumptuous attitude and heavy Jamaican patois, Viveca turned to Cornelius. "Who *is* this woman?"

His gaze shifted away from her. "Er—Winnie was Mrs. Fulton's housekeeper. After Grace died, I paid her and—er—the others—"

"What others?"

"Er—a small stipend to keep the place running."

"They runnin' it straight to ruin, all right," pronounced Emmett.

"Oh, hush, you useless mon!" Winnie scolded him. Turning to Viveca, she tried to explain. "You see, ma'am, after Mistress Grace died, we got no place to go, me and Miguel and Ruvi—"

"You and Miguel and—"

"Dey only be t'ree of us," Winnie pleaded, as if she were being eminently reasonable.

"Three!" Viveca turned to Cornelius. "Mr. Cornelius, I was barely able to purchase this, er—this—"

"Pigsty?" Emmett supplied for her.

Viveca shot Emmett a withering look. "And I cannot possibly afford to engage additional servants."

With a glance at Winnie's stricken face, Cornelius replied, "Well, perhaps you and the others can work something out."

"But there's nothing to work out. I—"

Cornelius pulled out a document from his breast pocket. "Here's your deed, Miss Viveca, signed, sealed and delivered. Hangman's House is yours."

Hangman's House, indeed! Taking the document, Viveca restrained a shiver. "Mr. Cornelius, I wish you had warned me about this place, and its condition, which is so much worse than I was led to expect."

Cornelius blinked rapidly. "Madam, I hate to contradict you, but the truth is, you got a steal. Now I must be going. As I mentioned, Mother was sinking when I left her."

"Yes, we wouldn't want you to develop a reputation for *abandoning* sinking vessels," Viveca shot back.

As Emmett snorted, Cornelius protested, "This house may be graying and dilapidated, but it's structurally sound. Good day, miss."

With as much dignity as he could summon, Cornelius turned and strode for the door, only to yelp as a floorboard buckled beneath him. He launched into an undignified little sidestep, then half his leg crashed through the floorboards into the crawl space.

Winnie gasped; Viveca crossed her arms over her chest. "Just what were you saying about this house being *structurally sound*?"

Cornelius glanced back at her in helpless embarrassment as Emmett stepped forward, grimly offering the trapped man his hand. With Emmett's help and much grunting and groaning, Cornelius managed to retrieve himself from the floor-boards. After brushing off his trousers, he plopped on his hat in a vain attempt to hide a red face.

"Perhaps a termite or two," he muttered, then fled out the front door.

"Mercy," Viveca declared.

Before she could consider the matter further, the Jamaican woman dashed up and patted Viveca's arm. "Oh, mistress, we give t'anks you be here at last."

"You're grateful, are you?" Viveca rejoined. "Well, evidently you're not thankful enough to avail yourself of a dust mop."

The woman flashed a tight smile. "Surely you be tired after de long journey. I show you your betroom. But first, you want t'see de rest of de house?"

Exasperated, Viveca waved a hand. "Yes, I suppose, why not? Do take me on a grand tour of my sumptuous new quarters."

"Yes'um." With a puzzled frown, Winnie led them down the hallway and pointed to their left. "Mr. Cornelius, he mention you teach de piano. Dat be de parlor for your instrument, ma'am."

Viveca gazed about the room, past debris and broken-down furniture, to a corner where a mouse skittered in the dust. "Yes, I'm certain my students will be enchanted."

Winnie motioned. "Dis way, mistress." Further along the corridor, she pointed at a vivid portrait of a woman. "Dat be Miss Fulton."

Viveca was struck by the beautiful Impressionistic oil painting of a regal woman in her fifties, with upswept gray-brown hair and aristocratic features. The brush strokes were exquisite, the colors vibrant. Staring at the signature, she murmured, "My heaven. This is a Sargent."

Winnie nodded. "Miss Grace, she say Mr. Sargent done her portrait in London, right before she move here."

Viveca was bemused on all counts. "But doesn't she have family—someone—who would want this?"

"No, dere be no one. She a spinster lady. No fambly."

"How sad," Viveca murmured.

Winnie pointed at a room to their right. "Dat be your dining room."

Viveca stared at the tarnished brass chandelier over the table, the grimy sideboard at the far wall. "Yes, I can hardly wait to sample my first feast there."

Grimacing, Winnie led them through an opened doorway into a large room with scarred wood floors and weathered cabinets. "Dis be your kitchen, mistress."

"Heavens," Viveca muttered, her gaze darting from the filthy cast iron sink crammed with dishes and fitted with an old-fashioned pump, to the sooty stove where flies buzzed at a disgusting frying pan filled with congealed gravy, to the aging pie safe. "Delightful."

After they moved back into the hallway, Winnie opened the door to a room near the stairs. "Dis be your bat'room, mistress."

"Bat room?" Viveca repeated, horrified.

Winnie snickered. "Ease up, mistress. We got dem, too, de bats, up in de attic. Dis be where you scrub yourself."

"Oh. The *bathroom*."

"Dat what I say, mistress. De bat'room."

Viveca ventured inside the small room. At least there was an indoor toilet, but it was filthy, and the porcelain sink had decayed into little more than a rust bucket. In the rectangular alcove at the rear, she spotted spigots for hot and cold water, even a small coal water heater on the floor. But there was only a large laundry tub where the bathtub should have been—she could spot its previous outline on the weathered floorboards.

Stepping into the vacant spot, she felt a sudden chill. Even though the day was muggy and she was warmly dressed, she found herself trembling, and rubbed her jacketed arms. "Why is it so cold over here?"

"Oh, dere be a cold spot right dere where de bat'tub us'ta

be," the woman replied matter-of-factly, as if that explained everything.

Casting Winnie a bemused look, Viveca retreated a few steps and at once shook off the chill. "How bizarre. Emmett, you'll need to check for a draft over there."

"Yes'um."

"And whatever happened to the bathtub?" Viveca asked.

Winnie's eyes widened and she crossed herself. "Dat be de haunted bat'tub, mistress."

"Haunted?"

"Spawn of the devil, dat t'ing. Mistress Grace, she have Ruvi and Miguel heave it outside to be done wit' its evil."

"You're joking!" Viveca declared. "She actually *threw out* her bathtub?"

Winnie's eyes gleamed with a frightening intensity. "Oh, yes, ma'am. Got duppies in it."

"Duppies?"

Winnie gulped and continued in a tense whisper. "Ghosties, mistress. First time she use it, Mistress Grace, she come flyin' out of dat t'ing and all but have apoplexy. Run through de house naked, she did." The servant leaned toward Viveca and whispered dramatically, "Got a mon in it, mistress, a *dead* mon—"

Viveca had had her fill of this loony woman and her crazy ramblings. "Heavenly days, enough! 'Ghosties' and 'duppies' indeed. I can't believe you've allowed your mind to wander so foolishly—or that Miss Fulton even ran through this house in—in such a state." She gripped her forehead. "May we please move on? Suddenly I have a splitting headache."

The servant appeared contrite. "Oh, yes, mistress, you be all tuckered out, nuh true? I show you de upstairs?"

"Yes, please."

With Winnie leading the way, the threesome climbed the flight of creaky stairs at the end of the hallway. Going up, Viveca was forced to bat at additional cobwebs and shreds of hanging wallpaper. On the landing she grimaced at the sight of a two-foot-high stone gargoyle squatting on the floor-boards. The statue oozed an expression of grotesque horror with its twisted mouth, sunken eyes and garish horns.

Weren't gargoyles supposed to scare off evil spirits? Instead, this one seemed to ooze malevolence, and the prospect was hardly comforting.

Upstairs, bedroom doors flanked either side of a shabby old hallway. A faded carpet runner meandered toward warped French doors leading to the outside veranda, light beams filtering through and dancing on the old scarred floor. Behind them, a steep staircase rose toward what Viveca presumed was the attic.

Winnie headed toward the farthest door on the right. "Dis be de bestest room, mistress. You stay here."

Mercy, this was the best bedroom? Inside, Viveca glanced from the sagging four-poster bed with ratty mosquito netting, to the equally decrepit daybed, to the battered bureau and wardrobe, to the oppressive velvet draperies shrouding the windows. The only redeeming light filtered through the gauzy panels on the French doors.

"Was this Miss Grace's room?" she asked rather anxiously.

"No'um, she slept in de room behind you." Winnie strode over to open the French doors, raising new clouds of dust. "Got you a nice veranda dat wraps 'round dis whole story."

Viveca sneezed. "Quaint, I'm sure, if one can manage not to fall through the floorboards like the unfortunate Mr. Cornelius."

"Yes'um." The servant appeared at a loss.

"By the way, where is your room?"

"In de attic. Ruvi and Miguel, dey bunk down in de basement—"

"You mean with the black cat?"

Winnie's face went blank. "We got no cat, mistress."

"Indeed, just as you have no mice in your parlor."

Winnie coughed. "Your mon can sleep in de basement, too, eh?"

Noting Emmett's dark frown, Viveca hastily corrected

Winnie. "Nonsense. Emmett will stay right here on this floor, in one of the spare rooms."

Winnie gasped. "A mon upstairs wit' you? Why, it wouldn't be fitting, mistress. Miss Grace would never—"

Viveca had had all she could bear of the woman's interference. "Winnie, I'm not sure what your arrangement was with Miss Grace, but you'd be wise to remember that this is *my* house now, and you are here only because of my generosity, not to mention patience. I shall decide on whatever sleeping arrangements I deem best for my mon—er, *man*."

Winnie had the grace to lower her gaze. "Yes'um."

Viveca removed her hat and began unbuttoning her jacket, smiling as Emmett came forward to take it. "Now I shall rest. As for you, Winnie, I'd advise you to gather up the rest of the—er—servants." She pulled her father's gold watch from the pocket of her skirt and flipped it open. "We shall have a staff meeting at four o'clock."

"Staff, er—"

"All of you be in the kitchen at four o'clock sharp. Is that clear?"

"Yes, mistress." Winnie actually curtseyed at Viveca's commanding tone.

"I'll just fetch in your portmanteau, ma'am," Emmett said.

"Leave it outside my door, will you, please?" she replied wearily.

"Yes, ma'am."

After the two had left, Viveca collapsed onto the ramshackle bed with a groan of its rusty springs and a rise of choking dust. She sneezed and brushed feathers from her hair, suddenly feeling exhausted and dispirited. It had been a long, arduous journey across country by train—too many drafty stations, bad meals and lumpy mattresses, in too many towns whose names she couldn't even remember.

Only weeks ago, she had actually looked forward to this sojourn—escaping San Francisco and the constant ridicule and gossip she'd been subjected to there. It was to be a fresh start in Savannah.

But now that she was actually here, she wondered what type of quagmire she'd gotten herself into. She'd known the house would be old, but not that it would be such an unqualified disaster. And although she'd never held a belief in ghosts, this place was spooky, to say the least: the black cat streaking across her path; the rocker with its unexplained source of motion; the hazy aura that hung about the square; the "cold spot" in the bathroom where the tub should have been.

And the old house came complete with three more servants to feed. If the two men were as strange as this Jamaican woman . . . mercy!

Once she felt reasonably rested, Viveca rose and went outside to the veranda to catch a breath of fresh air. Taking care to test each weathered plank as she moved, she ventured out to stand at the railing, her spirits lifting a bit as she inhaled the aromas of magnolia blossoms and cleyera and took in the scene beyond her. Her gardens were overrun but showed promise, especially the large rose bed a few yards beyond the house, with its many delicious colors—reds, yellows, violets and striking pinks. And she had many wonderful trees, large oaks and fragrant magnolias at the western boundary of her property. At the back, another stand of trees served as a gateway to what she presumed were the ruins of the old jail annex.

Glancing back toward the Beecher property, she feasted her eyes on the charming, lacy gazebo until a flicker of motion directed her attention toward the Georgian mansion beyond. Again Maxwell Beecher stood on his side gallery, staring in her direction. This time he was sipping something—a mint julep, perhaps? Could he see her through the trees?

Evidently he could, for he lifted his glass toward her in what appeared to be a mock salute, then once again turned and reentered his house.

Horrid man!

Viveca was about to retreat to her room when she spotted another set of double doors just down the veranda, and realized they must lead to the abode of the mysterious, deceased "Miss Grace." Curiosity spurred her to investigate. Although the heavily curtained French doors were weather-beaten and swollen, she managed to yank them open, then stepped into an oppressive niche of must and dark shadows. As her eyes adjusted, she spotted a carved mahogany bed covered in dusty burgundy taffeta, with a huge brass cross suspended over it, as if to ward off evil spirits. This was odd, she thought. Usually such a large religious artifact would be displayed in one's parlor, not bedroom.

Stepping closer to the cross, she heard a crackling sound and felt something crumbling beneath her slippers. Glancing down, she noted that the entire bed was outlined with crushed eggshell. How bizarre!

Turning away from the bed, she flinched as she observed that most of the room's pictures and all of the mirrors were shrouded in dusty black cloth, as if the occupant had been unable to bear the images or truths reflected there. The combined effect was most disquieting—the manifestation of a mind running amok, growing crazed.

Then Viveca was drawn toward a small, inlaid walnut card table with two chairs, positioned near a far wall. On the surface sat a dusty Ouija board with its idle planchette. Ouija, indeed! What tormented spirits had Miss Grace attempted to summon through the outlandish device?

Illogically, next to the table with its talismans of demagoguery stood a Bible stand with a large family Bible opened to Ezekiel, and a passage highlighted by the sign of the cross scrawled in a blurred, shaky hand: "Though they cry in Mine ears with a loud voice, yet will I not hear them."

Viveca shuddered. What voices had poor Miss Grace struggled to shut out—voices that may have eventually driven her to the edge of madness? Had she really run through the house naked, fleeing some unknown demons, as Winnie had claimed? Viveca had found the accounts outrageous, and yet . . . everything in this room belied the image of the controlled, confident "Miss Grace" she had seen in the portrait downstairs. She could almost feel the eerie presence of a soul in purgatory.

Viveca quickly retreated to the veranda and shut the doors. Thank goodness this creepy abode wasn't her room—at least Winnie had done her that one small kindness, it seemed.

She was about to reenter her own chamber when she flinched at a sudden sound. *Thwack! Thwack! Thwack!* Was someone chopping wood?

She headed further down the gallery toward the back of the house. There beneath her on a green patch she spotted a slightly built, dark-haired young man dressed in tan dungarees. He was pulling daggers from a leather pouch at his waist and hurling them into a massive oak. Why, there seemed at least a dozen blades protruding from the bark!

Was this Ruvi, the gardener? Or perhaps Miguel, the houseboy?

Then a flicker of motion drew her gaze to the decrepit stable beyond, just as another young man emerged, wearing only dark trousers and boots. A single earring gleamed at his ear; a large gold chain glittered about his neck. He looked like a gypsy.

With an unbidden shiver, Viveca noted that this man was taller, darker, hard-muscled, broad-shouldered. With his tight britches, shoulder-length jet-black hair and well-furred chest, he appeared downright wicked! At once he spotted her above him and started toward her. She struggled not to flinch as he drew out a pocketknife and cut a red rose from a trellis at the side of the house. Advancing further, he stuck the rose between his teeth, dipped into a bow, then grinned up at her. Even from here she could see the heaviness of his eyebrows, the blackness of his eyes.

With a gasp, Viveca retreated into the shadows. So this must be the gardener—a fresh and impudent rascal if she'd ever seen one. That meant the dagger-thrower was her houseboy. Two potential deviants, both with very sharp blades. Wasn't that just dandy?

Chapter Two

Viveca glanced about the crude kitchen table at her staff. She sat at the head, with Winnie flanking her on the right, eyeing her with mingled anxiety and mistrust. To her left sat the small, dark Spanish houseboy—a man of many daggers but few words, she'd discovered. Soiled dungarees hung about his slim frame, his black hair was mussed, his features even, though dirt-smeared, his gaze steady.

Then there was the gypsy gardener, Ruvi. Dark, intense, striking, he exuded the aura of an outdoorsman with his heavily tanned skin and strong, callused hands. She supposed he might resemble the brooding Heathcliff of Miss Bronte's famous novel. He appeared exotic and dangerous, from the predatory gleam in his eyes to the gold earring at his ear, the coin hanging on the heavy chain about his neck.

Another man of few words. Every time he grinned at her—which he did now—she had to stifle a shiver. Only one glaring flaw saved the man from total, devastating handsomeness: His front teeth were worn down almost to the quick!

Viveca stole a glance at Emmett, who stood lounging in

the archway, watching the scene with a troubled frown. She sighed, squared her shoulders and turned back to the others.

"Well, I suppose all of you must be wondering why I brought you here," she began stiffly.

"Yes, mistress," Winnie replied.

"When I purchased this—er—home, I had no idea it came with three servants. My circumstances are limited, you see."

"You letting us go, mistress?" Winnie asked, crestfallen.

Noting that both men were also watching her closely, Viveca fought an instinct to wring her hands. She knew how it felt to be abandoned, and detested the thought of doing so to others, even if they might deserve such treatment. "Well, I'm not sure," she answered candidly. "To be frank, my father left me only the most modest inheritance. Much will depend on how things proceed for me here. Once my piano arrives, I'm planning to support myself—and this household—by teaching music lessons. Accordingly, for the present, I can offer the three of you only room and board. Later, if things go well, we can discuss some modest recompense at that time."

Although the men remained silent at this announcement, Winnie clapped her hands. "Oh, yes, mistress, dat be fine!"

"And what do you men think?" Viveca asked, glancing from Miguel to Ruvi.

Miguel nodded solemnly and Ruvi grinned toothlessly.

Viveca cleared her throat. "Very well, we have an arrangement—for the time being. However, there are conditions."

"Conditions?" Winnie asked.

"Anyone who hopes to remain here must earn his or her keep," Viveca went on sternly. "This home is in deplorable shape. Indeed, its scandalous state makes me wonder what the three of you have been doing all these months since poor Miss Grace's death."

At last Ruvi spoke up in his deep, European-accented voice. "Why, we wait for you, *Gadji*."

Viveca restrained a shiver, wondering at the word *Gadji*

and whether it was a sign of respect or disrespect. Somehow she suspected the latter. "Well, I'm here now, and there will be no more sloughing off. I expect all of you to report to the parlor promptly at eight A.M. tomorrow. Together we shall inspect the house and grounds, and I'll assign duties to each of you accordingly."

"Yes, *Gadji*," Ruvi mocked.

Viveca was about to ask him to refrain from calling her *Gadji* when abruptly he stood, with Miguel quickly following suit. "Wait a minute," she ordered.

Both men turned to look at her.

"Ruvi, I prefer to be called 'Miss Stanhope.' "

"Yes, *Gadji*," he replied, bowing.

Grinding her teeth, Viveca addressed the houseboy. "Miguel, I trust you'll not be disfiguring any more of my oaks with your daggers?"

The little man flushed, then nodded rapidly. "*Sí*, senorita."

Watching the two men troop out, Viveca was convinced she was sending coals to Newcastle.

Winnie was about to follow suit when Viveca scolded, "As for you—"

Winnie snapped to attention. "Yes'um?"

Viveca waved a hand at the squalid kitchen. "You will clean up this disgusting room and prepare dinner for us."

The housekeeper appeared to go blank. "But, mistress, our larder, it be bare. Only a few black bean left, and a few scrawny chicken out in de coop—"

Emmett stepped forward. "Miss, I'll slaughter one of the birds, and I also spotted a few carrots and potatoes in the vegetable garden. Perhaps the woman can prepare a stew after she tidies up the place." He glanced meaningfully at the abandoned pan of gravy on the stove, now a haven for flies.

"Yes, thank you, Emmett," Viveca responded with gratitude. "Winnie, you will do precisely as Emmett has suggested."

Winnie gave a massive groan, but didn't protest further.

After Emmett trudged out the back door, Viveca turned

back to Winnie. "What is it with Miguel and his fetish for daggers?"

"*Fe-tish?*" Winnie repeated, perplexed. "Well, I t'ink for a time de dear bwoy travel wit' de circus and t'row de blades."

Viveca rolled her eyes. "Oh, great. A professional knife-thrower amongst us. Now tell me about Ruvi."

"What you need to know, ma'am?"

"For one thing, he has a pronounced European accent. And he keeps calling me *Gadji*, despite my admonition."

"He Rom," she explained.

"Rom? You mean gypsy?"

Winnie nodded. "*Gadji* is woman, but not gypsy."

"I see. It seems a sign of disrespect."

Winnie shrugged and lowered her gaze. "I not know."

Though Viveca suspected otherwise, she did not comment. "Do you know what his name means?"

"Ruvi? I t'ink it Rom for 'wolf.'"

"Splendid. Moreover, for an apparent outdoorsman, he certainly doesn't take much pride in the grounds."

"Ruvi, he prefer de horses, till Miss Grace, she sell them all to buy food."

Viveca rose with a weary sigh. "Yes, what lovely memories this house must hold. Step lively, then, Winnie. I expect supper to be served promptly at seven."

Viveca spent the next few hours unpacking in her bedroom. She could hear Emmett hammering as he repaired the down-stairs floorboards shattered by the hefty Mr. Cornelius. After putting away the last of her lingerie and washing up at the basin, she felt exhausted and starved, especially since she hadn't eaten since their rather meager breakfast on the train, a tepid repast of greasy rolls and weak tea.

Viveca found that the house, which had been so disquiet-ing all day, grew even spookier at eventide. The haze outside her window deepened, growing smokier and more sinister amid the bronze of sunset. Going downstairs, she found her-self swatting at a new crop of cobwebs that had miraculously sprouted from the ceiling, and the steps creaked even more ominously beneath her feet. On the landing, she stuck out her tongue at the hideous gargoyle, which, perhaps understandably, seemed to snarl back at her. She would have to get rid of that monstrosity.

Continuing, she wrinkled her nose at a strange, pungent odor curling up from the kitchen, as if a chicken were drowning in a witch's cauldron. *This* was to be her dinner?

In the downstairs hallway, she marched along, only to recoil as she walked straight through another spine-tingling "cold spot." Shivering, she stuck her hand out, only to find the draft gone. Shaking her head, she wandered out the front door, and found Emmett on the porch, sweeping away dirt and leaves amid the cloyingly sweet evening air.

"Emmett, come have supper with me," she invited.

He turned with a frown. "Miss Viveca, you know that wouldn't be seemly."

"Nonsense. You know darn well you dined with me most every night in San Francisco. I should have been lost without your company."

Briefly he smiled. "But that was when no one else about. Here, miss, you got them three."

"And I care not a whit what any of them think," Viveca asserted. "Moreover, I must say the feeling seems mutual, as these erstwhile 'servants' have allowed the house to disintegrate into such chaos. Now, regarding supper . . . will you offer me your arm, please?"

Here Emmett's innate chivalry won out over his discomfiture. He quickly set aside his broom and escorted his mistress inside to the dining room.

On the table, a single smoky candle cast sinister shadows on the scarred wood. As Emmett seated Viveca in a rickety chair, she stared at the chipped brown pottery plate, tarnished silverware and smudged napkin Winnie had set out for her. Nonplussed, she rapped her glass with a fork. "Winnie!"

The woman popped in from the kitchen, her face glossy with sweat, a grimy apron at her waist. "Yes'um?"

"Is this the best you can do for table settings?"

"Oh, yes'um, you should see de rest. Dey a fright."

"Very well. We shall scrub and polish everything tomorrow. Now set a place for Emmett."

Winnie gasped, casting the manservant a malevolent look. "You gonna let your mon eat wit' you?"

"Winnie! What did I tell you about not—"

Dodging the inevitable lecture, the woman ducked out, returning momentarily with a plate and silverware clutched in one hand, a steaming bowl balanced in the other. After dumping the place setting before Emmett with an unnerving clang, she crossed over to Viveca and slapped several clumps of a foul-smelling concoction onto her plate.

"My God—what is this?" Viveca asked.

"Your stew, mistress," Winnie pronounced with a glint of her gold tooth. "You want I serve your mon, too?"

Viveca gulped, still staring at the gruesome morass piled on her plate—a steamy gray mound, lumpy and distasteful. "Just leave us, please."

Winnie set down the bowl and left. Viveca and Emmett could only continue to grimace at their obnoxious "dinner." "Should we even try to eat it?" Viveca ventured. "It looks like swamp ooze."

Emmett bravely reached for the bowl. "I be first, missus."

She gently slapped his hand away. "No, no, I don't want your death on my conscience. If I weren't so darn hungry . . ." Digging into the primordial ooze with her fork, Viveca tentatively took a small bite, only to begin choking violently as fire invaded her mouth, throat and sinuses.

"Winnie!" she managed to croak out between fits of coughing. "Water!"

Emmett had already stood, rounded the table, and was beating on Viveca's back by the time a wide-eyed Winnie dashed in with a glass of water. Viveca grabbed it and gulped it down. Once the glass was empty she could finally breathe, albeit tears choked her eyes and her mouth still throbbed.

"Winnie, what are you trying to do? Kill us?" Viveca demanded hoarsely.

The Jamaican woman was crestfallen, hopping up and down. "Oh, no'um, no'um! I make you de aut'entic Jamaican chicken stew with de black beans, de jerk spices and peppers."

"Well, I'm jerking, all right! *What* peppers?"

"I not know, ma'am. Ruvi, he grow de t'ings outside—"

"Did he, eh? I feel as if I've been eating lava simmered in sulfuric acid. Tell me—when you cooked it, did you chant, 'Double, double toil and trouble,' like one of Mr. Shakespeare's witches?"

Winnie wrung her hands. "Mistress, what I do?"

"Please, just leave us in peace. Retire for the night before you murder us all."

With a frustrated grimace, the housekeeper scurried out.

"You all right, Miss Viveca?" asked Emmett.

Fanning herself, Viveca stared up at his lined, concerned face. "That woman is an atrocious cook—which has to be the understatement of the century." She pointed at the bowl. "Kindly take this loathsome repast outside and bury it. Lord knows, we wouldn't want some poor squirrel or field mouse to eat it and die an agonizing death."

"Yes 'um."

After he left, Viveca buried her face in her hands. She was still hungry, not to mention emotionally and physically drained. The stew had been the final insult capping off a truly awful day.

After a moment, clanging sounds in the kitchen lured Viveca there. Dirty dishes and abandoned pans cluttered the sideboard, and Emmett was at the sink pumping water into a large pot. "What are you doing?"

He turned, gesturing at the disorderly table, where a partially carved, boiled chicken sat abandoned on a chipped meat platter. "That no-account Winnie, she waste half the bird and just leave it there. So back in the pot it go, with some rice I find in the pie safe." He forced a smile. "We have us a fine chicken soup in no time, ma'am. Then I clean up this mess that lazy woman leave."

Viveca broke into a rare smile. "Well, I did send her on to bed. I'll help you tidy up."

"No, ma'am, that wouldn't be seemly."

Viveca crossed the room and hugged his back. "Bless you, Emmett. You're so dear. And I *will* help you."

He turned, awkwardly patting her arm. "It be all right, Miss Viveca. It be all right."

Viveca managed a brave nod, even though Emmett's troubled eyes told her otherwise.

Chapter Three

Despite the fact that the soup Emmett made was both delicious and nourishing, Viveca felt too unsettled to go straight to bed. She stood on the upstairs veranda and watched the evening fog rise up from the nearby swamps like an insidious malaise. The air was thick and stagnant. Only the raw cry of a swamp bird and the humming of cicadas punctuated the eerie stillness. Given the dense overcast, she expected rain by morning, and shuddered at the thought of how many leaks the old house might spring.

Once finally in bed, she tossed and turned between the clammy bedclothes and watched large mosquitoes dive at the mosquito netting, buzzing in their high-strung frustration. Reaching through the gauzy fabric, she took her father's beloved pocket watch from the night table and watched the moonlight glint off its gold, etched surfaces. She popped it open, listened to its comforting ticking and just made out the time on the Roman numerals—first ten o'clock, then eleven, then midnight . . .

As she lay there counting the hours, her mind drifted back to happier times in San Francisco: dining at Marchand's with her parents; learning the waltz at Lunt's Dancing School; listening to the band playing Gilbert and Sullivan at Golden Gate Park; hearing Adelina Patti sing at the San Francisco Opera; performing her own first piano recital in her parents' grand parlor. Most memorable of all had been her debut at the Cotillion, and her first kiss at seventeen, when Brent Hayden had stolen her breath beneath the mistletoe.

From a very early age, she'd been fascinated with the piano. She'd also loved the years she'd spent studying music at the Boston Conservatory, and living with an elderly aunt, now deceased. Although she'd dearly missed her parents and friends during those four years in Boston, her father had urged her to pursue her passion first, to complete her studies before contemplating a future family. "You'll have plenty of time for marriage and motherhood later on," he'd always assured her. Viveca had appreciated his enlightened attitude.

Then two years ago, right after Viveca's graduation, everything changed. Just as her parents had planned a celebratory trip to Europe for the three of them, her mother had suddenly taken ill with pneumonia—and had died within a week. Viveca had been stunned, devastated. Her father was inconsolable, and his spirits and health quickly failed. Viveca had devoted herself to him until his recent passing.

'Twas then she'd learned the awful news that her father's business was insolvent, when his partner Erskine Pendergraf had come to comfort her on his death . . . and the snake had seduced her instead! Rather than take charge of herself as she properly should have, she'd succumbed to the blackguard repeatedly. She's been so lost, so alone, so helpless against him.

How she'd hated herself for her weakness. And what a heavy price she had paid for her sins. Ultimately, Erskine's wife had found out, as had all of polite society. Her friends and suitors had vanished into the woodwork in the face of her shocking behavior. And the prominent friends of her parents—who had embraced Julia Ward Howe as a champion of women's rights and had sanctioned the budding movement toward a new feminine intellectualism—in the end had proven equally provincial in their judgment of a "fallen woman." Viveca had been ruined. As for Erskine, he had abandoned her without a backward glance. Afterward, she had even wondered if he might have been instrumental in her father's financial collapse, although, not having access to any of his records, she could never be sure.

But one thing was certain: Never again would she become the pawn, the toy, of a ruthless male. Never again would she allow any man to use her that way, much less give in to her shameful carnal side. These were the real reasons she had cut all her ties with San Francisco and fled here to Savannah. This was her opportunity for a new life—such as it was—and she would not squander it. This time, she would be strong, in charge of her own destiny.

Viveca was finally drifting off to sleep when the shrill sounds of a dog barking made her jerk awake. She crept out of bed, put on her slippers and wrapper and stepped outside onto the veranda. Tensely she scanned the boggy darkness in the direction of the howling.

The first thing she noticed was the full moon—it was huge, beaming a bright yellow-white up in the sky. By its glow she caught sight of Ruvi hunkered down before a small fire. He was throwing some sort of glittery dust at the blaze as a small mongrel dog barked and raced about him in circles. Viveca stared, mesmerized, watching each handful of seemingly magical sand make the fire hiss, snap and turn colors ranging from white to blue.

What on earth was this? Some sort of bizarre Romany ritual?

Even as she tried to make sense of the odd rite, Ruvi stood and cast his gaze up in her direction. Viveca recoiled into the shadows, watching him kick out the fire and stalk away toward the stable, the dog at his heels.

Mercy! What a peculiar man. Had he seen her standing here? She doubted it. No, it was more like he had *sensed* her. And what had he been throwing at the fire?

Viveca was about to give up pondering these imponderables when abruptly she jumped at a new, sharp sound—a gunshot! "Now what?" she muttered.

Although unnerved, Viveca felt equally determined to investigate. She retreated inside and headed downstairs. After tussling with cobwebs on the stairs, she finally made her way out the back door and down the steps. Eerie sounds throbbed about her on the moist night air—the screeching of birds and rustling of leaves. Her eyes scanned the murky copse of trees ahead of her, and at first she spotted nothing save the slight shifting of greenery.

Then she jerked at the sound of a second shot fired. Heavenly days!

Cautiously creeping forward, she spotted a gaslight gleaming, amid a haze of smoke, in the gazebo next door. Moving closer, she was appalled to spot her neighbor Maxwell Beecher standing inside the small pavilion, his strong, steady hand firing a pistol. With sickening precision, he was shooting branches off of an unfortunate young elm tree.

Why, the brute!

Although Viveca was far from appropriately dressed, and the sight of the gun-wielding man was both sobering and bizarre, by now she was too incensed to practice her usual caution. She stormed toward the gazebo. "What in God's name do you think you're doing?"

Her neighbor turned to her in astonishment, taking in her mussed hair and scandalous attire. "Well, what have we here, a ghost?" he inquired in a deep, Georgia-accented voice.

For a moment, Viveca stood as if transfixed, daunted by the power of his voice, the sheer handsomeness of him. Maxwell Beecher towered at least six feet tall. He was leanly, splendidly muscled, with a wealth of thick, shiny, slightly rumpled dark brown hair curving about a face of classic male perfection. He was younger than she'd expected, perhaps thirty years old. Like a corsair, he was dressed in snug black trousers and a flowing white linen shirt with several buttons left shockingly undone, revealing the tufts of dark hair on his sinewy chest.

He was hardly the curmudgeon she had expected, especially given his earlier atrocious behavior. What surprised her most of all was the glint of laughter—albeit cynical—in his gaze. That enticing glimmer made her treacherously wonder what color those deep-set eyes were. She couldn't completely make them out in the semidarkness. Were they sable brown? Midnight blue?

Shaking off her errant thoughts, Viveca squared her shoulders and marched closer. "A ghost, indeed! Sir, you're well aware that I'm your new neighbor. Why, you've been gawking at me all day."

"Gawking, have I?" he asked with wry amusement. "Madam, I commend your bravado. Has it occurred to you that you're trespassing on the property of a man with a loaded gun in his hand?"

Not intimidated in the least, she snapped back, "Sir, has it occurred to *you* that you're trying to wake the dead?"

"Wake the dead? Now there's an apt expression."

She strode closer to him. "What is going on here?"

He had the grace to grin. "Don't you think introductions are in order first?"

"I don't care to meet you, sir, only to silence your gun."

He chuckled, a wicked, throaty sound. "Hmmm. Silence my gun, eh? Now there's a provocative prospect."

Viveca's face flamed. Somehow he'd made it all sound quite depraved. "Spare me your insulting innuendos. And I repeat—what are you doing?"

"Oh, just a bit of target practice."

"Target practice? In the middle of the night?" She gestured at the sapling, which looked like the victim of an ax murderer. "Why, look what you've done to that poor tree."

He scowled magnificently. "Actually, the sapling is badly infected with cankers and needs to be taken down."

Viveca remained horrified. "Heavens, you don't have to murder it. Give it some dignity instead."

"Dignity for a tree? Well, I could always shoot you instead," he offered amiably.

She waved a hand in exasperation. "What is it about you men and trees, anyway? This afternoon I spied my houseboy hurling daggers at one of my most magnificent oaks."

"And did you give him what-for, as well?"

"Indeed I did. I made it clear such cruel desecrations will not be tolerated."

"Perhaps not on *your* property," Beecher drawled meaningfully.

"Not on anyone's property, if I have my say about it."

"So you're the new tree inspector, are you?" He turned, deliberately pointing his pistol away from her, and the tree, then fired again—this time at the ground.

Viveca flinched, and grimaced at the sting of smoke.

He pivoted back to her with a look of supreme self-satisfaction. "There. Now I've 'murdered' a dandelion. Are you happy?"

"Pity anyone who wants dandelion tea," she snapped back.

He stared at her as if she'd lost her mind. "What *are* you, madam? A crusading horticulturist?"

"What *are* you, sir? A sadist?"

He threw back his head and laughed. "Touché, then." He waved his pistol toward her property. "Perhaps I should just shoot down your house. Shouldn't be too difficult, you know. Talk about a blight that needs to be demolished—"

"Ah, yes," Viveca interjected smugly, "Mr. Cornelius told me you covet my house."

Devilment danced in his eyes. " 'Covet' is rather a strong word, though not of course when I'm in the presence of such beauty. Moreover, if I do 'covet' your house, miss, it's only to acquaint it with half a dozen sticks of dynamite."

"How chivalrous of you."

Chuckling, he stuffed the pistol in his waistband and climbed down the steps to join her. "Well, as delightful as this exchange has been, I'm forgetting my manners." He bowed briefly, mockingly. "Maxwell Beecher at your service."

She nodded stiffly, not offering her hand. She again felt rattled by the magnitude of his male presence, and his vibrant scent—male, musky and not at all unpleasant. "Viveca Stanhope."

"My dear Miss Stanhope," he murmured. "And now that we have introductions out of the way—"

Impatient to end their absurd banter, she finished shrilly. "May I have your word that you won't disturb my peace again tonight?"

"Not disturb your peace?" He stroked his jaw, his eyes gleaming with that same unexpected mischief. "Actually, I'm not sure that's something I want to promise. I must be forever prepared, since one never knows what perils may lurk in the darkness." He eyed her meaningfully.

"You mean there are more maniacs on the loose like you?" she inquired sweetly.

"Maniacs?" he laughed. "Well, there's haunted Savannah and all that."

"I don't believe in ghosts."

"Ah—then you've chosen rather peculiar environs for your new home, haven't you? All cozied up to the cemetery, the old jail and the Hanging Oak. Are you sure you don't want to accompany me to go dig up a few zombies tonight?"

"Not unless we bury *you* while we're at it," she snapped back.

He guffawed at that. "Bravo. You do have an outspoken way about you, my dear neighbor. And since we're being so very forthright"—he glanced toward her house, then grimaced—"tell me, Miss Stanhope, what made you purchase that monstrosity?"

She bristled at his words. "Not that it's any of your affair, but that 'monstrosity' is my new home. I expect you to accord it proper respect."

He gestured dismissively at the graying mansion. "Any woman who considers that hovel a suitable abode must not have two pennies to rub together."

"My, aren't you a man of considerable insight—and tact? Not that the state of my finances is any of your concern. And furthermore—"

"Furthermore," he cut in cynically, "let me be blunt. You were a fool to take on that pile of rubble—"

"Fool! Pile of rubble!"

"You're obviously one of those poor-relation types, someone's discarded aunt, sister . . ." Looking her over, his eyes gleamed with a wickedness that would have put Machiavelli to shame. "Or perhaps mistress?"

"Mistress? Why, I never!"

Resolutely he continued, "And you should have simply hired yourself out as a governess, or gone to live with family, as all such in your position must do."

For a moment Viveca was rendered speechless, so appalled was she by the man's arrogance, his hideously insulting comments, especially considering that he barely knew her. At last she managed to retort, "Sir, you are an impudent cad and you know nothing of my position."

"Well, I know what your position will be soon enough if someone doesn't rescue you."

The insolence in his tone made her burn to slap his face. "Rescue me? How dare you presume I need rescue."

He stepped closer, his male heat and scent enveloping her, his eyes gleaming cagily. "Whatever scandalous sum Cornelius managed to bilk from you for that dump—"

"Bilk! Dump!"

"I shall offer you . . . well, at least half as much to turn it over to me. And I'll personally put you on the first train to—whatever hinterland you hail from—"

"The hinterland of San Francisco!"

"Before I raze the eyesore."

Viveca was so stunned, so furious, she was actually trembling. His gall was unbelievable! And here she'd thought he had a certain charm.

"How dare you speak to me in such an atrocious manner?" she hissed. "You, sir, may take the first train directly to hell."

He grinned. "Again, Miss Stanhope, I must commend your spirit."

"Save me your commendations." She tapped the pistol at his waist. "Fire that gun again tonight and I shall come shove it down your throat."

The cad only chuckled. "Speaking of shove, may I suggest—"

She stormed away before he could finish, to the sounds of his infuriating mirth.

"Insufferable egotist!"

Viveca was tearing across her backyard, fuming at Maxwell Beecher's impertinence, when she gasped at a shimmer of movement in the trees ahead. She froze, peering intently into the darkness, listening to the low dirge of the wind, and an even more eerie echo, like a moan. A stagnant odor rose on the air, and she felt a sudden disquieting chill, much like the earlier cold spots.

What in hell?

In the greenery, a second quicksilver glimmer made her squint, straining to better see. Was that a shadow she spotted there? Mercy, was it the shape of a woman? Was it coming from the direction where the old death house presumably had been?

Gathering her courage, Viveca bravely stole into the trees at the back of her property, but encountered only dew-drenched branches and brambles that painfully scratched her ankles. Then at last an eerie glow low in a bush caught her attention; stepping closer and hunkering down, she found herself squinting at a pair of creepy green cat eyes that glowed back at her from the blackness. Even as she eased forward to get a better look, the eyes vanished.

So much for there being no cat on this property, she mused ruefully.

Nonetheless, Viveca frowned in puzzlement as she straightened herself and rubbed her injured leg. Her sighting of the cat eyes had brought momentary relief, but no real explanation. For she could have sworn she'd seen something

much larger only seconds earlier—a shape, an outline, a sil-
houette, *something*. It definitely hadn't been a cat. Moreover,
she'd felt cold, deathly cold, and now, wonder of wonders,
she was hot.

Rattled, Viveca hurried back to her house. She was rushing
in the back door when she collided with Winnie. The housekeeper recoiled with a gasp, her features wan, sinister, in the
reflected moonlight.

What was *she* doing here?

"Winnie, why ever are you lurking here in the darkness?"
Viveca demanded.

Undaunted, Winnie balled her hands on her hips. "What
you doin' out dere alone in de miasma, mistress? You tryin' to
catch your det?"

Viveca was tempted to laugh at Winnie's droll, dark references. "Whether or not I'm out strolling with miasmas is
none of your affair. Now tell me, were you just out in the
backyard?"

Aghast, the housekeeper shook her head. "Oh, no'um,
no'um. I ain't goin' out dere with all dem shadows 'n' such. I
jes' come downstairs 'cause I was scar't. I hear a gun be fired,
den low sounds, like folks was moaning."

"Moaning?" Viveca felt the blood draining from her face.

Winnie crossed herself. "What is it, mistress? You look
like you jes' seen a duppy."

"You don't say," Viveca mocked back.

"Mistress, what happen to you?"

Viveca waved a hand and started off. "Please, just go to
bed."

Leaving Winnie to frown after her, Viveca fled through
the darkness toward the stairs. The encounter with her
housekeeper had only worn further on her already frayed
nerves. She trooped up the steps, lashed by a new cascade of
cobwebs that had burgeoned forth like Rip Van Winkle's
beard. On the landing, she paused to calm her raging pulse,
and could have sworn she spotted the hideous old gargoyle
grinning at her. . . .

* * *

Maxwell Beecher had chuckled as he watched his new neighbor storm back to her own property, then pause, make a brief detour into the trees, and finally rush for her back door. Such odd behavior, but then a lot of folks in these parts chased shadows in the night.

Nonetheless, Viveca Stanhope was feisty and determined, and would not be easy to scare off. A pity, too, since Max knew he would know no peace until he wrenched that hovel away from her and burned it to the ground. It galled him that she'd invaded his territory, his peace, that she'd gotten to Hangman's House before he could. Indeed, he'd felt tempted to call out Agent Cornelius for selling the place out from under him.

Aside from her usurpation of the house, the mere presence of Miss Stanhope was an unwelcome distraction, a disruption to his normal routine. Though life on Hangman's Square definitely had its quirks, the isolation of his old family home had always suited Max's cavalier nature. Previously there had been no one around to monitor his comings and goings. Old Miss Grace had posed no threat, nor did poor benighted Miss Lilac, who lived across the square. The Cunninghams were gone on tour much of the time. Thus, if he wanted to have friends in for a raucous party, or tumble fair Lucy for a fortnight or two, there was never anyone around to know the difference.

Until now. What was the Stanhope woman doing here in Savannah, anyway? And why had she bought the ramshackle home next door? Gently bred young ladies didn't flee across country on their own, unless they had something to hide. Indeed, he'd definitely touched a raw nerve with her when he'd speculated that she might be someone's discarded mistress. But then, tact wasn't Max's long suit.

Still, she was a tempting baggage. Delectable, in fact, with that riot of red curly hair, that beautifully shaped long face with the lush mouth, large blue eyes, and features to put any French courtesan to shame. Her tall, slender body seemed to beg a man to claim its deepest recesses.

And so delicious-looking she'd been, in that sexy little wrapper and lacy gown!

Already his male instincts prodded him to pursue her. But even though she might be a mystery lady with something to hide, he couldn't afford to forget that ultimately, she still was a lady. He didn't need complications in his life, much less ladies. All his life Maxwell had cursed the yoke and gloried in the thrilling ride of the stallion. Besides, there were plenty of shameless fillies around, tarts he could bed at will with no risk of sullied reputations. His own was beyond repair, of course, but he rather liked it that way, especially thumbing his nose at the provincial society that felt duty bound to endure him with long-suffering tolerance.

Miss Stanhope was clearly trouble, and he should avoid her. Unfortunately, prudent behavior wasn't Maxwell's long suit. His adventurous streak too often led him down a self-destructive path. Part of him loved to shock, to seduce, to unveil. After all, that desire to conquer the fairer sex was pure raw male instinct. The stallion's greatest weakness, albeit its fiercest pleasure.

Chapter Four

Viveca awakened to clammy sheets, a sore back and the steady tattoo of rain on her roof. She grimaced, glancing overhead in search of leaks. Although the ceiling was grimy and tattered, to her surprise, she spotted no watermarks or telltale dripping. Otherwise, she felt sticky and miserable after a night spent struggling to sleep on the lumpy, sagging bed. How she longed for a cleansing, warm bath!

Donning her wrapper and slippers, she stole out onto the veranda, gazing at a gray morning, at trees quaking in the downpour amid the boom of thunder. The air on the veranda felt thick as honey, and despite the rain, fat mosquitoes buzzed at her. She batted at the pesky insects and muttered a curse. This was all she needed in her current depressed state of mind—the most melancholy day in all of memory.

At least there was no hint of the presence she'd spotted last night—or of her horrible neighbor, the tree assassin! The nerve of Maxwell Beecher, calling her a "poor relation" in need of rescue. Her blood boiled every time she thought about him and his outrageous comments.

Still, much as Viveca hated to admit it, the cad intrigued

her as much as he maddened her. Maxwell Beecher was a clever, handsome, even sexy, scoundrel. Another good reason to keep her distance from him. The rogue reminded her far too much of Erskine.

But what if she were only attracted to blackguards? What if she possessed a self-destructive streak? What if she were a harlot at heart, a slave to her own baser nature, like one of those pathetic creatures who strolled the Barbary Coast, seducing drunken sailors and picking their pockets?

Another reason to avoid Mr. Beecher, and possibly men in general, she mused wryly. Although twenty-three might be a bit young to give up on the institution of marriage, for now, she could certainly see advantages in becoming a spinster piano teacher. She'd had too much high drama in her life already.

Moments later, fully dressed, Viveca emerged from her room to spot Emmett standing near the stairwell, frowning up at the ceiling. How dear of him to share her concerns about the rain; it was almost as if they were of the same mind.

"Leaks?" she inquired anxiously, stepping toward him.

He turned and smiled. "Good morning, Miss Viveca. And no, ma'am, I ain't seen no leaks."

Viveca was taken aback. "You mean, not in this hallway?"

"Not anywheres in this house, far as I can tell. I've checked ever' room, ceptin' the bedroom of that witch, Winnie—"

Viveca restrained a chuckle. "No leaks—how amazing. And here I'd assumed the place would be a sieve."

He glanced overhead. "Well, the roof, it be slate, and slate last forever, ma'am. Maybe there be a broke tile or two up there, but that I can fix."

At once Viveca became irate. "Emmett Taylor, you'll do no such thing! Why, the very idea—you, at your age, scaling the roof! I shall send Ruvi aloft as soon as possible. Surely that man must be good for something—besides leering at me and flashing his gold jewelry."

"Yes, ma'am." Emmett gave her a quick grin.

"At least we have one a stroke of fortune—a sound roof.

That is, as long as the termites don't decide slate is a tasty meal."

Emmett shook his head. "There ain't no termites here neither, ma'am."

"What? But what about the broken floorboards where Agent Cornelius fell—"

"They ain't rotted, ma'am. Only the nails was rusted, so them boards busted loose. I already fix that." He strode over to rap his gnarled knuckles against a wainscoted wall. "This here house, it built of cypress and cedar. You ain't never finding no termites here, ma'am."

Viveca's spirits lifted. "Well, thank heaven for small blessings. The place may look a blight, but it seems to be structurally sound, just as Agent Cornelius advised us. Will wonders ever cease?"

"Yes, ma'am. She be an old lady, but she grand. All she need is some paint, wallpaper"—he paused, running the toe of his worn shoe over a scarred floorboard—"and some sanding and waxing of these old floors."

"Oh, Emmett," Viveca murmured, rushing forward to hug him. "Perhaps there's hope for us, after all."

"Yes, ma'am." Self-consciously he offered her his arm. "You ready for breakfast, Miss Viveca? I got us eggs boiling downstairs."

"You mean you've already gathered eggs for us?" she inquired, delighted.

"Yes, ma'am. I ain't letting that devil woman try to poison you again."

Viveca was actually laughing as she descended the stairs with her dear servant.

By mid-morning, Viveca had lost her earlier cheerfulness. "Disgraceful," she uttered. "Absolutely disgraceful."

In the steaminess following the rain, she stood in the backyard with her entourage of four servants. The air was thick and torpid, odiferous with the stench of a small fenced chicken coop on the eastern edge of her yard.

The five had just begun their tour of the house and over-run gardens, and Viveca was staring aghast at a pile of debris—everything from discarded clothing and carriage parts to a cracked toilet. She pulled a battered, rusty teakettle from the heap, grimaced, then dropped it. She smoothed down the lines of her blouse and skirt, only to realize she'd just deposited grime on both.

"Why hasn't any of this been hauled off?" she demanded of Ruvi and Miguel.

When Ruvi only grinned half-toothlessly and Miguel avoided her gaze, Winnie spoke up. "Miss Grace, she got no fee for de dump, and no wagon or workhorse for de haulin'."

"Well, I think we can afford some gate fees at the junkyard." Viveca turned to Emmett. "When you take the buggy back to the stable, try to rent out something to haul away this rubbish."

"Yes, ma'am," Emmett said.

Viveca proceeded toward the back of the property, noting that Miguel was following with a decided limp. Had he actually hurled one of his daggers into his foot? she wondered cynically. Then she frowned at the stacks of discarded building materials surrounding the cistern. "As for that rubbish heap, it's little more than an invitation to snakes."

Ruvi nodded. "Yes, *Gadji*. I've strangled a few water moccasins with my bare hands."

"How commendable," retorted Viveca, turning to glare at him. "And once again, Ruvi, it's 'Miss Stanhope' to you. Moreover, considering how *faithfully* you follow my instructions, I've just decided you're the perfect man to clean up this eyesore."

He merely grinned.

"And while we're addressing domestic matters, your dog kept me awake last night," she added sharply.

A shuttered, guarded look tightened his features. "I have no dog, *Gadji*."

"Right, just as you have no black cat in the basement, nor any problems with insubordination."

Ruvi merely stared.

"Well, keep your *nonexistent* dog quiet from now on!" Viveca turned to the houseboy. "Miguel, you can help Ruvi clear out the yard, and Emmett, you will supervise."

While Emmett nodded, Miguel shifted uneasily from foot to foot. "But, senorita, I work in the house."

"Perhaps you did, but I already have a manservant, as well as a housekeeper, such as she is." She cast a baleful glance at Winnie. "My point is, you're needed out here for the time being. And by the way, have you some impediment?"

"Im—" He paused, clearly confused.

She nodded toward his left leg and continued more tactfully, "I—er—I've noticed you're lame."

Miguel glanced helplessly at Winnie, and she grinned. "Oh, dat jes' de limp Miguel got on account of de shopkeeper dat shot de poor bwoy."

"Shot?" Viveca was thunderstruck. "Was that before or after Miguel traveled with the circus?"

While Miguel cast his gaze at his feet, Winnie replied with relish, "Afta'. 'Twas petty t'eft, you see."

"*Petty?*"

"Miguel, he stole a silver tea service, and de shopkeeper, he chase him out of de store and pepper him with shotgun spray—den de sheriff haul Miguel away. Miss Grace, she hear 'bout de poor bwoy's crosses and sufferations. She bail him out of jail and take him under her wing."

As Winnie spoke, Viveca's mouth dropped open. She found herself questioning the sanity of not only her new servants but also their former mistress. "Miguel was arrested for stealing the silver, and Miss Fulton still hired him as her houseboy?" she asked shrilly.

"De dear boy not really a t'ief, he just misguided," Winnie assured her.

"Good grief, what next?" Viveca glanced at Miguel, who remained abashed, while Emmett raised his eyes heavenward.

Despairing of making any sense of the matter, Viveca turned and strode deeper into the yard. About twenty feet ahead, she glimpsed a small, crumbling foundation choked with weeds. Was this what remained of the old jail annex? Although Mr. Cornelius had indicated that the ruins of the old "death house" were also part of her property, she was in no mood to venture closer. Instead she turned to a mound of earth in the foreground, where a weather-beaten trapdoor protruded at an angle from the caked dirt. "What is this?"

"The root cellar, ma'am," answered Ruvi.

Viveca stared down at the hasp lock. "I don't suppose any of you have a key?"

"Oh, no, ma'am, you don't want to go in dere," gasped Winnie, gazing at the trapdoor in fear. "It all chaka-chaka and full o' duppies."

What ailed the woman now? Viveca wondered. "Nonsense." Viveca turned to Ruvi. "Be kind enough to open the door."

Though Winnie wrung her hands, Ruvi grinned, strode forward and dispensed with the lock with a mere kick at what was clearly rotting wood. He leaned over and pulled at the door. At first the splintering panel resisted, but finally it gave way with a great cracking sound. He stepped back and motioned to Viveca. She walked over and peered inside, down an uneven row of earthen stairs. The smells of dank earth and rotting plant life assailed her nostrils. Through the dust and dimness, she spotted broken pottery and pots filling some kind of huge vessel.

"What's that down there?" she asked, grimacing up at the others.

Winnie crossed herself and replied in a fierce whisper, "Dat be de bat'tub, mistress. Miss Grace, she bury it away dere."

"She *buried* her bathtub in the root cellar? How bizarre."

"Miss Grace, she tell Ruvi, lock de t'ing up. Din' I tell you? Got ghosties in it."

"Ghosties, my foot," Viveca mocked. "You must know I don't hold with such balderdash." She nodded firmly to Ruvi and Miguel. "You two will retrieve this bathtub, clean it up and bring it inside. Then Emmett will find us a plumber to install it."

"Yes, ma'am," concurred her manservant.

But Winnie violently shook her head and pointed a trembling finger toward the tub. "By sweet Jesus sufferation, mistress! If you bring that spawn of de devil back inside, it—it steal your shadow fo' sure. An' maybe mine, too."

Viveca waved a hand. "Steal our shadows, indeed. For heaven's sake, Winnie, if I wanted to hear histrionics, I'd go to the theater. I need a *bath*, for heaven's sake. How long do you think a lady can endure life in this mosquito-infested swampland without a proper toilette?"

None of the others dared to answer that acerbic question.

Now the thud of hoofbeats directed Viveca's attention toward the street, and she smiled at the sight of a dray approaching from the west, with two burly men ensconced on the driver's seat.

She pointed at the large crate sitting on the wagon bed, with several steamer trunks stacked behind it. "Ah, I see my piano and wardrobes have arrived."

She marched around to the front of the house, the others falling into step behind her. She paused next to the conveyance just as a florid-faced man with a potbelly slid to the ground. "You be Miss Stanhope?" he asked in a heavy Irish brogue.

"Indeed." Viveca managed not to cringe at his pungent body odor.

The man took off his tattered cap and wiped his sweaty, dirty brow with his shirtsleeves. "William O'Dey at your service, ma'am. Well, Ducks and me 'bout busted our gizzards getting that there pianer on the dray. You reckon some of yer menfolk can help us out with heavin' her inside?"

"Of course—though kindly refrain from *heaving* my instrument." She snapped her fingers. "Emmett, Ruvi and Miguel, you shall assist these gentlemen in *moving* my piano inside."

Amid much grunting and groaning, the five set to work.

They managed to slide the huge box off the dray, through the gate and into the yard. Then O'Dey took a crowbar and pried open the crate, and with more twisting and moaning, the piano eventually emerged from its enclosure. Viveca breathed a sigh of relief to see that her beautiful red mahogany cabinet grand had arrived intact.

She glanced at Emmett, who was rubbing an obviously aching back. She turned to the others. "Gentlemen, you may carry my piano inside. Emmett, why don't you bring along the bench?"

"Yes, ma'am," he replied with obvious relief.

The other four grudgingly lifted the heavy instrument and bore it up the creaky front steps while Emmett followed with the bench. Viveca grimaced when Miguel, the smallest man, almost lost his grasp on one of the legs. The piano roiled precariously as the other three strained and grunted to hold it steady.

"Easy, men, easy!" scolded O'Dey. "Don't let's drop the blasted thing."

At last the four managed to regain control of it and continued without incident until they arrived at the door. But the large instrument would not fit through the opening. The men tried taking it straight through, only to be met by a screech of wood.

"Please, you mustn't scratch it!" Viveca beseeched.

O'Dey cast Viveca a surly look, then snapped his fingers to the others. "All right, men, let's try 'er on end."

"Must you?" Viveca protested.

"You think this here pianer's gonna sprout wings and fly into your parlor, ma'am?" O'Dey asked sourly.

"Very well. Proceed."

Although the men were careful, turning the huge instrument on its end created a discordant ruckus that made Viveca wince. But trying to shove it through the door, even at that angle, proved futile as well.

Heaving for breath, O'Dey scowled at Viveca. "Well,

ma'am, you'd best accustom yourself to playing yer pianer out here on yer gallery."

"On the veranda!" Viveca gasped. "Are you crazy? Have you no idea how delicate that instrument is, how damp the weather is here? Why, it will be warped, ruined, in no time!"

The man waved an arm in frustration. "Well, there ain't no way we're shoving this blame contraption through that door!"

Viveca was glaring at him when a familiar, annoying male voice inquired, "May I be of some assistance here?"

Viveca whirled to see Maxwell Beecher standing at the foot of the steps. Far from feeling justly irritated by his intrusion, she instead almost tottered in the shockwave of emotion that hit her on first viewing his beautiful eyes in the full light of day. Just as she had suspected, they were a deep, mesmerizing midnight blue, their impact bright, magnetic, devastating. Oh, Lord, this man was trouble!

He looked altogether too handsome standing there in his sharply cut black morning jacket and white ruffled shirt, his trousers perfectly creased, black boots gleaming, sunlight sparkling in his thick, silky hair. Viveca had to struggle mightily to recover herself.

"*You* wish to be of assistance?" she finally managed, albeit with a telltale quiver in her voice.

His expression gleamed with secret pleasure as he drawled, "Best of the day to you as well, my dear Miss Stanhope. And I cannot help but observe that you seem to be having some difficulty getting your piano through your front door."

"Brilliant deduction."

Ignoring her sarcasm, he climbed up the steps. "Gentlemen."

The four men glowered back and muttered unpleasantries.

Maxwell touched a gracefully turned leg on the piano, his touch almost sensual. "A fine instrument, though I've seen better."

He stared into Viveca's eyes with a boldly blue provocative

gaze. Viveca hated herself for the sudden thrill of excitement that warmed her belly. "I'd expect such a backsided compliment from the likes of you, Mr. Beecher."

He eyed the lines of her skirt. "Backsided, eh? As it happens, I'm also a connoisseur of backsides of all sorts."

"Oh!" Had there not been others present, Viveca might have slapped the cad, but she did not want to risk escalating matters, especially not by drawing poor Emmett into the fray.

Raising an eyebrow, Maxwell Beecher regarded Viveca briefly before speaking. "You know, before you bring in a piano, you might consider finding yourself a bathtub."

"I already have, thank you."

"Indeed?" He stepped forward, pulled out his handkerchief and dabbed at her smudged nose and cheeks. "Frankly, Miss Stanhope, you look rather like a chimney sweep, albeit a fetching one."

She recoiled. "Spare me your sarcasm, and your backhanded compliments. So do you wish to offer assistance with my piano or not?"

"Certainly, I do."

"How? By shooting off a couple of its legs?"

"No, I'm very much a connoisseur of limbs, as well." To confirm this, he stole a peak at her ankles. "Not that a shotgun wouldn't give your piano a nice nudge, but actually, I've a far better idea."

"Do enlighten us."

To her confusion, he turned and strode down the gallery to the large double parlor windows. He leaned over and yanked on one tall glass panel, which protested with a screech, then began to steal upward. His splendid muscles flexing, Maxwell continued wrestling with the pane until most of it disappeared into the second story. Then he repeated the procedure with the second pane, leaving a large double opening to the room. Turning to her, he mockingly bowed.

Viveca was amazed and humiliated, her face as red as a beet. "Oh, I had no idea that those windows were—"

"Jeffersonian doors?" he supplied amiably. He turned to the others. "Gentlemen, be my guests."

With a cacophony that made Viveca wince, the four men righted the piano, then easily rolled it into the parlor. Meanwhile, Maxwell Beecher strode over to rejoin Viveca. His scent wafted over her—pomade and shaving soap, and a deeper, more exciting male essence.

"Well?" she finally asked.

"Haven't you anything to say to me?" he teased.

"Yes. I think you're a sanctimonious blowhard."

He hooted a laugh. "Besides that."

She spoke through gritted teeth. "Thank you."

Feigning amazement, he cupped a hand around his ear. "Did I hear you correctly, madam?"

"Oh, hush."

"You're welcome, too." Tipping his hat, he ambled off down the steps.

Viveca was watching him, stewing and muttering under her breath, when Winnie stepped up to stare after him, licking her generous lips. "Quite a mon, eh, mistress?"

Viveca whirled on her. "Why didn't you tell me about the double parlor doors?"

Winnie grimaced. "Ma'am, I not know. I mean, Miss Grace, she never use de t'ings."

"And you, no doubt, never cleaned the parlor, much less washed the windows, eh?"

For once, Winnie appeared suitably contrite.

Chapter Five

"Oh, me achin' back!" declared the plumber.

Viveca grimaced at the sounds of Sean O'Murphy banging at the fittings to her bathtub, trying to attach the huge vessel to the spiggots and drain. The small, carrot-haired man crouching on the bathroom floor was actually the cousin of the dray driver, but what he lacked in size he made up for in bluster.

"You know, you don't have to kill my pipes," Viveca put in archly.

He waved a wrench at the scratched and stained bathtub. "This old iron heap is already done in, if you ask me."

Viveca's chin shot up. "Well, I didn't ask you. Besides, I think my servants did a fine job of cleaning it up. Anything else, a good scrubbing with Bon Ami will cure."

The man rolled his eyes at her, then deliberately banged a fitting.

Not one to tolerate such mutiny, Viveca scolded, "My good man, if you find this job so distasteful, I'm sure we can find another plumb—"

His derisive laughter cut her short. "You really think another bloke'll come out and work in this old spook trap?"

"Spook trap?" Viveca protested.

"It's well known this drafty old barn is the most haunted house in all of the Low Country. Were I not desperate for work—"

"That is quite enough," Viveca cut in, fighting an urge to chew her lower lip. "I've heard far too much nonsense about ghosts and duppies already."

He cast her a baleful look. "Ignore it at your peril, ma'am."

Viveca was poised to reply when she heard a distant rapping at her front door. Mercy, did she already have company? Lord knew, she wasn't expecting any more workmen. And she dearly hoped her contemptible though all too enticing neighbor hadn't made another appearance.

A moment later a wide-eyed Winnie skidded to a halt in the open doorway. Crossing herself at the sight of the bathtub, she breathlessly announced, "Mistress, a man of God has come calling on you. Mayhap he purge de duppies—"

"Indeed, I'll be sure to ask him for a friendly neighborhood exorcism," Viveca mocked. She stared down at her grimy clothing. "Mercy, I look a sight, but I suppose I must greet the caller nonetheless."

"Yes'um. He be in the parlor, ma'am."

Remembering the disgraceful state of the room, Viveca muttered, "Oh, splendid, our lovely parlor, all decked out in cobwebs and mice. Why didn't you just show him out to our cozy root cellar?"

With Winnie frowning after her, Viveca hurried off. So a clergyman had come calling. Here was her chance to make a good first impression in this community. But her house was an eyesore—and, as Maxwell Beecher had so charmingly put it, she looked like a chimney sweep. Oh, well, none of that could be helped at the moment. It would be far worse not to receive the gentleman.

Near the parlor, she paused at the pier table, anxiously eyeing her reflection in the crazed old mirror above. She might have been looking at someone's cleaning woman, judging from her disheveled red hair pulled back in a kerchief, not to mention the fresh smudges on her cheeks. She used the edge of her headscarf to tidy her face as best she could, then squared her shoulders and marched into the room.

Her quick perusal of the room revealed no skittering mice, thankfully. Then Viveca's gaze paused on a tall, blond man in a black suit. He stood with his back to her next to the piano, his shapely hands clasped behind him. Evidently hearing her enter, he turned and smiled in pleasure at what he saw.

Viveca returned his smile, similarly gratified to catch sight of the gentleman's youthful face, his handsome if sharply hewn features, pale blue eyes, even the prominent Adam's apple above his clerical collar. She noted that his suit was smartly cut, his shoes honed from expensive leather, and he exuded an aura of moneyed gentility.

"Miss Stanhope, may I welcome you to Savannah?" he greeted with an exaggerated bow and a barely discernible Georgia accent.

"Why, thank you, Father," she replied awkwardly. "I don't mean to sound rude, but may I ask how you came to know I'm here?"

"Why, certainly. A member of my parish, Mr. Cornelius, informed me of your arrival."

"Ah, yes, good old Mr. Cornelius," Viveca muttered. She glanced about the ratty, filthy room. "I'm sorry that we're . . . well, the dust is still settling here—"

"Oh, you mustn't apologize," he hastily cut in, stepping toward her. "You only just arrived in our fair city, I understand."

"Yes, that's true. And you are—"

"Father Aubrey Parish, of St. Bart's Episcopal Church."

"Father Parish." She extended her hand, which he shook briefly though firmly. "Good to meet you."

"And you, Miss Stanhope."

"So you're Episcopalian," she continued with interest. "As it happens, so am I. Grace Church in San Francisco."

He literally beamed at that. "Ah, the esteemed Grace Church—I'm impressed. How fortunate for our congregation to have another Episcopalian in our midst."

"Thank you." She indicated a threadbare settee. "Please, Father, won't you have a seat?"

"Certainly, thank you."

Waiting until she had ensconced herself in a lumpy, faded wing chair near the fireplace, he sat down and carefully crossed his long legs. He was about to speak when both flinched at the sounds of loud banging and florid cursing coming from the back of the house.

"I'm sorry—the plumber," Viveca explained.

"I see." The priest grimaced as a crashing sound shook the floorboards. "Have I come at a bad time?"

"Oh, no, not at all," she replied cheerily. "May I offer you a refreshment?"

"No, thank you, I shan't stay for long. I know you must be quite busy—with, well, the plumber, unpacking and so forth."

"Yes, it has been a rather hectic time," she admitted with a nervous little laugh.

"And your journey here must have been a long one. I mean, traveling all the way from San Francisco."

"Yes, it was."

"So what brings you to our fair city, Miss Stanhope?"

Although his question prompted a needle of anxiety, Viveca was prepared for such curiosity. "Actually, my father was a longtime friend of your Mr. Cornelius, who also happens to be the agent who sold me this property. He and my father attended Tulane together years ago. Back then, I believe it was still called the University of Louisiana."

"Ah, how fascinating. I must say Mr. Cornelius seems to be a most knowledgeable and capable fellow. He's also an esteemed member of our vestry."

Viveca bristled at this testimonial. "Is he? Well, I do hope the man has been more forthcoming with you than he has been with me."

The priest grew flustered, shifting his weight on the settee. "I—I'm not sure I know what you mean."

Regretting her hasty criticism, Viveca replied, "Well, let's just say that the—er, rather unkempt—state of this property was something of a shock to me on my arrival. Although my man does assure me the house is structurally sound."

"Oh." As she had spoken, Father Parish's coloring had deepened. "I—I'm so sorry."

"Don't apologize, it's not your fault," she quickly reassured him.

"Is there some way I can be of assistance?"

She waved a hand with bravado. "Oh, no, we'll be fine. And I never finished answering your question about why I settled here, did I? You see, recently, after my father died—"

"My sincere condolences," he cut in fervently. "Er—Mr. Cornelius mentioned your loss, as well."

"Ah—thank you. Anyway, I just felt it was time to make a new start elsewhere. I remembered Father speaking fondly to me of his visits here to Savannah. Then when I found Mr. Cornelius's address among his effects . . . well, one thing led to another and—"

"San Francisco's loss is our gain," Father Parish finished eloquently.

"Well, I shall hope so," she rejoined modestly, warmed by his compliment.

He gestured toward the piano. "Such a handsome instrument. I don't remember it belonging to Grace."

"Yes, it's mine. Er—did you know Miss Fulton?"

He nodded sadly. "Yes, poor soul. Grace attended our church faithfully until close to the end, when she became . . . well, I hate to say it, but rather unhinged. She never left the house and wouldn't receive callers. I tried to visit her many a time, but always ended up having to leave my card."

"How tragic." Feeling discomfited by his revelations, she nodded at the piano. "My instrument only arrived this morning, and we had quite a time getting it inside—"

"No doubt. But it appears to have survived your journey in splendid condition. Do you play?"

At once Viveca warmed to the subject. "Oh, yes. I must tell you that not only do I play, I was hoping I might teach here."

"Really? So you're a bona fide piano teacher." With an intrigued smile, he asked, "Tell me, did you study at the Boston Conservatory?"

Viveca was amazed. "Are you clairvoyant?"

He chuckled. "No, not at all. But unless one wants to study in Europe, the Boston Conservatory seems the only logical choice for any serious music student here in the States. Indeed, my cousin from Charleston studied piano there. Years ago Mother and I went up there for Claire's senior recital. She played the Tchaikovsky B Flat Concerto, which I'd also heard von Bülow play in Paris during my grand tour."

Now Viveca was so impressed, she clapped her hands. "Oh, I should have loved to have heard von Bülow! I was so saddened to hear of his death last year. And of course I'd adore seeing Paris, as well." With a poignant smile, she admitted, "My parents and I were going to go there after I graduated. But then my mother suddenly took ill . . . and we lost her."

"My, you have had your share of tragedies, haven't you, my dear?" He spoke gently. "Again, my deepest condolences."

She murmured a platitude.

"And I'm sure you will visit Paris one day. But I must add that Boston is quite a lovely city as well, with any number of cultural attractions. You were fortunate to have studied there."

"Oh, I agree," Viveca concurred, pleased to be in the presence of such a refined man. "And my elderly aunt was such a joy to live with, too, until she . . ." Not wanting to mention any more illnesses or deaths, she finished, "Yes, a fine town."

He grinned. "Well, I cannot believe our good fortune, to have such a gifted musician in our midst. Old Mrs. McCarthy has been this town's only real music teacher for over half a century, and if you don't mind my saying so, the poor thing has become tone deaf."

"Ah, what a shame," Viveca murmured, while thinking, *What a boon for me.*

"Not to mention we're always in need of someone to fill in for our pianist at church. Mrs. Buchanan has chronic pleurisy, you see. In a pinch, I can play a chord or two myself, though I always feel as if I'm imposing on my flock."

"Oh, I'm sure you're fine," Viveca gushed.

He snapped his fingers. "Perhaps I might partake of your services?"

This question delighted Viveca. "Why, Father—are you offering to become my first pupil?"

Although a telltale blush stained his cheeks, he replied firmly, "I am, indeed." An unexpected hint of mischief gleamed in his eyes as he added, "Although I must say that I think an audition of my new music teacher is in order."

"Oh, do you?"

Almost wistfully, he asked, "Would you play for me?"

That charming request Viveca could not refuse. "Well, I suppose I should check to make sure my instrument has arrived intact." She rose, smoothed her skirts and went over to the piano. She reached out to play a chord or two, then frowned. "It's a bit out of tune, you know," she murmured over her shoulder. "Most likely due to the jostling from the move here—not to mention the laborers turning it on end while trying to get it inside."

"Believe me, Ms. Stanhope, I'd be the last one to notice any discordance," he replied. "Please, do play, and before I leave, I promise to give you the name of the church's piano tuner."

"Very well." Viveca sat down and launched into "The Spanish Cavalier." She gave the spirited tune her best, her fingers moving strongly, precisely, over the keys, drawing out each trill and flourish. Inwardly she mused that she was auditioning not just for a job as a music teacher, but also for a new life.

She finished and turned to see him watching her, enraptured. Heartily clapping his hands, he stood. "Bravo! Bravo! My dear, you are gifted!"

She stood and dipped into a bow. "Why, thank you, kind sir."

"I cannot wait to introduce you to our parish. You will be coming to Mass this Sunday?"

"Why, I'd be honored."

Beaming, he stepped forward. "I should also be proud to introduce you to my prayer group. We meet every Wednesday evening to meditate and read the Scriptures."

Viveca had to struggle not to smile; he was so intently pious. "Why, yes, one of my favorite pursuits is, of course, studying the Bible. I eagerly anticipate meeting all of your parishioners." With an almost coy smile, she added, "And perhaps your wife as well?"

He blushed vividly. "So far, I haven't had that particular pleasure."

"Ah," Viveca murmured, her mind humming.

Haltingly, he confessed, "I—I suppose I've been waiting for the right lady to come along—you know, someone with whom I'd have, er, much in common."

"I see."

He broke into a shy grin. "At any rate, I must be going and let you get back to your unpacking."

"I suppose you're right," she agreed, "although this has been quite a pleasant diversion."

"For me as well. Again, isn't there anything I can do to be of help?"

"No, thank you, I think my four servants and I have it in hand. And you've already helped me considerably with your gracious welcoming visit." She lowered her voice. "Unlike my ghastly new neighbor."

He frowned in puzzlement. "You mean Max?"

"You know him?"

"He's my cousin."

Viveca's hands flew to her face. "Oh, no, I didn't mean—"

But the priest merely laughed. "Please, you mustn't apologize. Max is the black sheep of our family, much as he's considered a prime catch hereabouts. I must say in his defense that his mother was quite a harridan who henpecked poor Max's father to death. Perhaps that's why he has developed such an irascible character, particularly among the fairer sex."

Viveca sighed. "I guess I shouldn't be too hard on him. He did help the laborers move my piano into the parlor." She gestured toward the windows. "I hadn't realized those were jib windows, you see."

"Well, good for Max. Perhaps there's hope for him, after all. We might even see him at Mass one of these days."

"You mean he doesn't attend?"

"At Christmas and Easter, with the rest of the infidels."

She laughed. "Father, I look forward to getting to know you better."

He took her hand and warmly squeezed it. "Miss Stanhope, let me assure you, the feeling is mutual."

Moments later as Viveca showed him out, she had the distinct feeling that fortune had just smiled on her.

Chapter Six

There was something decadent about this bathtub, Viveca mused.

That night she stood in her bathroom, admiring her new tub amid the soft glow of two candles on the sink. All cleaned up, gleaming white, the vessel stretched before her, long and elegant with its voluptuous lines and carved claw feet. The plumber had managed to connect all the fittings. He'd also cleaned out the small coal water heater that was now percolating away on the floor. Whether it was due to the heat of the small boiler or some whim of the fates, the cold spot in the room was absent now—thank goodness.

Viveca went over and gently turned on the hot water. After a few sputters and spurts of dirty water, a pristine warm flow began streaming into the vessel. Smiling at the sight of steam beginning to curl, she eased on the cold water and put the stopper in the tub.

What a pleasure to anticipate a nice, leisurely soaking after such a long, arduous day. Of course, her moments with Father Parish had been most encouraging, but turning this ramshackle house into a livable home would not be easy. It did feel good to know she'd be able to think of the good father as a mentor—perhaps even more.

Did this mean she was willing to reconsider her doubts regarding the institution of marriage? Certainly, overcoming the massive shock of Erskine's seduction and betrayal, coming right on the heels of her parents' deaths, would not be easy. So far she'd planned only as far ahead as her move to Savannah, her desire to support herself here as a music teacher. But now she'd met a man who was clearly trustworthy—and practicality forced her to consider the possibility that becoming the wife of such a socially prominent clergyman could secure her future status here. Of course, men of the cloth tended to be an impoverished lot, but this priest's clothing, mannerisms and level of sophistication seemed to indicate otherwise. Poor-as-church-mouse clergymen did not travel to Boston for piano recitals, much less take grand tours of Europe. Besides, Father Parish was Maxwell Beecher's cousin, which once again indicated he hailed from old money.

Though thank God for the contrast between his courtliness and his cousin's beastliness!

Yes, the prospect of regaining the financial security and social prestige she'd lost in San Francisco was quite tempting. Of course, scheming possible matrimony with the priest did make her seem conniving. But perhaps it was high time she became mercenary and put herself first. Being naive, trusting and innocent had only brought her to ruin heretofore. She was determined that no one would learn of her previous fall from grace. Besides, if ever a match should develop between her and the good father, she would hold up her end of the bargain and perform her duties brilliantly. She would hardly exploit the man.

With the tub now full, she turned off the spiggots and removed her dressing gown. Naked, she shivered with the sudden odd feeling that someone was watching her. She glanced about warily. The small bathroom window was shaded and heavily curtained in faded blue damask; the walls with their graying silk brocade wallpaper sported no holes for prying eyes to peer through, even if the shifting shadows cast by the candles were spooky. The ceiling was yellowed, shrouded with the ever-present cobwebs, but otherwise seemed intact.

Shaking off the feeling of disquiet, she went over to her carpetbag and pulled out a small, cloth-wrapped bundle, wiping a tear away as she unwrapped the last bar of rosewater soap her father had given her—the final vestige of her former life of luxury and privilege. She'd allow herself this indulgence tonight; Lord knew it would be a long time before she could afford such extravagances again.

She crossed to the tub and sank her weary body inside. Oh, the pleasure! she thought, feeling the deliciously warm water enveloping her. Running the cake of fragrant soap over her body became a sensual feast.

Which was perhaps the real reason the entire subject of men, of romance, had been verboten in her mind: her own shameful weaknesses, the wickedness of her flesh. Oh, she did not want to think about such things now—her forbidden carnal side. The pleasures and the iniquities. The memories of Erskine, of how he had seduced her, taken advantage of her, callously broken her heart.

But he'd also roused in her lustful longings that she now knew might never quite be stilled. This was surely her punishment for the sin of adultery, whether or not she'd been naive and exploited at the time. This was why she must take care to never again become embroiled in such an imbroglio.

Of course, marriage to a priest might be another situation altogether, a union where coupling would be perfunctory at best, her guilty secret safe. How dear that blessed prospect of safety!

For now, she lay back in the tub and tried to turn her mind to neutral territory, more memories of home: the spectacular views of sunset on the bay from Russian Hill; the colorfulness of the Jefferson Street Promenade on Fisherman's

Wharf; the glory of the cherry trees in bloom at the Japanese Tea Garden; the sweet music floating on a summer day, the haunting strains of "The Lorelei" played on her piano . . .

The stirrings of enchantment, the twinge of secret longings. The thrill of fingers touching her, teasing her, caressing her. The tempting heat curling between her thighs, the tightness throbbing deep inside her belly, the overwhelming urge to surrender to the flood of ecstasy . . .

Viveca gasped and sat bolt upright in the tub, her eyes wide open. What on earth was going on here? She'd just felt herself drifting, slipping away, and then she'd felt as if someone—something—had been touching her! She could have sworn she'd felt the teasing caress of fingers—a man's hot, wicked fingers!—on her breasts, her belly, even between her thighs! She glanced downward to see that her nipples were tight and red as two small rosebuds, and her thighs trembled even in the heat of the water.

Mercy! She was allowing her imagination to run amok and would soon be in deepest trouble if she didn't regain control of herself. Had the priest unwittingly inspired this lapse? Was it the memories of Erskine? Or was the root of her sin her maddening new neighbor, Maxwell Beecher?

To her shame, she strongly suspected the latter.

Viveca hastily scrubbed herself, then rushed out of the bathtub.

Later, Viveca tossed and turned, unable to get her disquieting moments in the tub out of her mind. She had never held a belief in the occult, but this was an odd place, to say the least, and she had felt such strange erotic sensations while bathing, as if some unseen presence were indeed touching her amid that eerie refrain of sensual music. Now each teasing of the breeze at the curtains, each scraping of a tree limb against the side of the house, each shifting shadow on the bedroom floor, seemed charged with supernatural expectation.

The sounds were spookiest of all—the old house creaking and settling, shutters squeaking and rattling, her bedsprings singing. At one point Viveca even thought she heard the thud of footsteps overhead, unbalanced footsteps going *ker-thump, ker-thump, ker-thump*. She couldn't imagine skinny Winnie making such a robust sound. No, the noise definitely seemed masculine, like a man plodding along . . . and dragging a peg leg.

Could it be Miguel? Again she was skeptical. Despite his limp, Miguel seemed much lighter on his feet than this.

She chided herself for her foolish ramblings, flipped and flailed, beat her pillow, straightened her covers, and willed her eyes closed. When at last sleep came, her slumber was fitful at best. A man's face haunted her dreams, the face of a stranger—a dark, handsome, brooding visage with black eyes, jet hair and intense, tormented features. She saw his mouth move, heard his voice whisper, *Lorelei . . . Lorelei*, as in the song. But when she jerked awake, listening, the voice was gone.

Good Lord, who had invaded her dreams? Was it the same presence she'd sensed in the bathtub? Was it his footsteps she'd heard overhead? Whoever this strange spirit was, she'd sensed his pain, his wrenching sorrow.

Spirit? *What* spirit? She was imagining things, allowing this creepy old house to go to her head, and morning would come whether she indulged her fancies or not. With a groan she flung herself over, tried again to sleep, but still she was restless.

She could almost feel the moment midnight came. Midnight. The witching hour. The full moon . . . Abruptly she jerked awake at the sounds of howls. *Mercy*. The piercing barking shattered the night like the hounds of hell. Was it Ruvi's dog again? No, this din was much louder, deeper, like a wolf.

Was there *never* any peace to be had in this house at night?

Annoyed as much as she was alarmed, Viveca stumbled out of bed, drew on her wrapper and slippers and went out onto the veranda, her eyes scanning the misty, moonlit expanse in the direction of the awful cacophony. At last she spotted the hulking shape of a man in the distance. She gulped. Was her neighbor outside again? Did he howl at the moon?

Even as she mused cynically that she wouldn't doubt Maxwell Beecher would bay at the moon, she watched, appalled, as the distant figure fell to all fours and sprinted away toward the back of her property. At once the howling ceased.

"My God! What on earth?"

Viveca rushed down the veranda, hoping to catch another glimpse of the dog—the man, the dog/man—whatever it was. She almost couldn't believe what she'd seen—but why would her eyes deceive her? Still, when she reached the back side of the gallery, she spotted nothing other than the still-quaking leaves along the beast's path.

Bemused, she stood there for a long moment, determined to make sense of what she'd seen. Had it really been a man, a wolf—what?

Then a new flicker of motion near the foundation of the old jail made Viveca's spine tingle with dread and anticipation. It was the same spooky feeling she'd felt on returning from Maxwell Beecher's gazebo last night. She cupped a hand over her brow and peered past the silvery, sinister trees. Slowly the rustle of leaf and limb crept toward her. She swallowed hard, expecting a monster to leap out of the foliage any second now . . .

Should she run, hide? Somehow fear rooted her to the spot.

Then her heart leapt into her throat as she watched a tall, spectral figure emerge from the hazy trees, gliding with dogged steps into the moonlit clearing. Viveca gasped and cringed into the shadows, unable to believe her eyes. For beneath her shimmered the tall, malevolent image of a large woman, with strands of long, silver hair falling about her wide shoulders. Half shadow, half substance, the presence was dressed in a gray, gossamer, tattered dress. She held a long object in her hand, and was swinging it to and fro as she lumbered along. It was an ax!

Viveca watched, not daring to breathe, as the specter paused, then turned to stare up in her direction. She spotted deathly, wraithlike features—but no eyes, only black, sunken pits where the orbs should have been. Great God in heaven! Did she—*it*—see her there, cowering in the shadows of the veranda? Would it launch itself toward her now, and hack her to death? What should she do?

Just as Viveca feared she might faint, the presence turned and floated off into the next copse of trees.

Floated. Had it really floated?

"Oh, my heavenly stars," Viveca muttered, her hand clutching her chest. She was certain that right before the ghost, the wraith, whatever it was, had reached the trees, it had simply evaporated. Into thin air. This was incredible. The bizarre shenanigans at Hangman's House were becoming harder and harder to explain, much less understand.

Heart still thundering in her ears, Viveca ran for the safety of her room.

Chapter Seven

She was seeing things, imagining things. That was the only explanation that made sense. When sunlight at last dispersed the haunts of the night, Viveca awakened, determined not to tolerate such foolishness any longer.

Flights of fancy are the products of an overactive imagination and an underactive body. That was what her mother used to say. Whenever Viveca was subject to inane prattle or foolish daydreams, her mother would promptly put her to work polishing the silver.

Not a bad idea at all, she now realized. Not that she had much silver to polish. But no doubt she was restless at night due to her strange new environs, and all she needed was to become better acclimated, to pour herself into her new duties, her new life.

So that day Viveca drove her servants relentlessly, making Ruvi and Miguel sand and varnish the floors in the parlor, demanding that Winnie scrub every inch of the filthy kitchen. She had the gargoyle removed from the staircase landing—and when Ruvi suggested he might lock it up in the cellar, she didn't protest.

She polished her piano with beeswax until it gleamed, then sat down and banged out six renditions of Chopin's "Military Polonaise" until she was on the verge of exhaustion. She pulled weeds in the garden, and cut fresh roses for every room in the house. She even visited the crumbling foundation of the old jail annex, stomping about on the expanse of broken stone choked with weeds, as if to give the duppies their marching orders. She didn't retreat, not even when she strode through two more creepy cold spots that all but turned her drawers to ice.

This was her home, and *she* would become the possessor, not these so-called ghosts and duppies, she vowed fiercely. She was the new mistress here.

But when nightfall came, she did not take a bath. Somehow she just could not force herself . . .

Viveca hated herself for her weakness, but darkness found her in her room, cleansing her tired, sticky flesh in the hipbath by the light of a single candle. Somehow she just could not risk a repeat performance of her shocking sensual lapse last night.

Reasonably clean, she slipped on a handkerchief-linen nightie and collapsed beneath the mosquito netting. At once she felt herself drifting off to a deep, peaceful sleep. So much for hauntings, she mused . . .

But after midnight, just as had happened the previous nights, the sound of howls—even more shrill and bloodcurdling than before—made Viveca lurch out of her bed and stagger onto the veranda, while mouthing curses that would have shocked her father on his worst day.

Then she froze at the sudden deafening silence, glancing about in bewilderment. What on earth? The barking had completely stopped. Had it really happened at all, or had she dreamed it?

She acutely attuned her senses, looking, listening, sniffing the air. But she heard nothing beyond the sawing of cicadas, smelled nothing but the dank, swampy air, saw nothing but dark green, glittery shadows. No animal, no creature of any kind.

Then she shuddered at a shimmer of movement to the west, in the trees. Was it the woman with the ax again? Heart roaring in her ears, Viveca watched a new figure ease into view, smoke curling from its head. What on earth? Was this Lucifer himself? Where were his pitchfork and tail?

Viveca's heart thumped until she feared it might burst in her chest. At last a ray of moonlight betrayed the identity of the interloper. It was her detested neighbor, Maxwell Beecher. The scoundrel had paused about ten yards from her house, was smoking away as if he hadn't a care in the world—and staring up at her veranda!

Viveca shrank backward. Had he seen her? The sheer nerve of the man! He was clearly a voyeur, spying on her in this audacious manner. Well, she should go down there and shove his pipe down his throat, just as she'd threatened to do with his gun.

Only she might be eaten by the wolf or the cat or the non-existent dog, or whatever monster lurked in the shadows.

Then in the blinking of an eye, the gliding of a cloud over the moon, the figure vanished, making Viveca wonder if she'd seen him at all . . . or perhaps a ghost?

Enough of this nonsense, she scolded herself. She had a busy day ahead of her tomorrow. She marched herself back to bed, lay down and slammed a pillow over her ear.

But still, sleep wouldn't come, and the night grew even more sticky, oppressive and creepy. Viveca had a battle to the death with a couple of mosquitoes that managed to wend their way under the netting. She started at each small sound, each creaking of an old floorboard, each rattling of a window sash. Again, she thought she heard the odd *ker-thump* of foot-steps overhead, though tonight they were more muted—if no less unsettling.

An hour later, despairing of ever getting any rest in this benighted place, she went downstairs to the front porch, hoping to catch a breath of fresh air. Indeed, she opened the front door to a cooler, more bracing atmosphere on the downstairs gallery. But the old rocker was creaking away as she stepped onto the porch. She cast it a harsh look that actually stilled its treads. *Good*, she thought fiercely. She simply needed to take charge—of everything, but mostly of herself and her mind's foolish ramblings.

She sat down on the old chair and began to rock, watching moonlight glint off the old oak ahead of her, admiring gray cascades of Spanish moss that shifted in the breeze like a tattered shroud. She let her mind drift, relax, mentally playing several choruses of "Rocked in the Cradle of the Deep."

She was actually feeling serene and peaceful when a strange smell began to creep over her, like an oozing swamp. Grimacing to attention, she realized it was the cold, awful stench of death. With the stink was mingled a sickeningly sweet odor, like oleanders in full bloom, fragrant but lethal.

What on earth was happening?

Then her eyes were drawn to a massive branch on the oak, where she caught sight of a sinister form slowly twisting in the night, shimmering slightly in the quicksilver light.

Sweet heaven, surely it wasn't . . . ? She blinked, shuddered, blinked again. But yes, she was staring at a hangman's noose—and from it dangled the spectral image of a corpse!

Viveca shot to her feet without even realizing she had moved. She stared thunderstruck at the grotesque embodiment. She rubbed her eyes, stared again, but the wraith did not budge. It seemed to be the silvery image of a man, though with the heavy veil of leaf and moss cloaking it, she couldn't be certain.

Then the wind picked up a bit and the rope began to creak, slowly gliding to and fro. The presence turned toward her slightly, revealing garish features locked in a horrified death grimace.

Mercy!

Viveca rushed for the relative safety of the house, slamming the door behind her. On the stair landing she thrashed at cobwebs, then howled with pain as she stubbed her toe on the hideously grinning gargoyle, which had somehow reappeared on the landing. With a blistering curse, she kicked it away, and heard it go crashing down the stairs with an ear-splitting clamor.

If Viveca had hoped for any respite upstairs, she was sorely disappointed. At the top of the stairs, she froze in horror, staring up at the nebulous image of a man's leg, minus its foot, that had illogically sprouted from the ceiling above her. Heavenly days, weren't the everlasting cobwebs and the ghosts bad enough? She screamed, though no sound came forth.

Chapter Eight

Viveca awakened determined to find Ruvi and string him up from the Hanging Oak, especially when she saw the dark bruise on her right foot from her mishap last night. She was certain her impudent gypsy gardener was responsible for placing the hideous gargoyle back on the staircase landing. His little stunt wasn't funny at all—indeed, she could have broken her neck in the darkness.

Had he also been responsible for the disembodied leg she'd spotted hanging from the upstairs ceiling? She grimaced at the memory, recalling a vague, silvery stripe coursing down the trouser leg. The manifestation had seemed ghostly and diaphanous, but she supposed a man's pants leg stuffed with newspapers could have created the eerie illusion. Still, the leg had been there one second, gone the next. Nothing made sense.

Especially when she went downstairs, only to find no trace of the gargoyle on the staircase landing, not even a single shard from the shattered figurine on the steps or floor beneath her. Had one of the servants already swept up the debris? Not likely, since she hadn't heard Emmett stirring as yet, and none of the other servants was efficient in the least.

Then was the entire incident a hallucination? Was she losing her mind?

The bruise on her foot was real enough, as her slight limp attested. Doubtless she could go outside to the root cellar to determine the truth. But somehow Viveca couldn't bear the prospect of peering into that subterranean abyss again. Most of all, she couldn't face the possibility that the gargoyle might actually still be there—and intact. Then where would she be?

Deranged. Or, at the very least, on the verge of madness.

Bemused, she went out the front door and stared out at the square amid the balmy dawning of a late-spring morning. The image of the corpse was gone from the massive old oak, as was the cryptlike smell, but the spectral veil of Spanish moss, mingled with the spotty haze, made her shiver.

Viveca had never been one to tolerate tomfoolery of any sort. Her motto in life was to take the bull by the horns. There must be logical explanations for all these weird happenings. Possible mischief from her servants? Or perhaps her loathsome neighbor had hung a scarecrow of sorts on the square, hoping to spook her into leaving. After all, he wanted her house. Well, she would not abide such interference.

She needed to investigate, to find out what was really going on here. Perhaps some of her neighbors might be of assistance. She glanced at the other two homes on the square, the well-kept but shuttered Victorian to the south, the dilapidated Gothic Revival bungalow to her east. Judging from the curtain fluttering at a front window, someone likely lived in the old cottage—someone she hadn't seen or met. The rambling, one-story house was an eyesore, with its overgrown, cluttered yard and sagging verandas. Had Maxwell Beecher attempted to evict that neighbor too?

Half an hour later in the dining room, as Winnie served Viveca the grits and fruit Emmett had prepared, Viveca got straight to the point. "Tell me, Winnie, have you swept up any shattered gargoyles this morning?"

Winnie gasped. "Begging your pardon, mistress?"

"Did you find a shattered figurine in the downstairs hallway?"

Winnie shook her head. "I thought Ruvi put that evil t'ing in de cellar."

"As did I. So you didn't sweep it up?"

"No'um."

"I figured as much. Now tell me, do you know if there are any pranksters hereabouts?"

Winnie appeared perplexed. "Pranksters, mistress?"

"Purveyors of—er—practical jokes."

"I don't know what you mean, missus."

"Well, someone who howls like a dog, or hangs a scarecrow from the oak on the square."

Winnie crossed herself. "You seen a duppy on de Hanging Oak?"

"I saw the *dummy* someone put there."

But Winnie was wide-eyed, shaking her head. "On, no, mistress. Dat ghostie, it be real."

"There's no such thing as a real ghost," Viveca declared.

Winnie appeared more confused than ever.

"Tell me about my neighbors on the square."

Winnie frowned. "Well, there be de Cunninghams 'cross de square in dat big, fine house. Dey an older couple that travel a lot. Dey be in Italy 'til after Christmas. Oh, and Mr. Beecher—"

"Forget him."

"Yes'um." Wide-eyed, Winnie continued. "And over in de falling-down cottage is de old shut-in, Miss Lilac Tupper—"

Viveca's ears perked. "You're referring to the ramshackle bungalow to our east?"

"Yes 'um."

"Perhaps I should go calling on Miss Tupper."

Winnie crossed herself. "Oh, no, mistress, Miss Lilac, she is out'n her head."

"Like Miss Fulton was?"

"Yes'um."

Viveca harrumphed and sipped her tea. "You're one to talk about crazy, Winnie."

Wearing a puzzled frown, Winnie retreated to the kitchen.

In her neighbor's front yard, Viveca was greeted by a snarl of greenery strangling a leggy wisteria tree, along with the smells of honeysuckle and damp earth. She carefully navigated her way through the seedy expanse and climbed the sagging steps to the graying front porch.

Her repeated knocks at the warped old door brought no response. Finally she tried the knob. The panel creaked open, and she was beset by a musty odor from within.

She eased into the dimness, sneezing at the dust. "Hello? Anyone home?"

"Henrietta? Is that you?" called a frail but cultured feminine voice.

"No, madam," Viveca replied, heading toward the parlor to her right, from whence the voice had come. "It's your new neighbor."

"Ah, a new neighbor! How lovely! Do come in."

Viveca stepped into the room and blinked at the dimness. She found the old parlor crowded with threadbare Victorian furniture and shrouded with dust. Stacked about everywhere were newspapers and magazines—*Life*, *The Century Illustrated Monthly*, *The Saturday Evening Post*, along with numerous issues of *The Savannah Daily*—all in piles so thick she judged them to be fire hazards. She heard a plaintive "meow" coming from a distant corner, and watched a fat cat streak out from beneath a chair and skitter out of the room. At least it wasn't black, but a gray tabby.

As her eyes fully adjusted, she spotted a little silver-haired woman hunched in a scarred Windsor rocker near the fireplace. She was dressed in a drab gray dressing gown, her hair long, thick and snarled, unkempt like the room. But Viveca spotted real beauty in the woman's lined face, intelligence in the bright blue eyes.

"Good morning, Miss Tupper," she began. "I'm Viveca Stanhope, from the house next door. I hope I'm not intruding."

"Certainly not. Come closer, child, so I may have a look a you."

Viveca stepped closer and extended her hand. "I'm so pleased to meet you."

The old woman briefly squeezed Viveca's hand, her own fingers cool and frail. "Why, what a lovely thing you are! Please, do sit down."

"Thank you." Viveca slipped into a nearby high-backed chair.

Her hostess continued to eye her with keen interest. "You know, my dear, you rather remind me of myself back when my darling Wilbur first courted me. I've been meaning to come calling to welcome you to our little square, but these old legs don't work as they used to. Anyway, my man Alvin mentioned that Hangman's House had sold again."

Viveca restrained a wince at the reference. "Ah, yes. Were you friends with the previous owner?"

"Certainly, for many years." The old woman clucked to herself. "So sad about Gracie. She just went batty, poor lamb."

"So I've heard," Viveca muttered, frowning.

"Would you care for a refreshment, my dear? I'd offer you tea, but Henrietta and Alvin are off in town running errands."

"Oh, no, thank you, you needn't trouble yourself. I've just finished breakfast, and I can't stay for long." Viveca sneezed, again musing that this old woman's help must have attended the same school for domestic servants as had her own, since this home was in a deplorable condition.

"Bless you," Miss Lilac murmured. "Are you getting settled in?"

"Yes, slowly. Actually, I came here this morning because I have a favor to ask."

"Oh? Of course I shall help if I can."

Viveca leaned forward intently. "Can you tell me anything about the history of this square?"

The old woman laughed. "Well, I suppose I should know a bit, having lived here for most of four decades. Actually, there are only a few of the original owners left these days. I guess just myself and the Beechers—"

"Ah, yes, I've already met the *lovely* Maxwell Beecher," Viveca interrupted.

Miss Lilac picked up on Viveca's wry mood with a snicker of her own. "Quite a rascal that little Maxwell is, always trampling my petunias."

Viveca was taken aback. "But—the man I met was fully grown."

Lilac waved her off. "Oh, yes. My, how time flies. Has Maxwell trampled your petunias as yet, dear?"

"In a matter of speaking," she muttered, growing rather concerned about Miss Lilac's sanity. "But please, do tell me more about our square."

The old woman winked. "Well, you know it's rumored to be haunted."

"Yes, I've heard."

"No surprise at all, not with the cemetery, the ruins of the old jail, and the Hanging Oak all in the vicinity. Thus, the name 'Hangman's Square.'"

"Ah."

"Of course, I don't hold with such nonsense," the woman continued stoutly.

"Nor do I," Viveca seconded.

"But there have always been the ghost stories. Like the hanging victims."

"H-hanging victims?" Viveca hated herself for the stutter that betrayed her anxiety.

The old woman laid a finger alongside her jaw. "I suppose one of the most famous—or infamous, I should say—is the Oleander Man."

"Oleander Man?" Remembering the sickeningly sweet

scent of the flowers last night, mingled with the stench of death, Viveca felt her spine tingle.

"He was a gay blade who swept into town one spring, married several wealthy Savannah widows in turn, then poisoned each with oleander tea."

Viveca squirmed in her chair. "My God, how horrible! But who would be stupid enough to drink oleander tea?"

"Well, three of our flowers of the South did, before the sheriff caught the scamp just as he was about to poison the fourth. The man was tried and executed back in the early forties."

"Well, good riddance."

"I do agree. But some folks claim they still see the Oleander Man at night, swinging from the Hanging Oak. Supposedly his face is fixed in some sort of grotesque death grimace."

Now Viveca was on the verge of panic. Oh, mercy, she'd *seen* this man last night—his scowl, the smell of the flowers . . .

"Then there's the Quaking Lady," Lilac continued.

"Quaking?" Viveca shrilled out the word.

"Yes. It was seventy or more years back, I'm thinking. Legend holds she went crazy one night and set fire to the mayor's house, killing him. Thank heaven his wife and children were out of town at the time, and later 'twas revealed the poor lass had been his spurned mistress." Lilac clucked to herself. "Passions do run high here in the South, my dear. But still, he *was* the mayor, and he *did* slow-roast like a steer on a spit—"

"Heavenly days!" Viveca touched her suddenly tight throat.

"A band of irate citizens lynched the poor girl right here on the square. Evidently in their haste, they hanged her improperly. It took her most of an hour to strangle."

"Mercy."

Now a distressed quality tightened the old woman's visage. "To this day, some claim they see still her, twitching and jerking on the Hanging Oak. Thus her name, the Quaking Lady."

"How awful."

"And there's the third one."

"You mean three on a tree?" Viveca gasped, before realizing she'd just made an inane rhyme.

The old woman laughed dismissively. "Oh, Murfa isn't ever seen hanging from the oak, as far as I know."

"Murfa?"

"Murfa Divine, the Ax Lady."

Ax Lady? Viveca merely mouthed the words, for by now she truly was speechless.

"She was a mean one, Murfa was. Murdered her husband and in-laws, hacked them all to death with her ax. She was hanged on the square back in the thirties. Broke the rope the first time, she was so huge. At any rate, I understand her executioner lived briefly in your home—a boarder there, I think."

"Good grief," Viveca mumbled.

"Anyway, Gracie always used to claim she saw Murfa creeping into her yard from the ruins of the old jail, swinging her ax as she moved." She paused, sighing dramatically. "Which is why I knew Grace had gone loony."

"Ah." Viveca felt as if a boulder were wedged in her throat.

Lilac lifted her chin. "I, of course, am above such craziness."

"As am I," Viveca asserted, fingers clutching the arms of her chair. "So tell me, are *all* of these alleged ghosts former murderers?"

"Unfortunately, yes, though there's been gossip of a few other specters who were somewhat less colorful. Let me see . . . there's the Street Sweeper and the Poor Relation. The Street Sweeper is known to sweep the streets—and as for the Poor Relation, well, I don't know much about her, other than the fact that she was, of course, quite poor."

Viveca flashed a tight smile. "Of course."

"Then there are the rumors of the werewolves, what with

all the cats and dogs the sheriff has allegedly found around town, mutilated or with their throats slashed."

"Oh, dear." Viveca gulped, remembering how she had watched a man fall to all fours and sprint away into the night.

"Many who have lived here have heard the howling—though not I, of course."

"Nor I," Viveca quickly added.

Abruptly Miss Lilac grinned. "But of all the villains hanged on the square, the most notorious one of all was Alex Fremont. Fremont was the very scoundrel who built your house back in the early 1830's. A wealthy cotton planter—but quite a womanizer, that one. The devil incarnate with the fairer sex. Why, scandal stalked his every move until—"

"Yes?" By now Viveca was on the edge of her chair.

"He was tried for murder."

"You're jesting. *Another* murder? What is this town? The *murder* capital of the South?"

Lilac chuckled. "Well, sometimes it seems that way. As for Fremont's crime, legend holds it happened in broad daylight, on Oglethorpe Square. One of Fremont's former flames caught sight of him out with his latest paramour—what was her name?—ah, yes, Lorelei."

"*Lorelei*," Viveca whispered, falling back in her chair with a stunned expression.

"Of course, I remembered her name because of the famous Heinrich Heine poem, and the music by Frederick Silcher. As I'm sure you're aware, in mythology the Lorelei was a siren perched on a rock along the Rhine River, an enchantress who lured poor fishermen to their deaths. And this particular Lorelei certainly put her fatal spell on Alex Fremont."

"What do you mean?" Viveca asked tensely.

Excitedly, Lilac continued, "I mean that Fremont's affair with Lorelei was ultimately his undoing. When his scorned lover spotted the two of them together, she was so enraged, she attacked them with a knife. Alex pulled out a pistol and shot her straight through the heart."

Viveca cringed.

"Caused a horrible scandal hereabouts. Fremont was tried for murder, found guilty—"

"Wait a minute," Viveca interrupted. "Found guilty? But if she attacked him first, wasn't it self-defense?"

Miss Lilac leaned forward and wryly confided, "The woman Fremont shot was, it seems, the circuit judge's granddaughter."

"Ah."

"In any event, Fremont, like the others, was eventually hanged right here on our dear little square."

Viveca winced, struggling to absorb everything she'd heard. Then a sudden, sickening feeling swept her. "Fremont—er, he didn't have a peg leg, did he?"

"A peg leg?" The old woman pensively stroked her jaw. "No, never heard Fremont was lame, only handsome as Satan incarnate." She brightened. "But, speaking of missing members, there was the General, of course."

"What General?"

"Why, General Claude Hackberry, who lived in your house briefly after the war. That poor soul lost his foot at the Battle of Shiloh, and never did recover from his injuries, I've heard. Died within a year or so."

"And doubtless, never found his foot," Viveca muttered.

Lilac cackled. "Never found his foot—now there's a funny one. As for Mr. Fremont, well, I did hear something about him and a bathtub."

"Bathtub?" Viveca half shrieked.

With a naughty wink, Lilac explained, "Evidently, the old bathtub at Hangman's House was Fremont's favorite spot for—shall we say, frolic?"

Viveca could feel her heart pounding. "I—er—how do you know *that*?"

"Henrietta told me. That was years ago, when Gracie first moved in, and I sent my people over to help her. Apparently, the poor soul ran through her house stark naked, screaming out something about a naked man being in her bathtub— though of course no one was ever found."

"You can't be serious!"

"Oh, yes. Local gossip held it had been Fremont's bawdy ghost joining Gracie for her ablutions. Anyway, following that incident, she made the servants bury the hated vessel in the cellar."

Viveca could only stare.

Miss Lilac reached out to pat Viveca's hand. "You know, dear, I really should be offering you a refreshment. My people should return at any moment—"

But Viveca stood, unnerved and desperate to leave, although it was hardly Miss Lilac's fault. "Thank you so much, you've been so kind and more than helpful. But you see, I've barely begun to unpack, I have gargoyles on the loose, and . . . really, I must be going."

"Must you already?" Lilac asked wistfully. "It's so lonely here."

Viveca gently squeezed her hostess's frail arm. "I'll come again soon. I promise."

Viveca was relieved to see a smile light the old woman's face as she left. She fled the old house as if it were afire and all but vaulted across the square, giving the Hanging Oak a wide berth. Of course, it made no sense to retreat to her own particular house of horrors, but nothing was making sense anyway.

Or perhaps it was all making *too* much sense—especially what she'd just learned about Alex Fremont, his ghost, and his favorite spot for frolic—her own bathtub. Forevermore!

She entered the house to find Winnie laconically drawing a feather duster over the pier table. "So you met crazy old Miss Tupper, eh?" the housekeeper called over her shoulder.

"Crazy, you say!" Viveca scolded back. "As far as I can tell, the only real problem Miss Tupper has is one identical to mine. She has no reliable servants."

Winnie harrumphed. "You talking about old Alvin and Henrietta?"

"I am."

Winnie grinned, flashing her gold tooth. "Well, mistress,

they both been dead for nigh onto twenty year now. Yellow fever epidemic of seventy-six."

"Dead? Yellow fever?" Viveca muttered, reeling. "You're jesting."

"No'um. Now who crazy?"

Chapter Nine

Once Viveca calmed down a bit, she sought out Emmett. She found him in the backyard, on his knees, pulling weeds in one of the gardens.

"Hey, that's Ruvi's job," she called, arriving at his side.

With a pained grimace, he pushed himself to his feet, brushing off his trousers. "That Ruvi a lazybones if I ever seen one."

"Well, I shall speak to him. In the meantime, I've something else for you to do."

"Yes, ma'am?"

Viveca smiled gently. "The old lady across the square, Miss Lilac Tupper, could use our help."

"You talking about that old tumbledown shack? An old lady live there?"

Viveca nodded. "Would you kindly go over there, clear out the trash from her parlor and clean up the yard a bit? You should tell her I sent you, of course."

He blanched in obvious disappointment. "But I'm needed here."

She squeezed his arm. "Of course you are. But Miss Lilac's

home is so jam-packed with old magazines and newspapers, I truly fear it's a fire hazard. Also, for the time being, I think it's better if you're gone for a few hours each day. Otherwise, the other servants will never catch on to the routine here and just continue sloughing off."

He removed his cap and scratched his graying head. "I s'-pose."

"What's troubling you?" she asked gently.

"Sounds like you don't need me no more."

"Oh, Emmett." She fondly hugged him, inhaling his scent of earth and honest labor. "You are wrong. So wrong. Why, you're family to me and I shall always need you. I'd be lost without you."

He grinned shyly, and Viveca felt relieved that she'd redeemed herself.

"Besides," she continued, "that poor old woman . . ." With a sad smile, she confided, "she's living with two imaginary servants."

If Viveca expected Emmett to be shocked, she was in for a surprise when he merely rolled his eyes. "Well, we got that beat, don't we, Miss Viveca?"

"What do you mean?"

Almost matter-of-factly, he continued, "We gots us a porch chair off its rocker, a ghost dog, a wolf man, an ax lady, footsteps in the attic and dead folks swingin' from the Hanging Tree."

Viveca gasped. "Emmett Taylor, you don't mean you—that is, you've seen—"

"I go to Miss Tupper's house now, ma'am," he interrupted gruffly, turning and striding away, while Viveca stared after him, open-mouthed.

Maybe she wasn't crazy, after all.

On the other hand, maybe they *both* were.

Viveca began to dread nightfall. Learning about all the hangings on the square, the spooky goings-on in the vicinity, and especially, the sad tale of Alex Fremont and Lorelei, had only put her nerves further on edge. She was already far better acquainted with Alex Fremont than she ever wanted to be.

That evening as she crawled, exhausted, into bed, she found the stench of death again assailing her nostrils. It seemed to be coming from her very bedclothes! Recoiling, she searched frantically through the covers, scavenging beneath her pillow, and soon found herself clutching two small, foul-smelling cloth bundles tied with string.

What on earth were these? Somehow she knew just who to ask.

Hurriedly lighting a taper, she rushed into the hallway. At the base of the attic stairs, she yelled, "Winnie!"

Seconds later the housekeeper came bounding down the steps, her eyes large as two glowing coals, her hair mussed, her long nightgown trailing behind her. Simultaneously Emmett emerged from his room across the hallway, pulling his dressing gown over his faded pajamas.

"What be vexin' you, mistress?" Winnie cried, arriving at Viveca's side.

Viveca shoved the obnoxious bags under the housekeeper's nose. "What are these?"

Winnie gulped but, to her credit, did not recoil. "Dey grisgris, mistress."

Emmett stepped forward to glare at the housekeeper. "Gris-gris? Woman, are you trying to voodoo Miss Viveca?"

"Voodoo!" Viveca shouted.

One look at Winnie's stricken face confirmed her guilt. Nonetheless she pleaded, "But, mistress, it's de good grisgris. Dey ward off de evil spirits you set loose when you brung in dat wicked bat'tub."

"Evil spirits, indeed!" Viveca ranted. "Will you now put crushed eggshells all around my bed like you did with Miss Grace?"

Again, Winnie's abashed expression bespoke her culpability.

Viveca waved the obnoxious bundles. "Well, they smell like death themselves."

Winnie offered her hand. "I'll throw them out."

But Viveca tightly grasped the bundles. "No, I shall. Silly me, but for some odd reason, I find myself not trusting you. Now go on to bed and leave us in peace before I do something I regret."

"Yes'um." Winnie scampered back up the stairs.

Expression troubled, Emmett stepped forward. "Miss Viveca, you all right?"

She released a massive groan. "Yes, Emmett. I apologize for waking you."

He glanced about warily. "I don't get much sleep in this place nohow."

"I know just what you mean."

Viveca was eager to ask him more about what he'd said earlier, but he quickly nodded toward her hand. "You want me t' toss 'em out?"

She sighed. "No, it's bad enough one of us has to touch the odious little darlings. Go on back to bed, all right?"

"Yes, ma'am."

Back in her room, Viveca intended to toss the repulsive gris-gris off her veranda. Then she had second thoughts, instead throwing them into the potpourri jar on her dresser.

She groaned. She'd been rather harsh with Winnie, and was not proud of the fact that the goings-on in this house were turning her into a witch.

On the other hand, perhaps a screeching banshee would fit right in . . .

Alex Fremont haunted her, his tormented voice calling to her, his touch sending shivers through her body, his suffering and need drawing her toward a torrid fire, an uncertain fate. As if mesmerized she floated toward him, her will plundered, her body consumed by searing, powerful longings . . .

Viveca jerked awake right on schedule, just after midnight, but this time it was a familiar *thwacking* sound that roused her. Still half groggy from her unbidden erotic dream, she stumbled out onto her veranda and headed toward the back of the house, where she could just make out the form of a familiar small man standing beneath her. He was hurling daggers at the shed.

Viveca was enraged. "Miguel! What on earth do you think you're doing? After I warned you not to—"

At her words, the man did not even glance up, but instead ducked under a tree, turned and ran toward the front of the house.

Viveca tore after him. "Miguel! Damn it, I'm talking to you—"

At the front of the house, she froze. Miguel was nowhere in sight, as if he'd evaporated in the torpid night air. How could he have made his escape so quickly?

Then a shiver of movement on the Hanging Oak drew Viveca's attention to the square. Oh, damn, not again! But yes, there was no rest for the righteous—or for her weary eyes.

Viveca sucked in a horrified breath at the sight of the new silvery specter dangling from the huge tree, this one wearing a long dark skirt. Even as Viveca cowered and cringed, the awful being began to jerk and twitch, its woodlike arms flailing. She could even hear low moans shuddering forth from it. Panic urged her to run, yet she felt paralyzed by fear. She blinked, prayed the awful manifestation would vanish, but still the phantom writhed and heaved, its groans becoming howls of pain and despair.

Oh, God, it must be the Quaking Lady!

Then in a slight shifting of the breeze, the hooting of an owl, the wraith was gone. Viveca stared aghast at the nothingness where the specter had hung. Were it not for her wildly palpitating heart, she might have wondered if she'd seen the hideous being at all.

With a cry of horror, she whirled and retreated to her room. After what she'd just seen, lurid dreams would almost be a comfort!

Morning found Viveca in her kitchen, hastily dressed and groomed, with Winnie, Ruvi and Miguel gathered before her at the table. With purple bruises beneath her eyes revealing her lack of sleep, she paced about and read her servants the riot act.

"I want all of this nonsense to cease at once!" she declared.

"What nonsense, *Gadji?*" asked Ruvi.

"You and your dog, the one that doesn't exist." She whirled on Miguel. "You and your knife-throwing, awakening me in the middle of the night. Not to mention those outlandish footsteps in the attic—"

"But, senorita, I no—"

Skidding to a halt before him, she waved a hand. "Don't you dare lie to me! And that goes double for the rest of you! I'm sick to death of your denials—not to mention the corpses twisting in the wind."

"Corpses?" gasped Winnie, crossing herself.

Viveca shook a finger at her. "Who is responsible for those—just you tell me that!"

"Mistress, I not know," Winnie wailed.

"Poppycock. Now, all of you, listen carefully. I just want it all to stop. *Stop.* Do you understand?"

"Yes'um," Winnie croaked.

She glared at the men, who nodded in turn.

"Very well. Now all of you, go attend to your duties—that is, if you can manage to overcome your terminal laziness."

Exchanging confused glances, the men beat a hasty retreat. Winnie stood hesitating, biting her lower lip.

"What is it?" Viveca demanded.

"Mistress, I be sorry 'bout de duppies," Winnie offered contritely. "Mayhap I help you—maybe bring out de Obi-man to catch shadows?"

"Obi-man?" Viveca exclaimed. "What on earth is that? Some sort of voodoo witch doctor?"

Winnie actually cringed at Viveca's scathing tone. "He be . . . well, maybe I jes' make you a potion—"

"A potion? You mean the gris-gris and the poisoned stew weren't bad enough?"

Winnie continued to cower.

"Spare me your *help*, Winnie," Viveca rebuked. "I don't

want you concocting any more witches' brews, or summoning any voodoo charlatans, do you hear me? I just want the shenanigans to end."

"Yes'um." Winnie rushed over to the sideboard.

Viveca collapsed into her chair and buried her face in her hands. She wasn't particularly proud of herself for her diatribe, but she was beyond exhaustion, at her wit's end over the nightly hauntings and her servants' refusals to accept any responsibility. At least she'd managed to put a little fear into Winnie—she could hear her frantically working at the sink, clanging pots, pumping water.

And now all three of her domestics doubtless thought she was crazy.

Well, she wasn't. She was simply suggestible. The full moon, the rumors of ghosts, Miss Lilac's tall tales—all of this had gone to her head.

After all, Miss Lilac had suggested a Quaking Lady, and then she'd seen one.

As for the fact that she'd also "seen" the Ax Lady, the Oleander Man, the disembodied, footless leg, not to mention the bawdy ghost of Alex Fremont, *prior* to hearing Miss Lilac's stories . . . well, she didn't even want to think about all the contradictions in her logic there. She was impressionable. Gullible. That was all. She needed to take charge of herself, quit succumbing to fainthearted histrionics. She was not losing her mind.

Viveca was actually feeling somewhat calmer when suddenly she felt herself being drenched by a cold, sticky, slimy concoction. She screamed in shock and disbelief and stared up at Winnie, the obvious culprit, who stood above her, trembling and holding an empty glass. The witch had just poured a tumbler of goopy water—*something*—over her head. Whatever the disgusting mixture was, it stung her eyes, tasted awful on her lips and had soaked her to the waist. Even her corset felt sticky.

Shaking violently, she shot to her feet. "Winnie, have you totally lost your mind? What have you done now? Drenched me with oleander tea?"

Winnie frantically shook her head. "Oh, no 'um, no'um. I never try to poison you. I jes' mix a little raw egg in water, to ward off de evil spirits."

"You did *what*?"

Winnie was hopping from foot to foot. "De gris-gris, din' work, mistress. Prob'ly 'cause you cast dem from your bed—"

"So you anoint me with raw egg instead? After I told you, no more nonsense?"

"Yes'um," the servant shrilled.

Viveca took a long moment to calm her raging temper. At last she spoke in a measured, ominous voice. "Winnie, if you want to live, I'd advise you to *get out of my sight this instant*."

"Yes, mistress." The servant ran out the back door.

Viveca uttered a sound of frustrated rage. Raw egg in water, indeed. She was a revolting mess, and might never get clean. But she must try—afterward she would strangle Winnie and bury her in the root cellar!

She trooped into the central hallway, considered proceeding straight to the bathroom, then thought better of it. She detoured to the pier mirror, only to cringe at her image. She looked worse than one of the ghosts, like a drowned cat. Her hair was plastered to her head, bits of egg yolk clung to her eyelids, cheeks and throat, and her drenched blouse revealed the upper outline of her breasts above her corset. Worse yet, the egg was congealing and she was growing sticky, itchy, all over.

Then a rap at her front door sent her rushing forward before she really thought. She yanked open the panel to see Maxwell Beecher standing there, looking sartorially splendid in a smartly cut white Panama suit and matching hat. As he caught sight of her, his mouth fell open and he actually dropped the unlit cigar he held.

He looked her over with wide, astonished eyes, his gaze coming to rest on her scandalous bodice. She shoved her arms over her chest and glared at him.

"Having a bad morning, are we?" he inquired solicitously.

"What in hell do you want?" she gritted back.

He whistled. "I see you've answered my question. Actually, I'm playing country gentleman this morning. My poker quartet is due here shortly, and I was wondering if you might have some extra mint in your garden for the pitcher of juleps I'm preparing."

Viveca was beyond exasperation. She uttered a muffled curse, then slammed the door in the contemptible scoundrel's face.

Maxwell Beecher chuckled as he strode back toward his home. Quite a sight his lovely neighbor had been, soaked and dripping, and so very sexy with her voluptuous breasts straining beneath her sopping wet blouse. What in hell had she been doing? She looked as if she'd just taken a bath in raw egg. But that made no sense.

Oh, well. Who could understand women anyway—and the bizarre rituals they pursued for the sake of beauty?

Perhaps he should not have worried about scaring her away from the square, since surely madness would overtake her most any day now. She'd certainly appeared all but unhinged—indeed, Hangman's House had a way of making folks crazy all on its own.

Not that *he* could talk. He had his own demons to battle, much as he hated to admit it.

Besides, to be honest, he rather liked having the woman around now. He might even be able to find a way to offer her some good old-fashioned Southern comfort before she fled the greater-Savannah scene.

A new spring livened his step as he approached the steps to his side veranda. A fresh earthy scent drew his gaze to the garden. He glanced at a vibrant green bed and chuckled. Funny, he hadn't noticed that new patch of mint springing up over there. Enough for at least a dozen pitchers of julep . . .

Winnie made herself scarce for the remainder of the day. Relieved, Viveca didn't bother to look for her.

That night there were no hauntings at all—no footsteps in

the attic, no disembodied legs hanging from the ceiling, no Alex Fremont invading her dreams—and Viveca had her first night of deep, peaceful slumber since she'd arrived. When she woke the next morning she was stunned, grateful for having slept like a baby.

Of course it had nothing to do with the raw egg Winnie had tossed on her head, she told herself. Or the fact that the full moon had finally gone on the wane.

No, superstition played no part in this at all, Viveca told herself as she got up and placed the abhorrent gris-gris back under her pillow.

Chapter Ten

Sunday morning found Viveca church-bound in her best broadcloth suit and ostrich-feather hat. She was ensconced in the old buggy Emmett had retrieved and refurbished from her property's ramshackle stable. Wearing his brown Sunday suit and wide-brimmed hat, her servant sat on the seat before her, snapping the reins on the swayed back of the old gray horse he had rescued from the local slaughterhouse.

Emmett had always been a good scavenger, a skill she and her father had hardly needed during their posh San Francisco days, but one she greatly appreciated now. Her manservant had not only found her the horse, he'd also haggled with the rubbish man, trading a couple of old wagon wheels for a pair of scratched but otherwise intact rattan chairs that she'd sorely needed for her parlor. With an application of white paint, the two now looked lovely on either side of her fireplace. The floors in the room had also been sanded and waxed, the walls relieved of their shredded wallpaper.

Progress had been made. Hopefully, she'd soon be able to purchase additional supplies to refurbish her new home. She had no money for such luxuries now; indeed, she'd barely been able to pay the piano tuner when he'd come out the other day. If she didn't attract a base of students soon, she doubted she could buy food for her household next month. This was the main reason she was bound for St. Bart's today, in an attempt to launch herself in Savannah society. It seemed almost hopelessly naïve to pin her hopes on the presumed sponsorship of Father Aubrey Parish—but that was precisely what she was doing.

She had considered inviting Miss Lilac, her unfortunate neighbor, to accompany her to Mass, then had realized she would not aid her own cause by showing up with an apparent lunatic, a pitiful old woman who lived with long-dead servants and believed Maxwell Beecher was still a five-year-old trampling on her petunias. But Viveca couldn't feel too guilty, since over the past several days, Emmett had cleaned up Miss Lilac's yard and hauled off wagonloads of potentially hazardous paper from her parlor. Certainly Viveca intended to do far more for her needy neighbor; but she must establish her own place here before she could champion the causes of others.

At least the last couple of days had proceeded more calmly, even if the physical work had been backbreaking. Her loathsome neighbor Mr. Beecher had been curiously absent; and although she'd heard the same creepy footsteps and odd sounds at night, there had been no more dogs or wolves howling, and she'd spotted no more presumed ghosts on the hanging tree or in her yard. Her sleep had been relatively dreamless, and she hadn't felt the presence of any more visitors in her bathtub.

Actually, she hadn't taken a bath since that first disquieting experience. She'd continued to try to clean herself with the hipbath in her bedroom. Nonetheless, Viveca was determined to reclaim her own plumbing—in more ways than one, she mused wryly. She didn't believe in such folderol as ghosts, nor could she afford to succumb to the notion that she was simply a slave to a carnal side she couldn't repress. As for the duppies, she was simply suffering from exhaustion following her trip across country and the shock of adjusting to her stark new environs. Her psyche was overly suggestible, her mind playing tricks on her.

Now, as they moved past the cemetery to the north, Viveca admired the view of stately Regency and classical revival town houses surrounding shady old squares. She inhaled the aromas of honeysuckle and roses, admired azaleas dripping with pink and fuchsia blooms, watched the elite of the town glide by in their gleaming buggies and broughams. She even spied a gentleman in cap and ascot puttering past in a new-fangled horseless carriage. Viveca admired the statue of James Oglethorpe, Georgia's founder, on Chippewa Square, and the templelike stone facade of the First Baptist Church beyond. All over town, the mellow tolling of the church bells rose to calm her, taking her even further away from hauntings and duppies.

Soon they arrived on Episcopal Square, where the stone edifice of St. Bart's loomed prominently in the foreground. A neat two-story Georgian rectory stood next to it. That must be where Aubrey lived, she mused. Watching fashionably dressed families and couples gather and chat on the shady lawn near the church's front steps, Viveca squared her shoulders. She considered herself a stouthearted woman, but even she couldn't help but be daunted by the prospect of making an entirely new life here.

And as much as she loved Emmett and appreciated his support, the brutal truth was, she was making that start alone. Indeed, this was the first time in memory she had attended church, a social event, anything, without her father, an escort or a friend. It hit her now as never before how isolated she was, how she truly must champion her own cause.

Emmett slid down and offered her his hand. "I be back for you in an hour, Miss Viveca."

"I—er—you're welcome to come worship with me."

But he soberly shook his head. "No, thank you, ma'am. The rubbish man told me where the A.M.E. church be. I go there now, then come back for you later."

"Very well, if you're sure."

Leaning closer, he confided, "I ain't going with you to no white folks' church in this here town. I know what that hanging tree be for."

Viveca gasped. "Why, Emmett Taylor, I'm sure that's not true—"

He gave her gloved hand a tug. "Come on now, missy. You be late."

Viveca stepped down, raised her parasol and marched off toward the church, looking back to see Emmett regarding her with a troubled frown. She bravely waved back. Although she thought of him as practically a family member, he was doubtless right in his assessment of race relations here in Savannah. Attitudes were somewhat more progressive in San Francisco—a reality that wouldn't endear her to the citizens of this town, she suspected.

Nonetheless, Viveca advanced through the churchyard, nodding pleasantly to those who stared, and continued up the steps. In the vestibule, an elegantly dressed, white-haired gentleman greeted her. "Welcome to St. Bart's, ma'am. Are you a newcomer to our community?"

Viveca smiled brilliantly. "Yes, indeed."

He indicated the sanctuary. "Please, do join us, and don't forget to sign the visitors' roll."

"Thank you. I shall."

Viveca stepped inside the almost-full sanctuary to the soft glow of sunshine through stained-glass windows, the smells of beeswax, perfume and pomade. Numerous stylishly coiffed and hatted heads turned her way as she strolled down the center aisle toward the only vacant pews, at the front. She sat down next to a thin, lavender-gowned matron holding an elaborate Chinese silk fan. The woman nodded briefly and fanned her face. Viveca smiled back and opened *The Book of Common Prayer*, piously burying her nose in it.

Shortly the pianist began the refrain of "Onward Christian Soldiers," and Viveca was relieved to spot Father Parish at the rear of the processional, wearing his white cassock and

carrying a Bible. On spotting her, he broke into a sponta-
neous grin, and she could have sworn she saw a new spring in
his step. He really was quite a handsome man, she mused,
with his fair hair and fine features. He carried himself with
dignity and pride. She felt grateful to have him as a kindred
spirit, and was especially thrilled when he nodded at her
while passing.

Viveca was pleasantly lulled by the service and the hymns,
which reminded her of happier times in San Francisco. Father Aubrey gave a gentle, uplifting sermon on the subject of
devotion, reading several passages from the Song of Ruth.
Indeed, Viveca could have sworn she heard a few romantic
references, especially when he glanced tentatively in her direction while quoting the verse, "Blessed is the man who took
notice of you." At that moment, quite a few eyes turned in
Viveca's direction, and she felt too pleased to be embarrassed.

A highlight came after the sermon when Father Parish
asked that any visitors please stand. After a moment's hesita-
tion, Viveca rose, and amid a hum of expectation from the
congregation, Father Parish introduced her from the pulpit.
"My flock, I know I can count on you to welcome into our
bosom a newcomer to our town, Miss Viveca Stanhope of
San Francisco. She has just purchased Miss Grace Fulton's
house on Lost Lane." Amid excited murmurs, he added,
"Miss Stanhope is a piano teacher, trained at the prestigious
Boston Conservatory. I've already had the pleasure of hearing
her play, and I assure you she is quite gifted. She seeks to min-
ister to our community with her teaching skills, and I'm sure
both young and old amongst you will seek out her talents."

In the wake of more awed comments, the priest announced the next hymn. The lady next to Viveca chuckled
and murmured at her ear, "A music teacher, eh? Well, you
certainly seem to be playing Father Aubrey's tune."

Viveca was far too worldly-wise to blush, although she
slanted the woman a forbearing smile.

When church was dismissed, Viveca was cheered when a
woman walked up and offered her hand. "Hello, dear, wel-

come to Savannah. I'm Agnes Endicott, Judge Endicott's wife."

Viveca eagerly shook the dark-haired woman's hand. "I'm so pleased to meet you, Mrs. Endicott."

"Please, call me Agnes," she gushed. "I must tell you I was thrilled to hear Father announce that we have a new music teacher among us. As a matter of fact, I've wanted to study the piano myself for many years, and now that my children are grown—"

"Why, Agnes Endicott, I demand you stop monopolizing our visitor this instant," declared a second feminine voice, this one deeper, more commanding, with a heavy German accent.

Both women turned to watch a portly elderly matron in lavender satin march up to join them. Her round face and strong features revealed both charm and strength of character.

"Hello, dear, remember me? I'm Hilda Patertavish," she greeted, pumping Viveca's hand.

Since she'd never before laid eyes on this lady, Viveca was taken aback. "I—er—how do you do?"

"Welcome to St. Bart's, dear, and don't let Agnes here commandeer you," she continued forcefully. "She thinks she's the queen of all Savannah society, and doesn't realize I am."

While Viveca stifled a laugh, Agnes protested, "Hilda! Why, I never!"

Hilda wagged a finger at Agnes. "I'll have you know Miss Stanhope here has already agreed to accept my granddaughter Gertrude as her first student. Why, we're meeting at Miss Stanhope's house at—er"—she frowned at Viveca, then finished with a flourish of a ruffled sleeve—"ten A.M. tomorrow to get better acquainted."

"Is this true?" Agnes asked Viveca with a woebegone look.

"Are you questioning my honesty, Agnes Endicott?" Hilda demanded.

Viveca quickly took charge. "Ladies, of course, ten A.M. tomorrow sounds just divine. Why don't you both come calling then? We'll have tea and a nice chat."

"Why, yes, that will be lovely," agreed Agnes, clapping her hands. "Oh, I can't wait to tell Delbert my good news. He'd be here at Mass, of course, but he has an important case starting up next week."

"I understand," Viveca said graciously.

Agnes turned to Hilda and snapped her fingers. "You know, Hilda, we should acquaint Miss Stanhope with our prayer group."

"We should, indeed," agreed Hilda with a bob of her feathered hat.

Agnes beamed at Viveca. "We shall discuss it more tomorrow, my dear. Thanks so much for the invitation. See you then." Waving gaily, Agnes flitted away.

Viveca frowned after the woman, and muttered, "I do hope Mrs. Endicott knows where I live."

"Of course, everyone knows," Hilda assured her matter-of-factly. "We all knew Grace."

Viveca flashed Hilda a sympathetic smile. "Ah, yes. She was a member of this church, wasn't she? I'm so sorry you lost her. Were the two of you close?"

Hilda shrugged her fleshy shoulders. "Not really, although we were acquaintances—at least until the end, when Gracie grew so strange, locking herself away in that creepy old house and refusing all callers. Why, she became every bit as bizarre as that crackbrain Lilac Tupper who lives across the square from you. Have you met *her* as yet?"

"Yes, I have, poor dear," Viveca murmured, again grateful she hadn't invited Miss Lilac to church with her.

Hilda's lips twitched. "Then of course there's the rogue Max Beecher, living right under your nose."

"I've met him, too," Viveca confirmed drolly.

"What a rascal! The drinking, womanizing . . ." Hilda waved a hand in horror. "Let me tell you, if Max didn't hail from such a distinguished family, and didn't own half the banks in coastal Georgia, he would have been ridden out of this town on a rail long ago."

Viveca chuckled. Already she liked the outspoken Hilda.

"You seem to be quite an expert on the local scene, Mrs. Patertavish."

"Oh, my dear, you have no idea. There are no secrets at all here in Savannah." She gestured toward a tall, thin woman who was chatting with the elderly pianist. "Why, everyone knows Libby Aldersleeves lets the lamplighter in her back door each night at midnight—to, er, snuff out his wicks, if you know what I mean."

Viveca could barely contain her laughter.

"And you know that 'important case' Agnes said the judge is working on?"

"Yes?" Viveca prompted.

Hilda winked. "It's a case of sour mash."

"Oh, dear." Viveca grinned.

"My George was Delbert's partner in crime until the ague took him three years ago," Hilda continued. "No wonder Agnes wants to take up an instrument. She'll not get strummed by the good judge anytime soon."

Viveca was charmed but also amazed by the widow's unabashed commentary. Perhaps Mrs. Patertavish was socially prominent enough—or old enough—that it didn't matter to her what others thought. At any rate, she was quite an original. And she had more than sparked Viveca's curiosity.

"Mrs. Patertavish, tell me something," she murmured.

"Anything I can do to help, dear."

"When you came up, why did you pretend you'd already met me?"

Hilda chuckled. "Actually, Aubrey Parish asked me to take you under my wing."

"He did?" Viveca asked, pleasantly surprised.

"Yes. You've made quite an impression on our good rector, so of course I couldn't allow Agnes to think she'd gotten to you first." Glancing away toward the sanctuary exit, she sucked in her breath. "Tarnation! Speaking of Aubrey, just look at that shameless creature fawning over him."

Following the direction of Hilda's scowl, Viveca spotted a

horse-faced young woman dressed in a green silk gown and matching feathered hat. She was hanging on Aubrey's arm and apparently hanging on his every word. He was blushing and squirming, glancing about for any possible escape route.

"Who is that?" Viveca murmured.

"Our disgusting local sob sister, Beryl Bliss, a scandalmonger for *The Savannah Daily*."

"Sob sister?" Viveca repeated, perplexed. She watched as Beryl clutched Aubrey's hand while he stammered and genuflected. Finally he disengaged her clinging fingers and stepped away.

Straining to see, Hilda breathed a sigh of relief. "Oh, good, Aubrey has shaken off that odious baggage and is coming over."

But even as Aubrey Parish made a beeline in their direction, Viveca noted that the notorious Beryl Bliss remained by the door, arms akimbo as she glared at the women. Good grief—Viveca wouldn't want to meet *her* in a dark alley!

Arriving before them, Father Parish grinned from ear to ear. "Good morning, ladies. Viveca, I'm so glad you came today. And I see you're in good hands with Hilda."

"Only too happy to oblige, Father," Hilda put in. "Miss Stanhope is everything you told me she would be. And you know, she and I were just on the verge of dashing off to rescue you from that yellow journalist."

Aubrey blushed, glancing toward the door, where the woman still lingered. "You mean Miss Bliss? Hilda, where is your Christian charity? Doesn't she have as much right to seek redemption as anyone else?"

Even as Hilda opened her mouth to reply, Viveca smoothly interjected, "Father Aubrey, I must say your sermon was wonderful."

"Why, thank you," he rejoined in obvious relief.

"Indeed, Father, you chose such poetic subject matter," teased Hilda. "I almost missed your usual fire and brimstone."

"Hilda, I'm hardly a fire-and-brimstone cleric."

"Oh, no?" she needled. "What was it you were quoting last week from the Book of Daniel? 'Deliver us from the burning, fiery furnace'?"

While Viveca fought a smile, Father Aubrey coughed. "Tell me, Hilda, have you told Miss Viveca about our prayer group?"

"Of course Agnes and I have mentioned it. She and the judge are hosting us this Wednesday evening, you know." Hilda smiled at Viveca. "We'd love to have you join us, dear."

"Why, how nice," Viveca murmured.

"Yes, indeed," seconded Father Aubrey. "Hilda and her brother Myron are both members, and I do want you to meet the others." He pointed toward two couples who stood chatting across the aisle. "The Fitzpatricks and the Thorps. In fact, now seems an excellent time to introduce you. So, Hilda, if you'll excuse us—"

Hilda playfully elbowed the cleric. "Just what sin should I excuse, Father?"

He laughed self-consciously. "Viveca, shall we?"

Fighting a smile, Viveca placed her hand on his arm. "I shall look forward to seeing you tomorrow, Mrs. Patertavish."

"And you, too, my dear," Hilda responded.

As Aubrey escorted Viveca away, she noted with relief that Beryl Bliss had finally left. To Aubrey, she murmured, "Mrs. Patertavish seems to be quite a character."

"Yes, we have more than a few of those hereabouts," he responded rather wearily.

She could hardly disagree.

Chapter Eleven

Viveca's moments spent with Aubrey's prayer group proved quite pleasant, nabbing her several more invitations to try the group on Wednesday evening. Overall, she could not have been more pleased by her visit to the church—thanks to dear Aubrey Parish.

She offered him her gratitude as he escorted her down the church's front steps. "I cannot tell you how much I appreciate your sponsorship and support this morning. And your asking Hilda Patertavish to look out for me was wonderful, too."

"It's our pleasure, dear," he assured her with a grin, patting her hand. "Everyone in my flock just loved you, as I knew they would."

"Well, it didn't hurt to have such a glowing endorsement from the head of this church."

"Any praise I attributed to you was eminently deserved," he insisted. "Now, may I drive you home? Mind you, it will have to be a quick trip, since I'm already late for a meeting of the Sanctuary Guild—"

"Oh, please, don't concern yourself." She glanced about the shady grounds and spotted Emmett out in the street, hat in hand as he stood waiting by the buggy. "There's my man now. Do go on to your appointment."

"Very well. But I must insist on escorting you to the prayer meeting on Wednesday evening."

Viveca was delighted. "Why, thank you, that would be so kind."

He grinned. "I'll call for you at seven, then."

"I'll be ready."

He squeezed her hand and was off back up the steps.

Given her overall triumph, Viveca was tempted to jump in glee. But approaching Emmett, she noted his dour face, and hurried to his side. "Dear heart, what's wrong?"

He gazed at his feet, shuffling from one boot to the other. "Nothing, ma'am."

"Don't tell me nothing. Didn't you like your new church?"

"Yes, ma'am, I like it jes' fine." He hesitated, then added, "I seen that witch Winnie there, with some of her island friends."

"Ah. Is that why you're feeling so dour?"

"No'um. They plenty nice folk there, too."

"Then what's the problem?"

He avoided her gaze.

"Emmett, 'fess up!"

Guiltily he smiled. "Well, they be having a fried chicken dinner after the service—"

Viveca was crestfallen. "And they didn't invite you?"

"No'um, the pastor and his wife, they do."

"Then why didn't you stay? You know how much you love church dinners."

"Yes'um. But I come t'get you, missus, as I properly should."

"Oh, for Pete's sake." She waved a hand toward the square, where several small children raced after a hoop while their parents chatted. "Emmett, it's a beautiful, mild day and I'd love to walk home. Why, it's all of six blocks. I'm not some hothouse flower you must coddle."

His eyes widened. "Oh, no, ma'am, you can't go home unescorted. That ain't seemly."

Viveca was growing exasperated. "Emmett Taylor, don't you tell me what I can and can't do. Now, I insist you go on back to your chicken dinner—"

"Then you come with me, missy," he pleaded.

"Thank you, but I'm really not hungry, and I do prefer to walk." She made a shooing motion. "Go on, now, before I give you a nudge with my parasol."

He chuckled.

Settling the matter, Viveca turned and firmly started off. When she glanced back, shooting Emmett a fiercely stern glance, he gave a groan, then got into the buggy. Good. Both of them needed a chance to establish their roots in this town.

Instead of proceeding straight home, Viveca strolled down Bull Street into the Victorian section of town, where she admired huge, fanciful homes with high turrets and jaunty bric-a-brac, all decked out in charming color combinations—teal and mauve, robin's egg and cream. She smiled at the couples passing her, the men tipping their hats and the women graciously nodding.

Eventually she ended up in spectacular Forsyth Park. She smiled at the sight of families sharing the lovely day beneath the trees, their picnic baskets set out on colorful cloths, small dogs and children dancing about. She watched the comic antics of a group of couples playing croquet, the women in their voluminous skirts and small hats, the men in their sporty suits, caps and knickers.

She wandered up to the majestic French Empire fountain at the center of the park. With its lavish white pedestals, beautifully carved statuary and fine, gleaming sprays, it resembled a lacy glimpse of heaven.

All at once Viveca felt buoyed, happier than she'd been in months. The way things were proceeding, she'd have her station secured in this town very quickly. Why, within a few days, she wagered she'd have half a dozen students signed up, and their tuition deposited in a new bank account.

All in all—aside from the fact that she lived in a very peculiar house—she had not done too badly for herself.

"Well, you don't seem to be doing too badly for yourself," remarked an all-too-familiar, cynical voice.

Viveca turned, tension gripping her features as she spotted Maxwell Beecher striding up to join her. She supposed she should have known she couldn't avoid the cad forever. To her dismay, he looked handsome as the devil incarnate in his dashing black suit with pleated shirtfront, and derby hat.

She spoke coldly. "Mr. Beecher. May I ask why I have the pleasure?"

He chuckled in blatant acknowledgment of the sarcasm in her tone. "Actually, I spotted you here as I was riding to my club for an afternoon poker game."

"Lucky me." Noting his handsome brown horse tethered nearby, she harrumphed. "Poker again, eh? On a Sunday, no less. Tell me, are you meeting the same rogues you were entertaining the other morning when you sought to raid my garden?"

"Yes, those very rascals," he mildly agreed. Slowly he slid his gaze over her, rousing a perverse thrill in Viveca. "I must say you're looking far more presentable than you did then, Miss Stanhope."

She glared.

"You do clean up nicely. I take it you've just come from church?"

"You take it correctly. I've just left Mass, and you're bound for poker. Saint and sinner, then, aren't we?"

He winked. "Are you so certain you can tell one of us from the other?"

"Yes. Quite." Viveca was growing annoyed. "Now if you've finished harassing me, Mr. Beecher, I was actually enjoying my moments of solitude."

He gazed about at the lively goings-on. "Solitude, eh? Yes,

I shall be happy to relieve you of my harassing presence. But first I must wonder what you're doing out here on your own."

"Which is none of your business. Moreover, I might ask the same of you."

"But I'm not an unescorted lady."

"So you are not. Nor I am a shrinking violet." She raised her parasol. "Do you care for a demonstration?"

He raised his hands in mock trepidation. "Heavens, no. And I must say you're settling into your surroundings with considerable aplomb, much as it pains me to admit it."

"Well, I do relish causing you pain," she acknowledged sweetly. "And if I'm settling in well, it's no thanks to you, I might add."

To his credit, he broke into a sheepish grin. "I suppose we did get off on the wrong foot."

"Wrong foot? You all but kicked me with yours, firing at trees, then suggesting you would dynamite my new home."

"Calling it a home remains an exaggeration, in my humble opinion," he drawled.

"Humble, indeed. The truth is, you're a braggart who doesn't hesitate to denigrate the property of others. But that doesn't stop you from playing Peeping Tom at night, now does it?"

He blanched. "Peeping Tom? Whatever are you suggesting now, you wicked creature?"

"How dare you call me wicked." Her chin came up as she continued saucily, "I'm not suggesting anything at all, but stating a fact. I saw you the other night gazing up at my window, like Romeo gawking at Juliet."

He gave an incredulous laugh. "Madam, you delude yourself if you think I have any such foolish designs on your person."

"So you deny leering at me."

"Absolutely."

"You just want to decimate my house."

He lifted an eyebrow. "Well, if your respectable image today is any indication, perhaps there is hope for us all on Lost Lane."

"For me, anyway."

Clearly perturbed, he asked, "Just how are you planning to gain the funds to rescue that—er—eyesore? What skills do you have to bring to bear?"

She chose to ignore the naughty implication in his last question. "Actually, though it's hardly your concern, I'm planning to teach piano lessons."

"Are you?" He appeared taken aback.

"As a matter of fact, my first two students are already enrolled—Judge Endicott's wife and Hilda Patertavish's granddaughter."

He whistled. "So you've already snagged a connection with Queen Hilda, have you? Bravo, my dear. Quite the little social climber you are."

Viveca's voice grew deadly earnest. "I'm a survivor, Mr. Beecher."

"So it would seem." He paused, scowling. "But the Endicotts and the Patertavishes attend St. Bart's, my cousin's church."

"Indeed they do, as did I this morning. In fact, 'twas your cousin, Aubrey Parish who invited me to attend Mass there in the first place."

Thunderclouds loomed in Maxwell's eyes. "Did he?"

Delighted that she was getting to him, she straightened her cuffs in a deliberate attempt to further incite him. "An utterly charming man, your cousin. As a matter of fact, 'tis difficult for me to believe the two of you are related."

Maxwell smiled nastily.

"At any rate, Father Parish came calling earlier this week to welcome me to Savannah—a courtesy I was not afforded by certain of my—er—neighbors, I might add." Ignoring his glower, she continued primly. "Of course we missed your scintillating presence at Mass. Nonetheless, I thoroughly enjoyed the service. Father Aubrey introduced me to members of his prayer circle, and they invited me to come join them on Wednesday night."

"Prayer meeting, eh? So you've already entered the sanctum sanctorum. You don't waste a minute, do you?"

She all but smirked. "Of course, Father Parish will be escorting me then."

At that, Maxwell Beecher grew coldly silent.

"What's this? Cat got your tongue, Mr. Beecher?" she taunted.

Abruptly he loomed closer, his essence engulfing her, his intent gaze capturing her. "Look, miss, you may think you can fool my sappy cousin, but I'm wise to your game."

"I beg your pardon!"

"I'm not overly fond of Aubrey, but I do maintain some familial pride and loyalty, and I shall not allow the likes of you to exploit him."

"Exploit! Why, I never!"

"Don't tell me you never," he sneered. "Being a scoundrel myself, I can readily recognize a charlatan. And you, miss, are a charlatan."

"Of all the nerve!"

"You're clearly hiding something," he charged. "Else, why aren't you married at your age?"

"That is none of your damn—"

"How old are you anyway? Twenty-three?"

"—business!"

"It's downright scandalous for a woman such as yourself to be still unwed."

"You're one to talk about scandal." She stepped closer to glare up at him. "Moreover, I'll have you know I'm *eminently* respectable, from a highly esteemed Nob Hill family."

"Oh, really?" he taunted. "So tell me, if your pedigree is so pure, why would a socially prominent woman such as yourself flee San Francisco?"

"I didn't flee. I chose to come here. And you are an arrogant blowhard."

His voice grew deadly serious. "But a determined one, too. You'll be wise to remember that."

"Meaning what?"

"Meaning stay away from my cousin, Miss Stanhope."

"Or what?"

His next words came ominously soft. "You don't really want me to answer that, do you?"

Maxwell Beecher tipped his hat, turned and strode away.

Chapter Twelve

Viveca fumed as she continued walking home. How dare that cad threaten her. How dare he insinuate she had a tainted past—even if she did.

Why was he so suspicious of her? That answer proved easy. Clearly he was a black-hearted scoundrel who saw only wickedness in the hearts of others. Well, she'd be damned if she'd let him intimidate her.

Turning onto Lost Lane, she deliberately avoided gazing at his house. Closer to home, she was arrested by a splash of color on the square. She was surprised and intrigued to spot a woman in a pink dress sitting on one of the park benches, holding a gay, flower-printed parasol.

Curious, Viveca crossed over to the square. As she reached the center, the woman turned and smiled at her. Although she had to be pushing forty, she was pretty and slender, with long, light gold hair and a dusting of freckles across her pale, lined face.

"Well, hello," Viveca called, stepping closer.

"Hello," the woman called back. "Lovely afternoon, isn't it?"

"Oh, yes."

"Have you just come from church, dear?"

"Why, yes. From St. Bart's."

"Ah, so you're Episcopalian. I'm Methodist."

Viveca eyed the womanly curiously. "How nice. Do you live around here?"

"Actually, dear, I'm house-sitting for the Cunninghams." Reaching out, the woman patted the bench beside her. "Do take a seat. I'm Elvira Withersmith."

Viveca sat down and smoothed her skirts. "How do you do? I'm Viveca Stanhope. So, you say you're house-sitting?"

"Indeed."

"Have you been in town for long?"

"Only a few days, dear."

Bemused, Viveca glanced toward the Victorian house. "But the house looks all shuttered up."

Elvira laughed. "Oh, I only open the back windows." Self-consciously she touched her wan cheek with her gloved fingers. "I freckle horribly otherwise."

"Oh, yes, I've had that problem myself." Despite Elvira's explanation, Viveca remained curious. "Are you a friend of the family's?"

The woman's expression grew poignant and she twisted a handkerchief in her gloved fingers. "Actually, I'm Virginia's sister, but I'm afraid . . ." She glanced away, biting her lip.

"I'm sorry," Viveca quickly added. "I'm prying."

"No, you aren't. I mean, you can't have known." Breathing a deep sigh, Elvira bravely turned to face Viveca. "I'm afraid the sad truth is, my sister and I haven't spoken in over twenty years."

Viveca was shocked. "Oh, my. Why—why, I'm so sorry."

"It was all my fault, you see," Elvira went on, sniffing. "I made an unfortunate slip of the tongue about my sister's—er—girth in front of Jonathan, who was at that time her fiancé. Afterward, Virginia was livid, and I'm afraid she has never quite forgiven me."

Viveca was stunned by the account. "You mean you and

she haven't spoken in twenty years, just because . . . ? Why, how terrible. But if you and Mrs. Cunningham are estranged, then how—"

Forcing a smile, Elvira pulled a silver chain from her bodice and flashed a gold key at Viveca. "Years ago, Jonathan gave me a key and told me I could stay at their home whenever they're gone. Which is most of the time, it turns out, now that the twins are grown and married."

"Ah." Noting the woman's morose expression, Viveca slowly shook her head. "Not to mind your business, Miss Withersmith, but I must say I find your story tragic. It's so heartbreaking. You and your sister not speaking, all these years. Over something that, frankly, seems rather trivial."

Swallowing hard, Elvira nodded. "I know. I've tried to apologize to Virginia many a time, but she always turns a deaf ear."

"Again, I'm so sorry—but at least you've tried your best." Forcibly, Viveca brightened. "Please, while you're here, come call on me—or if there's anything else I can do to help, just let me know."

The woman flashed a brave smile. "Thank you, dear. But my Bible keeps me company—that and Jonathan's extensive library. I'm working my way through his classics, and have not even gotten past Dante and Chaucer as yet. Besides, dear, you already brighten my days with your music."

Viveca grinned. "You've heard me playing?"

Elvira patted Viveca's sleeve. "Oh, yes, dear, and you're wonderful. I especially love it when you play Strauss." With a dreamy sigh she added, "Reminds me of my debutante days, back when I truly was the belle of the ball."

"Why, what a wonderful compliment. And you're so pretty, I'm sure you were the center of attention."

"Thank you, dear." She nodded toward the Tupper house. "I imagine Miss Lilac loves your music, as well."

"You know her?"

"We've met a time or two." Elvira inclined her head toward the Beecher property. "Now, Maxwell Beecher—he's the cock of the walk, eh?"

Rolling her eyes, Viveca drawled, "In his own estimation, at any rate."

Elvira wagged a gloved finger at Viveca. "Be careful of him, my dear. You must know he once made a play to seduce me. Of course that was years back when he was but a fresh lad and before my beauty began to fade."

Viveca made a sound of outrage. "Why, I think you are absolutely lovely just as you are. And a pox on that dreadful man, anyway!"

Elvira actually laughed.

"Are you sure there's nothing I can do for you?" Viveca asked.

The woman regarded her wistfully. "My dear, you have a generous heart. That will always serve you well."

"Why, what a lovely thing to say."

"Just be careful of that rogue living next door to you—"

"Oh, believe me, I will."

"And why don't you go home now and play another waltz for me? I can't think of anything better to cap off this perfect day. Some Schubert would be nice, don't' you think?"

"Why, I'd be honored. And I do hope to see you again."

"Oh, yes, you certainly shall."

The two women said their farewells, and Viveca returned to her house. In the parlor, she played the Schubert Waltz in B-Flat Minor, followed by selections from Chopin and Strauss. But when she looked back out at the square, Elvira Withersmith had gone home.

Maxwell left his poker game early, in a foul humor as he rode home. He'd lost over a hundred dollars, and he never lost at games of chance—indeed, he never lost at anything. But his tormenting, delectable new neighbor seemed to haunt him everywhere he went. Not only had he encountered her en route to his club, but one of his poker buddies, Judge Endicott, had related that his wife Agnes had returned from church all abuzz regarding Savannah's "delightful new piano teacher" and her potential romance with their rector, Max's cousin, Aubrey Parish. Delbert and the others had speculated over the budding love affair, bedeviling Max with taunts and innuendos whenever possible, especially since the lovely Miss Stanhope was known to be his new neighbor. Would he want to compete with his cousin? they'd teased. Would he take her flowers from his garden, or swoon over her in his gazebo? Even Max's calling the four of them "gossiping old maids" had not slackened their appetites for prattle. Max's mood had gone darker as the afternoon progressed, and his concentration had been skewered.

Why had Viveca Stanhope so quickly gotten under his skin? Of course, she'd looked unspeakably lovely today in her crisp fitted suit and feathered hat, her stylish attire showcasing her figure, that mass of red hair, that full, saucy mouth. Seeing her again had only reinforced the sense of potent attraction he felt toward her. Indeed, he wouldn't at all mind having a go at Viveca.

But he may as well hoist himself on his own petard; trying to seduce the prim though enticing Miss Stanhope would only defeat his own purposes. He wanted to be rid of her, not draw her closer. Besides, society dames struck him as a frigid lot—much as he was tempted to melt those layers of ice.

Already Miss Stanhope disturbed his sleep, his peace. And he'd lied to her earlier. Shameful though it was, he had been the one who'd stood outside in the moonlight several nights ago, watching her veranda. He'd stood there brooding, smoking in the darkness, wondering why the stubborn lady was so determined to hold on to the derelict house.

To add insult to injury, it seemed that the conniving little baggage had set her cap for his cousin Aubrey. She'd invaded his territory in more ways than he could count. Max had always found Aubrey pretentious and boring, but also naïve and guileless. As Max had told Miss Stanhope, he felt a familial duty to protect his nincompoop relative from a woman who was surely a gold digger.

At last, a noble motive he could assign himself!

Turning his horse onto Lost Lane, he automatically glanced

toward her house, and saw no visible signs of life there. If she was back from church, she was likely taking her Sunday siesta. Of course, he couldn't allow himself to fantasize about a prospect as tantalizing as joining her.

As the horse made a smart clip down his driveway, his young groundsman, Ely, came sprinting around the corner in his dungarees. "Afternoon, Mr. Beecher. How was your poker game?"

Max slid off his horse and handed over the reins. "I've known better ones, I fear."

"Sorry, sir. Wilda, she come by right after you leave and cook up a potful of chicken and dumplings for you."

"How many times have I told that woman she doesn't have to prepare dinner for me on Sunday?"

Ely broke into a grin. "If you not hungry, sir, I am."

Max patted the lad's shoulder. "Don't fret, she always leaves enough food for several armies."

"Yes, sir."

As the servant led the horse away, Max crossed the lawn, climbed the steps to the side gallery and approached the French door to his downstairs suite. When he opened the door, the familiar, tantalizing scent of jasmine wafted over him, along with the low tinkle of a woman's laughter.

Hell and tarnation! She was back—the minx—ready to torture him again. Max didn't know whether to be intrigued, or annoyed.

Obviously, she wasn't going anywhere, so he might as well face the music. "Hello, you little tart," he murmured, stepping inside . . .

Chapter Thirteen

Viveca had decided it was high time to show the bathtub who was boss. Perhaps her newfound courage stemmed from her surely silly and superstitious hope that Winnie's gris-gris and raw-egg-drenching might have banished the spooks from her abode—but, whatever the reasons, she was ready to deal with her demons.

She poured in some eucalyptus oil—perhaps hoping to ward off evil spirits—and filled the tub almost to the brim with steamy water. She gazed at the pristinely clean tub filled with hot, clear water and could scarcely believe Miss Lilac Tupper's account of Alex Fremont's ghost haunting the bathtub. Indeed, there was nothing here now to explain the weird, wicked sensations she'd felt while bathing here previously.

Surely those odd stirrings had been only a fluke, a flight of fancy. Yes, she'd been rattled, but that didn't mean she should tolerate such inner mutiny. She must take control of her own will, her capricious sensuality, just as she'd taken control of her life in coming here. Lord knew, her lot here was difficult enough already, and she'd be damned if she was going to forgo the pleasures of a good, hot bath!

Though she knew it was a sinful concession to foolishness, she glared about the room, wagged her finger as if to scold an unbidden spirit, and ordered, "Don't you dare try to invade my bath tonight!"

Silence was her only answer. So much for hauntings, she mused wryly.

With a grim nod of her chin, she removed her wrapper and sank into the tub. The warm water enveloped her, and at first she thoroughly enjoyed herself, sliding the sponge up and down her arms, applying the rosewater soap. She inhaled the medicinal scent of the water and could feel her lungs and throat clearing. She'd always contended that eucalyptus was an excellent restorative at bedtime.

Then gradually she found herself relaxing even more, slipping away, dreaming. In her dream she smelled the cloying sweetness of lilac, stealing over her slowly, sensuously, like a lover's caress. Soon she was drenched, overwhelmed with lilac—and warm, so warm she felt as if she were glowing. Music drifted over her again, the poignant strains of "The Lorelei." This time she clearly heard the words, sung in a woman's haunting, silvery voice, the tune so poignant and beautiful, her eyes welled with tears:

> *"I know not what spell is enchanting*
>   *That makes me sadly inclined;*
> *An old strange legend is haunting*
>   *And will not leave my mind;*
>   *The daylight slowly is going,*
>   *And calmly flows the Rhine.*
> *The mountain's peak is glowing*
>   *In evening's mellow shine."*

Long, somnolent moments later, Viveca began to glimpse the hazy image of a beautiful woman standing in the bathroom. Some distant vestige of Viveca's pious, sober self scolded her to awaken, to shake off the spell that had bewitched her, but somehow she could not summon the will to stir herself.

Gradually Viveca's nebulous visitor grew more real, revealing brilliant red-gold hair, tawdry painted cheeks and wicked, bright green eyes. She seemed to be laughing, beckoning some unseen lover with her generous mouth and coy smile.

Most shocking of all, the woman was fully naked. Soft light gleamed on her voluptuous flesh. Her breasts were full, the nipples rosy, her belly gently curved, her thighs smooth and supple. Viveca could even see the thatch of curly, shiny hair between the woman's legs—and strangely felt more intrigued than scandalized.

Then a man moved into view. Viveca could see him only from the back, but he was naked and tan, magnificently muscled, with strong, long legs and hard, chiseled buttocks. His thick, jet-black hair curved about his splendidly formed head, the swath culminating in a sensuous curl at his nape.

Confidently he glided toward the woman until his body enveloped hers. His long fingers gripped one of her breasts, kneading roughly; she sighed dreamily, her red sensuous lips falling open on a gasp. Her beautifully shaped hands stole around his splendid buttocks, shamelessly exploring, skillfully caressing.

Appalled and disgracefully aroused, Viveca watched the man go rigid from head to toe. He tossed back his head, and she even thought she heard him moaning. Indeed, she moaned aloud herself.

Then the woman fell to her knees before him. Mercy, what were they doing now? The woman literally latched herself onto the man, her face hidden, her arms tight about his waist—and then he began to arch to and fro in the obvious, vigorous thrusts of the sex act. At last Viveca realized precisely what the couple was doing! Mortification prodded her to run, to break free, to escape, but still she was powerless, rooted to the spot, locked up within her own trance, melded into the couple's wanton coupling. Tingles of hot pleasure pulsed and arched within her own breasts, her own belly. Her stomach quivered, and her fingers helplessly thrashed the water. She could barely swallow, her throat was so tight.

Then, just as she heard her own raw cries and felt herself on the verge of surrendering to a shattering climax, the entire scene splintered before her eyes into a thousand silvery shards. . . .

Viveca sat bolt upright in the tub, struggling to breathe, reality hitting her with a massive thud. What on earth had she just witnessed? Had she seen what she thought she had seen, or was it another dream, an hallucination?

Whatever had happened, Viveca was shaking so badly, she felt she might never get out of the tub. She was also bereft, in a torment of frustrated need. Whoever her mysterious visitors had been, they had teased her, remorselessly toyed with her, roused her to unbearable desires, then left her hanging, ravenous, unassuaged. If she had ever doubted the weakness of her own carnal flesh, she could no longer.

When Viveca finally regained control of her raging emotions, she climbed weakly out of the tub, tore on her wrapper and darted out the bathroom door. She didn't draw a sane breath until she was upstairs in her room, the door shut behind her.

What on earth was going on in this house? She'd just somehow witnessed the most appalling act—no, she'd been a *part* of it. Was she being punished for the sins of her past? Was she reliving them?

Of one thing she was certain: The culprit had again been the ghost of Alex Fremont—the same mischievous phantom that had haunted her dreams and joined her during her ablutions before. Miss Lilac had been right about him and his preferred spot for seduction. Only he'd brought along a companion this time. A courtesan par excellence. And yet Viveca had warned him not to invade her bath!

He hadn't, she realized with a sudden shudder. She'd

scolded him away, so instead of joining her in the tub, he'd wreaked his vengeance in the most depraved fashion, bringing along a paramour to torment her. He'd made her a voyeur . . . as well as a participant. Even now, she wantonly, brazenly, hungered for more. And she could just picture the devil, laughing at her.

The middle of the night found Viveca prowling her veranda, again unable to sleep. If anything, the sexual frustrations and stark yearnings she'd felt in her encounter with the naughty, bawdy ghosts had only intensified over the last restless hours. Moreover, she couldn't believe she was on the verge of accepting as commonplace something utterly bizarre: that she lived in a haunted house.

But no other explanation made sense. The ghosts in her bathtub, the specters hanging from the square, the man/wolf she'd seen howling in the night, the wraith with an ax stalking across her backyard, the leg suspended from the ceiling, the things that went bump in the night—on and on it went. The countermeasures Winnie had supplied—the loathsome gris-gris and raw egg in water—may have alleviated the situation temporarily. But the phantoms were back with a vengeance. The evil confronting Viveca was obviously too pervasive and insidious to be banished by the charms or incantations of a half-crazed Jamaican woman.

It was bad enough that she lived in such a run-down house. But a haunted hovel—this was beyond the pale!

She peered into the distance, through the thick, inky night. Her neighbor next door had his light on. But she didn't spot him, or his familiar cigar, out on the veranda. Why was he up so late? Couldn't he sleep, either? Or was he entertaining a female caller?

Viveca's stomach churned at the thought, although not entirely with revulsion. Actually, she wouldn't put anything past the brute who had insulted her today. It made her more than a little uneasy that Maxwell Beecher had so quickly guessed that her past might be less than pristine. But it also gave her a welcome sense of power to think he might be so hostile toward her because *he* had something to hide. That might be an interesting avenue to investigate. As for his warning to stay away from his cousin, she'd give that admonition all the consideration it deserved—none at all.

At least Maxwell Beecher was a little better behaved than her naughty bathtub ghost.

Viveca continued to stare, brooding, into the darkness, until a flutter drew her gaze beneath the spooky trees at the back of her property, near the broken foundation of the jail. What nocturnal beast was prowling about now? Was it the gardener's dog, her Peeping Tom neighbor, or the wolf? Her heart pounding, Viveca stood transfixed, watching the foliage flutter, listening to it crackling and snapping as if someone were passing there.

After a moment, a familiar, shadowy figure emerged from the vegetation. Viveca stared, gasped, hardly believing her eyes. Yes, the ax woman was back, stalking across the lawn with her lumbering gait, slumped shoulders and sharp ax. Then about ten yards away from Viveca's veranda, the woman paused and shifted her face upward. She seemed to stare straight through Viveca with her empty eyes—taunting her, daring her.

At first Viveca recoiled, fearful the spirit might harm her. Then, realizing how absurd the thought was, she gathered her courage, stepped forward and raised a fist. "Whoever you are, get out of here! This is my property, my home! Leave me in peace!"

Viveca could have sworn the wraith actually hissed at her before it floated off into the night.

"What is going on in this house?"

Storming into the kitchen the following morning, Viveca confronted Winnie. She realized she was unkempt, her hair untidy, her dress misbuttoned, her toilette incomplete, but she was half crazed from fright and lack of sleep, and she could not bear another moment of suspense.

At the sink, Winnie turned with a laugh. "Mistress, you look a sight, like you seen another—"

"Precisely!" Viveca waved a hand. "Now tell me what ails this house."

Winnie wiped her hands on her apron and stepped forward. "You seen de light, eh, mistress?"

"I see darkness all around me—and specters in that darkness."

Winnie nodded. "You a believer now?"

Viveca tore a hand through her hair. "I don't know. Well, I suppose. There are the wolf calls, the corpses on the square, the ax woman, the leg minus its foot, not to mention that damned bathtub—"

"Aha!" Winnie stepped forward with dark eyes zealously gleaming. "Din' I warn you, mistress? It be a wicked bat'tub, nuh true?"

"Well, true."

"What it do to you?"

Viveca loudly cleared her throat. "I—I have no intention of discussing the particulars with you. Just tell me why my house is infested with spooks."

Winnie gazed about, sadly shaking her head. "Well, it be where dey die, mistress, where spirits lose deir shadows, where dey try to catch yours."

"Oh, splendid."

"Dey be many here," Winnie went on in a low, eerie voice. "Ones that hang from de square. Others murder, steal. Some just lost. Dey all haunt de night."

"Yes, it's rather like bedlam in hell, isn't it?" Viveca quipped.

"De spirits be restless," Winnie continued soberly. "An' sometimes dey not know dey dead."

"Should we tell them?" Viveca mocked.

"Mayhap we should. When de duppy roam de night, usually it be sad, lost. Usually it want something, need something."

Viveca was not in the mood to hear anything profound, especially not coming from her questionably sane housekeeper. She wanted—needed—practical solutions, short of incinerating her new home. On the other hand, she supposed she couldn't afford the luxury of complete disdain toward Winnie's opinings, either.

"So what are you trying to tell me?" she inquired, voice rising. "What can we do about this—this most disquieting situation?"

Winnie gave her an uncertain look.

"How can we get rid of the—the duppies, or whatever?"

"Ah." Lowering her voice, Winnie confided, "Sometimes, back in de islands, we talk to de duppies, ask why dey prowl de night."

"You mean like a séance?"

"Yeah."

"Heavenly days," Viveca declared. "I'll not have a séance in this house. We can't solve this craziness with more insanity."

Winnie clucked to herself. "Den what you call de duppies?"

What, indeed? Viveca could only stare. She had no answers, only a torment of doubts and additional questions.

In the meantime, reality awaited her. She squared her shoulders and clenched her jaw. "Thank you, Winnie, you've been so informative and immensely reassuring. Now I'd advise you to get moving. Mrs. Endicott and Widow Patertavish are due here for tea at ten A.M."

Winnie's brows shot up. "Dey is?"

"Indeed they are. I shall personally brew the tea, of course, and Emmett will go to the bakery for scones, as we don't want to risk poisoning the dear ladies with your culinary delights. You will tidy up the parlor—that is, if you can manage to do so without killing anyone."

Winnie's gulp more than demonstrated that she well understood Viveca's tone.

"In any event," Viveca continued archly, "since both ladies are coming to inquire about piano lessons, bear in mind that my future livelihood—and yours—will depend on the quality of the hospitality we extend to them today."

"Yes, ma'am." Wide-eyed, Winnie hastened to the pantry and grabbed a feather duster. Viveca collapsed into a chair.

Chapter Fourteen

"My dear, I can't believe what you've done with the place," Agnes Endicott gushed as she sipped tea and nibbled at a pastry.

"Thank you," Viveca murmured.

Gussied up in a silk dress and feathered hat, Agnes was ensconced across from Viveca on the threadbare settee. Next to her, Hilda Patertavish, also regally attired, sat with her granddaughter, Gertrude, a fair-haired, polite child of nine. Both women had arrived simultaneously, promptly at ten, and Viveca was pleased that she'd managed to complete her own toilette and prepare tea before her guests appeared.

Hilda was gazing about the decrepit though tidy room. "Well, you've swept it up nicely, my dear, and put out fresh flowers, but I must say this whole house looks rather like a corpse decked out in lace and ribbons."

Agnes blushed vividly and drew a hand to her breast. "Hilda, must you make such appalling comments?"

"You do articulate colorfully," Viveca added, lips twitching.

"Well, I'm one to speak my mind, as everyone in this town knows." Hilda winked at Viveca. "I'm just pointing out the obvious. This house needs work, my dear. And you need students."

Viveca seized this cue to smile at Hilda's granddaughter. "So tell me, Gertrude, are you interested in music?"

The girl nodded in a bob of her sausage curls, and was about to reply when her grandmother stepped in. "Doesn't matter if she's interested or not. Any proper young lady of her age should be taking music lessons—otherwise, folks will think she's being raised a heathen."

Viveca stifled a laugh. "I see. And you, Mrs. Endicott? Are you an aficionado of song?"

"Oh, please call me Agnes," the woman replied graciously. "And yes, I've wanted to play the piano ever since I took lessons briefly as a child. You see, my mother was quite a gifted musician. We had a beautiful cabinet grand, much like yours, and she filled our parlor with music each evening after dinner. I'll never forget those glorious old tunes Mother played—'Swanee River,' 'Beautiful Dreamer,' and 'Jeanie with the Light Brown Hair.'"

"Ah, yes, Mr. Foster's wonderful compositions. I'm sure your mother's performances must have been quite memorable."

"They were indeed." Agnes breathed a wistful sigh. "Then, during the awful war, Mother died of scarlet fever. When Father returned from battle to find her gone, he couldn't bear to look at her piano any longer, so he sold it." She paused, sniffing. "That was the end of music in our lives—and of so much else."

A poignant silence fell. Viveca gazed at Agnes with compassion, noting that even Hilda appeared sympathetic, bereft of her usual clever reply. There was nothing funny about the fragility of life—Viveca well knew this herself; and although thirty-plus years had passed since the end of hostilities, feelings about the War Between the States obviously still ran quite deep here in the South.

"I'm so sorry," she said at last. "And so happy I may be able to help you find music in your life once again."

"Ah, yes, and what a lovely thing to say," declared Agnes, brightening. "I can't wait to start my lessons."

But Hilda shot her a withering glance. "Wait a minute, Agnes Endicott. My Gertrude is going to be Viveca's first student."

Viveca gritted her teeth, fully expecting a catfight. She was relieved when Agnes graciously acquiesced, smiling at Gertrude. "But of course. Children should always come first."

"Good, then," Hilda continued imperiously. "I take it you're available to start instructing my granddaughter immediately, Viveca?"

"I am indeed," came her smooth reply. "The piano tuner came out last week."

"Splendid. Now for the financial arrangements," added Hilda.

Viveca had already mentally set a modest price for her piano lessons, so she might quickly build up her clientele. So she was pleasantly surprised when Hilda offered her twice that amount per lesson, and insisted Gertrude be taught twice a week. Agnes promptly insisted on the same arrangement for herself, and within moments deals had been made in which Viveca would receive for two students the income she might normally expect for eight!

Once all the details had been settled, and bank drafts handed over for the first month's lessons, Viveca could only sit in intense relief as Hilda continued to dominate the exchange. Reaching out to pat Agnes's hand, she directed, "Now, Agnes, dear, why don't you run along, and drop Gertrude off with her mother? I have some additional business to discuss with Miss Stanhope."

Agnes grew flustered, twisting her handkerchief in her hands. "Well I, er—"

"Are you saying you don't want to escort my granddaughter home?" Hilda demanded with a scowl.

"No, of course not, but—"

"We can visit more at your first lesson, if that's convenient," Viveca put in tactfully.

Once again the woman yielded with a smile. "Oh, yes, I shall look forward to that. Thank you so much for the tea, Miss Stanhope."

"You're most welcome."

"And I shall anticipate our first lesson with great relish."

"As shall I."

Agnes stood. "Gertrude, shall we go?"

Viveca also rose to show her guests to the door. When she returned she noticed a secret gleam of mischief dancing in Hilda Patertavish's green eyes.

Viveca frowned back; much as she appreciated Hilda's help, she felt her guest had truly been rude this morning. "Hilda Patertavish, I have a question for you," she began sternly.

"Yes?"

Setting her arms akimbo, Viveca demanded, "Does everyone in Savannah tolerate your behaving like a martinet?"

To Viveca's surprise, Hilda Patertavish burst out laughing, slapping her plump sides. "Oh, I like you, my dear. I do indeed. And yes, *everyone* in these parts tolerates my tyrannical streak, although I do have a feeling I may have just met the exception."

Despite herself, Viveca laughed.

Hilda patted the empty space beside her. "Oh, come now, dear, quit grumbling and sit down. We've much scheming to do."

"Scheming?"

Hilda winked. "What else do we females do over our tea?"

With some trepidation, Viveca took her seat.

Hilda set down her teacup and saucer. "Now to get to work. We shall address your future shortly, but first, you must tell me why you fled here to Savannah."

Viveca had been taking a sip of tea and all but spit it out. "What?" she asked hoarsely.

A knowing light gleamed in the older woman's eyes. "Let's not mince words, my dear. A properly bred young lady such as yourself does not skedaddle cross-country unless she's running away from something."

Viveca felt a chill. The contemptible Maxwell Beecher had already arrived at this same conclusion, although she was not about to admit this to Hilda. Nonetheless, it was quite daunting to think that all of Savannah society might already be suspicious regarding her motives in settling here.

"I—I'm not hiding anything," she asserted. "And besides, not to be rude, but even if I were, why would I tell you?"

"Because I like you, my dear," the woman reiterated. "And I can't help you if I don't grasp the true gravity of your—er—situation."

Viveca was stunned. "Mrs. Patertavish—"

"Hilda."

"Hilda, you hardly know me. Why would you say you like me, much less that you want to help me—especially if you think I'm hiding something?"

Hilda merely rolled her eyes. "My dear, I've lived a long, long time, and have learned to rely on my instincts. From the moment I first laid eyes on you, I recognized a kindred spirit. You're a strong woman, Viveca—indeed, you remind me of myself at your age. I've had my fill of wilting lilies, and it would be a treat for me to watch you flower here. Indeed, Aubrey Parish asked me to mentor you, and I take such requests quite seriously. Not to mention I can already tell the good parson is quite taken with you—"

"He is?"

Hilda waved her off. "Of course he is, silly girl. The lad all but drools at the mention of your name. Accordingly, I wish to join in on the fun. When you and the handsome cleric are wed, I want all of Savannah to know that this is a match I made—and, of course, endorsed. Why, in these parts, folks don't put their mares out to stud without my prior blessing."

Now Viveca did laugh—in disbelief.

"Oh, don't just sit there gathering flies," Hilda scolded. "Say something."

"B-but why would you assume that either the good father or I are seeking a partner in marriage?"

Hilda gave a cynical groan. "Every young lady worth her salt is seeking a husband, my dear. Why do you think the good Lord put us females here? As for Aubrey, of course he needs the right wife to help advance his career with the church."

"And you think a woman with something to hide—at least in your estimation—is the right candidate?" Viveca asked skeptically.

"That we shall determine shortly," Hilda rejoined. "But in my opinion, Aubrey needs someone worldly-wise. That boy is hopelessly naïve, and no giddy young virgin will be able to protect him from the likes of Beryl Bliss."

Viveca scowled. "You're referring to the woman journalist we saw fawning over him yesterday at church?"

"Precisely. Beryl thinks she's Savannah's answer to Nelly Bly, when actually she's as morally bankrupt a little scalawag as I've ever laid eyes on. And she has her claws aimed straight at poor Aubrey."

"Oh." Viveca was taken aback. "So you think it would be in my best interests to pursue Aubrey, and thereby rouse the antagonism of this female reporter?"

Hilda waved a plump finger. "Aha! So you do have something to hide."

Flustered, Viveca protested, "Well, I didn't say that. My point is, I'm trying to establish my place here—make friends, not enemies."

Hilda stared her straight in the eye. "My dear, you know how to articulate, and dodge issues, quite adeptly. But let me be brutally frank. No newcomer is accepted into Savannah society without my blessing, if not my outright sponsorship. I'm willing to help you, but I shall not work with a stacked deck. Now I want to hear the full details about your background in San Francisco and the *real* reason you came here."

Viveca stifled a groan. Hilda Patertavish was relentless. She was also wickedly smart and formidable. Her ultimatum was likely not an empty one. Even Maxwell Beecher had called her "Queen Hilda." If Viveca had any hope of making it here in Savannah, she might have to admit the truth.

"Well, my dear?"

Viveca sighed. "Are you certain you want to open Pandora's box? You may well hear something that will change your feelings regarding me."

"I doubt it, unless you've murdered someone—"

"I haven't."

"At any rate, your secrets will be safe with me."

Viveca wondered about that, but realized she had little choice but to trust the woman. Gathering her courage, she spilled out the entire sad saga of her life back in San Francisco, how she'd lost her parents, how Erskine had ruthlessly taken advantage of her, seducing her and forsaking her afterward.

Once the entire tawdry tale had been revealed, Hilda snapped her fingers and clenched her jaw in outrage. "Aha! I just knew you were the victim of some cad. Why, I could practically smell it on you. You know, the very same thing happened to my cousin Enid's daughter. The two of us were all atwitter, about to launch Rose here at her first cotillion, when a Savannah scamp seduced and ruined her. Why, we had to ship the poor child off to live with her grandmother in Charleston, with all of those snooty, highfalutin' folks. Rose has done well there, has made a good match for herself—but my point is, these matters must be handled with the greatest of delicacy."

Viveca was amazed and warmed. "You mean you don't blame me for my transgressions?"

Hilda patted her hand. "Of course not, dear. Your experiences have only made you stronger, much less likely to succumb to such a scoundrel again. And do you really think your story is that unusual?"

"Well, I don't know," Viveca admitted. "I really haven't had anyone to talk with these past months."

"Which is why you need me," Hilda put in smugly.

Viveca smiled.

"Besides, at my age, I have no illusions left regarding men. Aside from a few gems like Aubrey, they're all rascals, in my view. Indeed, had not my George succumbed to the ague, I might have shot him over one of his little peccadilloes."

Viveca shook her head wonderingly. She was liking this woman more by the moment. "Still, why would you choose—well—a soiled dove for Father Aubrey?"

"Oh, poppycock. Aubrey's far too artless to ever know the difference. My point is, you're a seasoned fighter now. You'll be able to protect him, nurture him, help advance his station, as well as your own. And your heart's in the right place, unlike Beryl, who cares about nothing beyond the tip of her snooping little nose. She's only pursuing Aubrey to secure entrée into our society, and unearth more gossip."

"Yes, but what if she decides to point that 'snooping nose' toward me?"

"She wouldn't dare. I'd paper my outhouse with her ugly face."

Viveca burst out laughing.

"Now, I take it you'll be joining us at prayer meeting on Wednesday evening?" Hilda continued brightly.

"Yes. As a matter of fact, Father Aubrey is escorting me."

"Splendid. After the meeting I'll announce that I'm hosting a dinner party on Saturday night to introduce you to our community."

Viveca was delighted. "Why, how kind of you."

"I'll see that all the proper folks are invited, of course."

"That's so generous of you."

"After dinner, you'll perform some sort of brief program on the pianoforte—an excellent way to impress everyone with your talents and build your clientele."

Viveca was impressed. "My, you think of everything, don't you?"

"In the meantime, just watch your p's and q's, get this place in better order—and, of course, avoid your neighbor."

Viveca laughed. "You mean Maxwell Beecher? Believe me, I want nothing to do with the man."

"You're wise there." Hilda sighed. "A pity, too, since Max is such a handsome rake, and can be a real charmer when he wants to be. But his mother ruined him—Charlotte was such a witch toward him and his poor father. Max is definitely a blood brother to your cad in San Francisco. But at least he's gentleman enough not to ruin our ladies here—although everyone knows he consorts openly with his harlot."

"His . . . ?" Viveca's eyebrows shot up. "He does?"

With a forbearing look, Hilda confided, "Yes, her name's Sally something-or-other, from one of those hen houses along the river. Utterly disgraceful, the way that man carries on. But we have to tolerate his lapses because Max has his hands in so many prominent pockets—all those banks, you see." She sighed. "Which means I'll likely have to invite him for Saturday night, as well."

"Oh, dear."

"Don't fret about that now. Just give Max a wide berth and plan to wear something pretty." Hilda glanced at Viveca's quite presentable green teal muslin frock. "Or do you need assistance there?"

Viveca shook her head. "I still have quite a respectable wardrobe from my better days in San Francisco."

"Good." Standing, Hilda glanced about the room. "You know, dear, speaking of life's little luxuries, I've tons of discards in my attic that you could use to spiff up this house—wallpaper, furniture, art. I'll have my man start bringing things over."

Viveca was stunned and touched. "You would do all that for me?"

Hilda waved a hand in deprecation. "My dear, they're just the castoffs from my attic, although they'll look downright regal compared with your current accoutrements, I must say."

"Why, I can't thank you enough."

Hilda winked slyly. "You can, if you help me play the game as I love to play it."

By now Viveca knew precisely what she meant. "Then I shall try my best."

"Splendid. Well, dear, Gertrude will arrive promptly at nine on Thursday for her lesson. I'm so excited. Until Wednesday evening—"

Viveca squeezed her guest's hand. "Thank you, Hilda."

"Thank *you*, my dear."

Chapter Fifteen

Savoring her victory in gaining her first students, Viveca sent Emmett off to town to buy a plump chicken and fixings for a celebratory dinner. She also kept a watchful eye on the Beecher mansion next door. How dare Maxwell Beecher accuse her of being tainted, when from what Hilda Patertavish had told her, the miscreant openly consorted with harlots! Well, she'd definitely keep her eyes peeled to get the goods on him. The next time the cad tried to threaten her, she intended to be prepared.

Unfortunately, the day brought no useful observations or surprises until late in the afternoon, when Mrs. Patertavish's driver pulled up with a dray loaded with his mistress's "castoffs." Viveca was delighted to find herself the proud owner of four rolls of gold silk brocade wallpaper, along with a lovely burgundy velvet settee, matching armchairs, several inlaid French occasional tables, a gold leaf mantel clock, even a magnificent walnut Victrola. She marveled over some exquisite art nouveau figurines and several sterling silver gewgaws. Watching Hilda's man and her own servants bring her treasures into the parlor, Viveca mused that, if these were

Mrs. Patertavish's discards, the woman must live a life to parallel Lady Astor. When Hilda's man left, promising more tomorrow, Viveca could not believe her own good fortune. She felt intensely grateful to Hilda, and to Father Aubrey for asking the woman to sponsor her.

She and Emmett enjoyed their sumptuous dinner in the dining room, and afterward she had him take a plate to Miss Lilac next door. When he didn't return right away, she glanced out a window to see him seated with the old woman on her front veranda, the two rocking away and chatting. Pleased, Viveca made a mental note to call on the widow soon.

Even sunset, with its rising mists and ubiquitous promise of hauntings, could not dampen Viveca's gay mood. She played some of her favorite pieces on the piano, with an eye toward selecting a repertoire for Saturday night, and tumbled into bed pleasantly exhausted, with bright hopes for the morrow.

Alex Fremont's face mocked her with his dark, erotic eyes. His deep, mesmerizing voice called to her—"Lorelei, Lorelei," as if she were his long-lost love. His fingers caressed the length of her body, raising shivers. His darkness drew her, threatening to consume her soul. Unbidden longings drenched her, and she lay half slumberous, quivering with unassuaged desires . . .

Viveca wasn't sure just what awakened her, but sometime after midnight she jerked to awareness, her heart pounding, her loins throbbing with shameful need. Her eyes scanned the gloomy shadows of her room, searching for something she already *knew* was there. At last her gaze settled on a spectral haze that hung about the French doors to her veranda. What on earth? She gulped and stared, intensely frightened, baffled by the embodiment hanging there.

The misty, murky reflection was large and dense, about half the size of her armoire. Its outline was indistinct, like a shifting vapor. Even as she struggled to discern what it was, why it was here, the bizarre mist floated out through her closed French doors and disappeared!

Aghast, Viveca tumbled out of bed, crossed the room and tore open the French doors. There it was—the fog, the miasma, whatever it was—in the garden beneath her.

Enough! she vowed fiercely. She was sick to death of being taunted by these beings, these spooks, these . . . whatever they were. And this time she would brave the night prepared.

Grabbing her slippers and wrapper, Viveca hurried out of her room and down the stairs, colliding with a fresh curtain of cobwebs on the landing. Muttering curses and hacking at the gossamer fibers with her arms, she proceeded down to the kitchen, rummaged through a drawer and extracted a large butcher knife. Features grimly set, she stole out the back door.

The thick, damp night enveloped her, throbbing around her; the cicadas seemed to scream in her ears, loud as her own roaring heartbeat. As she rounded the house toward the spot where the apparition had settled, at first she saw nothing. Then she caught the barest outline of the haze just to the west of her, floating into the trees. Firmly gripping her knife, she followed the apparition, proceeding through the greenery and onto the Beecher property, past the gazebo . . .

Intrigued and appalled, Viveca watched the mist emerge on Maxwell Beecher's manicured lawn. Even as she continued steadily toward it, abruptly the mist lifted, melting away into the atmosphere. Astounded, she tiptoed closer. She glanced all around her, frantically searching, but could spot no vestige of the fog monster.

Damn! Where had it gone? And what *was* it?

Suddenly it occurred to her that she was only about ten yards away from Maxwell Beecher's house. She was a skimpily attired female with wildly tumbled hair and a large knife in her hand, trespassing on her neighbor's properly— and he was a man known to stalk the night with a gun.

But it was as if she'd been obsessed to follow the strange fog wherever it led her. Now if she were caught red-handed, her irascible neighbor would surely be absolved for shooting an alleged madwoman with a knife. She must turn for home at once.

Then the sound of moans—male moans—made Viveca pause, listening intently. She was certain the echo was coming from Maxwell Beecher's house—indeed, from just beyond the French doors on his side veranda. Good heavens, was he sporting with a woman in there? The cad! Well, hadn't Hilda told her how he consorted with his "harlot"? The very thought roused Viveca's righteous anger and made her face burn with both shame and fascination.

Peering through the murkiness, she could see a soft glow flickering through the gauzy curtains on his French doors. Again, Viveca felt compelled to continue. Quietly she moved closer and tiptoed up the steps, smelling mint, thick, sweet jasmine, and hearing the calls of a night heron.

The moans were louder now—a man groaning, grunting, as if in pain. Pausing by the curtained French doors, Viveca shamelessly stared. Inside, she could just make out the shadowy environs of a bedroom. The eerie glow she'd spotted bathed a large, four-poster bed; she could see the dark form of a man reclined there. Over him hovered the soft outline of a woman, her long, thick, tumbled hair partially obscuring his face, and her own. In her hand the woman held a small, lit candle.

Mercy! Both players in this bizarre little game were quite naked.

As Viveca stood there, shocked but mesmerized, the woman drew the candle up and down the man's body, laughing devilishly as the man howled in pleasure/pain. Heavenly days! Was the creature actually dripping hot wax on him? Did he enjoy such torment? It was depraved!

And yet she couldn't turn away.

After a few more moments of this hot-wax torture, the woman snuffed out her wick and lazily settled her voluptuous form over the man, until they became one twisting, writhing being. His cries of pain became groans of arousal, at first blissful, transported, but soon more visceral, agonized, as the two continued their decadent dance, wantonly rolling about and grinding their bodies together on the bed. All the while the woman laughed her evil laugh. Viveca clutched a pillar and felt herself trembling from head to toe. The need consuming her was overpowering now.

And she was so confused. The ghost of Alex Fremont had tried to seduce her in her dreams, then the vapor had led her here—to gaze at Maxwell Beecher's bawdy bed. What did everything mean?

Hearing Maxwell utter another searing sigh, Viveca softly cursed. Merciful saints! She had seen quite enough. Muffling a cry of outrage and frustrated passion, she fled for her house. She was certain she'd just observed Maxwell Beecher and his cheap floozy engaged in the most pernicious fornication. Well, her reprobate of a neighbor would never again be able to threaten her. She had him by the ear now.

Marching into her backyard, Viveca skidded to a halt as she spotted another all-too-frequent nemesis: the hideous, ax-swinging specter of Murfa Divine stalking toward her, emerging from the trees at the back of her property. Couldn't the wraith take a hint?

Too incensed to feel fear, Viveca decided to borrow a page from Winnie's book. Bravely striding forward, she raised her butcher knife at the awful creature and yelled, "Hey, Murfa! In case you haven't heard, you're *dead!*"

Murfa snarled at Viveca before vaporizing back into the trees.

The remainder of Viveca's night was tortured by more erotic dreams. Alex Fremont, naked, beckoned to her with his wicked eyes. When she moved as if hypnotized toward him, his face shifted, features twisting into the devilishly handsome countenance of Maxwell Beecher. Then it was Maxwell caressing Viveca's breast with a firm hand, Maxwell stroking her buttocks with bold fingers, as all the while his masterful eyes held her spellbound.

Viveca awakened, sobbing softly, in a ball of pain, a knot of twisted desire. By candlelight she filled the hipbath with cold water and soaked her aching private parts—to no avail. Back in bed, she quivered with unconsummated desire and tore at her sheets. Oh, Mercy, she needed help. Somehow she must get help with this!

The next morning, determined to seek answers, Viveca gathered tea and pastries to take to her shut-in neighbor, Miss Lilac. Emerging on the front porch with her small tray, she spotted no one stirring at the Beecher house next door. Doubtless the scoundrel was still sleeping off his late-night exertions. Part of her was tempted to go hurl a rock through his window, though she supposed it wouldn't do to rouse him, or tip her own hand. She didn't even want to consider the possibility that a spark of jealousy may have partially roused her righteous indignation.

Crossing the square, Viveca spotted Elvira Withersmith out in the Cunninghams' front yard, trimming the roses. She waved and Elvira waved back. Moving into Miss Lilac's fragrant front yard, Viveca noted with pride how well Emmett had cleared away the snarls of greenery. On the porch, she rapped briefly, then slipped inside, calling, "Miss Lilac?"

"In the parlor, dear," came the frail response.

Stepping inside the room, Viveca was pleased to note how tidy it was—even the gray tabby cat seemed content as it dozed on the settee. Even more gratifying, her hostess looked like a new woman, all decked out in a clean housecoat, her hair freshly washed and combed. There was even a pretty blue ribbon tied about her silvery locks.

"Why, Viveca," the woman greeted brightly. "Do come in."

Pleased that Lilac remembered her name, Viveca stepped forward. "Thank you. I brought you some tea and pastries."

Lilac clapped her hands in delight. "Oh, you do too much for me."

Viveca carefully set the tray in the old woman's lap. "Miss Lilac, believe me, it's my pleasure."

"Do sit down, my dear. Will you share this with me?"

Viveca settled herself on the settee and petted the sleeping cat. "Oh, no, thank you. I've just finished breakfast."

The woman lifted the teacup and took a long sip. "Ah, divine. Can't remember when I've tasted such a fine cup of tea."

The sight of the old woman delighting in such a simple pleasure twisted Viveca's heart. "My mother always believed tea is good for all that ails one."

Miss Lilac smiled. "And she clearly passed on her generous nature to you. Why, I'm overwhelmed by all you've done for me. Sending dear Emmett over to clean up this place—and that wonderful dinner you dispatched with him last night. He's fine company, too."

"I'm so glad you enjoy him. He's a family treasure, all right."

"And I've heard your wonderful playing, too," Lilac went on wistfully. "Last night wasn't it Bach, along with some Scarlatti?"

"Yes, indeed," Viveca acknowledged, impressed by Lilac's musical acumen.

"Emmett told me you'll be giving piano lessons soon."

"Starting on Thursday."

"Splendid, my dear," the old woman declared. "You're bringing Hangman's Square back to life, you know. It's been dead long enough."

Viveca regarded Miss Lilac thoughtfully. Previously, she'd feared the woman was demented, but now she wasn't so sure. Perhaps all Lilac had needed was a little attention—and now, like her wilted property, she, too, was springing back to life.

The old woman stared back, her gaze canny. "You came over here to ask me something, didn't you, dear?"

Viveca laughed rather nervously. "Are you a mind reader?"

"I can tell there's something on *your* mind."

"Well, I suppose you're right." Twisting her fingers together, Viveca remarked, "A moment ago you spoke about bringing this place back to life. Obviously, the dead play quite a role in this square's history, too."

"Amen," Miss Lilac agreed with a rueful laugh.

"And I was just wondering if you'd ever seen . . ."

"Yes, dear?"

"Well . . ." Feeling ridiculous, Viveca burst out, "any vapors hereabouts."

"Vapors?" Lilac laughed. "You mean like Mr. Foster's 'vapor on the summer air'?"

"Now, there's an apt analogy." Viveca chuckled, despite herself.

Miss Lilac slowly shook her head. "Around here, my dear, we have fogs, we have bogs, we have reports of doppelgangers luring folks away, and bogeymen stealing them off into the night. As for vapors, well, there is the classic Savannah 'miasma,' of course."

"Miasma," Viveca repeated. "You know, my housekeeper mentioned that recently."

"In Savannah, the miasma is considered something of a local character," Lilac confided wryly. "It consists of the noxious vapors rising up from the swamps in the evenings. At dusk around here, folks always tell their children, 'Get in before the miasma gets you!' The fog is rumored to carry yellow fever, you see."

"Well, according to Dr. Finlay of Cuba, it does carry the mosquito responsible for spreading the disease, eh?"

Lilac chuckled. "You're a very smart girl." She paused, regarding Viveca quizzically. "Now tell me what's troubling you."

Viveca swallowed hard. "It's just that—well, last night I did see a vapor, a miasma, *something*, but it wasn't a blanketing fog . . . more like—well, an embodiment."

"Ah."

"It led me on quite a chase, then just evaporated. And there have been other odd occurrences, usually just after midnight—sightings, I suppose you could call them—"

"Sightings, eh?"

"Yes, in particular, er . . ." Releasing a heavy sigh, Viveca abruptly asked, "Can you tell me anything more about Alex Fremont?"

Lilac appeared fascinated. "Alex Fremont? What else would you like to know?"

"Well, perhaps what he looked like?"

Lilac snapped her fingers. "Are you telling me you've seen Fremont's ghost, young lady?"

Viveca wasn't about to reveal the shocking secrets of what she'd actually seen—*felt*. "Well," she hedged, "I have seen a face in my dreams, a face that might be Fremont, along with someone else—a woman—"

"You're thinking this would be his Lorelei?"

"Yes." Viveca's fingers dug into her skirts. "At any rate, I—I've heard the song, too. 'The Lorelei.' "

"I see."

"Do you think I'm crazy?" Viveca asked anxiously.

Lilac laughed and waved her off. "Oh, my dear, I'm in no position to judge anyone. As for this square—it has been known to do strange things to people's minds."

"No kidding," Viveca muttered. "So, tell me, Miss Lilac—do you happen to know what Fremont looked like—or anything more about his history?"

Lilac shook her head sadly. "Sorry, dear. As I told you before, he was rumored to be a handsome devil, but he lived here before my time." Abruptly she brightened. "You know, I think there may still be a painting of Alexander Fremont—of his execution, in fact—down at the courthouse."

Viveca could feel the blood draining from her face. "A picture of—of his execution? Surely you jest."

"Not at all, dear. Evidently, some local artist painted it on the day he was hanged. Lordy, it's been over twenty years since I've been in that building, and I can't recall any details about the portrait. But it may be there yet—"

"At the courthouse," Viveca managed to repeat.

"Yes, dear. On Bull Street."

Viveca rose, shaking Miss Lilac's hand with her own trembling fingers. "Miss Tupper, I can't thank you enough."

Lilac squeezed her hand. "If I can repay you even in small part, my dear, I'm the grateful one."

An hour later, standing just inside the entrance to the Chatham County Courthouse, Viveca wasn't so certain she should have thanked Miss Lilac. She was staring at a vivid oil painting entitled *Tragedy on Hangman's Square: The Execution of Alexander Fremont*.

Viveca might have expected that the artist would portray a crowd of sneering spectators in the foreground, waving their fists and demanding justice. And there they were, complete with fire in their eyes and bloodlust gripping their faces. What she didn't expect was the visage at the center of the portrait.

She was gazing at the face that had haunted her dreams, the figure that had invaded her bath: Alex Fremont was every bit the dark, handsome devil of her visions; he stood proudly on a scaffolding at the center of the painting, a hangman's noose around his neck, the old oak towering above him. Behind Fremont loomed the black-cloaked hangman; at Fremont's knees knelt a sobbing woman with red-gold hair in a chignon; one of Fremont's strong hands was extended toward her in apparent pity. Viveca could feel the anguish of this couple to her very soul—their love, their heartbreak, their torment over the fleeting quality of life.

"I'm sorry," she whispered, without even thinking.

Then she gasped as she recognized the kneeling woman. It was the creature that had cavorted with the ghost of Alex Fremont in her bathroom! Her clothing and hairstyle were much more sedate, refined; but it was definitely the same person. Still, Viveca was puzzled: Surely this "Lorelei" hadn't actually been there with Fremont on the hangman's platform?

Then, glancing into the foreground, Viveca spotted a tiny inset portrait, like a cameo, off to the right; it was of a fair-haired woman lying dead on a grassy knoll, eyes wide open as blood trickled from her breast. This had to be Fremont's victim, his former mistress. Viveca realized then that the painting was an allegory, the artist detailing through his brilliant brush strokes the entire shocking tale of Fremont's descent from grace.

Now it hit Viveca as never before that the hauntings she had experienced were real, that the tormented souls who had visited her were still locked up in their purgatory. The emotional connection she felt toward all the characters in the scene was overwhelming, and the impact made her totter slightly as the portrait seemed to blur in and out.

An elderly gentleman gripped Viveca's arm to steady her as he passed. "Miss, are you all right? Should I fetch some smelling salts?"

Viveca shook her head at the kindly man dressed in his fine coat and silk top hat. "Thank you, sir, I'm fine."

"Well, you look as if someone just walked on your grave," he teased.

The best Viveca could manage was a frozen smile.

Chapter Sixteen

Father Aubrey knocked on Viveca's door promptly at seven on Wednesday evening. She opened it to see him standing there in his sharp black suit and clerical collar, his hat in hand, his fair hair gleaming, backlit by sprays of light sifting through the sunset trees on the square.

"Good evening, Father Parish," she greeted him brightly.

"Please, call me Aubrey." He took in her starched, lacy white blouse, lightweight crocheted shawl, black and white checked taffeta skirt and high-heeled black pumps with ivory spats. "My, how fine you look, Viveca."

"Thank you."

He offered his arm. "Ready to go?"

"Indeed."

She slipped outside, shutting the door behind her and placing her fingers on his arm. She noticed his corresponding blush as he escorted her down the steps and through the yard. His fingers felt moist and trembled against her wrist as he assisted her into his cozy buggy. She sat down on the narrow bench, smoothed her skirts and her chignon and smiled at him in welcome.

He colored again and got in beside her, perching himself so far away from her that she feared he might fall off the seat. Gently he flicked the reins, and the horse plodded off.

Passionate the good father wasn't, she reflected ruefully. Polite, yes.

"How has your week progressed?" she asked.

"Oh, not well," he replied with a sigh. "Old Mr. Hammersmith died, so I've a funeral to prepare for tomorrow."

"I'm so sorry. I do hope I'm not taking you away from your duties tonight."

"No, not at all," he quickly reassured her. Clearing his throat, he added, "Actually, I've been looking forward to this evening all week."

"Have you?" Viveca asked, her spirits lifting.

He nodded fervently. "Tonight we're studying St. Paul's Epistle to the Ephesians, my favorite of all his sacred letters." Piously he quoted, " 'And do not get drunk with wine, for that is debauchery; but be filled with the Spirit, addressing one another in psalms and hymns and spiritual songs, singing and making melody to the Lord with all your heart.' "

"My, how very inspirational," Viveca agreed with forced cheerfulness.

As they passed the Beecher house, Viveca noted several lights were on, and she dearly hoped Maxwell Beecher was watching them pass by. Indeed, after he'd warned her away from his cousin, she took perverse delight in the prospect of thumbing her nose at him. She didn't see him peering out any windows—but she could always hope.

Then as they rounded the corner, she detected a slight stirring in the trees at the back of her own property. Her pulse quickened. Was Murfa Devine on the prowl again? Or was it some other wraith or bogeyman?

So far, Viveca hadn't broached the subject of ghosts with Aubrey, for obvious reasons; but now she realized it might not hurt to feel him out a bit on the subject. After all, who could have lived in Savannah for long without having heard about the notorious hauntings? And actually, a mention of her neighbor Lilac Tupper might make an excellent launching point for their discussion.

"Aubrey, are you acquainted with my neighbor, Miss Lilac Tupper?" she asked casually.

He sighed. "Yes, poor soul."

"Emmett and I have been trying to help her—you know, bring her food, clean up her place and all that."

"How kind of you. Our women's fellowship has extended her various charities, as well."

"Anyway, she seems such a sad, lonely old lady. On a couple of occasions when I've visited her, she has given me quite an earful about"—with an offhand gesture, she finished—"well, you know, *haunted* Savannah.'"

He raised an eyebrow. "My dear, surely you're not taking seriously the rantings of a woman who allegedly lives with two dead servants?"

Viveca's eyes widened. "You know about that?"

"All of Savannah knows about Miss Lilac and her bizarre flights of fancy," he replied archly. "Not that there aren't plenty of other benighted souls hereabouts to spin ghost stories, tell tall tales, and invent all the other, usual malarkey."

"Malarkey?" she repeated carefully. "So is that how you would characterize the occult?"

He nodded, eyes gleaming with religious fervor. "I am a man of God, Viveca. I believe the occult—as you might refer to it—does not exist. The devil, yes, he's always there to tempt us, with his minions. But as for ghosts, wraiths, zombies and so forth, I find them all to be products of crazed or demonized minds."

"You do," she murmured.

"Yes, I believe that anyone who gives credence to such heresy may well be possessed of a demon herself. There's nothing I can do for such a lost soul unless she's willing to see the error of her ways and seek redemption." Meaningfully he added, "That is something you might well remember in choosing your associations, my dear."

Viveca was tempted to ask him what had happened to his

sense of Christian charity. "Are you suggesting I should avoid
Miss Tupper just because of her ghost stories?"

He reached out to pat her hand. "By all means, dear, take
her food and such and have your man tend to her gardens.
But otherwise, I think you would do well to avoid her possibly deleterious influence."

Viveca just managed to smile back at Aubrey, although she
was tempted to stick out her tongue at him. She mused that
the fire-breathing witch hunters of Salem could have used
the good father way back then. So much for finding a kindred
spirit in him, she realized soberly. The man who appeared so
close to perfection had at least one glaring flaw—his highly
pious, self-righteous streak. Any potential life she might
share with Aubrey would not be without its sacrifices.

Viveca opened her fan and cooled her face, reflecting that
she might well need help from above to get her through this
evening.

Viveca was impressed by her first glimpse of Judge Endicott's
house, an enormous yellow stone Victorian mansion in a
posh neighborhood only blocks away from the Savannah
River. As Aubrey escorted her through the fragrant, gaslit
yard, he informed her that the house, like a number of
prominent Savannah properties, had been designed by the
renowned Boston architect William Gibbons Preston.

A butler in black admitted them to the mahogany-paneled
rotunda; there Viveca admired stained-glass windows with
panels of vibrant peacocks, colorful flowers and exotic jewels, all lit by exquisitely fitted brass chandeliers. Then in the
overwrought, mauve and black Victorian parlor, Agnes Endicott rushed forward to greet the just-arrived couple like
long-lost relatives, with Hilda Patertavish close on her heels.
Viveca met Agnes's florid-faced husband Delbert and Hilda's
rather foppish brother, Myron; she and Aubrey then exchanged greetings with the effusive Fitzpatricks and the taci-
turn Thorps.

Afterward, seated on the uncomfortable settee between

Agnes and Hilda, Viveca struggled to stay alert during the interminable scholarly discourse on the Book of Ephesians. Her only source of comic relief was their host, the judge. The portly man, with a face full of spider veins, kept slipping away to chug more sour mash, if his slurred speech and strong whiskey odor were any indication.

At last the session ended with a group prayer, after which the men all but vaulted away to the veranda for cigars and brandy, with the exception of Aubrey, who remained behind, discussing a biblical passage with Hilda. Viveca settled herself with the other women at a card table near the fireplace.

At once Agnes began to gush while patting Viveca's arm. "Cleo and Alice, I'm sure you've heard that Miss Stanhope is a very talented music teacher. I'm beginning lessons with her on Friday."

"Are you, indeed?" asked Cleo Fitzpatrick, a vivacious blonde with sparkling blue eyes. "You know, Miss Stanhope, my sister's boy, Dalton, has been begging Mary Lou to sign him up for lessons for ages now."

"I'd be delighted to meet with your sister and her child," Viveca murmured.

"Splendid, then. Shall we set a date?"

After exhausting the subject of Viveca and her lessons, Agnes turned the conversation to local gossip. The ladies commented on the recent crop of debutantes presented at the annual Christmas Cotillion; they dropped the names of a couple of prominent couples who had attended the Bradley Martin society ball in New York City; and they chatted about several more local families who had recently gotten newfangled telephones.

Growing restless, Viveca glanced at Aubrey and Hilda on the settee, and noted he seemed uncomfortable. He was squirming, his face flushed. After he excused himself and left to join the men, Viveca watched Hilda rise and cross the room to sample cookies at the buffet.

Viveca murmured a "Pardon me" to the other ladies and went over to join her friend. "I see you and Aubrey had your heads together over the Scripture," she teased. "I wasn't aware you were such a biblical scholar."

"Oh, bosh!" Hilda scolded, nibbling on a macaroon. "I had far more to discuss with that young man than greed, licentiousness and the wickedness of the flesh."

Viveca stifled a laugh. "Did you?"

Hilda tapped her fan on Viveca's arm. "You look quite fine tonight, Viveca."

"Thank you, Hilda."

"Indeed, Aubrey was just commenting to me on what a lady you are, how well you present yourself."

"Was he?" Viveca asked, pleased.

"He definitely favors you, my dear. And I urged him to forge ahead full steam."

"My, you are the matchmaker."

"Of course, it's rather hard to imagine Aubrey with a head full of steam for anything, unless it's the Scriptures," Hilda continued ruefully. "He'll be a dullard of a husband, but a faithful one. At any rate, passion and lust are the weaknesses of the lower classes, don't you agree?"

"Oh, of course," replied Viveca, though she felt not nearly as convinced as she should have been.

"I've invited everyone to my buffet on Saturday evening. In the meantime, see what progress you can make with him, my girl."

Viveca chuckled.

Hilda took a sip of tea. "All set for my Gertrude in the morning?"

"I can't wait."

"Splendid. Now go rescue Aubrey from those men before the judge hopelessly corrupts him with Cuffs and Buttons or some other equally perverse liquor."

Viveca squeezed Hilda's hand. "Thank you."

"My dear, once again I must thank you. Having you to sponsor has put a feather in my cap."

Viveca had to shake her head in astonishment as she headed off for the veranda.

* * *

When Aubrey walked Viveca up the path to her porch, he again grew flustered, his fingers trembling as he assisted her up the steps in the moonlight. At her front door, he shifted from foot to foot and finally cleared his throat, the uncertainty of his expression reflected in the wan light drifting through the glass-paned door.

"A fine evening, Viveca."

"Indeed. Thank you so much for inviting me, Aubrey."

"Er—Hilda suggested I might escort you to her gathering on Saturday evening—"

"Yes, that would be just lovely," Viveca cut in effusively. "It's wonderful to have a gentleman such as yourself to help me get acclimated to the community."

"Er—yes." He glanced away miserably.

She touched his arm. "Aubrey—what is it?"

He swallowed hard, then finally met her eye. "I—I'm afraid I feel rather like a wolf in sheep's clothing—"

"You do? But why? You're obviously a man of very high moral standards—"

"Thank you, Viveca. But—well, as Hilda made me realize tonight, I'm not squiring you about Savannah strictly out of Christian charity or the kindness of my heart. I—I—the truth is, Viveca, I'm looking for . . . a wife."

The word came out of Aubrey's mouth half strangled. Despite his utter lack of romanticism, Viveca couldn't resist a coy smile. "Oh, are you?"

He coughed miserably. "Yes, I'm in need of—er, a life mate to help me better serve my church and community. And I—I beg to hear your thoughts on a possible—er—courtship between us. Would that be—agreeable to you?"

Although Viveca was less than transported by his tepid declaration, she maintained an outward cheeriness. "You wish to pay suit to me? But that is absolutely nothing to be ashamed of, Aubrey. Indeed, I admire your honesty."

"You do? Then you—er—"

"I should be delighted to have you attend me, sir."

He broke into a shy grin. "Well—well, that's just wonderful. Until Saturday, then."

Even as she inclined her cheek for a chaste kiss, he shook her hand, then hastily took his leave.

Back inside her house, Viveca felt unsettled. She'd made excellent progress tonight in her goal to find a place for herself in this community. She even had an esteemed local clergyman paying court to her. But as Hilda Patertavish had pointed out, there would be a price to pay: Her life would be passionless.

Well, who needed passion, anyway? It had only wrecked her life before.

Aubrey was basically a good man who might have faith, but was totally lacking in spirit, in zest for life. He also had a mercenary side—he wanted a wife to advance his standing in his church and community.

But wasn't she equally predatory? She felt no real spark of attraction toward him, yet she was prepared to become his wife to secure her own security and prestige. In the end, it would be a devil's bargain made between two purported Christians.

And passionless . . .

Bemused, Viveca drifted outside to the backyard. Tonight the mists were lighter than usual, the setting quite serene. She inhaled the sweet potpourri of nectar on the night air, watched moonlight dust the roses and magnolias and strike the gazebo on the hated Maxwell Beecher's property. All at once she felt unbearably sad, thinking of all she had lost in her life, all she would never have here in this new, alien environment. She had lost the love and companionship of her parents, and would never know the love of an ardent, vital man.

The distant gaslit gazebo seemed to mock her, bringing poignant memories of San Francisco—of Hill Park at sunset, of ships at harbor, the fog on a winter night, fireworks in the summer, moonlight gleaming on the lily pads at Golden

Gate. She could almost see a laughing couple dancing on a far pavilion as in those earlier festive days.

It took Viveca a long moment to realize that she actually *was* looking at a couple dallying in the gazebo—a *ghost* couple in diaphanous evening clothes. Fascinated, she stepped closer to the shocking yet mesmerizing scene. Nebulous but discernible, a man and a woman glided about in a mist of lacy shadows and glittering moonlight. Bodies locked, they spun in a sensual embrace, their soft laughter echoing in the night, her hair trailing after them like a wistful cloud. Closer and closer together they waltzed and whirled, becoming more and more defined as they converged, sparkles of light glimmering on their wispy, gossamer clothes. And just above the delicate trill of laughter and the droning of cicadas in the night, Viveca could hear the strains of "The Lorelei," played on some distant, celestial strings, the tune so sweet and poignant it made her throat ache.

Good heavens, it was the couple who had haunted her bath, the doomed lovers she'd seen in the painting. Alex Fremont and his Lorelei, the woman he had killed for, twirling through the eternity of the night. Once again, the emotion, the sense of connection she felt on viewing the tragic pair, was heartrending for Viveca. Without realizing it, she ventured closer, ever closer.

And then their dance began in earnest.

Viveca watched, captivated, as the man lifted the woman high in a pirouette, then slid her down against him; with a moan of delight she locked her body around his. Viveca's mouth went dry as she realized what was happening. The male ghost eased into a slow, sexy glide while the female began rhythmically bobbing up and down upon him, crying out wantonly. Together they spun and glided, dipped and lifted and cavorted, all the while singing out their love, like the ethereal music of heaven. At last their rocking reached a crescendo, their sighs mingled, and then they melded in a flash of brilliance, like multicolored lightning. Afterward only a haze of smoke lingered, the embers of a love well sated.

Viveca stared at the emptiness, unable to believe what she had just witnessed. It had been brazenly carnal yet unbearably sweet. Worst of all, she had been a *part* of it. She ached inside—ached with frighteningly intense, shameless desires. She was lost, bereft, and in a moment of weakness she might normally forestall, she succumbed to tears, and finally to heart-wrenching sobs.

How could the restless spirits be so cruel, yet so utterly bewitching?

A long moment passed before she heard a man's voice wryly ask, "Ready to cry uncle now, are you?"

Viveca whirled to see the hated Maxwell Beecher standing just a few feet beyond her, his thick, dark hair framing his face, his handsome features outlined in moonlight. He wore no jacket, and his white dress shirt again lay rakishly open, revealing a dark thatch of hair on his muscled chest.

Viveca was in no mood for his mockery. In a fit of pique, she responded, "Oh, why don't you just go to hell?"

He whistled and stepped closer. "My, but you're in a feisty temperament tonight."

Viveca recoiled as the sexy scent and enticing heat of him raised even hotter twinges deep inside her already aroused body. "Have you any more comments on my character, or will you leave me in peace?"

"Leave you in peace, must I?" he mocked. "My dear, you're again trespassing on *my* property—and I haven't even shot you as yet, may I point out."

Though sorely tempted to smile, she retorted, "You may take your property and go choke on it."

He actually grimaced. "Good Lord, woman, what ails you tonight? Obviously, living on Lost Lane has not at all improved your disposition." He nodded toward her house. "Speaking of which, I'm still willing to take that monstrosity off your hands."

"If you must know, it's being in your presence that sours

my disposition, Mr. Maxwell Beecher," she shot back. "As for your buying my property, my answer remains no."

He smiled nastily. "Too set on snaring my pious cousin to consider moving, eh?"

Viveca had been expecting this. "Were you spying on us tonight?"

He gave a shrug, belied by the tension in his shoulders. "I heard Aubrey's buggy pull up earlier this evening." His voice deepened with an undeniable menace. "Didn't I warn you to stay away from him?"

She balled her hands on her hips. "Haven't you figured out by now that your dictates hold not the least bit of sway over me?"

He advanced angrily. "So you think you've nothing to fear from me, eh?"

She held her ground with a sneer. "Other than having to abide your obnoxious presence as my neighbor? No."

He loomed even closer, eyes blazing. "You know, you're a clever little minx, Miss Stanhope, but you're not too sly for me. Don't you forget that I can see beyond your snooty façade, that I know what you're really about inside—"

"And what, precisely, is that, sir?"

"This."

Too late, Viveca glimpsed the passionate intensity in Maxwell Beecher's eyes. A split second later she was hauled forcefully against him and kissed, thoroughly, punishingly. She tried to resist him. But her every nerve ending was already on fire with a voracious thirst that had been building for days. When his tongue brazenly sought entrance to her mouth, she beat on his back with her fists, fighting him, but mostly fighting herself. Still, he was so determined, so strong . . .

So hard, so warm, so sensual . . . Ultimately, the strength and heat of him against her, the torrid intimacy of his kiss, made the longing inside Viveca burst into fiery flames of need. She felt her defenses melting away in the flood of erotic heat pulsing through her. Panic assailed her—she felt dangerously close to succumbing to him, yet somehow the feeling was too glorious to resist.

Maxwell took advantage of her softening, pushing his tongue into her mouth, then slowly, devastatingly, teasing and arousing her unbearably, until her nipples tingled and her belly quivered.

Viveca's knees buckled. His hands gripped her hips, steadying her, boldly exploring, brazenly snuggling her up against his tantalizing hardness. At last, with a wince of desperation, she threw her arms around his neck and kissed him back as if she would suck the soul out of him. . . .

When they finally broke apart, she was gasping for air and he was smiling in triumph. "There. Now we both know."

Face burning, Viveca drew back and slapped him full force across the face. He merely grinned, and didn't even touch his cheek, which she knew must smart terribly.

His impudence and gall only fueled her outrage. "You despicable cad!" she ranted. "How dare you kiss me, much less threaten me. And for the record, I do have nothing to fear from you, Mr. Maxwell Beecher, since I know all about you and your illicit activities. Your gambling, your drinking, not to mention your—your slut."

"My slut?" he mocked. "Been gossiping with Hilda Patertavish, have you?"

She was tempted to ask him if he knew *everything*, but instead demanded, "Do you deny it? Besides, I heard the two of you fornicating last night, like cats in heat—"

He was thunderstruck. "You *heard* us? Why, you little voyeur! Little did I know a female Peeping Tom had moved in next door to me. Why didn't you just waltz into my bedroom and offer to join us for a ménage à trois?"

"So you don't deny it."

"I don't deny I'm a blackguard of the first order, my dear, but by God, if you spy on me again, I'll blister your delicate backside—"

"Hah! As if you don't spy on me!"

"I don't."

"Liar."

He advanced on her, breathing hard. "Threaten me if you will, Miss Stanhope, but the truth is, my place in this town is assured."

"So now you own the town?"

"In a manner of speaking, I do. You, on the other hand, are the Jennie-come-lately, the interloper—and if you don't heed my warnings regarding my cousin, I shall wreck your prospects here."

"How? By attempting to ravish me as you just did with that—that disgusting kiss?"

"Me, ravish you?" he mocked. "I was about to ask *you* to kindly return my tongue to me."

Mortified, she slapped him again, hard. He caught her wrist and spoke with soft menace. "Strike me one more time, Viveca, and it's over my knee with you. In fact, *please* give me that pleasure."

She yanked her hand free and squared her trembling shoulders. "I think what I said to you initially bears repeating. Go to hell."

He merely grinned. "It will be my pleasure to drag you there with me."

As he turned and strode back into the night, Viveca felt frighteningly close to believing him. Oh, the beastly man! Now he knew her secret—he knew her weakness. And the brute had aroused her as no man ever had before—not even Erskine.

What on earth was she to do? Why had the heavens visited on her the trial of dealing with Maxwell Beecher?

Maxwell muttered curses as he continued toward his house. Damn that outspoken baggage next door—damn her eyes for defying him. And watching him at sport—she deserved a thorough tumbling herself for that audacious act of voyeurism.

He remained incredulous that she was ignoring his warnings about Aubrey, thumbing her nose at him and shamelessly pursuing his cousin. Clearly she was no lady, but a crafty little gold digger.

Well, she wouldn't get her hooks into his cousin if he had anything to say about it, even if he had to personally chase her tail out of Georgia.

Why was he feeling so irate, anyway? Was it because he wanted her for himself? He cursed silently.

Kissing her was not something he'd intended to do, and the heated contact had aroused him far more than he'd anticipated. Though she had squirmed, her breasts had been supple against him, her mouth heavenly hot, wet, on his. Then when she had kissed him back, her tongue taking free rein in his mouth . . . ah, the thought of having her in bed with him had seemed worth dying a thousand deaths. Her supple body writhing against his had only poured fuel on the flames of his ardor, and he throbbed with frustrated lust.

Damn her! Thanks to the maddening siren, he would sleep little tonight. His dreams, if he had them, would be tortured, haunted. If only he could tumble a certain hot little piece beneath him—ah, then he would dream.

Chapter Seventeen

Gertrude Patertavish, Viveca's first student, proved to be a sweet-natured nine-year-old who took to the piano like a squirrel to nuts. She readily understood the concepts of scales and chords. Indeed, by the end of their first lesson, Gertrude was skillfully executing a C-major scale. Viveca found her mind wandering as the child practiced.

She couldn't stop thinking about the contemptible Maxwell Beecher and the way he had kissed her last night. Ostensibly, he'd done it to show her what she was really about—and now she feared he knew, too! Oh, why did she have to be saddled with such a maddening nemesis just when things were going so well for her otherwise?

The worst part was, she did feel a spark of attraction toward the rogue. No, more than a spark. His kiss had definitely curled her toes and warmed the pit of her belly. And after she'd kissed him back so recklessly, he must surely wonder what type of wanton she was. She'd likely confirmed all his suspicions.

Had the potent attraction she felt toward Maxwell been

sparked by the sensual, ghostly scene she had witnessed earlier? Or had it been—horror of horrors—genuine? Somehow she strongly suspected the latter, even though it did seem as if her two bawdy ghosts were conspiring to shove her into Maxwell Beecher's arms.

What was she going to do?

"Was that good, Miss Stanhope?" Gertrude asked brightly, intruding on her thoughts.

Smiling, Viveca rose and went to the girl's side. Gertrude looked so pretty with her blond hair in perfect corkscrew curls, wearing a crisp pink gingham gown with a lacy white pinafore. Patting the girl's arm, she assured, "That was excellent for a beginner." Turning, Viveca picked up a workbook from a nearby table. "Now, here are some practice chords and scales I've composed for you to take home."

"Oh, thank you, miss."

Watching Gertrude clutch the practice book as if it were the rarest treasure, Viveca felt touched, poignantly recalling happier days when music had filled her, too, with such wonder. "I'm pleased you like it."

The girl nodded. "By the way, Grandma asked me to remind you not to forget to practice, since you'll be playing for our guests on Saturday night."

"Yes, indeed, I shan't forget. I'm so looking forward to going to your grandmother's house. I take it you'll be there?"

"Oh, yes, and my parents, too. Mama said I can stay up to hear you play. I'm so excited."

"Well, it will be a treat to see you again, dear. Now you be sure you practice, too, before next Monday."

The girl bobbed a curtsey. "Thank you, miss, I certainly shall. Good day, Miss Stanhope."

Viveca saw her student out the front door, watching as the manservant who had brought her assisted her into her family's awaiting brougham. Viveca's first lesson had been a great success, yet she felt melancholy. Perhaps it was the prospect of performing in public again—something she hadn't done since her father's death. But Gertrude had been right that she needed to prepare for Saturday night. She'd started to select her repertoire the other day, but hadn't made much progress.

Back in the parlor, she picked up a stack of sheet music from the stand next to the piano. She quickly set aside her favorites, the romantic waltzes, nocturnes and songs of Chopin, Strauss, and Schubert. Too passionate, too angst-riddled, all of it. And currently, too painful a reminder of the side of herself she was determined to repress.

Far better to stick with the precision of the Baroque, she mused soberly. With a sigh, she pulled out a Bach two-part invention. Her fingers lightly drilled the keys as she refreshed her execution of the piece to perfection. Then she turned to Scarlatti and Vivaldi.

Viveca wasn't sure just when she became aware that she had traitorously pulled out a certain favorite, fervent Chopin nocturne. The poignant song was filled with sadness and repressed longing. Indeed, much later, she would conclude that she'd acted as if hypnotized. She poured herself into the bittersweet strains, her fingers moving with passionate mastery over the keys—and she could feel her breath quickening, excitement stirring in her nipples and between her thighs. Never had she felt such raw emotion, such torment, such tenderness, while playing her piano. It was as if the instrument itself had become her lover, seducing her with each bittersweet note, undoing her in the most audacious sensual encounter. Just as her desire peaked to unbearable levels and she felt herself about to go over the edge and succumb to ecstasy, the mood abruptly shattered, and she found herself pounding the piano keys in loud, discordant frustration.

Face hot, Viveca shot to her feet, at last realizing what had happened. That damned ghost! First he had invaded her bath, then her dreams—and now her piano! He had actually ravished her through the keys, reducing her to a mass of trembling longing.

Breathing heavily, she paced the room, her hand slicing through the air. "Damn you, you cad! When will you leave me in peace!"

Although the room was silent, once again she could almost hear him laughing at her. She was tempted to hurl a vase across the room, then realized this would accomplish nothing except prove she was losing her mind.

Then abruptly Viveca smiled as a deliciously vindictive idea occurred to her . . .

"Think you have me outwitted, do you, you phantom of the bathtub?" she ranted at the unseen ghost. "Well, I have news for you!"

She was about to spill the beans, then thought better of it, clamping her mouth tightly shut.

"Remove this monstrosity," Viveca ordered the plumber.

Two hours later, Sean O' Murphy, complete with soiled dungarees and toolbox, stood in Viveca's bathroom. The little man glanced in stunned disbelief from the tub to her. "Have you gone daft, lady? I almost broke me back installing the bugger, now you want it gone?"

"Precisely."

"But why?" He looked at her as if she'd lost her mind.

Viveca flushed. "I don't see how that's any of your affair."

"Ain't it working proper?" he asked.

"*Properly*," she repeated irately. "Indeed it is not."

"Then why not let me fix the blame thing?"

"I . . ." Reduced to stammering, Viveca retorted, "Because I want it removed. Gone. Do you understand?"

"Women," grumbled O'Murphy, settling to his knees and pulling a wrench out of his toolbox.

For a few moments he yanked at the fittings and banged at the pipes, struggling unsuccessfully to loosen the plumbing, while Viveca stood on the sidelines wringing her hands.

"Holy saints, but she's in there tight," O'Murphy muttered. He reached out with his gnarled fingers to give a stubborn fitting a twist, only to yelp in pain.

"What is it?" Viveca cried.

He shot to his feet, wild-eyed. "It's blazing hot, miss! Take a look!"

Viveca stared at the tub in amazement and horror. Heavenly days, he was right! The fixtures attaching the vessel to the plumbing now glowed a fierce red, and steam was rising from the bottom of the tub. "My God, what could have caused this?"

He was crossing himself and backing away. "Mary, Joseph and Jesus, 'tis the spawn of the devil."

Viveca gulped. "Don't be ridiculous. It must be just— well—excess hot water."

With his wrench, he tapped the water heater on the floor. "Feel the boiler, miss—'tis stone cold."

She touched it and gasped. "You're right. What on earth . . . ?"

With a sneer, he handed her the wrench. "Here, miss, have a go at it yourself, with my blessings. No job is worth braving the fires of hell."

"But—but Mr. O'Murphy—"

Her plea was futile. Crestfallen, she watched the little man turn, grab his toolbox and rush out of the room. With a sound of frustration rising in her throat, she turned back to the bathtub to see the fixtures still glowing. She reached out tentatively to touch the side of the tub, only to cry out in pain. The entire tub was hot as a griddle!

Hell and high water! She was living in the house of the damned!

And she had two cads tormenting her—one living, one dead. Plus she seemed powerless to control or evict either of them! Oh, why hadn't she listened to Winnie when the housekeeper had warned her never to bring this cursed bathtub inside?

Well, Maxwell Beecher might well be right about one

thing: she needed to get out of this house. But she wouldn't leave until she could exit with her head held high—which meant, not until she could move to that prosperous rectory on Episcopal Square.

She had no time to waste.

Chapter Eighteen

Viveca took particular care with her appearance on Saturday night. She donned her best evening gown from her San Francisco days—a Worth triumph of blue velvet with a low, beaded bodice and a white lace overskirt. She arranged her shiny red hair in tight curls on top of her head, securing her stylish coiffure with a slender pearl tiara complemented by modest pearl earrings. She lightly rouged her cheeks and mouth and applied generous amounts of rosewater to her bodice and earlobes. Blue satin slippers and a matching beaded reticule completed the regal image she sought.

Even Winnie seemed impressed, her eyes going wide when she came upstairs to tell her mistress Father Parish had arrived. Downstairs, as Viveca stepped into the parlor, Aubrey at once rose, his expression pleasantly astonished, a red corsage in his hand.

"My dear, you look wonderful," he murmured.

"Thank you. You look quite handsome yourself." She gazed with approval at his elegant black suit and clerical collar.

He gestured at the refurbished surroundings. "I was just admiring this room, your new settee and chairs."

"Actually, Hilda Patertavish graced me with some lovely furnishings she no longer needs."

"How kind of Hilda." He stepped forward, handing her the corsage. "For you."

"Why, thank you," she murmured, sniffing the delicate tea roses. "These are wonderful. Will you pin the corsage on me?"

He grew flustered. "Well—well, of course, dear."

She deliberately moved closer, smiling up at him rather saucily as he fumbled at her bodice, his fingers cool and trembling beneath the lacy fabric of her dress, his face growing hotter by the moment as he struggled to attach the flowers.

Done, he all but leapt back, drawing in a harsh, relieved breath. "There, I think I've got it."

She glanced down at the corsage, pinned at a corner of her bodice. "Thank you, it looks lovely. And the red tea roses are a perfect complement for my blue gown, don't you think?"

"Of course." He coughed. "That's quite an extraordinary evening frock. Is it a Worth?"

"Yes, a Christmas gift from my father a few years back." She winked. "So, Aubrey, are you a connoisseur of couture, among your numerous other talents?"

He flushed even more vividly. "Well, er, yes, my sister . . . my mother . . . you see, they subscribed to *Godey's* Magazine, and—shall we go, Viveca?"

But Viveca was getting a perverse thrill out of rattling him. She'd had quite enough of his pious reserve. She strolled over to the sideboard, where a carafe of brandy and two snifters had been set out. "I thought we'd have an aperitif first."

"I—er—we wouldn't want to be late—"

She laughed gaily. "But isn't being fashionably late *de rigueur* in these enlightened times?"

"Well, I suppose . . ."

Viveca stepped forward with two filled snifters, depositing one in his hand to forestall further resistance. She crossed the room and seated herself on the settee, patting the place beside her. Deliberately she batted her eyelashes. "Please, Aubrey, have a seat."

Swallowing hard, he strode to her side. When he seated himself at least a foot and a half away from her, she scooted closer. "Shall we have a toast?"

"Yes, of course," he managed, lifting his snifter. "To your successful debut in the Savannah community."

"Hear, hear," she seconded, clinking her glass against his.

Silence fell as both took a sip. "Ah, an excellent spirit," he murmured.

"Yes, excellent." She leaned back lazily. "So, tell me about your week, Aubrey."

She watched sweat pop out on his brow. "Oh, please, I would only bore you."

"Nonsense. I'm ravenous to hear."

He took out his handkerchief and mopped his forehead. "Well, if you must know, my week began with a meeting of the vestry . . ."

As he recited a chronology of his daily activities that was, indeed, dry as toast, Viveca sipped her brandy and tried to appear engaged. This became more difficult as she became aware, gradually, of a teasing sensation beneath her skirts. The odd tingling began at her ankles and slowly traveled up her silk-stockinged legs. Mercy, what was it? she asked herself, struggling not to squirm. Was it a mosquito, a moth?

No, this sensation was much more subtle, sensual, wicked even. It felt like the lazy caress of a feather, tickling her knees, slowly trailing upward to tantalize her thighs, then tormenting her higher still, somehow even penetrating the hot, forbidden terrain between her tightly clenched thighs.

With a cry of horror, Viveca shoved her glass at Aubrey, then lurched to her feet and began beating at her skirts.

Aubrey popped up as well, his face red with mortification. "Viveca, what is it?"

She was still performing her ludicrous little dance and thrashing at her skirts. "I—I think a bee is under my skirt."

"Oh, heavens!" he gasped, setting down the snifters. "May—may I help?"

She expelled a huge breath and placed a hand over her fluttering bosom. "I—I think it's finally gone."

"Er—did it bite you?"

"Well—not exactly." Red-faced, she managed a tremulous smile. "But I do think you're right, Aubrey. Do let's go. We mustn't be late."

"Indeed."

Quickly he offered her his arm, but cast her a perplexed look as they left the room together.

Viveca remained horrified, infuriated. For by now, she knew precisely what had been beneath her skirts, and it hadn't been a bee, but a very determined prankster. She couldn't wait to get home tonight . . . and *roast* a certain ghost!

The Patertavish mansion off Washington Square was a Georgian masterpiece of red brick and fluted white columns. As the tuxedoed butler escorted Viveca and Aubrey into the lavish double parlors with their silk brocade wallpaper, cast plaster ceiling medallions and crystal chandeliers, she found she could hardly see over the expanse of beautifully coiffed heads and fluttering fans. The rooms buzzed with gay laughter and hummed with the liveliness of a string quartet playing Strauss.

Although Hilda had claimed this would be a modest affair, Viveca counted at least twenty couples milling about and sipping cocktails in the enormous salon. Noting the regal costumes of the attendees—the women in their finest jewel-tone evening gowns, sumptuous pearls and feathered headdresses, the men in their dashing tuxedos—she felt grateful she, too, had dressed to the nines.

Before Viveca could take everything in, Hilda rustled up, looking quite prosperous in a gown of striped plum silk with matching jeweled headdress. She shook their hands in turn. "Why, my guest of honor! Good evening, Viveca. Aubrey."

"Your home is beautiful, Hilda," Viveca murmured.

"Thank you, dear. I'm so thrilled to have you both here. Now I must introduce you around. All of Savannah is quite breathless to meet you, Viveca."

"I'm sure they are," enthused Aubrey.

But even as Hilda was about to lead them away, she glanced toward the entry hallway and grimaced. "Oh, no, there's Herman Hargrove, editor of *The Savannah Daily*, along with that abominable Bliss woman. What rotten luck."

Viveca hastily took in the rather odd couple standing in the columned archway—a rotund, balding middle-aged stranger with a large black handlebar mustache, and the more familiar figure of a tall young woman with outrageously curly brown hair, a receding jawline and dark eyes gleaming with avid curiosity. Viveca remembered Beryl Bliss from church, when she'd been fawning over Aubrey. Tonight she was dressed in a rather silly-looking red satin gown with exaggerated puffed sleeves and a gaudy spiked feather headdress with fake ruby stones.

Aubrey was also staring at the newcomers. "Now, Hilda, isn't that a rather unchristian thing to say?"

Hilda leveled a stern glance on him. "I invited the man, 'tis true, but I never gave him license to bring along that *creature*."

"Ah, yes, Miss Bliss," Aubrey muttered. "I recall meeting her at church."

Hilda lowered her voice. "She's the sob sister who wrote that lurid exposé on the Oglethorpe Avenue Orphanage—the one which, as you're aware, St. Bart's so generously supports."

Scowling, Aubrey again glanced toward the archway. "Ah, *that* article." Loudly he cleared his throat. "Yes, I must agree, Miss Bliss's diatribe was ill-appreciated."

"Oh, Aubrey, you're such a sheltered little lamb," Hilda went on with a long-suffering air. "You have no idea how despicable that little upstart is. Why, all of the ladies on the Cotillion committee are still abuzz regarding her horrid editorials espousing the views of Marx, Freud, Susan B. Anthony and Elizabeth Cady Stanton. Why, the woman is a Communist, an atheist—and a suffragette."

Viveca was tempted to chuckle at Hilda's down-the-nose attitude toward suffragettes—a disdain she suspected Hilda held only for Beryl Bliss. Otherwise, the widow seemed a champion of strong women, and was definitely one herself.

Aubrey, however, appeared suitably horrified by Beryl's alleged affiliations. "My, my," he muttered. "But if Miss Bliss truly is an atheist, then why do you suppose she visited our church?"

"Because of you, dear heart," Hilda answered forthrightly.

"What?" he inquired, paling.

Hilda elbowed him. "Such a babe-in-the-woods you are, Aubrey. Can't you tell when a woman has her sights on you?" She slanted Viveca a wink over his head.

"Well, I—er," he stammered, glancing from Hilda to Viveca and back.

"Did I neglect to mention that Beryl's a ruthless social climber, and a gold digger?" Hilda warned. "So beware, my good man."

Aubrey gulped.

While Viveca struggled not to chuckle over this exchange, Hilda glanced beyond them, then waved a hand in exasperation. "Oh, rats, they're coming over."

The threesome grew tensely silent as the two stepped up. Beryl sourly took note of Aubrey and Viveca standing together as her calculating, predatory gaze came to rest on Viveca. Viveca instinctively knew when another woman was sizing her up as a competitor, and she was definitely getting the evil eye here.

"Herman," Hilda acknowledged stiffly.

The man fidgeted in obvious discomfiture. "Hilda, so good to see you. I do hope you don't mind my bringing along

Beryl. You see, my dear Ellie is attending to her sick mother tonight—"

"I'm sorry to hear of it." Deliberately ignoring Beryl, Hilda gestured toward Viveca and Aubrey. "You know Aubrey, of course. And I'm delighted to introduce you to my guest of honor, a newcomer to our community, Miss Viveca Stanhope of San Francisco."

"Miss Stanhope, how do you do?" Hargrove shook the hand Viveca offered, then turned to his companion. "And this is my star reporter, Beryl Bliss."

"Miss Bliss," Viveca murmured, extending her hand.

"Miss Stanhope," Beryl replied in a harsh, nasal voice. Ignoring Viveca's still-extended hand, she turned to the cleric with a coy look. "Aubrey, dear, so good to see you again. You do gad about, don't you?"

He colored. "Good to see you, as well, Miss Bliss."

"Please, call me Beryl," she simpered.

With Aubrey appearing ready to eat his hat, Hilda at last addressed the obnoxious woman. "Well, Miss . . . *Bliss*, whatever are you up to these days? Planning any more attacks on our revered Savannah institutions?"

"Oh, you do run on, don't you, Mrs. Patertavish?" Beryl parried back with a high-pitched laugh.

"Perhaps you're aiming to excoriate Father Parish next?" Hilda simpered poisonously.

"Why? Has he been naughty?" Then, noting Hilda's murderous scowl, Beryl hastily added, "Ah, I see Mr. Clayborne over there, and I've been meaning to ask him about his new ventures in land speculation." She winked at Aubrey. "Toodle-oo, dear."

With her jaw slowly falling open, Hilda watched the woman stroll away. She turned her ferocious visage on Hargrove. "Herman, have you taken leave of your senses? How dare you bring that disgusting baggage into my home!"

He winced at her tone. "Hilda, as I told you, Ellie was called away tonight—"

"Then you should have gone with her, or come alone. And you should discharge that uppity hoyden at once. Let Beryl Bliss practice her yellow journalism with the likes of Joseph Pulitzer and his miserable hireling, Nelly Bly."

Hargrove pulled out a handkerchief and wiped his sweaty brow. "I'm sorry, Hilda, but Beryl's my Ellie's first cousin once removed, and I pretty much have to tolerate her."

"Well, I never . . . Oh, dear." In mid-sentence, Hilda jerked her head toward the foyer. "Speaking of the devil, there's Max Beecher. Herman, I'll deal with you later." Urgently she began making shooing motions toward Viveca and Aubrey. "You two go have some planter's punch while I steer Maxwell southward."

Aubrey spoke up in confusion. "Is there some reason I should avoid my cousin?"

Hilda merely snapped her fingers at him. "Go!"

At once Aubrey snapped to attention. As he led Viveca away, she glanced toward Maxwell, who grinned back at her before dipping into a mocking bow. She seethed. Oh, why did the cad have to look so devastating—his thick shiny hair so wickedly long about his collar, his features so angular, strikingly handsome, his eyes reflecting such mischief? Just the sight of him quickened her pulse and warmed the pit of her belly, bringing unwanted memories of their torrid kiss the other night.

Why couldn't Aubrey affect her this way?

Chapter Nineteen

Despite the presence of the hated Maxwell Beecher and the already annoying Beryl Bliss, Viveca felt that the evening proceeded well. After greeting Maxwell and steering him toward the bar, Hilda returned to take Aubrey and Viveca on the promised round of introductions. Viveca met the distinguished president of the Cotton Exchange, William Washington Gordon, his wife, Nellie, and their daughter and son-in-law, Julia and William Low, who were visiting from England. She was introduced to the esteemed Judge Peter Meldrin, who was chatting with his colleague Judge Endicott. She met Carl Brandt, director of the Telfair Academy; insurance agent William Daniels and his wife, Anne; phosphate czar and prominent socialite George Johnson and his family. All of the attendees graciously greeted Viveca and Aubrey, and several inquired about her piano lessons. She made it a point to show an interest in the lives of all those she met, and soon found herself caught up in conversations ranging from the price of phosphates and cotton to the revolution in Cuba to the burgeoning fire insurance industry here in Savannah, even the debut of Puccini's *Manon Lescaut* at the recently renovated Savannah Opera House.

Afterward she and Aubrey sampled the buffet—a sumptuous feast sporting every Southern delicacy from shrimp-stuffed mushrooms to okra soup to fried chicken with praline sauce. The lavish fare was topped off by richly brewed *café brûlot*, along with Georgia peach pie and whipped cream. Soon the waist of Viveca's gown seemed to be strangling her. When she stole another glance in Maxwell Beecher's direction, she was bemused to note several pretty debutantes buzzing about him like colorful butterflies, while he shamelessly flirted with one and all. The snake!

After dinner, the servants pulled back the furniture and set out chairs in the double parlors. Taking her place at the magnificent grand piano, Viveca played her Bach and Scarlatti repertoire to an enthralled audience. Throughout her brief recital, she remained calm. She knew that her posture was flawless, her performance impeccable. Gertrude Patertavish, looking adorable in a pink party dress with lavender ribbons and lace trim, beamed with pride as she sat in the front row between her parents and hung on every note her teacher played. At one point Viveca caught sight of Maxwell Beecher watching her from a gold-leafed archway, and almost missed a trill.

Following her performance, well-wishers besieged Viveca, and several more families indicated they wanted to sign up their children for piano lessons.

She and Aubrey managed to avoid Maxwell Beecher most of the evening, until the gathering began to thin and he stepped up to join them near the sideboard. As she regarded him coolly, his roguish gaze swept her from head to toe, making her feel undressed. To her shame, she felt her heart flutter.

"Good evening, Cousin," he murmured to Aubrey. "Viveca, how lovely you look."

"Thank you," she managed.

"Maxwell," Aubrey stated woodenly, shaking his hand. "Good to see you. I take it you know Miss Stanhope?"

"Ah, yes." He turned to Viveca with a rather menacing smile. "So, you two are becoming quite the item, eh?"

Viveca couldn't resist grinning back at him, while Aubrey loudly cleared his throat. "Not that it's any of your affair, Maxwell, but I am now formally courting Miss Stanhope."

Still, Maxwell's sardonic gaze did not leave Viveca as he thoughtfully stroked his jaw. "Paying suit to her, are you? Such an inspired idea. You know, Cousin, I might just have a go at her myself."

Viveca's smile turned to a glower; Aubrey sucked in an outraged breath. "'Have a go!' Cousin, what a crude, contemptible thing to say to Miss Stanhope! I must insist that you apologize at once."

Still ogling Viveca, Maxwell chuckled. "Are you going to call me out if I don't, Cousin? Pistols at dawn and all that?"

"No, I am a man of the cloth, not the sword," Aubrey rejoined sharply. "I shan't call you out—although you, Maxwell, obviously need to be *re*called to worship, to repent your sins."

"My, my, Cousin, you're on a sanctimonious tear tonight." Eyes dancing with amusement, Maxwell dipped into another bow. "Miss Stanhope, my sincere apologies for insulting your—er—delicate sensibilities and *obviously* high moral standards."

Before either could respond, he slipped away.

Outside on the Patertavishes's nectar-drenched veranda, Maxwell stood smoking a cheroot, staring at the moon shining down on a huge magnolia tree. He hated to admit it, but he could no longer avoid it. He had been jealous as hell, seeing Viveca with Aubrey tonight. When she'd grinned at him, flaunting her relationship with his cousin, he'd been tempted to throttle her, kiss her . . . and much more.

Damn, but the woman looked ravishing in that wonderfully

cut Worth gown, which beautifully highlighted her flawless curves, her exquisite skin. How he'd ached to tumble that perfect coiffure and bury his face in those luscious, sensual locks. He wondered what Hilda's grand potentates would have thought if he'd grabbed Viveca, hauled her close, yanked down that naughty décolletage and latched his mouth onto her bosom in front of God and everyone. Damn, but the woman could drive him to drink with one bat of those long, sexy eyelashes. Such was the state of his tormented arousal these days.

His cousin was far too much of a lamb for that wicked little temptress. Maxwell needed to set her in her place. Beneath him in bed would be a good place to begin, he thought with wry humor and a potent surge of excitement. It maddened him that she defied him at every turn, yet it aroused him even more. He wanted her, wanted his revenge, wanted to level her pride, but most of all, he just *wanted*. Hell, the minx was making him crazy!

"Why, hello, Maxwell."

Maxwell whirled to see that a woman had joined him, not the one he coveted, but an unwanted interloper. "Well, hello, Nelly Bly."

Beryl Bliss's laughter shrilled forth, sounding all too hyena-like as the moonlight illuminated her cold green eyes and pointed nose. "Maxwell Beecher, you're a scamp, calling me Nelly Bly."

"But isn't Miss Bly your heroine?" He deliberately whistled a few notes from the Stephen Foster tune.

Beryl chortled. "Perhaps I prefer to catch a *hero* in my cap."

More likely in your trap, Maxwell mused wryly. He stared at the fresh creature, unable to believe she was playing the coquette with him. But in the brief time he'd known Beryl Bliss, he'd realized this woman had no shame. She never hesitated to flirt with him, with Aubrey, with anything in pants. Obviously, she sought to secure a good match for herself, thereby gaining further entrée into Savannah society—and access to even juicier prattle.

He often wondered how she summoned up so much gall when she was such a sight to look at, especially with that large mouth and those hideously prominent teeth. The woman looked like a horse with a receding jawline, if that were possible.

"So, what do you think of our new piano teacher?" Beryl asked peevishly.

"Miss Stanhope? She's also my new neighbor."

"Yes, I've heard. And obviously she fancies your cousin."

Noting the woman's pout, Maxwell raised an eyebrow. "As do you, Nelly?"

Proudly she raised her chin. "Well, I must question Aubrey's being in the hands of such an upstart."

Maxwell grinned. "And I must say it takes one to know one."

She bobbed her short eyelashes at him. "Maxwell, please, must you tease me so?"

"You think I'm teasing?"

"You know I come from an esteemed family," she whined.

"Ah, yes," he mocked. "If memory serves, you were spawned from one of the original Natchez nabobs, eh?"

"Not to mention I'm cousin to Ellie Hargrove and all."

"Indeed. Impressive."

"It just vexes me to watch that nervy woman waltz into town and plot to get her hooks into Aubrey. He's such an innocent, and she's such a—"

"Femme fatale?" Maxwell supplied.

Beryl snapped her fingers. "Precisely. She's a ruthless social climber who plans to use him shamelessly to achieve her own ends."

As are you, Maxwell was tempted to retort. But aloud he said merely, "Ah, yes, it does seem Miss Stanhope is determined to snare dear Aubrey in her sinister web."

"And surely you can't approve, Maxwell, being Aubrey's cousin and all."

If only you knew, Maxwell thought wearily. "Well, I'm certainly no fan of gold diggers."

If Beryl caught this pointed reference to herself, she betrayed no sign. "And we mustn't forget that this Stanhope creature arrived here quite suddenly, her background clearly questionable."

Her background clearly questionable. Hmmm . . . Suddenly Maxwell grinned as a delightfully evil idea occurred to him. But could he really do it to her?

She would to him in a heartbeat, he realized.

With a low chuckle, he murmured, "You know, you're right, Nelly. Someone really needs to investigate Miss Stanhope—for Aubrey's sake, of course." He snapped his fingers. "As a matter of fact, you're an investigative journalist, aren't you?"

She snorted a laugh. "Maxwell, you sly thing!"

"Me, sly?"

"Are you suggesting what I think you're suggesting?"

"Why, never."

Beryl tapped his arm with her feather fan. "Don't you go acting holier-than-thou with me, Maxwell Beecher. I know you have ample motivation to interfere in the romance between your cousin and that interloper."

He flinched. "What do you mean?"

Beryl's cagey eyes gleamed with secret triumph. "I saw the way you looked at Viveca Stanhope tonight—as if she were the cherry on your jubilee." Giggling, she raked her conniving gaze over him and released a heady sigh. "You do have a certain intensity about you, my dear. I'd go for you myself, except that I have no illusions regarding the type of cad you really are."

"Pity me," he mocked back, "to be deprived of your coveted attentions. And speaking of the pot calling the kettle black . . ."

Unabashed, Beryl opened her reticule and drew out her notebook and a small pencil. "Let's see, I overheard Mrs. Endicott mentioning that Miss Stanhope is from San Francisco. As it happens, one of my college chums settled there, and works for the *Courier*."

"So it appears you have the situation well in hand," he drawled.

The woman stared at Maxwell and licked her lower lip. "Ah, yes, dear, well in hand."

Later, at home, Maxwell stood sipping brandy on his veranda. He'd had far too much to drink tonight, thanks to *her*. Watching Viveca make her public debut while flaunting her budding relationship with Aubrey, and looking like such a gorgeous little social butterfly in the process, had been driving him crazy. And it wasn't as if he didn't have another nymph tormenting him as well, one he was now eager to be rid of . . . if only he knew how.

He wasn't too proud of himself for inciting that Bliss woman against Viveca. But she deserved it for her sheer stubbornness in not selling him the house, not to mention the way she'd thumbed her nose at him several times now. He had any number of reasons to be rid of her—not the least of which was preserving his own sanity.

All at once he stiffened to alertness as he heard his cousin's buggy round the corner. Grinding his jaw, he watched the conveyance glide by his house, then saw Aubrey pull up before Viveca's home and help her disembark. Maxwell muttered expletives at the sounds of her laughter as the two crossed the yard together.

On her porch, more giggles, more flirtations; then the little minx stretched on tiptoe and kissed Aubrey's cheek. He genuflected, obviously flustered, and hastily took his leave.

Not until he heard a shattering sound did Maxwell realize he'd hurled his brandy snifter against one of his fine Georgian pillars. On the gallery next door, his lovely nemesis turned to glare straight at him, then flung open the door, went in and slammed it shut behind her.

The war was on.

Indeed, Maxwell was about to abandon all shreds of good sense and go charging after her when the soft purr of an all-too-familiar female voice stopped him. "Oh, Maxwell, darling? Come on in."

Her again. Maxwell hesitated, mouthed a curse, then turned and entered his house.

Chapter Twenty

Life assumed a routine for Viveca over the next couple of weeks. She was quite busy teaching her new slate of pupils, and Hilda Patertavish saw to it that she was constantly caught up in the Savannah social whirl, attending church meetings, teas and soirees, being presented at various hallowed ladies' clubs and civic organizations. Viveca also substituted as church pianist on Sunday when old Mrs. Buchanan's pleurisy kept her bed-bound. Viveca's performance brought her a fresh surge of admirers and even more new students for her burgeoning enterprise. She wasn't nearly as thrilled to note Beryl Bliss's presence once again at church—to watch her glare in Viveca's direction throughout the service, and fawn over Aubrey afterward.

Viveca did see Aubrey frequently as he continued to squire her to prayer meetings and various social functions. He even signed up for a refresher course of piano lessons. Viveca refused to accept any recompense from him, as it felt good to be doing something for him for a change. However, she found him an uninspired, if technically competent, student. At times it was difficult not to wince when he pounded out chords and hymns in his wooden, mechanical fashion; at such moments she felt tempted to bemoan the general lack of passion and vitality in their relationship. Although she had dared to kiss his cheek recently, the best she could expect from him these days was a chaste peck on the back of her hand, or a pat on the arm—hardly portents of a future robust union.

As if to remind her of what she was missing, Viveca would often catch sight of Maxwell Beecher when Aubrey saw her to her door. He would watch them from afar, his cigar glowing on his veranda. At least he was keeping his distance, for now.

Otherwise her nights were not particularly pleasant. Despite Viveca's warnings, Murfa Divine still stalked the yard at night. Viveca still heard the howls of dogs or wolves, and sometimes spotted cat eyes glowing at her from the inklike murk. Cobwebs still spewed from the staircase ceiling like spindrift in a storm, and the General's leg continued to taunt her with its quicksilver manifestations, along with the *kerthumping* sounds overhead—noises she was now convinced his spirit must be making.

Most tormenting of all, the ghosts of Alex Fremont and his Lorelei still haunted her dreams. Sometimes he came to her alone, tormenting her, mocking her with his dark smile; sometimes she saw the two of them together, making love. Invariably she awakened bereft, confused, quivering with longing.

Then late one May night, Viveca was stirred by the sounds of "Dixie," drifting through her window in a man's low whistle. Bemused, she cautiously left her bed, tiptoed out onto the veranda and followed the soft notes around to the front of her house. She steeled her spine, half expecting to see another corpse swinging on the square. Instead she spotted a gray, nebulous figure floating about in the street. It was the shadow of an old, bent man, wearing raggedy clothing and a tattered straw hat. He was gliding about to his own ethereal rhythm, pushing a large broom to and fro while whistling the famous anthem of the Old South in a bittersweet refrain.

Even as he worked, she could see the rays of dawn beginning to creep over the trees from the east.

Viveca's heart thudded. Why, this must be the "Street Sweeper"! Had the ghostly municipal servant been out all night, prowling greater Savannah, keeping the thoroughfares clean?

"Well, he ain't just whistling 'Dixie,'" she muttered to herself with a touch of wry humor. But just as she eased forward to get a better look at him, a golden spray of light hit the square, splintering his image.

Though astounded, Viveca had to smile. At least this spook wasn't as frightening as the others. Indeed, there had been something sweetly poignant about him, as if he'd been indeed a benevolent spirit.

Should she go ask Miss Lilac about him tomorrow? Now, there was a touch of irony, she mused; dawn was breaking and tomorrow was already becoming today. She was standing here ruminating about the occult, when this very evening Aubrey would arrive to take her to a prayer meeting.

As far as the otherworld was concerned, she hardly needed any further encouragement!

Maxwell Beecher had been watching Viveca's comings and goings and was slowly working himself into a hard boil of pent-up frustration. Wednesday evening proved to be no exception as he prowled his veranda and gulped whiskey.

He'd tried to keep his distance from her ever since the night of Hilda's soiree, when he'd been so sorely tempted to storm over to her property, kick down her door, carry her upstairs . . . and ravish her. He'd scared himself with those reckless thoughts and wanton urges. But ever since, he'd been unable to resist watching, drinking, brooding.

There had been little respite for him. Savannah's most highfalutin' ladies and their children had come and gone from her house like a never-ending Easter parade. Sounds of her piano had constantly drifted out through her windows to taunt him—children playing discordant scales and chords, even Aubrey popping by to pound out "Rescue the Perishing." And of course the prima donna herself had performed her precise Bach and Scarlatti selections, which, just as had happened on Saturday night, belied the true passion in her soul. Just one kiss had convinced Max that Viveca Stanhope was a far more sensual, earthy creature than her frigid repertoire—and demeanor—would suggest. But wasn't that the sum total of her existence these days—running from her true self? He knew what she was *really* about, and it was hardly frilly tea parties and delicate trills of Vivaldi.

What drove him most insane was that the more she played the society queen—the ice princess—the more he hungered to melt her. When she had left with Aubrey for prayer meeting earlier tonight, his blood had boiled at the sight of the two of them so cozily ensconced in Aubrey's buggy. Though it shamed him to admit it, he'd been pacing this veranda ever since, lying in wait like a jungle cat stalking its prey, desperate to get another glimpse of her—just to *see* her, and especially to see if the two would kiss. He was working himself into a fine froth, he knew. And he still had that other nymph tormenting him, and had no clue how to get rid of her.

He had to protect Aubrey, of course. More than that, he needed to protect himself from an attraction that was becoming overwhelming. Unfortunately, everything about the minx drew him to her—her beauty, her wit, her strength of character. Most of all, her stubborn refusal to allow him to dominate her. He was unaccustomed to spirited women who could hold their own with him. It was amazing, maddening, all too sexy.

Suddenly he paused, his senses growing acutely attuned to the sound of hoofbeats. He pivoted to watch Aubrey turn his buggy into Lost Lane. Viveca was there beside him, hanging on to his arm, laughing gaily.

He ground his jaw.

In front of her house, she continued her absurd patter as Maxwell's artless cousin helped her alight and the two proceeded up the walkway together. At her door, they talked and laughed for what seemed an eternity. Even Aubrey was chuckling, waving his hands in an animated fashion, unlike his usual stiff self.

Max's breathing quickened as he watched Aubrey take Viveca's hand, bow and gallantly kiss it. Then as he straightened, she wrapped her arms around his neck, stretched on tiptoe and kissed him back . . . on the mouth!

Strangled sounds rose in Max's throat.

This time Aubrey did not genuflect; he did not flinch. Although Viveca's kiss was brief and seemed fairly chaste, Aubrey stood it like a man.

Max muttered curses.

After an everlasting purgatory, when Aubrey finally turned and strode away, she waved to him gaily, blowing kisses, while he gallivanted along with a new spring to his step.

A red haze of jealousy all but blinded Max, and logic flew straight off the veranda. Enough! This was quite enough!

Viveca was in a fine humor as she waved at Aubrey and watched him drive away. Tonight's prayer meeting had been far more engaging than previous installments. Granted, the continuing discourse on Ephesians had been as dry as ever. But their host and hostess, the charming Fitzpatricks, had been great fun. During the refreshment hour, something of a melee had ensued when the couple's three Yorkshire terriers had gotten loose from the butler's pantry, chasing each other around the house and creating general havoc. One of them had even landed in the punch bowl. Poor Cleo Fitzpatrick had been mortified, but the guests had had a grand time helping her and husband Charles gather up the culprits and put the house to rights. When Aubrey had dropped her off, they were both still laughing over the incident.

Which was probably why he had let her kiss him tonight— she'd caught him off guard in a rare moment of exhilaration. Yes, his lips had been somewhat wooden against hers, but at least he hadn't recoiled or pulled away. She was making progress with him. At this rate, she might soon close the deal and become his fiancée.

Then why wasn't she filled with delight at the prospect? Because the personal price she would pay would be dear. It continued to bother her that, in seeking marriage with Aubrey, she was in a sense almost prostituting herself.

Viveca went inside, locked the door and took a lit taper from the hallway table. She was about to proceed upstairs when she heard an angry banging at the front door. Had Aubrey forgotten something? No, this pounding sounded far too aggressive to be him.

Peering through the glass panel, she gasped as she recognized Maxwell Beecher's dark, incensed features. A traitorous wave of excitement swept her—he appeared so passionate and irate—but her fury over his intrusion was greater.

"What are you doing here?" she called out.

"Open this door," he demanded, his voice slightly slurred. "I must speak with you—now."

"Are you crazy? Go home!" she retorted. "It's late, and you're drunk."

"You know nothing about my current state," he shot back, rattling the lock. "I said, let me in."

"And I said, go away." With her free hand, Viveca picked up a heavy iron doorstop. "By God, if you try to force yourself into this house—"

With that, he at last gave up. Waving his hands, he turned and strode away.

"Why, I never!" Viveca caught a raspy, relieved breath, watching his dark form disappear into the night. The nerve of the man, showing up at her door and trying to break in! What possible motive could he have had?

Then realization dawned. Surely he'd been watching her again, the scamp—and had seen her and Aubrey kiss good night. Why, the voyeur! She almost wished he had broken in so she could have applied the doorstop to his delicate skull.

Setting it down, she rechecked the lock, then stomped up

the stairs with her taper, in her angry haste almost setting afire the newly hatched harvest of cobwebs on the landing. Stifling unladylike comments, she continued on up to her room. At once she snuffed out her taper, not wanting to alert her obnoxious neighbor if he was still on the prowl. She undressed in the darkness, all the while muttering to herself and wishing she could throttle Maxwell Beecher.

She had just stripped down to her camisole and bloomers when she jumped, screeching, at the sound of her French doors banging open, flooding the room with moonlight. She watched, aghast, as a dark, powerful figure strode into her room.

"Very well, I'll pay full price," snarled an all-too-familiar voice.

"Maxwell Beecher!" Viveca cried, backing away toward her dresser, her heart hammering wildly, her hand fluttering to her chest. "What in hell do you think you're doing?"

"Why, paying you a little nocturnal visit, Miss Stanhope," he drawled. He strode closer to her, swamping her with his scent—an intoxicating mix of man, whiskey and potent arousal. Brazenly he raked his gaze over her skimpily clad body. "You refused to speak to me—remember?"

"Why, of all the . . . Get out of here!"

"No."

Pulse fluttering wildly, she dodged his advancing body. "But—I'm not dressed!"

"I've noticed."

"How did you get in here?"

"I scaled pillars as a child," he replied, breathing hard. "It's not a talent easily lost, I've learned. I might have come through one of your windows, but there are all those pesky servants I might have alerted—"

Viveca shook a fist at him. "Get out of here or I shall call my man."

"That poor old soul? Please don't inflict me on him—especially not in my current indelicate state." With a sudden swift movement, he caught her about the waist and pinned her against the dresser with his hard body. "You see, I'm in the mood to strangle someone, and I'd much prefer it to be you."

Viveca was horrified and yet scandalously aroused. Much as he maddened her, his hot body stirred her so, she could barely catch her breath. Even his anger perversely inflamed her. "M-my housekeeper will come—"

"And doubtless broadcast the scandal to the entire community. In case you hadn't heard, the woman has a reputation for a rather loose tongue."

"What do you want?" she wailed.

He eased closer. "Isn't it obvious?"

Oh, God, he was glorious—glorious and so hard! This couldn't be happening. "Please, please no," she managed.

With a low curse, he backed away. "Very well, then. Getting back to what I *want* . . . Let's begin with this: I want you to hear me out. If you do, I'll leave quietly, and no one will ever know of my little sojourn to your boudoir. If you don't—"

Viveca was not prepared to hear the consequences—indeed, in her present state, she might *demand* them. "Very well," she retorted in a quavering voice. "But make it quick or I shall kill you myself."

He chuckled, fumbled about at her dresser, finding and lighting the taper. He turned to admire her in the soft glow. "My, my. How fetching you look."

Face burning, Viveca hastily grabbed her wrapper and pulled it on. She was equally impressed by the sight of *him* in the candle glow. He was unshaven, hair tumbled, shirt askew, and he looked dark, dangerous, magnificent, like some exotic cat on the prowl. But one with eyes so searing and vividly blue they threatened to melt her soul.

Oh, heavenly days, she could not afford to succumb to his potent pull on her senses. "S-speak up. We haven't got all night."

"Would that we did, my love," he teased. When she would have protested, he raised a hand. "Very well. Once again, I've come to tell you I'm prepared to offer you full price."

Viveca's pulse dove straight into her belly at his provocative statement. "For what?" she rasped.

His gaze gleamed with devilment. "Should I say 'for you'?"

"Say it and die."

He grinned. "For this house, of course."

She blinked angrily. "Mr. Beecher, I'm beginning to question your sanity—or rather, the lack thereof. As you're more than aware, this property is *not* for sale. And you've wasted yet another trip over here."

His gaze slid insolently up and down her body. "Oh, I wouldn't call it wasted."

She slapped his face.

He seized her wrist. "Damn you, Viveca! Do you realize that, prior to my meeting you, no woman ever dared to strike me? Now you've done it thrice."

"Would that I could do it a thousand times."

"You witch!" Releasing her, he began angrily pacing. "You're an uppity baggage, aren't you? Gallivanting about Savannah like you own the place. When are you going to get it through your stubborn head that you're not going to succeed here?"

"I am succeeding here just fine," she flung back at him.

"You're going to fall."

"And you're the man who's going to trip me?"

"I'm not going to allow you to hoodwink my cousin."

She laughed as comprehension hit her. "So that's what's really stuck in your craw, isn't it? Can't stand to see your cousin besting you, eh?"

"Aubrey couldn't best me finding his way out of the outhouse," Max sneered. "And besides, you're presuming I'm the least bit interested in you myself."

She was incredulous. "You're standing in my bedroom, aren't you?"

For a moment they glared at each other. Then Max snapped, "That's beside the point—"

"And what, pray tell, is the point?"

He waved a hand. "You're dead wrong for Aubrey. A woman

like you will never be satisfied with a pantywaist like him. So, yes, I must protect him from himself—and from you."

"Indeed? Have you asked yourself who might protect *you* from *me* if you try to thwart me?"

"You think I have something to fear from you?"

"Well, something has made you desperate enough to scale my pillars."

Abruptly he turned and resumed his pacing, tearing his fingers through his rumpled hair and muttering, "I, miss, know precisely what I'm doing. You are the one who is totally out of her depth, who will eventually lose control and betray her own tawdry nature—"

"What? You mean, breaking into a woman's bedroom isn't losing control—"

"And I am the man who is going to make you do it."

Viveca gasped as she heard the steely intent in his voice. Before she could react, he closed the distance between them and hauled her close. She squirmed and pushed against his chest, trying frantically to break free, to no avail.

But the expected, ravishing kiss did not come. Instead Max stared down into her eyes, so intensely that she shivered, and a sweet, hot aching curled deep inside her belly. Heavens, this was worse than being ravished!

"Kiss me," he ordered hoarsely. "Kiss me now."

"Go to hell."

Her bravado seemed to amuse him; he toyed with a curl at her nape. "Consider it your Christian duty."

"*What?*"

"You're driving me to drink."

"Well, I'm not Carrie Nation," she flung at him.

"Thank God for that."

Despite her bravado, when he caressed her thigh through the thin layers of her wrapper and bloomers, a soft sob of longing escaped her. Then when his strong fingers grasped and roughly stroked an aching breast, she shuddered.

Viveca was drowning. Why, oh, why wasn't she fighting him? Perhaps because the heat of his palms, the erotic stroking of his fingers, was shattering her—and the diaphanous silk of her chemise only acted as a conduit for the erotic fire his touch spread over her. Her nipples tautened and her toes curled; she moaned in mingled anguish and desire.

He pressed his mouth against her ear, the heat of his breath tormenting her. "You kissed him tonight and now you're going to kiss me. But not chastely. *Carnally*. Let me feel the wetness of your mouth on mine, the heat of your tongue stroking mine."

"Stop it!" she cried. Then, almost helplessly, "*Please*, stop it."

"Now," he reiterated. "Kiss me."

At that Viveca snapped. With a raw cry, she thrust herself upward and kissed Max almost violently. He groaned and crushed her tightly, so tightly she almost couldn't breathe. Mouths mating ravenously, they stood there for what seemed an eternity, devouring each other. Viveca's heartbeat roared in her ears; never had she known such sweet glory as this hot, rapacious, never-ending kiss. Maxwell's hands roved her breasts, her belly, her bottom, rousing decadent thrills as her fingers stroked the hard muscles of his back.

She hardly even realized what was happening until he locked his hands beneath her derriere and lifted her. They fell across the soft mattress together and he yanked down the bodice of her chemise and latched his mouth onto her bare nipple, his rough face raising riotous chills. She screamed softly and writhed beneath him. Oh, his tongue was wicked, so brazenly wicked, on her breast. She was on fire, in the sweetest, most everlasting hell, her flesh throbbing with need, her breathing tortured.

Then when his fingers slid up her bare leg, she grasped his errant hand. "Don't, Max," she pleaded.

He merely drew back and smiled at her. "You're flushed, panting, my love. You want me. You're burning for me. Admit it."

Viveca was drowning. "Please, I can't bear it when you speak of—"

"Making love to you? Kissing you? Undressing you?"

"Stop it!"

"Why, Viveca? Because you can't bear to hear the truth?"

She could only wince.

"Do you think you'll ever have this with Aubrey?" he continued hoarsely. "Do you think you'll ever know anything with him beyond chaste kisses? Will you ever feel his mouth on your body, his hands caressing your most intimate places, his tongue—"

"God, stop torturing me," she begged.

But he caught her face in his hands and forced her to meet his fervent gaze. "You need to be tortured. You need to be humbled. Unmasked. You need to be driven to heights where you'll abandon your foolish pride and silly pretensions. He'll never demand your utter surrender—he'll never bare the soul of you. But I will."

Viveca was terrified of precisely that. Nonetheless, another scorching, kiss from Max practically tore that soul out of her. She almost lost all control, so drugging was his tongue in her mouth, so tantalizing his hard, hot body crushing hers. But when his hand slipped between her thighs, his rough fingers teasing her tiny inflamed nub through the cloth of her bloomers, she tossed her head free and begged this time. "No, *please stop*."

Evidently he heard the raw panic in her voice, for at last he drew back, his gaze fierce, boring into hers. "Why, Viveca?"

"Because—because I can't. Because you only want to shame me."

He smiled sadly. "Perhaps I do. But you will glory in it."

Viveca fully expected a renewed ravishment at that point. Instead, Maxwell abruptly moved off her, stood and was gone, leaving her a mass of throbbing, unassuaged longing.

Chapter Twenty-one

Viveca soon realized it might be years before she outlived her shame over her shocking lapse with Maxwell Beecher. The passage of days did nothing to diminish her mortification—or her traitorous, secret yearning for him. What had happened between them on Wednesday night had been the realization of all her fears. She had been wanton, utterly without shame. Only a last burst of sanity had saved her from complete ruin.

And she had enjoyed it—enjoyed having the rogue all but ravish her! She was attracted to him—treason though it be. There was no more denying it.

She was falling for a scamp who could only bring her disgrace just as Erskine had—possibly even worse this time. Somehow she must protect herself. It was a matter of survival. She would have to avoid him like the plague.

Luckily, she did not see him over the next few days. She poured herself into her duties—teaching her lessons, refurbishing her house. Hilda Patertavish, bless her heart, sent her additional furnishings, and also dispatched a crew of three laborers with paint to whitewash the exterior of Viveca's home.

Outwardly, things were going well for her. Inwardly, she was a mess, terrified that Maxwell Beecher would gossip about what had happened between them, or demand even more indignities for his silence. She continued to fear that her past might catch up with her, that the house of cards she had built might collapse at any moment.

And at night she still shuddered in her bed, flinching at every odd sound—the thud of footsteps overhead, the distant howls of dogs or wolves, the low whistling of the Street Sweeper outside. When the hauntings sometimes forced her from her bed, she might catch a glimpse of Murfa Divine stalking across her backyard, or the Quaking Lady out on the hanging tree. More than once, she was sure she spotted Ruvi or Miguel slithering about in the darkness.

Alex Fremont's spirit granted her no respite, either, although his presence was usually more emotionally wrenching than truly frightening. One night she awakened to see him standing beside her bed, his ghostly image glimmering softly as he stared at her with reproach and pain in his eyes. Another time she walked straight through him while entering the bathroom—afterward she felt enervated, drenched with his heat, totally caught up in the unfulfilled desires that still blazed between him and Lorelei. She felt tormented on every level.

On Sunday mornings, Viveca was dismayed to note Beryl Bliss ever present at church, freezing Viveca with her hostile glares and gushing over Aubrey after each service. One morning as Viveca chatted with Agnes Endicott following Mass, she spotted Beryl at the church door, clinging to Aubrey so tenaciously that she was tempted to go rescue him. Then, watching Hilda Patertavish march up to intercede, Viveca chuckled with relief. The widow actually made shooing motions at Beryl, then firmly steered Aubrey away.

Viveca joined them near the vestibule just in time to hear Hilda scolding Aubrey. "Whatever was that tawdry creature doing here again? How dare that brazen little atheist sully this sacred place?"

Face red as a beet, Aubrey stammered, "W-well, Miss Bliss

just confessed to me that my sermons have inspired her to—er—reconsider her rejection of a deity. After all, Hilda, we must always extend our hand in Christian charity to those unfortunates who are willing to repent." Even as Hilda opened her mouth to reply, Aubrey noted Viveca's presence and flashed her a relieved smile. "Ah, hello, dear. How lovely you look today."

"Thank you, Aubrey. Another great sermon."

With Viveca steering the subject matter into neutral territory, the threesome chatted a few moments longer. Afterward, as Aubrey drove Viveca home, he broached the subject of Beryl. After clearing his throat at least a dozen times, he stammered, "Er, Viveca, I do hope it's not an embarrassment to you—I mean the way Miss Bliss keeps—er—"

"Throwing herself at you?" Viveca supplied sweetly.

At that, even Aubrey's fair hair seemed to blush. "I—er, Viveca, I do hope you don't think that I've—"

She patted his arm. "Aubrey, I know you haven't encouraged her."

He heaved a huge sigh of relief. "Thank God."

"But you're an attractive man, so I'm not surprised she's making a play for you."

He scowled worriedly. "But—this is most unwelcome. Not that I wouldn't treat her with Christian charity, but . . . do you have any suggestions regarding her—er—forwardness?"

"Just try to keep things polite, professional—"

"Believe me, I do."

"And if I were you, I certainly wouldn't allow myself to be alone with her."

He went wide-eyed at that, then nodded vigorously. "I shall try my best."

Viveca smiled back, but inwardly she felt troubled, especially as she remembered Beryl Bliss's scathing glares at her. Beryl wanted Aubrey, and Viveca was clearly an obstacle.

On Monday morning Viveca was composing a lesson in the parlor when she heard the front door bursting open. Fearful that Maxwell Beecher had intruded on her again, she dropped her chord book and surged to her feet. To her puzzlement, she watched Hilda storm in, a folded newspaper in hand.

"Have you seen this?" she demanded, waving the paper at Viveca.

"Seen what?"

Hilda hastened over and shoved Beryl Bliss's column into Viveca's hands. "This."

Viveca quickly scanned the column and soon found what had so alarmed Hilda:

> *Rumor has it Savannah's newest music teacher has fled a less-than-pristine past in San Francisco, where she was illicitly linked with a prominent married man. My, my, such a shady lady amongst us, eh, dear readers?*

"Oh, my God," Viveca murmured, aghast. "How did she find out?"

"Don't you have any ideas?"

Viveca scowled. "Well, there were some innuendos in the San Francisco newspapers regarding my affair with Erskine—but who would have thought Beryl Bliss would go to these lengths to dig up that sort of smut?"

"She's a human weasel, all right. I think we underestimated her determination to snare Aubrey."

"Heavens, this is awful," Viveca moaned. "Is there anything we can do?"

Hilda gave a massive groan. "Well, I've already been by the *Daily* office to threaten Herman Hargrove with keelhauling—or worse. But the man refuses to discharge her. She must have something on him."

Viveca was crestfallen. "Oh, Hilda, I'm so sorry."

"Why should you be sorry?"

"Because you've been kind enough to sponsor me—and now I've been publicly disgraced, which will surely reflect badly on you."

Hilda waved her off. "Oh, bosh. You're only disgraced if you take this lying down. Everyone knows that woman is a yellow journalist, and if we all staunchly maintain your innocence, there's a good chance it may just blow over."

"You really think so?" Viveca inquired with frail hope.

"My dear, there are ample skeletons in numerous closets in this community. You've been well received so far, and no one wants to ruin you—except for that Bliss woman. The problem, however, will be Aubrey."

"Yes?" Viveca bit her lip.

"He's so holier-than-thou, and with his position, he does have to be above reproach, beyond scandal."

"Meaning I could lose his support?"

"Not if we don't allow it to happen. I hate to say the man is a pantywaist, but the truth is, he'll care much more about what the community thinks regarding this than what he may think himself."

Viveca nodded dismally. "I've been afraid he could display such wishy-washy tendencies."

Hilda patted her arm. "Don't fret. Once I'm home I shall telephone around and arrange some social calls for the two of us for tomorrow afternoon, so we may mend your fences with some of Savannah's better-known grandes dames."

Viveca was touched. "You would do that for me?"

"Of course. What time do you finish your teaching?"

"I'm actually free for the afternoon, but I must be back by five-thirty for Aubrey's lesson." She sighed. "If he even shows up."

"He shall come, I'll see to it," Hilda promised staunchly. "I'll take care of the good father, and in the meantime, why don't you start planning to host prayer meeting here next Wednesday evening?"

"Here? Do you really think I'm ready for such a big step?"

"Why wouldn't you be ready? What do you have—a ghost in your closet or something?"

No, only one in my bathtub, Viveca almost replied. "I—er—of course not."

Hilda firmly bobbed her chin. "We mustn't allow this little bump in the road to break our stride—not for an instant."

"Indeed." Viveca forced a smile.

"I'll call for you tomorrow at one, then."

After Hilda left, Viveca paced the parlor, keenly agitated. She was horrified about the newspaper article, terrified her future here was about to be drowned in yellow ink. Damn that little witch, Beryl Bliss! Why did she have to target Viveca?

As for Hilda's suggestion that she host a prayer meeting . . . murder! Not only was she up against a vindictive journalist and besieged by the occult, but now she would have to entertain her pious new friends in a house infested with spooks?

And it wasn't as if she could ask anyone for advice. Viveca had never fully confided in Aubrey about the ghosts, not since their first cursory conversation on the matter had revealed how closed-minded he was. As for Hilda, the woman had already been far too kind to her. Viveca couldn't expect miracles. If she confessed to her friend that she'd seen wraiths jerking about on the hanging tree or stalking across her backyard, the woman might ride her out of town on a rail.

But what would she do if the ghosts interrupted her first social gathering here? Perverse as these spirits were, they might just do it, especially the naughty, bawdy phantom of Alex Fremont.

A sharp rap at the front door interrupted her musings. A moment later, Viveca's stomach clenched when Winnie showed Maxwell Beecher into the room. In stark contrast to his mussed appearance last week, he was clean-shaven, freshly groomed, wearing one of his classic white Panama suits.

Oh, mercy, this was all she needed now!

As he stepped toward her, his gaze boring into her intently, traitorous desire swept her and her heart skipped giddily. Damn her own wanton nature! But far more devastating than the passion sweeping her at the sight of him was the emotion battering her pride, her entire being—the torrid memories of their kisses urging her to rush into his arms. She had missed him—actually missed him. This was awful!

"What are you doing here?" she managed to ask.

"I came to talk to you," he answered carefully.

She lifted her chin. "Winnie, Mr. Beecher is not welcome here. Show him out."

Even as the housekeeper glanced about in confusion, Maxwell stepped closer. "You will talk to me."

"Or what?"

"Do you really want me to answer that?"

The soft menace in his tone ran a shiver down her spine, and Viveca couldn't afford to contemplate how he might retaliate. "Winnie, you may leave us now. If Mr. Beecher isn't gone in five minutes, send in Ruvi and Miguel."

"Yes 'um." Wide-eyed, Winnie dashed out.

Max smiled tightly. "Aren't you going to offer me a chair?"

"No. Say your piece and go."

Ruefully he shook his head. "Very well. Actually, I'm on my way out of town for a couple of days. Delbert Endicott invited me to his summer house on Tybee Island. We thought we might do a bit of fishing."

"For 'Cuffs and Buttons'?" she asked sweetly.

He chuckled, drawing out a slip of paper from his breast pocket and handing it to her. "I wanted to give you this before I left."

Viveca glanced at the generous bank draft and whistled. "What is this? Guilt money?"

A muscle jumped in his strong jaw. "It's a very generous payment for your house, my dear. All you have to do is to accept it, and leave."

She shook the check in his face. "Damn you! When will you get it through your thick head that this house is not for sale?"

"When will you get it through yours that you need to sell?" He flashed her a grim look. "I read today's paper, you know."

Viveca caught a sharp breath. "So you believe Beryl Bliss's smut?"

"I believe you need to be on your way."

Rage at his audacity all but blinded Viveca. "Or what? Or you will ruin me like—like—" Realizing her terrible slip of the tongue, she clamped her mouth shut.

But the damage was done. Maxwell strode closer and gripped her arms. "Like whom? Is what Nelly Bly said true?" More gently, he added, "Did someone hurt you, Viveca?"

Although the concern in his voice all but decimated her, she managed to retort, "You think you haven't?"

He blinked rapidly and released her, and she took perverse delight in the spasm of guilt that crossed his face. "That's precisely my point," he said thickly. "You're far too tempting, my dear."

Bravely she raised her chin. "That's hardly my fault."

"Perhaps not," he conceded. "But I think you'll agree with me that this . . . this reckless attraction between us must be nipped in the bud."

"So nip it."

He gave an incredulous laugh. "So you think it's that simple? Just nip it, eh? Tell me, Viveca, what do you think will happen between us if you *don't* leave?"

"Nothing will happen," she asserted with bravado.

"Just as nothing happened following prayer meeting?"

Hot color scalded Viveca's face. "You—you climbed into my bedroom and all but assaulted me."

"And you beat me away with your pillow."

She was silent, chest heaving.

He regarded her with unexpected tenderness. "What *do* you think will happen the next time, Viveca?"

She almost burst out sobbing, so emotionally torn by his unexpectedly sincere questions, his show of emotion. "I repeat, *nothing* will happen, because there won't be a next time."

"Really? So you're that strong?" She could see the pain in his eyes as he whispered, "I'm not."

Viveca knees almost buckled then. Oh, he could turn a phrase and twist her very heart. "Maxwell, please—"

"Why do you think I accepted Delbert's invitation?" he continued with surprising humility. His gaze swept her with anguish and desire. "I must get away from you, for God knows what I'll do otherwise."

Viveca knew precisely what he meant, as she was in an equal torment herself. In self-defense she turned away from him, her pulse racing, her stomach hurting. Almost helplessly she clenched her fists. "I—I hardly think we're slaves to our so called 'carnal' natures, Maxwell."

He came up behind her, reached for one of her clenched hands and kissed it. She winced with longing. "Then you're lying to yourself, and to me. You're just as caught up in this as I am. But you're scared, Viveca, damned scared. Why, I'm not entirely sure." Gently he turned her to face his searching gaze. "But, darling, sometimes what we most fear is also what we most *need*."

Again she couldn't speak, as his honesty was devastating her.

He stroked her cheek and smiled. "Viveca, do you really think I like myself for the way I've treated you? Let me maintain what little shred I have left of my honor. I'm not a marrying man—I'll ruin you if you stay. I can't help myself. Accept the money, and go."

Viveca swallowed hard, then squared her shoulders. She tore the draft to shreds and let them flutter to his feet. "I'm not a quitter, Maxwell."

Shaking his head, he regarded her almost sadly. "Unfortunately, my dear, neither am I. This isn't over. You're going to pay a heavy price for your pride."

Reeling, she argued, "It's not pride, it's—"

"Pride. Don't say I didn't warn you."

He turned and left the room. At the archway, he pivoted. "By the way, Viveca, any time you want the money, just say the word."

He left and her hot gaze followed him out.

Chapter Twenty-two

When darkness fell, Viveca paced her room in her night-gown, unable to face the prospect of going to bed as her conversation with Maxwell Beecher replayed itself through her mind in a thousand tortured choruses. Was he right? Was it inevitable that she succumb to him if she remained here?

The bank draft he'd given her had been extremely generous. Was it merely false pride that had made her tear it into shreds before his eyes?

No, it was the fact that she wasn't a quitter, that she wouldn't allow him to chase her away. She would succeed here, despite his doing everything he could to sabotage her.

Yet what would happen if they did have another encounter? She winced at the very possibility. The ghosts scared her, but it was Maxwell who seemed to *devour* her. And what would remain of her when she lost herself to him? When she yearned to present her heart and soul to him like a feast on a platter? The attraction between them was so devastatingly potent. This morning, it had been all she could do not to fly across the room into his arms—and tear off his clothing. Even as much as he maddened her. Even as much as she *thought* she hated him.

Of every menace she faced here, he was surely the most formidable. But she couldn't allow another womanizer to ruin her. She just couldn't. What could she do?

Her restive moments brought no answers. Realizing at last that she couldn't resolve this by working herself into a froth or wearing holes in the rug, she marched to her bed and pulled back the coverlet. That was when she screamed her lungs out.

A dead bat lay on her pillow.

Simultaneously, Winnie and Emmett burst into her room. "My God, Miss Viveca!" Emmett cried, slack-jawed.

Winnie was violently crossing herself. "Sweet Jesus sufferation, it's a sign of de devil!"

Viveca was gasping, a quivering hand braced against her heart. "Did you put it there?" she demanded of Winnie.

Winnie adamantly shook her head. "Oh, no'um, no'um. If I touch that demon seed, it steal my shadow."

Viveca waved a fist. "If you're lying to me, by damn, *I'll* steal your shadow."

Winnie shuddered. "Miss Viveca, there's somet'ing *wrong* in dis house."

"No kidding."

"We need de Obi-mon to come out and pull Obeah from dis place."

Grimacing, Viveca remembered Winnie's previous reference to the Obi-man. "Don't give me more of that voodoo mumbo jumbo."

"But we need 'im to rid dis house of its evil," Winnie pleaded.

"Well, we might just begin by ridding it of *you*," Viveca scolded. "But for now, I'll settle for someone dispensing with"—she gazed at the bed and grimaced—"that hideous bat."

Emmett stepped forward. "I'll take it away."

Viveca slapped his hand. "Don't you dare touch it. Bats are known to carry diseases." She raised an eyebrow at Winnie. "And there are already far too many rabid creatures out howling at the moon in these parts."

Winnie flinched.

"Yes'um," Emmett said. "But what you want I do?"

"Carefully wrap up that creature in the bedding, then burn everything," Viveca ordered.

"Yes, ma'am." He went to work.

Winnie pointed at the bed. "You still gonna sleep dere?"

"No, I shall sleep in Miss Grace's room tonight."

Winnie nodded. "Aren't you scar't of her duppy?"

Viveca glared.

"I go change the bedding for you."

"No, I'll do it," Viveca retorted.

"But, mistress—"

"Let's just say I don't like the way you turn down the covers."

"Yes'um." Although she pulled a confused frown, Winnie fled out the door.

Watching Emmett work, Viveca could only shake her head. Who could have put that awful creature on her pillow? Someone with a sick, perverted mind and a twisted sense of humor.

Although she'd given her housekeeper the third degree, she doubted the culprit had been Winnie, since she'd seemed as horrified over the dead bat as Viveca was. The woman didn't seem artful enough to fake such abject terror. That left Ruvi or Miguel—but could either of them have gotten inside her room undetected?

She'd have to leave the investigation for tomorrow, although she did wonder why she bothered. She'd only hear a new set of denials.

At one time, she might have suspected Maxwell Beecher of such treason, but now she realized this type of cruelty was beyond him. Yes, he was a scamp, but following their emotional encounter today, she actually understood why he wanted her to leave—even believed he was trying to act the gentleman—and she couldn't accept that he'd stoop to these tactics. Indeed, she was tempted to run to him for comfort, for help—and from that standpoint, she was darn glad he was away at Tybee Island.

Watching Emmett shake his head, then stride out with a huge bundle of linens, Viveca was struck by another possibility: What if her tormentor wasn't worldly at all? So far, the spooks on Hangman's Square had not attempted any direct physical threats, unless she counted the cobwebs and the gargoyle on the stairs.

What if the atmosphere here was growing even more menacing?

Later, lying in Miss Grace's bed, Viveca still felt disquieted. Yes, the bed was more comfortable, the cross hanging above it somewhat reassuring. But it was unnerving sleeping in a dead person's room. Clean sheets or not, she could still smell Grace Fulton—faded essences of lavender sachet and lilac water—and she could still sense her presence. She even wondered if she might encounter Miss Grace's spirit tonight.

Despite Viveca's trepidations, eventually the exhausting day and the harrowing moments in her room took their toll, and she succumbed to slumber. Yet within seconds, a scratching sound made her jerk upright in bed. What now? Was there a mouse on the loose?

She listened intently for a few seconds, barely able to hear the low screeching over the pounding of her heart. Soon she realized that the sound came from the direction of Miss Grace's small game table. Mercy! Was the planchette moving about on the Ouija board? But that was crazy. How could this be, unless the suspected mouse was holding a séance?

Even as rattled as she was, Viveca was tempted to laugh over that image. She lit a taper, got up and went over to the small table. The planchette was still on the Ouija board, but she was stunned to discover that a letter had been etched in the dust.

The letter "A," written in a man's bold script. Heavenly days! All at once Viveca knew she'd received a message from beyond. Alex Fremont wanted her to know that this had once been *his* room! It was as if he were branding the space as his for all eternity.

Viveca glanced about frantically but saw no other signs of him. She was tempted to flee, but the prospect of returning to the scene of the crime, sleeping in that same bed where those gruesome bat remains had been discovered, proved too much for her. Wryly she mused that avoiding some particular night terrors was worth braving ghosts.

And brave ghosts she did. When Viveca finally dozed again, she saw in her dreams not the spirit of Grace Fulton, but once again the tortured face of Alex Fremont. Again he whispered, "Lorelei"; again she felt his pain.

Then Viveca found herself standing in this very room, Miss Grace's room, with tapers lit all around her. But the setting was different, more dated, the expanse filled with magnificent carved rosewood furniture and vivid European art. A moan drew her attention to the bed. Although she was almost afraid to look, she turned and stepped closer, gazing through the wispy mosquito netting. Oh, heavens, it was the ghostly couple. They were naked on the bed, their golden bodies gleaming with sweat in the soft light; he was kneeling on the mattress while she straddled him. They were copulating fiercely, wantonly, crying out, devouring each other. She was wrapped around him, her gleaming, fire-streaked hair falling across his bare, muscled back. She moaned with animalistic abandon and rode him hard; he dug his fingers into her buttocks and claimed her deeper still. It was the most unabashed mating Viveca had ever witnessed—horrifying, electrifying, tantalizing.

Then Alex Fremont gazed up at Viveca and smiled even as he continued thrusting into Lorelei. *Join us*, she heard his deep voice whisper. *Join us*.

Longing gnawed at Viveca's soul. As if she'd lost all will of her own, she felt herself floating toward the lovers. Then

abruptly the scene splintered into a thousand fiery shards . . .
and Viveca jerked upright in bed, darkness swimming all
around her as she moaned in pain and terrible desire. She was
trembling all over, and even worse, the front of her nightie
clung to her most private parts with shameful carnality.

Oh, God, when would this torment end? She was being
driven insane—her desires fueled by the salacious couple's
desires, and her own never-ending adventures in voyeurism.
All of it combined to put her in an agony of need, of
want . . .

And, shame that it was, she wanted Maxwell Beecher most
of all! She longed to crawl on her knees to him, all the way to
Tybee Island if necessary. How could she find release from
this purgatory?

With a cry of anguish, Viveca pummeled the pillow, then
fell onto it with a low sob. She wasn't one to cry uncle, but
she couldn't take much more of this nightly inquisition.

But, if she expected any respite at all that night, she received none. When her dreams came again, they were again
of Alex and Lorelei. This time the scene shifted to a shady
square. Viveca saw Alex standing there with his lady love,
both of them dressed in elegant costumes. They were embracing, kissing, near a blooming lilac tree. The scene had a
special poignancy, almost an innocence, to it.

Viveca spent long moments caught up in their dream, hypnotized by their need for one another. Then abruptly a third
figure, edged in sinister shadows, moved into view—it was a
woman with a knife, her face gripped with such anger that
Viveca twitched in her sleep. With a cry of rage, the woman
launched herself at Fremont and Lorelei. Quickly he drew
out a pistol and shot her. She fell, dead, at the couple's feet.

Afterward Alex and Lorelei clung together, trembling.
Viveca could feel their terrible pain and regret. Then the
square swarmed with citizens—vengeful men grabbing Alex
and Lorelei, appalled ladies bending over the fallen woman.
As Lorelei was dragged in one direction, Alex in another, he
struggled at his bonds and she at hers.

Lorelei! he silently screamed. *Lorelei!*

Then, turning directly to Viveca, he cried out from his dream, *Help us.*

Viveca sat up, her heart thumping, aching, in the darkness. She spent a long moment choking on tortured breaths that were more like sobs. At last she fully understood her bawdy ghost. She'd *been* there with him.

Help us, he'd pleaded.

But what could she do? Although his soul might be in purgatory, although he might haunt her dreams nightly, Alex Fremont—and his lady love—were both quite dead.

Chapter Twenty-three

Once daylight scattered the terrors of the night, Viveca tried her best to put its unsettling events behind her. She did question both Ruvi and Miguel regarding the dead bat found on her pillow, but both, as expected, denied all guilt.

She was thankful when most of her morning piano students showed up; only one mother sent a note stating her child was ill. At least if she was being harmed by Beryl Bliss's poison pen, it seemed the ripple effects had not been fully felt in greater Savannah as yet. Between students, she began preparing for her role as hostess for Bible study next week. She dispatched the men to wash all the windows, ordered Winnie to bleach, starch and iron all the curtains and dresser scarves, and began planning her refreshment menu.

That afternoon she accompanied Hilda on the slated round of social calls to Savannah's various matrons. En route, Hilda reassured Viveca that she had already spoken with Aubrey and convinced him that Beryl's venomous writings were shocking lies motivated strictly out of spite and jealousy. Hilda preached much the same sermon in every parlor where they sipped tea and nibbled pastries that afternoon.

Portraying Beryl Bliss as a villainess proved an easy enough task, given Savannahians' general dislike of the woman.

All in all, the two women accomplished a great success. By late afternoon when Hilda dropped her off, Viveca hugged her mentor and effusively thanked her.

Although tired, Viveca was feeling in much better spirits as she entered the house. Thanks to Hilda's rescue mission, she felt as if she could face the community—and especially Aubrey—now. In fact, the sound of low voices in the parlor made her wonder if he hadn't already arrived for his lesson.

Instead, she stepped inside the room to see Winnie standing near the fireplace with a visitor—not Aubrey but a tall, striking, middle-aged black woman dressed in a flowing costume of printed red silk accented by a purple tignon. Closely huddled, the two women were gazing ominously at the walls and ceilings of the room while speaking in hushed, conspiratorial tones.

"Winnie, I wasn't aware you were expecting company," Viveca remarked.

Both women turned. Winnie looked like a thief caught in the act, but her guest appeared quite at ease, even in command, and intrigued by Viveca's presence. Viveca found herself equally absorbed by the newcomer. The woman literally glittered with gaudy jewelry—gold hoop earrings, a large, flashy cross, numerous bangles, beads and rings. Her dark eyes shone with intelligence and a dash of mischief; her high cheekbones lent her a queenly air, as did the slight smile curving her generous lips.

Tentatively Winnie stepped forward. "Miss Viveca, meet my friend from de A.M.E. church, Sista' Taheisha."

"Sister," Viveca murmured, still quite bemused.

"Greetings, madam," the woman intoned in her deep, Jamaican-accented voice, bowing before Viveca.

"Sista', she come to help us," Winnie rushed on. Lowering her voice, she whispered urgently, "You know, wit' de duppies."

"Ah, the duppies." Viveca flashed the sister a tight smile.

"Winnie, you really should have asked me before—er, presuming to entertain guests here."

Before Winnie could apologize, the sister shook a beringed finger at Viveca. "Din' ya be scoldin' de girl. Winnie tell me you fin' de sign of de devil on your pillow, ma'am. Ya need our help."

Although annoyed by the woman's presumptuousness, Viveca was also grudgingly impressed by her spirit. "Do I? Well, Sister, have you some wisdom to impart regarding our dire situation?"

The woman drew herself up with great dignity and spoke in woeful tones. "I walk dis house wit' Winnie and 'vine it wit' my amber. I find it plague wit' lost spirits. Much pain. Much sufferation. God save."

"God save!" Winnie echoed vehemently, crossing herself.

"Really?" Viveca inquired. "And what do you suggest we might do about this—er—plague of sufferation?"

The sister raised her strong chin. "We need de Obi-mon come out, bless dis house, pull Obeah and catch de shadows."

Viveca rolled her eyes. "Not the Obi-man again."

The woman dramatically moved her hands through the air, flashing jewels on her splayed fingers as her eyes gleamed. "I see much bad sasa here. Evil duppies, spirits caught in the fiah. I see danger in dis house for you, madam."

"Danger," Viveca repeated, more daunted than she cared to admit. "Have you ever heard of the power of suggestion?"

Her guest flung a hand outward in a gesture of contempt. "Turn ears hard, reap de bloodfire."

Totally confused, Viveca turned to Winnie. "What does *that* mean?"

Winnie gulped. "Not listen, burn in hell."

"Oh, great." Viveca was about to thank the woman for her less-than-questionable assistance and show her to the door when she heard a familiar rapping outside on the porch. "Heavenly days, that must be Aubrey!"

"The sista', she 'bout to leave," Winnie declared.

"Splendid. Will you kindly show her out the back door?"

But even as the three women hurried into the central hallway, Aubrey, evidently spotting them through the glass-paned door, opened it and stepped inside. Expression anxious, he glanced from Viveca to Winnie to the sister.

"Viveca, forgive me for just barging in, but when I saw . . ." His gaze pausing suspiciously on Taheisha, he asked, "Are you all right, my dear?"

"I'm fine," Viveca assured him, though she shoved her hands behind her skirt to keep from wringing them.

"What is Sister Taheisha doing here?" he added sharply. "You know her?"

"Fad'er." Taheisha greeted him with a smug look and an exaggerated curtsey.

"She jes' leavin'," reiterated Winnie, grabbing her friend's arm and tugging her away.

"My, my," murmured Aubrey, shaking his head and watching the women retreat down the hallway.

"Well, won't you come into the parlor?" Viveca asked brightly.

"Of course." But Aubrey was scowling as he followed Viveca inside the room. "My dear, I must say I'm rather shocked. Do you have any idea who that woman was?"

She turned to face him with bravado. "Yes, a friend of Winnie's from the A.M.E. church."

He gave a bitter laugh. "Would that it were true. Sister Taheisha happens to be one of the most notorious Obeah priestesses in all of Savannah."

"Oh." Viveca blanched. "And you know this . . . how?"

"Well, I'm hardly a friend of the woman's," he hastily assured her. "But everyone hereabouts is aware of Taheisha and her reputation. You see, there's a small, unsanctioned splinter group in the African Methodist Episcopal church, mostly Jamaicans involved in an Obeah cult. The sister is one of their leaders."

"That sounds ominous," Viveca muttered.

"Indeed. She didn't ask you for any money, did she?" he continued worriedly.

"Well, no."

"Good. Because these people are often involved in frauds and swindles, bilking their victims with promises that they'll remove evil spells and so forth."

Viveca grimaced. "I see. You seem to know a lot about this."

He nodded. "A colleague of mine, David Lindley, spent three years as a missionary in the Caribbean. Through David I learned how the natives of Jamaica practice their ghastly voodoo-style religion and ofttimes try to disguise it as Methodism."

"Ah. So that's the reason for their association with the A.M.E. church?"

"A sham association, of course. Theirs is a history of fetish oaths, insurrections, black magic, snake and devil worship. Stealing souls, and pretending to bring the dead back to life."

Viveca shuddered. "Pretending to bring the dead back to . . . you mean, like zombies?"

He nodded dismally. "I'm afraid so. Of course they're not really dead at all, just participants in the crazed hoaxes these charlatans perpetrate. The worst crimes of all are the poisonings—"

"Poisonings?" Viveca's hand rose to her throat as she remembered Winnie's culinary debacles.

"The Obi-men and women poison their victims by means of ground glass and other vile substances. Sometimes the women even hide the poison in their fingernails, then add it to their victim's drinks when they dip their fingers."

"How awful." Unwittingly Viveca clutched her throat.

"For the right price, a priest or priestess will 'put Obeah'— in other words, a curse—on a man or woman's enemy. Then for an equally proper incentive, they'll also 'pull Obeah,' or banish the spell."

"I see. But the spells don't really work . . . do they?"

He gave a sober sigh. "Well, ofttimes these priests and priestesses succeed in simply scaring their poor victims to death. Why, David said his manservant went into a decline right after he spotted crow feathers in his path. The miserable soul claimed the Obeah man had caught his shadow and pinned it to the cotton tree. He died soon afterward."

"How ghastly."

"Yes, my dear. You must proceed with great caution," he continued sternly. "If Winnie has befriended this Obeah witch, then she's likely involved in the sect, as well. You should definitely consider discharging her."

"Well—I shall certainly question her."

"Good." He patted her arm. "You know, we must do everything we can to safeguard your repetition, especially under—er, present conditions."

"Oh." Viveca was crestfallen. "Are you referring to Beryl Bliss's article? Aubrey, I'm so sorry—"

"Please, dear, you mustn't apologize," he cut in earnestly. "Hilda has already explained matters to me. I didn't believe that creature's vengeful lies for an instant, and neither does any other respectable citizen in this town. I'm simply pointing out that with that disgraceful woman targeting you, you don't need—"

"To be associated with an Obeah cult?"

"Precisely," he concurred heavily.

Viveca nodded. "Thanks so much for your advice, Aubrey. You've helped me immensely. Shall we begin our lesson?"

"Of course."

Although she remained quite unnerved, Viveca managed to retain her composure during their session. Nonetheless, Aubrey's frightful revelations and admonitions kept replaying themselves through her mind.

After he left, she stormed into the kitchen to confront Winnie. "Why did you bring that—that voodoo priestess to our home?"

As Winnie turned from the pie safe, Viveca gulped at the sight of her long, sharp fingernails, surely fertile hiding grounds for poisons. "I'm sorry, mistress," she stammered. "Sista' Taheisha, she jes' want to help."

"Help!" Viveca ranted, pacing about. "Do you realize how

you both made me look to Father Parish? Like some sort of lunatic."

"I ast' her to come while you out. I not know de fad'er—"

"Are you a member of an Obeah cult?" Viveca cut in heatedly.

Winnie shook her head. "No cult. Only worship."

"Ah, so you *worship* Obeah?"

Winnie nodded. "We worship de god of de skies, de goddess of de earth. And what ail dis house, we can cure."

Viveca felt at her wit's end. "Damn it! I don't know if you're really trying to help me, or if you're making bad things happen."

"Mistress, no, jes' want to help," Winnie implored.

Viveca searched the woman's pained, bewildered face for answers, but could find none. Throwing up her hands, she left the room.

She was so hellishly confused about all of this. But whether Winnie and her friend intended good or evil, the priestess had said great danger awaited Viveca in this house. *That* she couldn't doubt for an instant.

She knew a terrible malaise gripped this house, and that it was rooted at least partly in the supernatural. But should she resort to witchcraft to find a cure? What if, instead of banishing her resident demons, she drove them to even greater heights of mayhem and insurrection?

That evening Viveca faced a new dilemma: Where would she sleep? Should she return to Miss Grace's room, and possibly spend another night with Alex Fremont and his Lorelei—or should she brave the bed where the dead bat had been found? The alternatives were equally daunting.

She soon decided she would try to avoid both potential pitfalls by having the beds switched. Miss Grace's bed was much more comfortable, anyway.

Of course, Ruvi and Miguel looked at Viveca as if she were crazy when she ordered them to switch beds, and they grumbled and groaned as they went about the task, but the feat was accomplished in short order. Soon Viveca was in her own room, tucking herself into the previous owner's bed.

Lying there in the darkness, she found her mind treacherously drifting to Maxwell. Memories of their passionate words and heated kisses haunted her. Yes, he was a thorn in her side, but now that he'd been gone for two nights, she missed him terribly—even the torment. What was he doing with the judge on Tybee Island? Was he missing her, as well?

Eventually her tumultuous thoughts quieted. The exhaustion of past days and weeks caught up with her as she lay cocooned on the soft mattress, and she fell deeply asleep. When midnight came with its plethora of spooky night sounds, she barely heard them enough to stir. But then she gradually became aware of low sounds much closer to her, as if in her room—first a soft thumping, then the echo of an eerie voice, as if someone were moaning.

Aie, came the soft, dirgelike sound. *Aie . . .*

It continued, growing louder, more ominous. *Aiiiiiie. Aiiiiiie!*

At last Viveca jumped awake, her hands frantically clutching the covers. Heavenly days! The sound was coming from her armoire!

She looked around for a potential weapon, grabbing a star-shaped brass paperweight from her night table. She crept out of bed, raised the paperweight and opened the door to her wardrobe. She heard a soft but bloodcurdling scream—*Aiiiiiiiiiiie!*. Then a dark figure leapt out at her, grabbed her arm and knocked the weapon out of her hand.

Viveca was stunned to find herself grappling with a woman cloaked in black, her face covered with a veil. And she was wielding a knife over Viveca's head!

"*Aiiiiiie!*" the presence rasped in a blood-chilling voice. "Be gone!"

Panic consumed Viveca, but thankfully not enough to immobilize her. Realizing her attacker was about to plunge the knife into her body, she rammed her fist upward, grabbing her attacker's wrist just as the dagger was descending. The two struggled violently, the figure hissing and growling at Viveca. The assailant was unbelievably, almost supernaturally, strong. Though small, she seemed to possess a demonic drive.

"Help!" Viveca screamed, still trying to keep the sword from descending on her throat, her heart. "Someone please help me!"

"Miss Viveca!"

Thank heaven, her bedroom door burst open and Emmett rushed in. The figure released Viveca, spun to snarl at Emmett, then fled across the room and out the French doors. Both Viveca and Emmett raced over just in time to watch the attacker slide down a pillar, jump to the ground, then scramble off in the direction of the Beecher mansion.

"Miss Viveca, are you all right?" Emmett asked anxiously.

She fell into his arms, shivering violently. "Oh, Emmett, Emmett—she—it—tried to kill me!"

"I saw. Did she hurt you?"

Viveca caught several ragged breaths. "No, I don't think so."

"Let's get you inside."

Inside, he lit a candle and stared horrified at her arm. "Miss Viveca, you bleeding!"

She pulled up her sleeve and winced at the sight of a slender cut along her wrist. "It's only a scratch."

"We tend it. Then I go get the sheriff."

Terrified as Viveca was, she found this prospect sobering. "Should we, Emmett?" In a frantic whisper, she pleaded, "I—we both know what goes on in this house, don't we?"

He pointed at the cut. "That be real, Miss Viveca."

Electrified, she nodded, although she far from shared his certainty. Yes, her wound was definitely real, but as for her assailant . . .

All at once both tensed as a new figure dashed into the room. "Miss Viveca, you all right? Oh, God, you bleeding!"

Winnie stood there, features tight with fear.

Emmett turned aggressively on the woman. "Winnie, did you just try to hurt Miss Viveca?"

She violently shook her head. "Oh, no, I never hurt Miss Viveca."

"Was it your voodoo priestess friend?" Viveca demanded.

"What friend?" Emmett added.

"No, ma'am, the sista' not harm you," Winnie cried.

"Then who did?" Emmett asked.

"I—I not know," Winnie stammered. "But—but I go get bandages for you, Miss Viveca."

After she dashed out, Emmett regarded his mistress with perplexity. "What's this about Winnie's friend?"

Viveca sighed. "While I was out this afternoon, Winnie brought a Sister Taheisha to our home."

He scowled fiercely. "You mean that witch she sit with at the A.M.E. church?"

"So you've met the sister, too, eh? Evidently, while she was here the good sister divined our home with her amber and decided it is thoroughly infested with evil spirits and needs . . . well, an exorcism of sorts."

Emmett rubbed his forehead with his hand. "Sweet Jesus, help us."

"What do you think?"

"I think you need to drown both them witches in the same gunny sack," Emmett advised.

Although she smiled sadly at Emmett, Viveca remained torn. She couldn't know who had tried to kill her tonight, but she doubted it had been Winnie or her friend Taheisha. Taheisha was too tall to fit in the wardrobe and Winnie could not have gotten back inside that quickly after running off. Plus Viveca did have to consider the possibility that the being might have been otherworldly. It had just been so ghastly, so formidable.

Yes, she feared Winnie's potential for mischief, but in some ways she was even more daunted by the prospect of declining the help Winnie and Taheisha had offered. Which meant this spooky old house was corrupting her brain, tempting her to believe in malarkey like evil duppies stalking her, bad sasa, and shadows on the loose, needing capture.

Indeed, after Viveca's wound was tended to, after Emmett left and Winnie helped her into bed, when the housekeeper scattered broken eggshells around the bed while chanting in some exotic patois, Viveca didn't even comment, much less protest. Curling up in a ball of pain and confusion, she again treacherously ached for Max. . . .

Maxwell Beecher was yearning for Viveca as he sat in a rocker on the magnificent front veranda of Delbert Endicott's large beach house on Tybee Island. Ahead of him rolled the silvery waves of the Atlantic Ocean, lapping against the shoreline beneath the cloudy silvery haze of the moon. Behind him, the Tybee Island lighthouse flashed its beacon toward sailors navigating the mouth of the Savannah River.

It was a blessedly serene scene that hardly mirrored the turmoil in Max's mind. He'd come here to do some fishing and get his mind off Viveca Stanhope; he'd failed on both accounts. He couldn't stop thinking of her, craving her. The woman truly haunted him now—and that was quite an ironic admission coming from him.

He couldn't seem to chase her away. Nor could he seem to resist her. And part of him was actually glad. *Glad.*

He heard the screen door squeak open, along with the thud of Delbert Endicott's boots as he crossed the planked gallery carrying a tray with highball glasses and a bottle. "Well, Maxwell," he greeted in a deep though slurred voice, "we're now officially on our third bottle of Cuffs and Buttons."

"You mean *you're* on your third bottle, Your Honor," Max drawled back. "All I've had is a delicate quaff of each, rather like being the king's royal whiskey taster, I presume."

Delbert guffawed, laid the tray on a small table between them and settled heavily into his rocker. He poured himself and Max a highball, then took a long sip. "Splendid night, eh, Maxwell?"

"Indeed," Max replied with feigned gratitude. "This little jaunt has been a welcome respite."

"Aside from the bass not biting."

Max fought a smile. "Yes, a double tragedy, our having to amuse ourselves with cards and liquor."

Both men laughed. "Ah, there's no pleasure like a good sour mash," the judge drawled. "And speaking of sour—"

"Yes?" Max inquired testily.

"You've been in an acerbic frame of mind the entire time we've been here, Beecher."

"I have not."

The judge rolled his eyes. "Brooding on the veranda . . . pacing on the beach. Max, do you think no one has noticed how you're agog over your new neighbor?"

"Agog? I take it you're referring to Viveca Stanhope?"

"Whom did you think I meant? Lilac Tupper?"

"Delbert, I think all that sour mash is polluting your brain."

"I think not. I saw the way you were gawking at the girl at Hilda Patertavish's soiree, as she flitted about so brilliantly with your dear cousin. I'd say you appeared about ready to jump out of your skin . . . and murder poor Aubrey."

Max gulped whiskey. "You do exaggerate."

"Oh, I think not. I know a fellow male of the species in pain when I see one. Tell me, dear friend, why don't you just stop fighting old Cupid and pursue the girl instead?"

"Pursue her?" Maxwell echoed in disbelief. "The woman has made it patently clear she's chosen my cousin."

Delbert laughed. "Since when have you given a damn about such niceties, or what any female thinks? Besides, Miss Stanhope and Aubrey Parish? A pretty poor match, in my view. That scintillating young creature can't be happy with such a . . . forgive my crudeness, Max, but we both know Aubrey is a sap."

"But it's a bed she's obviously made, nonetheless."

Delbert chuckled wickedly. "Then it's your job to change her mind—and her bed."

"Change her mind? But I've been trying to get her to leave town."

"Leave? Why?"

Max waved a hand. "Isn't it obvious? As you've just so delicately insinuated, the woman is driving me toward . . . well, passions I'm not prepared to pursue—"

"And why not pursue them?" the judge prompted.

Max was incredulous. "Delbert, are you deaf, dumb and blind? You of all people should know that I'm not proper husband material for any lady, by any stretch of the imagination."

Delbert merely guffawed. "You think *I* am? But my Agnes has managed to survive, even thrive, by my side."

Max was silent, brooding for a long moment. "At least you married her. As for my designs on Miss Stanhope . . . well, Delbert, you know me well enough to realize that propriety can't be one of them."

"Then change those designs." Gazing out at the beach, the judge sighed deeply. "Life is short, my boy. You're clearly miserable as matters stand, so my advice is, do whatever you need to do to get what you most desire. That's what I did with my Agnes, and believe me, it's been worth it."

"Worth marriage?"

Delbert chortled. "Don't say it like it's a death sentence, son. Swallow your pride, Max. Quit trying to chase Viveca Stanhope away and take her some roses instead."

"Roses?"

Delbert sloshed his liquor. "Yes, roses, candy, all those dainty little favors ladies adore. And heed my warning: Keep brooding and hesitating this way, and she'll be married to Aubrey by summer's end. Is that what you really want?"

Max scowled. His problem was, in large part, that he wasn't sure what he *really* wanted.

Delbert gave a shrug. "Well, enough said. You figure it out, my boy." He creaked his rocker into motion. "I presume we'll arrive home tomorrow in time for my dear Agnes's prayer meeting. Perhaps I can claim dyspepsia and duck the festivities. By the way, Max, how do you manage to avoid all things holy in our fair city? Especially with Aubrey being our rector."

Max shrugged. "Well, I'm not married to your dear Agnes, jewel that she is. And I couldn't care less what my cousin thinks."

"Except, perhaps, when it comes to what he thinks about Miss Stanhope?" the judge inquired. "I presume Aubrey will escort her, as usual."

Max glared.

"Which will leave you at loose ends. May I suggest we host our 'five-in-hand' for poker at the DeSoto?"

Max pulled out a cheroot and bit down hard on it. "Poker at the DeSoto? I'll have to let you know. Possibly I'll have other plans."

The judge scowled at Max a moment, then burst out laughing.

Chapter Twenty-four

Daylight brought Viveca no answers regarding her attacker. She considered every possibility—from her assailant's being a woman, a large boy, or a small man pretending to be a woman, to a ghost wielding a knife. She thought of the unknown woman who had attacked Alex Fremont and Lorelei in her dream, the woman Alex had murdered; was that female specter stalking *her* now, seeking some sort of twisted vengeance?

Terrifying as all these prospects were, the evidence seemed to argue that the culprit was real, as real as the gash that still stung her wrist. Thus as the morning passed and she conducted her lessons, she began to have second thoughts regarding her decision not to inform the authorities about her would-be assassin. She still wasn't sure she should make the bizarre incident public—but shouldn't she at least warn her neighbors about a potential marauder on the loose?

At noon, she sent Emmett next door with a plate for Miss Lilac, instructing him to caution her to keep her doors and windows locked. Then, as she was finishing her ham sandwich on the front gallery, she watched Elvira Withersmith, in calico dress and large slat bonnet, round the corner of the Cunningham house and kneel to pull weeds from a flower bed surrounding a large crepe myrtle. She got up, intent on visiting with the woman—and cautioning her, as well.

In the Cunninghams' front yard, Viveca called out pleasantly, "You can come weed my garden any time you want."

Elvira straightened and smiled. "I've been meaning to tell you that your place is looking so much better."

Arriving at her neighbor's side, Viveca murmured, "Thank you. Have you heard from the Cunninghams lately?"

Elvira went pale, then busied herself dusting dirt off her gardening gloves. "No, no word at all, I'm afraid."

Viveca bit her lip. "I'm sorry. I know it's painful, the matter between you and your sister." She gestured expansively. "But surely she must appreciate how well you care for her home."

Elvira sighed. "I can only hope so." She glanced at Viveca's sleeve and gasped. "My dear, you're bleeding!"

Viveca grimaced at the sight of her splotched right cuff, where blood had oozed through the bandage. "Oh, gracious. Really, it's nothing. I just had a bit of an accident last night."

"Accident?"

Taking a deep breath, Viveca confessed, "Miss Elvira, I know this may sound bizarre, but have you ever heard of a woman with a knife trying to attack folks in these parts?"

Elvira's hand fluttered to her heart. "Oh, horrors! Is that what happened to you?"

Viveca nodded. "Crazy as it seems, an attacker somehow infiltrated my bedroom last night. It was a woman with a knife—and she leapt out of my armoire and tried to stab me."

"Forevermore!" Elvira gasped.

"Fortunately, my manservant scared her away."

"Well, thank God for that." With an expression of grave concern, Elvira patted Viveca's arm. "You poor lamb. How terrified you must have been. Are you all right?"

Viveca nodded. "Only this scratch."

"And the woman didn't harm anyone else, or try to steal anything?"

"No."

"Well, bless your heart."

"Thank you. Er—getting back to my question . . . does my account sound at all familiar?"

Elvira hesitated a long moment, then sadly replied, "You know, I have heard of such a woman."

"Really?" Viveca tensed.

A faraway, pained look lit Elvira's pale eyes. " 'Twas at least ten years back, I'm thinking. They say she went crazy with fever one summer night and ran through the streets of Savannah with a dagger."

"My God!"

"She broke into a home, confronted a couple in their bedroom—"

"Oh, heavens! How awful!" Viveca was thunderstruck, left gasping at the parallels to her own situation. "But who is she? *Where* is she? Perhaps I should inform the authorities about this—"

"But there's nothing to tell them," Elvira cut in sadly.

"What do you mean?"

Elvira's visage reflected anguish and regret. "I didn't finish my account. You see, when the woman attacked, the husband moved to disarm her. Rather than be caught, she turned the knife on herself." Elvira nodded to the west. "She's buried yonder in Colonial Cemetery."

Viveca staggered, grabbing the trunk of the crepe myrtle for support. "Good heavens! Then this . . . last night, this must have been someone else."

"Could be." Cryptically Elvira added, "Though one never knows."

No kidding, Viveca thought. "So you're aware of the—er—the hauntings hereabouts?"

Elvira laughed ruefully. "Oh, my dear! On Hangman's Square? Of course I am."

"And you will take care?"

"Indeed. But don't worry, dear, I'm fine. Always, always fine."

Something about the way Elvira said it left Viveca uneasy. She strongly suspected that the woman knew more than she was letting on.

"Well, good day, then." Flashing Elvira a weak smile, Viveca turned for home. Great. So now she had another name to add to the long list of suspects—alive and dead— who may have attacked her last night.

Once Viveca tidied up her dinner dishes, she returned to the parlor to prepare for her next piano lesson. Bemused, she noticed that someone had closed the lid over the keys. Without thinking, she flipped it open.

Viveca jumped back, stunned. A huge snake was slithering about on the keyboard! She screamed so loud, the creature actually jerked and twitched.

Simultaneously, all four of Viveca's servants converged on the parlor—Winnie with a broom, Ruvi with a rake, Emmett with half a sandwich in his hand, and Miguel dragging a snarl of greenery with one foot.

At once four sets of eyes became fixated on the squirming reptile. "Cottonmouth!" Winnie yelled, pointing a trembling finger at it.

Although Winnie and Miguel shrank away, Ruvi quickly stalked across the room, knocked the snake off the piano with his rake handle, picked up the writhing creature from behind its neck, and with a cruel, swift twist, killed it. Viveca winced at the gruesome sight.

By now Emmett was by Viveca's side and frantically patting her back. "You all right, Miss Viveca?"

"Y-yes." She turned to Ruvi. "Who did this?"

"Not I, *Gadji*," he quickly replied, as Winnie and Miguel added their own tense denials.

Viveca had had her fill of the shenanigans in this house, and the repeated refusals of all three of her inherited servants to accept any responsibility. "So none of you had anything to do with it, eh? Don't give me that folderol."

"But, Miss Viveca—" pleaded Winnie.

Feeling at her wit's end, Viveca began to pace. "Listen to me, all of you. I can't take any more of this, do you hear me? Today is Wednesday, for heaven's sake. Do you understand?"

"No'um." Winnie looked totally confused, and Ruvi and Miguel merely shook their heads.

Viveca waved her hands. "What I'm saying is, exactly one week from today, I'm hosting prayer meeting in this house. *Prayer meeting*, for heaven's sake! And we have maniacs on the loose, banshees, ghosts, poisonous snakes, God knows what else, and—"

She wasn't allowed to finish. Everyone jumped as the front door blasted open and a charged male voice called out, "What in hell is going on here?"

Viveca turned to watch Maxwell Beecher storm into the room, a huge bouquet of red roses illogically clutched in his hands as he took in the scene with horrified eyes. Spotting Ruvi with the dead snake, he strode to Viveca's side while staring daggers at the gardener. "Sweetheart, are you all right? Is this man trying to hurt you?"

His use of the word "sweetheart," along with his vibrant, virile presence, warmed Viveca's belly with an unexpected tenderness. He looked so gorgeous and masterful, standing there with frantic concern in his dark blue eyes. She had missed him, she realized with traitorous longing. Missed him terribly, and the gnawing instinct to close the distance between them was all but overpowering.

But, noting Rudi's near-panicked look, she quickly replied, "No, I'm fine. Ruvi just killed a snake that somehow managed to insinuate itself inside my piano."

"What?" Max glowered fiercely at the servants. "Which of you did this?"

Four heads were violently shaken.

Max muttered a curse. "All of you, please take away that odious carcass and leave Miss Stanhope and me alone."

All four looked to Viveca for guidance; she almost protested, then a look at Max's grim face convinced her he was in no mood to be crossed. She nodded to the servants, who quickly took their leave.

"What are you doing here?" she asked him.

"What am I doing here?" he repeated in disbelief. "I just returned from Tybee Island and was coming to bring you roses when I heard you screaming as if you were being burned at the stake. And I repeat, are you all right?"

But Viveca was staring raptly at the gorgeous bouquet of roses, inhaling their tantalizing scent—and that same strange softening was again threatening to dissolve her will. "You were coming to bring me flowers?"

He shook a finger at her. "Oh, no, you don't. We're talking about *you* here." Laying the bouquet on the piano, he demanded, "Well, Viveca? What on earth has been going on?"

She flung her hands outward. "I don't know what happened. I—"

"My God, your sleeve!" he cried.

Viveca glanced at the spreading blotch of blood on her cuff, then at Max's thunderstruck face. "I—it's nothing. I cut myself slicing bread—"

"Liar!"

With surprising gentleness, he took her hand, pulled back the cuff and winced at the sight of the blood-soaked bandage. "What happened to you, Viveca? Did someone try to hurt you?"

Reeling at his nearness, the undeniable worry in his voice, Viveca knew she couldn't afford to tell him the truth about what had occurred in her bedroom last night. "Really, I'm fine."

"Fine, hell. We need to change this bandage."

She pulled away, mostly in self-preservation. "I—I'll get Emmett to do it."

Max appeared incredulous. "Viveca, tell me what is going on here. And what is the meaning of that dead snake?"

"I don't know," she replied in helpless frustration. "When I came in from having dinner on the porch, I found someone had closed the lid on the piano keyboard. When I opened it—"

"You had a cozy introduction to a venomous snake?" he tensely supplied for her.

"Well, yes," she admitted.

"Good Lord, how could this have happened?"

"I have no idea."

He waved a hand. "Well, the hideous creature couldn't have slithered inside the keyboard all by itself and then shut the lid."

"Precisely."

He began to pace. "Damn it, Viveca, this is most unacceptable."

"No lie."

"Why didn't you tell me you're in danger here?"

She gave an incredulous laugh. "What? How could I know the danger wasn't from you?"

He appeared stunned. "Viveca, that's not fair."

She realized it wasn't—indeed, it was difficult not to wilt at the reproach in his eyes. But, despite her fear that she might reveal everything to him, she forged on. "Well, you shoot trees, don't you? And you threatened me with dynamite."

"I threatened your *house* with dynamite."

"Is there a difference?"

He hesitated a moment; then a guilty smile pulled at his lips. "Perhaps I was hasty."

"Just hasty?"

A muscle jerked in his jaw. "Let's get back to the issue at hand. What else has been going on here?"

She glanced away. "Nothing."

"Rubbish." He stepped forward, seizing her by the shoulders. "How can I protect you from these obvious perils if you won't tell me the truth?"

His magnetic presence, the heat and strength of his fingers clutching her shoulders, again threatened to undo her resolve. But she shuddered to think of his response if she confessed all—especially, how he might protect her from any future assailants in her bedroom. Her boudoir was already too often invaded by another bawdy male presence.

Drawing a deep, steadying breath, she said gently but firmly, "Max, much as I appreciate your concern, it's not your job to protect me."

"Well, someone needs to take on the task."

Lips twitching at his near-comical exasperation, she asked, "Why did you come here?"

"Viveca, you're changing the subject—"

"*Why*, Max?"

He actually smiled, turning to retrieve his bouquet. "As I said, to bring you these."

She took the sheaf of fragrant blooms, smelled them, then gently laid them back down. "They're lovely. I can't wait to put them in water. Now let's hear your ulterior motive."

"Why, Viveca, I never—"

" 'Fess up, Max."

His eyes gleamed with that familiar mischief. "Very well. I came to implore you not to go out with Aubrey tonight."

She ground her teeth. "As I might have known you would."

"Well, you can't enjoy his dry company or those dull prayer meetings." He reached out and caressed her cheek with his fingertips, his expression revealing a touching vulnerability. "Come out with me instead."

"What?" She backed away. "Well, this is a change of heart."

"I suppose it is."

She gave an incredulous laugh. "You've been trying your best to chase me out of Savannah. Now you want me to go out with you?"

"Yes."

"But I thought I was 'too tempting.' "

"Oh, you are," he replied huskily. "Which is precisely why I'm here."

The passion in his tone, his eyes, made her gasp. Viveca's stomach fluttered, aching with desire. Instinctively she eased farther away. Max pressed closer until his intense face hovered just inches above hers and his warm breath sweetly teased her cheek.

"I tried not to think of you while we were out at Tybee Island," he went on fervently, "but you burned ever brighter in my mind. No wonder, love—I should have been here, defending you." He cupped her chin in his hand and smiled down into her eyes.

Viveca caught a raspy breath; this sort of Southern-gentleman chivalry was totally unexpected from Max, and equally devastating. "I—I'm really all right," she managed weakly.

"Are you? Then instead of reciting meaningless litanies with Aubrey tonight, why don't you really do your Christian duty and save me from another evening of cards and sour mash with Delbert Endicott?"

Viveca gazed at him in amused perplexity; he definitely had a way of needling her conscience. Too bad he was no candidate for redemption. "How convenient of you to place responsibility for your corrupt behavior on me."

He chuckled, his voice dipping to an even lower, more seductive note. "Come along with me, Viveca. Tell Aubrey you have . . . well, dyspepsia or something."

"Dyspepsia?" she repeated, aghast.

"It works for my friend the judge. We'll take the buggy down to the river, spread out a blanket, have a picnic. I'll ply you with champagne, caviar, fresh fruit, and"—he leaned over, whispering at her ear—"we'll see what develops."

Though tempted more than she would have dreamed, Viveca at last managed to squeeze past him. "I might have known you'd suggest such a lurid assignation. And don't think for a moment that I'm fooled by this . . . this devious shift in tactics. Browbeating me didn't work, so now you try flowers and sweet talk instead?"

He gave a groan. "Viveca, do you hate me so much?"

At once she felt contrite. "Max, I don't hate you at all. But forgive me if I don't believe that you have my best interests at heart. A blind man could see that any potential relationship between us would be disastrous. I trust you about as much as I do that snake. And I just don't think this . . . this attraction between us is right."

She heard a soft curse escape him; then he closed the distance between them, pulled her into his arms and kissed her—a ravishing, ardent kiss that seemed to go on forever. Viveca became conscious only of him and the fierce aching in her heart. Oh, what was she going to do? Just one touch of his lips and she was all but lost.

When he pulled back, his eyes blazed down into hers. "Tell me this isn't right, Viveca."

She was breathless, rattled. "Max, that isn't the point."

"Oh, but it is precisely the point."

To illustrate, he kissed her again, this time in a slow, drugging, intimate fashion. She moaned and pressed herself eagerly into him. At moments like this she felt as if she had no will of her own—they did feel so right together.

After a moment, he tucked her head beneath his chin. "Change your mind, Viveca?"

Though miserably conflicted, she whispered back, "No, Max. I'm sorry."

With a frustrated groan he released her. As he strode for the door, she watched him with anguished eyes.

At the archway he turned. "Damn it, Viveca, when are you going to stop lying to yourself—and to me? I'm going to make you face the truth. And I'm going to find out what's really going on in this house. Mark my words."

Watching him stride out, she collapsed onto the piano bench. She couldn't doubt Max's departing vow. Indeed, part of her was tempted to rush after him, apologize, beg him for help—beg him to release her from this crazed desire he'd fired in her. But the personal price she would pay would be too great. As touching as his concern had been, he'd also made clear what he really wanted from her, and it was hardly something respectable like marriage. No; although Max might be a better person than Erskine, in too many ways that counted, he remained a huge pitfall for her.

A moment later, Emmett eased inside the doorway. "Miss Viveca, you all right?"

She stood, gazed at his deeply troubled face and flashed him a wan smile. "Yes, Emmett."

"I worried. First that woman with a knife attacked you, now this . . ."

"We'll get through it."

He shook his head. "Them folks needs to go."

She bit her lip. "You mean Winnie, Ruvi and Miguel?"

He nodded.

Viveca felt intensely torn. "Emmett, I see your point, but I hesitate to discharge any of them without proof. We both know what it's like to be harshly judged."

"I know, miss." He shook a finger at her. "But them folks *still* needs to go."

Viveca sat back down with a groan, reflecting dismally that perhaps he was right.

Moments after he left, Winnie tiptoed in. "What now?" Viveca asked the woman irritably.

Though Winnie trembled, she held her ground. "You think I hurt you, mistress?"

Viveca sadly shook her head. "Winnie, I don't know. Why don't you tell me?"

"I not hurt you," the woman asserted.

"Well, splendid."

"You not believe me?"

"I don't know what to believe."

Winnie stepped forward. "What you do next week when you have your Bible ditties if dem duppies show up?"

Viveca's eyes implored the heavens. "Please, don't remind me. I'm already half ill about it."

Winnie continued sternly. "You gots to start listenin' to me, mistress. We gots to catch de shadows, pull de Obeah.

Let me gather up some folkses for you. Den you see we help, not hurt."

At the moment, Winnie's suggestions actually sounded palatable, making Viveca realize she was surely standing at the gates of abject defeat—or incurable insanity. Nonetheless, she had pretty much exhausted all potential solutions herself. What else *could* she do?

With a great sigh, she at last acquiesced. "You know, Winnie, you're right. This house is thoroughly infested, and I'm sick and tired of being the whipping boy for a gaggle of ghosts. So bring on the Obi-man."

"Yes'um."

"Tonight. After prayer meeting."

Chapter Twenty-five

Preparing for prayer meeting, Viveca was about as calm as a cat with its tail on fire. She was all thumbs, shattering a bottle of perfume and tearing a button off her best linen blouse. She couldn't believe she was actually going to allow some "Obi-man" to perform an exorcism of sorts in her house. But sheer desperation had brought her to this terrible pass.

When Winnie rapped on her door, Viveca all but jumped out of her skin. "Come in!" she ordered shrilly.

The servant entered, wary-eyed. "Mistress, de fad'er downstairs waitin' for you."

Viveca pinched her cheeks and grimaced. "Very well."

"You need t'be back by ten," the woman added. "De Obi-mon be here den, long wit' Sista' Taheisha and a few more folkses."

Viveca turned in her chair. "Back by ten? But I thought these—er—observances began at midnight."

Urgently Winnie whispered, "First de Obi-mon walk de house, take off ghosts and bugaboos. Den we drop legs at de Nabbing."

"Oh, brother. What's that—some sort of séance?"

"You see, mistress."

Viveca chewed her lower lip. "Gracious, Winnie, I—I'm having second thoughts about this."

Urgently Winnie stepped forward. "Be too late now, mistress. I already tell de Obi-mon you pay him five dollar to catch duppies."

"Five dollars? Must I?" Viveca grimaced as she recalled Aubrey cautioning her against paying these practitioners of Obeah.

Winnie nodded. "In Jamaica we say two t'ings, mistress: 'Neb'er slight de cook' and 'Neb'er cheat de Obi-mon.'"

Viveca decided she was already in too much trouble to risk any such mutinies. "Very well, I shall pay him. Just get everyone inside before we return at ten, as Aubrey is already suspicious of what may be going on here."

"Yes, ma'am."

Moments later as Viveca left with Aubrey, she felt stiff and awkward, finding it almost unbearable to attempt to smile at him or make her usual small talk. As their buggy turned the corner, she noted that the Beecher mansion was darkened. It appeared that, just as he'd threatened, Max had given up on her and gone off to play poker. Even though she traitorously wished she was with him now, and not Aubrey, she realized his absence was a blessing. The last thing she needed was for him to come storming over later tonight during the exorcism.

Viveca felt as if she might jump out of her skin during the lengthy prayer meeting at the Thorps' home; she was anxious regarding the planned exorcism, afraid she wouldn't make it home in time, terrified she'd be found out. Then when Aubrey read several scathing passages from Lamentations, she *really* sat up and took notice: "'She weeps bitterly in the night . . . All her gates are desolate . . . Her foes have become the head . . . her enemies prosper . . . she has been made to suffer for the multitude of her transgressions.'"

Oh, heavens. The fire-and-brimstone verses turned Viveca's stomach to ice; they seemed a horrible portent of a disaster to come. Had she made a terrible mistake in planning to host a séance following prayer meeting? Would she be made to suffer horribly for her sins?

The meeting ran late, and by nine-thirty Viveca was squirming on the couch beside Aubrey. "Are you all right, my dear?" he asked as the other couples finally got up. "I must say you look rather wan."

"Actually, I have a terrible headache," she confided. "Would you mind taking me home now?"

Although his features revealed his disappointment, he at once patted her hand. "Of course. Poor dear."

Viveca felt intensely relieved as they thanked their hostess and hastened out the door. When Aubrey pulled up his buggy in front of her house, she was grateful that everything looked normal, and there were no callers standing on her porch.

However, as he escorted her to the door, he frowned at the sight of a bundle of twigs that had been nailed next to the framing. "What do you suppose that is?"

Staring at the strange charm, Viveca was equally bemused. "Actually, I've never seen it before."

"It looks like some sort of pagan talisman. Perhaps Winnie placed it there while we were gone?"

"I—I really have no idea. But I'll have Emmett dispose of it."

"So you haven't discharged your housekeeper as yet?"

"I—really, Aubrey, should I send her packing just because she had a visitor from her church? That seems harsh."

"Not harsh at all, considering the caller's reputation," he scolded. "Really, Viveca, you must deal with this—"

"I know, but . . . just not now, all right?"

He flashed her a contrite smile. "Of course. I'm sorry, dear. You do have a headache, don't you?" He leaned over, chastely kissing her brow. "Feel better, now. Good night."

Watching him retreat down the walkway, Viveca wrung her hands. Again she wondered what madness she might have unleashed by giving Winnie permission to set up this exorcism, this séance, whatever it was. Perhaps she could still back out.

But wouldn't the Obi-man get angry and "put Obeah" on her?

She just needed to pay him. Surely that was all he *really* wanted—her money.

She waved at Aubrey, then went inside. Hearing a thrum of voices, she ventured into the parlor.

She gasped and stopped in her tracks. Present were at least twenty black women and men, all extravagantly attired in brilliant jewel-tone costumes of silk or satin, embellished by glittering gold jewelry. One young man toted a large drum, while another held a shiny trumpet. A couple of attendees had brought along wicker baskets; low clucking sounds made Viveca suspect live chickens were inside.

Good grief! Then Viveca's gaze became riveted to the area near the hearth, where Winnie stood wearing a yellow silk blouse, a purple skirt and matching tignon. Viveca was amazed, as she'd never seen her housekeeper so splendidly attired. Next to Winnie stood Sister Taheisha, gowned in crimson silk and a gold bandu; she acknowledged Viveca with a regal nod.

But it was the sister's companion who took Viveca's breath away. He was a wizened black man, small, bent and frail. Proudly he stood in his red linen robe and white headdress, his dark, crafty gaze fixed on Viveca. In his hand he held a black staff; at its hilt hissed a gold serpent. On the coffee table before him had been placed a large, scarred, black wooden chest.

His bag of tricks, no less?

Taking note of her mistress, Winnie rushed forward. "Miss Viveca, I so glad you back. We all come in real quiet-like, just like you ast'. Dis be de Obi-mon, Tamos."

Viveca flashed the man a quick smile, and he grimly nodded back. "How do you do? Winnie, may I have a word with you?"

"Yes, mistress."

Half frantically, Viveca tugged the housekeeper out into the hallway. "Winnie, why did you invite so many people here tonight?"

"Dey be needed for de ghost-catching."

Viveca grimaced. "You know, Winnie, I—I'm still having second thoughts about this entire—er, tomfoolery."

Winnie seemed to panic at that, waving her hands. "Oh, no, mistress, no," she begged hoarsely, inclining her head toward the Obi-man. "You want him snatch your duppy?"

Viveca stared in trepidation at her bizarre guest; the last thing on earth she wanted was for this sorcerer to "snatch her duppy," whatever that meant.

"Miss Viveca, what is going on here?"

With gratitude, Viveca whirled to watch her beloved Emmett come trooping down the stairs. But before she could speak, Winnie charged toward him. "What you doin' down here, mon? Din' I tell you, stay in your room?"

"You don't tell me what to do, woman," Emmett all but snarled. He turned to Viveca. "Miss Viveca, what all them strange folks doin' here? This witch has been letting 'em in all evening long."

Viveca patted his arm. "I know, Emmett, but . . . well, she did so with my permission."

"*What?*"

He tottered on his feet, making her fear he was on the verge of apoplexy. She gripped his arm. "There, there, dear heart. Do calm down. You're aware that we've had problems with—er—the restless spirits in this house?"

Emmett glowered but didn't comment.

"So Winnie and I have decided to organize an exorcism of sorts, and the dear gentleman over there, Mr. Tamos, has agreed to lead the proceeding, for a modest fee."

Glancing at the parlor, Emmett was shaking his head. "Miss Viveca, you done lost your mind."

"Perhaps so," she conceded, "but I won't lose my soul."

"Your *soul?*"

"Forgive my indelicacy, Emmett, but it seems Mr. Tamos is not a gentleman to be crossed. He's been known to steal duppies and pin them to the cotton tree."

Emmett glanced in dismay at the Obi-priest.

"Please, Emmett, don't interfere," she pleaded.

"But, Miss Viveca—"

"Come along, we've guests waiting," she ordered briskly.

With Winnie and the reluctant Emmett following, Viveca stepped inside the room. Sister Taheisha strolled up to her, inclining her head toward Tamos. "You pay?"

"Oh." Viveca dug in her reticule and pulled out a five-dollar gold piece. Before she could offer it to Tamos, Taheisha snatched it up and stuffed it into her bodice.

Taheisha nodded to Tamos, who pounded the floor with his staff and spoke up in a deep, ominous voice. "We walk de house now."

"Praise God!" uttered Sister Taheisha.

"Of course," stated Viveca.

As Tamos started off with his slow, lopsided, but somehow majestic gait, two of his disciples hastily grabbed his wooden chest and followed. Winnie motioned for Viveca to queue up next, and she did so, Emmett by her side. Next came Winnie and Sister Taheisha; the rest of the entourage fell into place behind them in twos, several carrying lit black candles.

The hour that followed was the strangest Viveca had ever experienced. By candlelight, amid the soft beating of the drum, a monotonous dirge of trumpet and an occasional, punctuating squawk from one of the chickens, the Obi-man led them from room to room, chanting in his patois while his island entourage softly hummed behind him. His mutterings were sprinkled with alien-sounding words such as "Sasa," and "Accompong," weirdly mingled with the more familiar sayings of Christianity—"bloodfire and brimstone"; "Fad'er, Son and Holy Spirit"; "God have mercy on us."

His actions were even more peculiar. In each room he drew charms from his chest, depositing them in various critical places: in the dining room he plugged up several "holes" in the wall with buzzard feathers; in the hallway he tossed broken eggshells at the portrait of Miss Fulton; pungent, smelly herbs were strewn generously about several more rooms.

Just inside the bathroom door, he paused to sniff the air, then turned to Viveca with a fierce expression. "Bad sasa. Bad, bad sasa."

"I'm aware," she mumbled back, ignoring Emmett's baleful look.

Tamos snapped his fingers and his two chest-bearers stepped forward with his cache of sorcery. This time he extracted a small wooden miniature of a casket. He said a litany in patois, then whooshed the small vessel through the air, repeatedly opening and then snapping its jaws shut like the snout of an alligator. Viveca jumped back as one of his passes came dangerously close to snipping off the tip of her nose.

"Sasa be gone!" he chanted. "Sasa be gone! God save!"

"*God save!*" wailed his company.

Viveca was horrified and enthralled. Behind her, Winnie whispered, "De Obi-mon, he catch de shadows now, mistress."

"How lovely," she managed.

Upstairs, more strange substances were deposited, to ward off duppies and "pull Obeah": a parrot's beak beneath Viveca's bed; grave dirt outside on her veranda; several lizard bones on Emmett's dresser; a sprinkling of egret feathers on the front veranda. Afterward, handfuls of odious dead plant and animal matter were strewn all over Miss Grace's room, amid much ranting about evil sasa and the like.

Eventually the procession wended its way back downstairs, out the back door and down the steps into the basement. Not having visited this particular abyss before, Viveca garnered no more than a fleeting glimpse of a dank, smelly expanse with a scattering of crude furnishings.

At the sudden flood of candlelight, Ruvi and Miguel jumped up from their bunks, and a black cat sailed, screeching, out the window, sending a shudder through the entourage. While the nightshirt-clad servants regarded the bizarre newcomers in consternation, Winnie dismissed the two with a wave of her hand. "G'long to the stable, boys. We got duppies to catch."

Needing no further prodding, both men dashed for the door.

Meanwhile, the shaman's wooden chest had been deposited on a scarred table. A gasp rippled over the gathering as the Obi-man drew out a long black rat snake, which slithered, hissed and undulated in his hands. Viveca cringed as the Obi's disciples stared in awe and fell to their knees, wailing and supplicating.

Tamos raised the twisting serpent over his head, then commanded, "Bredren and sistren, drop legs."

With a collective shout, everyone popped back up, and the dancing began in earnest. Viveca stood watching with Emmett, both of them dumbstruck. Amid loud shrieking, the pounding of the drum and the wailing of the trumpet, the group gathered in a circle and joined hands, stomping their feet, singing, chanting, gyrating about. Sister Taheisha led the incantations in a patois/Christian jumble. Meanwhile, the shaman, with the snake coiled about his neck, pranced about the dungeon like a man reborn, snapping his miniature coffin and ostensibly catching many more loose shadows.

Soon the dancers worked themselves into a frenzy. Some fell moaning on the floor, while others broke apart and assumed animal presences—squawking parrots, barking dogs, hissing cats. The drummer beat out a frenetic pace while babbling in a strange tongue; Sister Taheisha raced about, features transfixed, chirping like a bird. Hearing a high-pitched squawk, Viveca didn't even want to think about what might be happening to those unfortunate chickens.

Amid the cacophony, the Obi-man began wailing passages of Scripture, colorfully embellished: "Oh, generation of vipers, you cannot flee de wrath to come. Depart from me, all ye workers of iniquity. Out of de serpent's root shall come forth a cockatrice, and his fruit shall be a fiery flying serpent."

With that, Tamos hurled his snake across the room, to an uproar of shrieks and exultations. Cringing next to Emmett, Viveca watched Sister Taheisha catch the twisting reptile and begin dancing with it undulating about her neck.

Next the Obi-man summoned over the young trumpet player. The man knelt beneath Tamos and, at his bidding, tore off his own shirt. The wizard then rubbed down the lad's face and chest with some vile-looking, pasty gray substance. The poor victim began to choke, jerk and heave; soon the man rolled about on the floor as if in a fit, and at last grew deathly still. At this, the exultant Obi-man turned away to lead his flock in a raving cheer.

Eyes delirious with excitement, Winnie rushed up to Viveca. "Look, mistress, de Obi-man, he kill Edwin to show his power."

Viveca felt she might faint. "*What? Kill?* B-but couldn't he have killed the snake, for heaven's sake? You didn't warn me there would be human sacrifices tonight!"

Winnie cackled. "Ah, din' you fret, mistress. Ever't'ing be fit 'n' frock, you see."

Viveca stared in horror at her housekeeper, quite certain the woman was insane. By this juncture, she was not just worried, but frantic. She rushed to the fallen man's side and began slapping Edwin's face, desperately trying to rouse him from his lifeless state. But he reacted not at all, his countenance fixed in a deathly pallor. Anxiously she felt his throat, but could detect no pulse.

By now Emmett had joined Viveca. Feeling the man's wrist, he soberly shook his head. "He gone, Miss Viveca. Them crazy folks done murdered him."

"Oh, my God!" she gasped. Hosting an exorcism was one thing, but now she had a death on her conscience. Still, hadn't Aubrey mentioned something about followers of Obeah "pretending" to be dead? But this man seemed truly dead.

Despite Emmett's grim pronouncement, Viveca refused to give up. Madly she glanced about for the Obi-man. "Sir! Sir! I think we have a small problem over here!"

The Obi ignored her, leading his followers in a new, harried dance. Meanwhile, Edwin continued to resist all of Viveca's efforts at resuscitation. After what seemed an eternity, the dancing and wailing finally abated. As the others raptly hummed, the Obi-man marched over to Edwin carrying a small cask. Shooing Viveca and Emmett out of his way, the Obi knelt, wailed an incantation, then poured some odious dark substance into the man's mouth.

At once Edwin began to choke, quake and stir, as the room erupted in renewed cheers and shouts. The "dead" man's limbs began to twitch, his eyes flew open, and within a minute he staggered to his feet! At last Edwin grabbed his trumpet and blew a discordant wail as he lurched about.

"Praise Accompong, Tamos, he raise de dead!" yelled an exultant spectator, and an even more furious dance began.

Viveca and Emmett stood watching in stunned disbelief. Winnie sailed up to tug at Viveca's sleeve and grin jubilantly. "See, Miss Viveca, din' I tell you, all fruits ripe? De Obi-mon, he 'vive Edwin. Now he anoint you wit' oil."

Staring across the room at Tamos, who was busy retrieving another small flask from his sorcerer's chest, Viveca sucked in a horrified breath. Was she to be this witch doctor's next victim?

Before she could respond, Emmett exclaimed, "Oh, no, Miss Viveca! He gonna poison you now."

"No, he bless you wit' oil to keep you safe," Winnie protested.

Gazing at the fearsome warlock, Viveca gravitated between cooperating or losing her duppy. She finally decided she had less to fear from the former. She touched Emmett's sleeve. "I'll be all right."

His eyes went wild. "No, Miss Viveca."

"Stay here," she ordered, and stepped away.

"Miss Viveca!"

Before she could lose her nerve, she crossed the room to face the slyly grinning Obi. Well, here came eternal damnation, for sure. At Winnie's urging, Viveca knelt at his feet. The Obi chanted a long, prayerlike discourse, then opened the vial, pouring a foul-smelling concoction over Viveca's head. She struggled not to gag. The oil was so obnoxious and putrid, dripping into her eyes, her ears, her mouth, that it was all she could do not to anoint the Obi's robe with the contents of her stomach.

Then in that very instant, there was a mighty flash of light, like lightning, at a basement window just beyond Viveca. The attendees issued a collective cry and fell to their knees, shrieking praises. Winnie knelt beside Viveca, hugging her, shuddering and sobbing.

"De duppies be gone now, mistress—kill me dead."

In that moment, even Viveca was a believer.

Chapter Twenty-six

The house seemed strangely at peace.

The next morning the air seemed clearer, the sun brighter, the cobwebs gone from the stairs—and seemingly from Viveca's mind, as well. She stepped out on the front porch to view a beautiful, balmy late-spring morning. For the first time in memory, the old oak tree on the square stood splendid in the pristine clear light, the usual ominous haze gone. Flowers were springing up all over her and her neighbors' yards—daisies, periwinkles and marigolds. Yard birds—robins, sparrows, jays—were hopping about and singing. Most amazing of all, the old porch rocker was at peace, not moving at all. Bemused, Viveca strode over and tapped a tread with her slipper. It rocked a moment, then grew still again. Astounding!

The exorcism had worked.

"The duppies be gone, eh, mistress?" Winnie asked cheerfully as Viveca went into the kitchen. "Old Tamos, he know what he doing, give t'anks."

"Well, something definitely seems different," Viveca agreed.

All day long, throughout her piano lessons, her noonday meal, her time spent listening to Dvorak's *New World* Symphony on the Victrola, the absence of gloom was notable. That night, Viveca even dared to take a bath again, and after some initial tense moments, she realized that the phantom Alex Fremont would not be joining her.

She almost missed him. Almost.

She did miss Max, shameless creature that she was. She felt bad about their argument. And she'd defied him, going out with Aubrey. But she was fighting for her emotional survival here—she couldn't afford to let Max swallow up her will as Erskine had. She even yearned to run to him and spill all, share her delight over the successful exorcism, but had no doubt as to how another encounter between them would end.

Despite these poignant regrets, she went to bed with a heightened sense of well-being. However, remembering her recent attacker, she hid a butcher knife under one of her pillows.

Much later, she flinched at the sound of a board creaking. Glancing in the direction of the sound, she spotted a shadow on her veranda, the glimmery image of a woman. Hellfire and damnation! Just when she thought the worst was over. Would she never be left in peace here? By heaven, she had had enough!

Viveca grabbed her knife, crept out of bed, donned her slippers and wrapper, then tiptoed toward the veranda. The visage, evidently spotting her, froze in its tracks, uttering a low hiss. Then it sprang back, whirled and leapt over the railing.

Knife raised, Viveca stormed the veranda. She arrived at the railing just in time to view the trespasser shimmying down a pillar. The interloper landed, sprang to its feet and sprinted into the trees.

Damn, the prowler was getting away, and there was no time to go downstairs. Well, if scaling pillars was good enough for Maxwell Beecher—and the intruder—it was good enough for her. After all, she had climbed trees as a child, although that seemed a lifetime ago. And the ground did look awfully far down.

Nonetheless, quashing a grimace, she dropped her knife to the ground, then hooked her leg over the railing. Reaching for the nearest pillar, she more or less flung her body around it. No sooner had she mounted the rough column than she began to slide, squealing as the coarse cypress hiked her nightgown and scratched her inner thighs on the way down.

At last, with a grunt, she landed on the ground, sore, a bit disoriented, but otherwise intact. Moonlight glinted off her knife in the grass; she quickly retrieved it and ran for the trees separating her house from Maxwell's property.

Running through the silvery expanse, she spotted no trace of her tormentor. Then at last, as she emerged in Max's yard, she caught sight of a woman's dark skirt disappearing through the open French doors to his bedroom. As on another recent night, she could see a candle glowing within.

Why, the cad! Had he sent his paramour to torment her, to scare her away? Well, she would not stand for it!

She ran to his side veranda and climbed the steps. She was prepared to charge into his room, knife raised, when she was again arrested by the sound of moans. She froze at the opened doorway and peered inside to see Maxwell Beecher thrashing about on the bed and groaning passionately. Obviously, there was a woman lying beside him, although his body shielded her from Viveca's view. Mercy, it might be the creature who'd just tried to invade her room. Nonetheless, the guttural sounds he emitted were so lurid they made her cheeks burn—and her belly churn with hot, unbidden desire and unwanted jealousy.

The miscreant! Here he was fornicating away again, when only yesterday he'd tried to ply her with flowers and sweet talk. And he was doing it with a woman he'd just sent to terrorize her!

Outraged, she stepped inside the room and grabbed the lit taper from the dresser, charging toward the bed. "Why, you scoundrel!"

As Max jerked awake and opened his eyes, Viveca noticed several things at once: He was naked, flushed, breathing hard; he had a very large erection straining against the sheet; and he was quite alone.

He spotted her and drew his astonished gaze up and down her skimpily clad body. "Well, well," he muttered hoarsely, "what have we here? A woman in a nightgown intruding in my bedroom, complete with a lit taper and a butcher knife. Tell me, are you planning to set me on fire or impale me?"

For a moment Viveca was too taken aback to speak, so rattled was she by his carnal appearance, his rumpled hair, the sexy line of whiskers along his jaw, and most especially, his distended shaft. However had he gotten himself into this lewd state all alone?

"Or do you wish to impale yourself?" he continued mildly. "From the way you're gawking at my attributes, my dear, I do have my suspicions."

Viveca's face burned, and she struggled to find her voice. "Can't you do something about that?" she finally managed with a curt nod toward his erection.

He smiled. "Do you wish to be a witness or a participant?"

She gulped. "Where's the woman?"

"I think she's standing in front of me with a knife."

Viveca waved her knife. "You know what I mean, you cad."

"I'm afraid I don't."

"The woman you just sent to kill me!"

"My heaven, have you lost your mind?" He tore off his covers.

She backed away. "What are you doing?"

"Getting up."

"But you're already—"

He grinned devilishly. "Up? So it would appear. You don't think I wish to discuss this lying down, do you?"

She winced. "But you're—you're—"

"Naked? Yes, quite. And if you don't want to become even more of a voyeur than you already are, I'd suggest you hand me my dressing gown."

In a panic, Viveca set down her taper and glanced about the room. Spotting a silk brocade dressing gown folded across a chair, she rushed over and grabbed it, then turned, hurling it at him.

With deliberate disdain, he flung the robe away and stood—totally, magnificently nude. Viveca gasped in shock and fascination. Max loomed before her, tall and splendid, from the wealth of thick, soft hair on his proud head, to his wondrously chiseled face, to his hard, burnished shoulders, muscled chest, flat belly and . . .

Heaven help her, his erection!

As he slowly, laconically picked up the dressing gown, her gaze became riveted on his staff, so large and tantalizing. The tiny nub between her thighs throbbed to its own painful awareness. She almost sobbed aloud, so agonizing was her response to him.

"How dare you!" she declared at last.

He grinned, donned the robe and tied the sash. "You, my dear, are the one who has invaded my bedroom, so take the consequences." With a meaningful gleam in his eyes, he stepped toward her.

Heart hammering, she backed away. "I repeat, where is the woman?"

"I repeat, she's standing in front of me—and about to be ravished."

From his tone of voice, he meant it. Half panicked, she held up her knife. "Stop right there and explain yourself."

Without missing a beat, he grabbed the knife from her hand and slammed it down on the dresser. His features were fierce, gleaming with an intensity that was maddening and devastatingly sexy. "Woman, you defy all logic! How dare you ask me for explanations, treat *me* like a trespasser, when you're the intruder here—"

"You sent an intruder to kill me."

"I did no such thing."

"Then—then how did you get into this—this state?"

His expression shone with mischief. "Do you really want me to tell you?"

Viveca hesitated a long moment before answering that loaded question, again wondering just what she might be unleashing. At last, with a calm she hardly felt, she murmured, "Yes."

She expected him to taunt her, torture her, then likely throw her down on the floor and have his way with her. Instead, surprisingly, she watched uncertainty cross his dark face. Then he turned away, strode to the side of the room and began to pace. Drawing his fingers through his disheveled hair, he muttered, "Crazy as it sounds, I'm tempted to tell you the truth."

"I want the truth."

He turned, giving her a hard stare. "Do you, my dear?"

"Yes. Of course."

"Then I must have your word that you won't use it against me."

She was outraged. "Hah! All you've done since I've arrived here is threaten me, undermine me, even try to seduce me into leaving."

"You're wrong there." His hot, intense gaze swept over her. "I wasn't trying to seduce you into leaving—only to seduce you."

"W-whatever." Again her face flamed.

"And I didn't gossip about our little—er—lapse together, did I?"

"Well, give the man a ribbon," she sneered. "The truth is, you've been playing games with me, Max, playing unfairly, playing to *win*—doing everything you can to force me out of town. Now you want me to give up all ammunition against you?"

"If you want the truth, yes."

In exquisite frustration, she sized up his implacable face and realized she must make at least some concession. "Very well. If you'll tell me the truth, I won't use what you say tonight against you."

He groaned. "It's not all I'd hoped for—"

"It's all you'll be getting."

Resignedly he nodded. "The truth, then. Actually . . . well, there is a woman."

"Aha! I knew it."

"But she's not what you think."

"Oh, she isn't?"

"She isn't"—he regarded her with unexpected anguish, drew a deep, bracing breath, then finally whispered, "*real*."

A chill streaked down Viveca's spine. "What do you mean, she isn't real?"

He began prowling the room again, waving a hand. "I mean every night I'm tormented by something . . . a presence."

"Presence?" Viveca barely whispered the word.

His next words came out in a rush. "She's the most hellish, shameless vixen you could ever imagine. She comes to me in the night, sometimes even during the day. She's half real, half . . . hell, I don't know what she is. She strokes me, teases me, drives me"—he turned to face her with fists clenched—"*mad*. But she stops just short of giving me the satisfaction I crave."

"Oh, my God," Viveca murmured. This tale was sounding all too hauntingly familiar.

He continued through clenched teeth. "She is a cruel, beautiful siren. I've even seen her at times—reddish-haired, voluptuous—why, I've heard her name—"

"Lorelei," Viveca whispered.

He gazed at her, thunderstruck. "You've seen her, too?"

She glanced away. "I—I've heard the name."

He stepped forward. "No, there's more to it than that." Suddenly he laughed. "Well, I'll be damned!"

"What?"

"It's all making sense to me now. You running around in circles in your backyard. The cut on your wrist, the snake on your piano. Your house is haunted, too, isn't it?"

She floundered, not sure how to respond.

He seized her by the arms. "Well? Isn't it?"

"Yes!" she admitted miserably. "It's haunted. By a veritable shipload of lost souls."

"Damn." For a moment he stood in stunned disbelief. "Then it seems we share much, you and I."

"Yes, we share much."

"Then you've seen—"

"The undead swinging from the Hanging Oak? The ax lady stalking about near the old jail?"

"So I'm not crazy!" he cried. "You know, it's all been so outlandish, I was afraid to tell anyone about it—"

"Tell *me* about it," she urged.

"I am."

They both laughed, and Viveca actually delighted in the keen sense of camaraderie and connection she felt between them at that moment.

He shook his head in awe. "I still can't believe it, both of us seeing the same . . . You know, this Lorelei has a partner—I sometimes see him, as well—"

"Yes. Alex Fremont."

"Fremont? Why is that name familiar?"

"Lord, if only it weren't."

"Tell me."

Viveca explained all she knew regarding the history of Alex Fremont—the love triangle, the alleged murder he committed, how he was tried and sentenced to death, the execution portrait she had seen at the courthouse.

Max listened in fascinated silence. "So you've seen this Fremont at your home?"

"Yes. He haunts . . ." she halted.

"What, Viveca?"

Keenly embarrassed, she stared at his dresser. "Never mind."

Firmly she was turned to face his brooding countenance. "What?"

"My bathtub," she admitted miserably.

"Your bathtub!" He appeared alarmed. "Has he hurt you?" Voice dipping to a tormented level, he added, "Ravished you?"

Embarrassed, she shook her head. "No, he has only taunted me, enticed me, much like your Lorelei."

"But, damn, Viveca, in your *bathtub*—"

"It hasn't just been there," she cut in, wanting to steer away from such lewd issues as her plumbing, but not sure just how. "Why, one time when Aubrey came calling, Alex even teased me in the parlor—with, well, you know, a feather or something."

"I'll kill him," Maxwell uttered.

"Fool, you can't kill a ghost."

Although a smile pulled at his lips, he countered, "You think not? Do you presume you're the only one around here with a violent streak? On the night we met, do you really think I was shooting at that poor tree?"

Viveca gazed at him for a moment, electrified. Then she snapped her fingers. "You were shooting at the ghosts!"

"Indeed. Not that it's done me much good." At that, he paused, looking her over with a lascivious gleam in his eyes. "But you know, my dear, I've been known to shoot at burglars, too."

She gulped, caught totally off guard by his abrupt change in tactics. "That's quite interesting. Now—er—getting back to the ghosts—"

But Max was advancing with a definitely sexy gleam in his eyes. "To hell with the ghosts. We've got all night to talk about them." He reached out to trail a fingertip over the low bodice of her nightgown. "For you see, my dear Miss Stanhope, I've yet to make you accountable for trespassing in my bedroom."

"Max, be fair," she pleaded, gasping. "I'm really not a burglar, I'm—"

"An enchantress," he interrupted fervently. "Armed and dangerous—as I am." He pulled her close, his eyes gleaming with an intensity that was both frightening and irresistible. "You know you're fair game." He drew his hand through her hair, messaging her scalp with his strong fingers, and she winced with longing. "At my mercy now. I could kiss you or kill you."

Even as she was about to ask which he preferred, he kissed her so passionately she feared he might swallow her whole. Discovering Max tonight as she had—so brazenly aroused— couldn't have been more titillating. And the shocking, intimate disclosures they'd shared had drawn them closer still—so close that she feared she had no ammunition left against him.

His mouth was hungry, hot, demanding over hers. Her nipples tingled against the heat of his chest. His arms were clamped tight around her, so tight their two bodies seemed melded as a single being. She wondered how much more of this she could bear. Her pulse roared in her ears and she yearned to devour him.

At last she managed to push at his chest. "Max, we mustn't."

His gaze burned down into hers. "Why did you come here, Viveca?"

"I was chasing—to find the woman—"

"You were chasing your desires—"

"I was chasing a ghost," she said in tortured tones.

He stroked her cheek with his fingers. "No matter. You're here now, and I am not a noble man. Not fair, either. Which means, at long last . . . you are mine."

He crushed her against him and kissed her again. This time Viveca knew she was lost. The attraction they'd fought for so long, fueled by the amorous ghosts and by their own runaway desires, had at last raged out of control. How could she ever have thought she could resist him, resist this overwhelming need between them?

She felt his manhood, so hot and delectable against her, and ached to feel him inside her. Her fingers dug into the strong muscles of his back. He moaned, his hand catching the skirt of her nightgown, raising it . . . and then he cursed.

"My God, you're bleeding!"

"What?" Backing away from him, she glanced down and saw the streaks of blood on her gown.

"Did you hurt yourself with that knife?" he demanded. "Hellfire and damnation, woman, you are a menace. I should keep you under lock and keep. But mostly, I should keep you."

At his words, Viveca at last became conscious of a burning sensation on her inner thighs that wasn't just passion. "No, no, I didn't hurt myself. I slid down the pillar chasing the . . . whatever it was on my veranda."

His jaw dropped open. "You could have broken your fool neck."

"As could you when you scaled that same pillar," she flung back.

He laughed then, a low, wicked sound, and drew her hand to his erection. "Come scale *my* pillar, Viveca. It's time, my love."

She gasped and knew she should snatch her hand away, but she was captivated by the feel of his rigid shaft in her fingers. "I—we can't, Max."

Shamelessly he clasped her hand tighter around him. "Of course we can, my dear Miss Stanhope. I'll show you precisely how. But first we must see to your wounds. Take off that gown so I may swab them."

"No—I've nothing on underneath!" Now she did recoil, and could have sworn her fingers still burned from the intimate contact with him.

His grin was wide. "That's precisely the idea, my pet—you with nothing on and me joining in the fun."

"No—no, I'll see to the wounds myself."

He winked gravely. "As you wish." He indicated the dresser, where there sat a bowl with water, and a towel.

Viveca hastened over, wet the towel, lifted her gown as discreetly as possible and began dabbing at her abrasions. All the while, her breath came in mortifying pants and her insides ached with raw lust for him.

At instant later she sensed his heat behind her, felt his hot breath on the back of her neck. He reached for a drawer. "I think I've some salve here, darling."

The word "darling" almost sent her staggering against him.

Max rummaged a moment, then said, "No, I've a better idea."

In a smoothly choreographed movement, he leaned over, clutching the hem of her nightgown and pulling it high over her head.

"Max, no!" she cried.

Too late—her nightgown was already gone, tossed across the room. Roughly she was turned to face him. As she stared breathlessly up into his eyes, he dropped his own robe.

Viveca was reeling. Max's eyes devoured her, slowly, intimately, as if she were the most incredible feast, while she stood before him, spellbound. "Beautiful, just beautiful," he whispered in awe. He grasped her breasts, kneading them, puckering the nipples, rolling each between a thumb and forefinger.

Viveca could not breathe, his touch was so unbearable. Then his mouth followed, teasing a tautened nipple, sucking it inside his hot mouth, his slight beard delightfully abrading her aroused flesh. She sobbed and pulled at his hair, wondering how a being could be so caught between heaven and hell . . .

To her shame and fascination, he sank to his knees before her, clasping her thighs in his arms, pressing his mouth to her belly, raising quivers. "So soft, so lovely. Relax, darling."

A violent shudder rippled over Viveca. Suddenly she knew just what he intended, and she couldn't bear it. Nor could she bear to stop him. "Don't do this—oh, please, don't."

"Relax," he reiterated.

He stared up at her, smiling, then pressed his face to her trembling thighs. She bucked violently, and he chuckled and clutched her even tighter. He thrust out his tongue and drew it in slow, tantalizing circles over her tender skin. "So lovely."

Viveca almost collapsed then, hoarse cries rising from her tight throat. Max shoved her back against the dresser and moved upward, latching his mouth at the joining of her thighs. His beard prickled her, and she felt herself on the verge of climaxing then and there.

"Oh, Max!" she cried, pounding a fist on the dresser.

His fingers sought entrance, roughly, urgently. "Open to me now, Viveca," he commanded. "Open to me."

Shamelessly she spread her thighs with all the abashment of a two-bit harlot.

"There . . . better." His fingers teased her, nudged her. "Arch forward now, so I can better taste you."

A spasm of searing ecstasy shot through her at his words, sending reality, lust, everything spinning all about her. Oh, he was wicked, and she was powerless. Wantonly she arched her hips. His lips latched onto her nub, his tongue so wet, so rough. She writhed in shattering pleasure. The rapture surging within her was like nothing she'd ever felt before, and the exquisite rhythm continued without end. Soon she was beating her fists on his strong shoulders, climaxing again, again, yet again. He only chuckled, a deep, throaty sound. His hands slipped behind her to grasp her buttocks and hold her helpless to his rapacious mouth.

"We need this. We both need this so," he murmured.

Just when Viveca could bear no more, she was seized and hauled down full-thrust onto Max's hot shaft. She cried out at the exquisite pleasure of joining herself with him, body and soul. Never had she felt anything so fulfilling, so very right. As he gripped her hips and pushed her into a powerful rhythm, his eyes blazed with a fire that melted her soul. His mouth locked onto hers, tasting of her deeply. She kissed him back, searching, seeking with her own voracious tongue, while meeting his thrusts fully, letting his love consume her. Soon, shattered gasps escaped her; he moaned as her nipples streaked fire across his furred chest. They rocked there, locked in a brazen, endless pleasure, mating with all the savage abandon of two wild animals.

When at last he spilled himself inside her, she fell on him, sobbing softly, utterly sated.

Chapter Twenty-seven

The night had no end . . .

Soon after claiming Viveca, Maxwell gently disengaged, picked her up and carried her to the bed. He fetched the basin and towel and cleansed her, washing not just her wounds but every sensuous part of her. Viveca thought she might swoon at the erotic, intimate attentions he paid her. When he tested the folds of her womanhood with a naughty finger, she whimpered.

"Sore?" he asked, smiling down into her eyes. "Sorry, love, but I'm not sure I can resist you."

She held out her arms and fought tears. "Neither can I."

With a groan of deep pleasure, he eased inside her, smothering her soft cry with his mouth. Thus they spent the night, mouths fervently locked, with him rocking and spending himself alternately, until she was far too sore to move but didn't care. He tried his best to be gentle, and the tender concern he demonstrated touched her soul. Yet he was powerless to resist her, just as she was helpless to stop loving him. Their thirst for one another knew no beginning, no end. Never had Viveca felt so close to anyone, so cherished, so treasured. It was as if all the pain of her life, her past, was starting to ebb away.

Toward dawn, Maxwell stirred next to Viveca. His face was pressed to her hair, fragrant and dusky smelling. She looked incredibly lovely with her perfect features in repose, the soft light dusting her rosy skin and glinting highlights in her lush red hair.

He couldn't believe she had finally come to him. And could hardly comprehend the ecstasy they shared. She was such a precious, intriguing bundle of contradictions—innocent yet passionate, shy yet adventuresome, bittersweet yet joyous. He'd learned so much about her, including the fact that, as sweet and tight as she had been to possess, she hadn't come to him a virgin. This hadn't surprised him—he'd always suspected some sort of trauma in her past.

One thing was for certain: He would see to it that the cad who had harmed her—whoever he was—got his due. He felt an amazing obsession to kill the bastard—and an equally and unexpectedly tender urge to protect her, to hold her close forever.

Even then, she opened her eyes and stared up at him, her gaze wide, languid, uncertain.

"Why, hello, darling," he murmured, kissing her mouth.

She caught a sharp little breath. "Goodness, it's getting late, I should leave—"

"Please, not yet," he said, nuzzling her cheek.

She laughed. "You want more of this?"

"Always, darling. But—er—perhaps we should talk."

He felt her tensing in his arms. "About what?"

He hesitated a moment, then said quietly, "I want to know who hurt you, Viveca."

He could feel her emotional and physical withdrawal as she sat up, pulled the sheet up to her neck and thrust her fingers through her tumbled hair. "What makes you think someone hurt me?"

He sat up beside her, taking her hand. "Viveca, don't be

coy. It doesn't suit you. You must know you came to me . . . well, deflowered."

"Deflowered?" she repeated in outrage.

He gave a groan. "Viveca, I meant no criticism. I'm the last one to condemn anyone for alleged misconduct. But I can't find a delicate way to put this. Someone—someone hurt you."

She glanced away, as if fascinated with the glass panels on the French doors.

"Viveca?"

"Yes, there was someone," she admitted hoarsely.

"What was his name?"

"I don't think that's any of your business."

Max felt as if he'd been gut-punched. "Not even now?"

She met his troubled gaze and sighed. "Very well. His name was—is—Erskine Pendergraf."

"Pendergraf? Of the famous San Francisco family?"

"One and the same," she acknowledged bitterly.

Already Max hated the man. "What did he do, Viveca?"

She raised an eyebrow. "What do you think?"

"Viveca, please, you know what I mean."

She breathed a heavy sigh. "Actually, Erskine rather reminds me of you."

"Oh, ouch!" he cried.

"Well, not completely," she amended with a contrite smile. "But, like you, Erskine is considered a rascal but is socially prominent enough to get away with it. He was my father's business partner. The two of them imported furniture and fine art from the Far East and sold the items at auction."

"Go on."

"When Father died, I had expected him to provide for me. Instead"—her fingers clutched the sheet—"I found out his business was insolvent."

"Ah." Max was silent a moment. "And did the illustrious Mr. Pendergraf have anything to do with this apparent debacle?"

"Believe me, I've considered the possibility," she replied ruefully. "But I never participated in my father's business, and following his death, it was declared bankrupt and closed by the courts. As for Erskine—if he was involved in any shenanigans, I couldn't really tell. You see, he's quite wealthy in his own right, having wed an heiress whose family owns hotels, a couple of railroads and various other enterprises."

"Giving him any number of convenient ruses for hiding stolen assets," Max commented wisely.

"I suppose. At any rate, I didn't see that at the time. After Father died and his attorney informed me of the scandalous state of his financial affairs, Erskine became my lifeline— paying for the funeral, advancing me living expenses—"

"Seducing you?" Max asked darkly.

She swallowed hard and stared at her lap. "Yes."

Maxwell pounded his fist on the coverlet. "Damn the scoundrel."

Bitterly she continued, "Then, after society found out, he begged his wife for forgiveness and abandoned me without a second thought."

Max's heart went out to her; it killed him to think she had suffered so, that such a conscienceless miscreant had so badly misused her. "Darling, I'm so sorry." He clutched her close, albeit she was stiff in his arms. "And that's why you came to Savannah?"

"Yes."

"That scoundrel deserves to be drawn and quartered."

She laughed ironically. "And you don't?"

That barb hurt, especially since it carried a grain of truth. "Viveca, I may be a scamp, but I've made no pretenses regarding who, *what*, I am."

"That's true," she conceded with a half smile. "You admit you're a rogue, while Erskine is a conniving snake in the grass."

"Is that the only difference you see between us?" Max asked sadly.

A smile lit her face. "No. Erskine lacks your—your passion, your vitality, your zest for life. Your straightforwardness. He was much more insidious, calculating, even when . . ."

"He took you to bed?" Max asked tensely.

"Yes."

He took her hand and tenderly kissed each finger. "Viveca, he's a bastard, and I wish he were here right now so I could call him out."

With a touch of wry humor, she replied, "But you're here, and I don't see you calling yourself out."

He slanted her a reproachful look. "Moreover, much is making sense to me now."

"Oh?"

He stared her in the eye. "So this is why you want Aubrey."

Her chin came up. "You mean because he's so different from Erskine? Well, yes."

"He represents safety for you."

"There's much to be said for safety."

"Possibly. But safety is also cold, passionless. It will never do for an earthy, wanton creature like yourself."

She made a sound of contempt. "Thanks for the compliment, Max."

"But it *is* a compliment," he replied firmly. "There is no shame in enjoying your sensual side, Viveca—even exploiting it to the fullest depths of pleasure."

Although she appeared intrigued, even adorably flustered, by his unabashed suggestion, she asked, "When it brought me to ruin before?"

He caressed her cheek. "Viveca, what that cad did to you was unforgivable, but I'm not him."

"I know that, Max."

"Do you? Because I have my doubts."

She was silent, appearing perturbed.

"Please don't allow what happened with him to spoil our chances."

"You mean we have a chance together, Maxwell?" she asked hesitantly.

His brow knitted. "Of course we do. Believe it or not, Viveca, I'm thinking about just that." He nestled her close and kissed her fragrant hair.

Daylight brought Viveca a stunning sanity.

She awakened with a start, sitting up in bed. She spotted Max across from her, naked on the window seat. Heat seared her from head to toe at the sight of him. He appeared utterly magnificent, brazenly sensual, reclined there on one arm, staring at her so solemnly, sunlight pouring over his splendid body. He truly was a shamelessly carnal, handsome man. And after all they'd shared, he was still turgid!

But what insanity had possessed her to abandon all logic, all instincts of self-preservation, and give herself to him last night? Had one of the demons on the loose possessed her brain?

"What are you doing?" she whispered at last.

His grin was wide. "Watching you sleep, my love."

Despite her doubts, she still ached to fly into his arms again. Instead she stammered almost shyly, "I—I guess I should be going."

Scowling, he came over to sit beside her and clutched her hand. His voice dipped low, seductive. "First, tell me when you'll be coming back, darling."

"I . . ." Viveca's head was whirring, especially from his sexy nearness, the sensual scent of him.

"Viveca?"

She swallowed hard and struggled to get up. "Mercy, my servants may already be up, I must—"

He caught her wrist. "Viveca, stop it. What's wrong?"

She hesitated a long moment, then miserably met his probing gaze. "I'm afraid last night was a mistake."

A flicker of pain crossed his eyes. "Really? If it was, then it's one we repeated at least a dozen times."

Feeling hellishly confused and more than a little guilty, she nodded. "I realize that, Max. We—we both got carried away by—well, the emotion of the moment, the sharing about the ghosts and such. But the truth is, we're just so different, like night and day, and—"

"Don't give me that nonsense," he cut in passionately. "Viveca, we came together last night because we were meant to be together. And we're much more alike than you want to admit. You're just not willing to give us a chance."

"Maybe I'm not," she admitted.

"Because I'm too much like him?" he asked bitterly.

"Well, maybe you are." In anguish she gazed up at him. "Max, you have some very good qualities, I don't deny that. But you're a hedonist at heart. You're also headstrong, determined. Even if we did stay together, I'm afraid that ultimately you'd swallow up my will, just like Erskine did."

"More nonsense. Viveca, you're plenty strong yourself— indeed, I've never met a woman with your backbone. You just need to start believing in yourself, and consign that brute who harmed you to his eternal damnation. Moreover, I think we're perfectly matched, you and I."

"Really? Perfectly matched? That doesn't keep you from trying to tell me what to do."

"Well, I sure as hell want to keep you from seeing Aubrey. Can you blame me for that?"

She gave a groan. "No, I can't blame you. But you're going to offer me . . . what in exchange?" She gestured at the bed. "More of this?"

He scowled. "I'm not sure, Viveca. But what we have now sounds like a pretty wonderful place to begin."

"Oh, I knew you'd say something cavalier like that."

He waved a hand. "Viveca, give me a chance. This is new to me, too." He raised her chin and stared solemnly into her eyes. "I want you to give him up."

"Give up Aubrey?" she murmured.

"Right." Sternly he added, "And the ghost, as well."

She was tempted to smile—he looked so fearsomely irate. "Max, obviously, I need to do some thinking. I have a choice to make. I can't in good conscience continue seeing both you and Aubrey."

"Bravo," he mocked. "So think, then."

She bit her lip. "Now you're angry at me."

"Damn right, I'm angry. And while you're *thinking*, my love, think about *this*."

Abruptly Max pulled the sheet from her hand and tumbled her beneath him on the bed.

Chapter Twenty-eight

Viveca found it hard to leave Max. He looked both angelic and fierce sleeping next to her, his warm breath on her cheek, his strong forearm possessively clamped about her middle. But as emotionally torn as she was, she knew she had to leave. She did have much thinking to do.

Gently disengaging his arm and easing out of bed, she donned her nightgown and wrapper and tiptoed out his French doors onto the veranda. It was still early, and she spotted no one about. She quickly ran for the edge of his property and dashed through the trees. Once in her own yard, she debated whether to go in through the front or back door. Then the sound of a man whistling at the back of her property propelled her toward the front. Heavens, the servants were already up. At least Ruvi or Miguel was, since she couldn't remember Emmett ever whistling "Sweet Genevieve."

She hastened on, but just as she arrived on the front lawn, she watched Elvira Withersmith emerge on the porch of the Cunninghams' place; at once the woman paused and stared at Viveca.

Viveca's stomach took a dive. Realizing that retreat would only make her look worse, she stepped forward and bravely waved. "Good morning, Elvira. Are you, too, up smelling the roses?"

"Indeed, the Lord has blessed us with a lovely day," Elvira called back.

Viveca strode toward the street, pulling her wrapper more tightly about her. "Yes, so lovely that I just had to take a peek outside before—er—preparing for my day."

If the sight of Viveca in her nightclothes took Elvira aback, she revealed no sign. "Have you heard the house is for sale?" she asked, heading down her front steps.

"Really?"

"You didn't see the sign?"

Viveca quickly crossed the square and met Elvira in the Cunningham front yard. She glanced at the placard, which had been blocked from her view by the huge oak: "Offered by Cornelius Properties." So her old nemesis was at work again.

Viveca gazed with keen sympathy at Elvira, but couldn't really read her features beneath the large brim of her slat bonnet. "I'm so sorry. How long has it been up for sale?"

"Not long," Elvira muttered woodenly. "Evidently, Virginia and Jonathan are gone in Europe too much of the time to hold on to it any longer." With a tragic sigh, she added, "Though I'm not sure what I'll do once the house is disposed of."

Viveca stifled a wince, remembering what it had been like to face the prospect of homelessness. "Oh, what a shame. Is there anything I can do to help? My house has plenty of extra rooms—"

"Please, you mustn't concern yourself," Elvira cut in proudly. "I'll make out. I always do."

Viveca flashed her a sad smile. "Just promise me you'll keep me informed. I'll be happy to help if I can."

"Thank you, I shall try," Elvira replied stiffly.

Viveca turned for home. What a shame about Elvira. She

hoped she would be able to do something to assist the kindly woman.

Inside, she could hear Winnie singing a spiritual in the kitchen, but no one else seemed to be about. She hurried up the stairs and to the safety of her room. Seconds later she heard Emmett's door squeak open across from her. Thank heaven, she had made it back in before *he* had caught her!

Viveca had a heavy slate of piano students that day, but found it hard to concentrate. Endlessly she relived her shocking, wonderful night with Max. She was certain they had made a terrible mistake—that no good could come from their reckless passion. But somehow she couldn't regret it, either. Their moments together had been wondrous, even strangely healing for her. And although she hated to admit it, he had sated a sexual need that had been torturing her for weeks now. Her desire for Max. For him alone. There, she'd acknowledged it fully. Yes, Alex Fremont's ghost had titillated her, driven her toward Max, but she'd taken those final steps entirely on her own.

But how could she trust him with her life, her future, when he did remind her so much of Erskine? Yes, he had a heart, where Erskine had none; yet he remained the type of cavalier rogue no sane woman should pin her hopes on.

Midday found Viveca in her parlor finishing a piano lesson with Agnes Endicott. Agnes had just completed an A minor chord when abruptly Viveca heard her front door *whoosh* open and someone stride heavily into the house. Oh, heavens, was it Max, come to claim his due?

She was almost relieved when Hilda Patertavish stormed into the room. Then a look at Hilda's stricken face, not to mention the newspaper folded under her arm, renewed Viveca's sense of panic.

Standing, she stammered, "Hilda, I—to what do I owe—"

Hilda cut her short with a flourish of the newspaper. "This is horrible, Viveca! Horrible!" Then, spotting Agnes at the piano, she added, "Oh, hello, Agnes. Why don't you go have a snort of bourbon or something?"

"I beg your pardon!" Agnes gasped.

Hilda waved her off. "Oh, it's good enough for the Gibson Girls, isn't it? These are the enlightened nineties, after all." As Agnes sat slack-jawed, Hilda again flourished the paper. "At any rate, I must speak with Viveca alone, so if you'll excuse us—"

"Why, I never!" declared Agnes. "You're shooing me out of Viveca's house—*again?*"

"We're almost done, and can make up the time during our next lesson," Viveca offered diplomatically.

"Of course." Although she offered Viveca a stiff smile, Agnes shot Hilda a scathing look as she angrily gathered up her workbooks and stood. "We wouldn't want to offend *Queen* Hilda." Hurling Hilda a final glare, she marched out of the room.

Hearing the front door slam, Viveca winced. "Hilda, did you have to be so harsh with Agnes?"

"Oh, never mind that simpering little ninny. We have much greater problems at hand." Hilda shoved the paper in Viveca's face. "I take it you haven't seen this yet?"

Viveca gulped. "No, and I'm almost afraid to look."

Hilda thrust it into Viveca's hands. "Well, look, my dear. Avoiding the truth will do you no good. This is a disaster."

With a feeling of sick dread, Viveca sat down on the settee, unfolded the newspaper and glanced down, only to utter a cry of disbelief and mortification. On the front page of *The Savannah Daily* was a picture of herself kneeling in her basement before the Obi-man, Tamos. He was anointing her with oil, his robed arms extended, his dark eyes gleaming fiercely. Around her were gathered the drummer with the bongo, the erstwhile dead trumpeter, and the rest of the Jamaicans in various throes of the Obeah frenzy—some in unnatural, twisted positions, others posing as birds, cats or dogs. All bore transported, near-crazed expressions.

Good Lord, how had anyone taken that picture? she wondered frantically. Then with a groan she recalled the "bolt from beyond" she'd spotted through the basement window just at the moment Tamos had blessed her. Why, it must have been the glare of flash powder!

But even worse was the headline: "Voodoo on Hangman's Square," followed by Beryl Bliss's byline. Viveca feared she might become physically ill as she began reading the article:

> *Take heed, dear readers, and listen well. It seems righteousness and sanity have gone the way of the devil on Lost Lane, as this intrepid reporter has discovered. Viveca Stanhope, our fair city's presumed answer to Clara Schumann, is actually a charlatan and a sinner. While feigning piousness as she teaches piano lessons and pursues a prominent local rector, this deceitful woman has been holding séances in the basement of her home—shocking, ghastly voodoo rituals harking back to the days of Negro insurrections here in the South . . .*

"Oh, my God!" Viveca declared, crumpling the paper in her lap.

"*Now* you see why I've interrupted you?" Hilda demanded.

"I can't believe that little witch was actually skulking about on my property—and playing Peeping Tom at my basement window!" Viveca cried. "What else did she say?"

"You mean you can't *read* the rest?"

"I don't think I can bear to."

Hilda began to pace while waving her hands. "Well, only that you're been practicing black magic, witchcraft and sorcery in your home, inciting the local Negro population to rise up, do violence and poison the corrupt aristocracy, *and* that you should be hanged from your own petard—er, square. That pretty much sums it up."

"Oh, murder," Viveca muttered, burying her face in her hands.

"Indeed. Before, I was certain I could save you from Beryl's sly innuendos, but this—this, my dear, is going to be the worst scandal since the Yazoo Land Fraud! Folks here remember all too well those days of Negro uprisings—"

"Good grief, Hilda, I wasn't trying to organize a revolt," Viveca interrupted distraughtedly. "And I think it's patently unfair of Beryl to imply that the others were, either."

"I'm sure the word 'fair' isn't in that creature's vocabulary. At any rate, does it matter? The well has already been salted—Beryl's poisonous remarks are out there, spreading like a miasma."

"I'm ruined," Viveca declared dully.

"Well, let's not go that far," Hilda remarked a bit less harshly. "But the question remains, what shall we do?"

Helplessly Viveca glanced up. "Is there anything we *can* do?"

"I'm not sure." Plodding over to the settee, Hilda seated herself beside Viveca and drew several harsh breaths. "But first, I must ask, whatever possessed you, Viveca?"

That question proved Viveca's undoing. She shook with bittersweet laughter until tears rolled down her cheeks. "Indeed, whatever *possessed* me."

"Well?"

"If I tell you, you'll for sure give up on me."

"If you don't, there's no hope."

Viveca nodded dismally. "You know, you're right; what do I have to lose? The truth is, I enlisted my housekeeper's help and she organized the . . . the séance or whatever it was. I resorted to this madness because my house is infested with . . . spooks."

To Viveca's shock, Hilda waved her off. "Well, everyone knows about that."

Viveca was agog. "They do?"

"Of course they do," Hilda rejoined with a long-suffering air. "My dear, Savannah dates back to the seventeenth century. We have more dead souls here than you have citrus trees in your state of California. The entire town is plagued by restless spirits, and has been ever since Governor Oglethorpe laid out our squares. We even have our secret spiritualist societies, closet occult enclaves . . . although that's not to say I'm a member."

Viveca's mouth was hanging open. She'd had no idea Hilda was a believer. And from the way she'd spoken of spiritualist societies, Viveca even suspected her friend might well be a member of some paranormal organization.

"Why, at my house I've been battling with the poltergeist of a German parson for over twenty years now," Hilda went on, fluttering a hand in agitation. "Refuses to leave my third-floor sewing room." She paused, smiling slyly. "Although we have had some interesting theological discussions on Martin Luther and Philipp Melanchthon."

"You're jesting!"

"Not at all. Most homes here have their resident specters. *However*"—sternly Hilda wagged a finger—"that doesn't mean it's discussed openly in polite society, much less that any of us resort to voodoo, with its links to black magic and insurrection. Shame on your housekeeper; she should have known better. Indeed, the entire paranormal movement has been frowned on of late, especially with the poor Fox sisters being exposed as charlatans back East."

"But—what do folks here do about their—er—hauntings?"

Hilda shot her a withering look. "Well, they take care of it politely, discreetly, in the Savannah style. A proper exorcism by a priest, or a low-key séance—there are some possibilities. Savannah definitely has its history of those. But *voodoo*. My dear, never voodoo."

"Actually, it was Obeah."

"Same difference," Hilda retorted. "The bottom line is, you've now been exposed in the newspaper as some sort of heretic, being doused by a witch doctor while your Jamaican entourage prances about in their crazed ecstasies."

"I know."

"Now let's decide how we can fix this."

Viveca was incredulous. "You mean you still want to help me?"

"Of course. I have too much invested in you to give up now." Hilda patted Viveca's hand. "Besides, as I've told you many times, I like you, my dear."

Viveca smiled at her straight from her heart. "You're a kind and loyal friend, Hilda. But I feel rather like Humpty Dumpty at the moment. I'm not sure even you can put me back together again."

"Nonsense, we'll muddle through it." She laid a finger alongside her cheek. "Let's see, with Aubrey, I suppose you should just tell him the truth and throw yourself on his mercy. May or may not work, though I still have some pull with the boy."

"Yes." Viveca grimaced. "I can't imagine he'll be pleased to learn that his lady love has hosted a Jamaican-style exorcism. When I raised the possibility of ghosts with him before, he seemed quite disapproving."

"Of course he's a sanctimonious snoot, but still a good catch. As for how you respond to the rest of society—well, blame it on your housekeeper and discharge her."

Viveca was horrified. "No, I can't! I gave Winnie permission for all of this."

"Then you're even more of a ninny than she is. However, if you want to hold your head up again in this town, my dear, my advice is to send the wench packing. Throw yourself on your sword with Aubrey, take your medicine, then ask him to bless your house or something, so he won't feel quite so incensed by the pagan aspect." Abruptly Hilda stood. "Now we're going to go see Herman Hargrove."

"We are?"

Hilda nodded adamantly. "Yes. And this time we're going to force him to discharge that abominable Bliss woman!"

Following a quick trip downtown, Viveca stood with Hilda before Herman Hargrove in his dark, cluttered office. Her friend was pounding her fist on Herman's desk while he cowered in his chair.

"How could you have allowed that despicable little she-devil to libel my dear friend Viveca?" Hilda ranted. "You will discharge Beryl Bliss at once, and print a retraction of her entire scandalous diatribe!"

Herman grimaced, struggling unsuccessfully to shrink further into his seat. "Hilda, I realize Beryl can be exasperating, but as I've explained before, I cannot simply fire her. She's my Ellie's cousin—"

Hilda cut him off by shoving her florid face a mere inch away from his pudgy nose. "Speaking of Ellie, I hadn't wanted to use my trump card, but now I shall."

Recoiling, Herman blanched. "What do you mean?"

Triumphantly, Hilda straightened herself and smoothed her silk skirts. "I mean, if you don't discharge that lying little baggage, and print a retraction of the entire article in your next issue, I shall tell your *darling* Ellie about the little peccadillo you and my George indulged in with those two trollops up in Charleston."

Now even Viveca was amazed, both by her friend's pluck and by Herman's mortified reaction. Indeed, from his scarlet color and the gurgling sound rising up in his throat, she feared he might have a heart attack at any moment.

"You knew about that?" he whispered.

"Oh, yes," Hilda declared.

He mopped his brow. "The woman will be gone tomorrow."

Hilda beamed. "Splendid, then. Come along, Viveca."

Viveca followed her friend out of the room, shaking her head at the widow's audacity.

Chapter Twenty-nine

Back at home, Viveca was disappointed when her two after-noon piano students failed to appear. Their parents had sent servants with notes: Melissa Osbourne had developed a blinding headeache; Billy Morrison had badly skinned his knee. Viveca assigned the absences to what she knew must be the truth: Both the Osbournes and the Morrisons had read the newspaper article by now. As Hilda had said, Beryl's pre-vious perverse insinuations had been one thing, but her pro-viding such blatant evidence of Viveca practicing the occult was something else altogether.

Oh, heavens, would she now lose all her students? Would she be ruined, socially and financially? She paced the parlor, half panicked.

In mid-afternoon, Aubrey came calling. Viveca felt her stomach churning as Winnie showed him into the parlor. Of course he held the newspaper in his hand—and his expres-sion couldn't have been more disapproving.

With his reproachful gaze following Winnie out of the room, Aubrey held up the paper and slowly shook his head at

Viveca. "My dear, I don't know what to say. Whatever possessed you?"

"That's what Hilda asked," Viveca murmured.

Sternly he continued, "Indeed, just as I was about to leave to come see you, Hilda came calling on me. She told me of Herman Hargrove's promise to discharge Beryl Bliss and retract the article. She also swore that you were under the influence of that ungodly Jamaican housekeeper of yours when you did . . . well, whatever you did on Wednesday night. But Viveca . . ." Appearing devastated, he whispered, "You held an Obeah ritual in your home—and you did it after *prayer meeting.*"

She winced. "I know. I'm sorry."

He waved a hand. "How could a woman of your stature and apparent presence of mind succumb to this sort of—of barbaric black magic? Didn't I warn you about Sister Taheisha and the others?"

"I . . ." Miserably Viveca prowled the room, then turned. "Aubrey, my house is haunted."

He laughed. "What? You can't seriously believe that?"

"Oh, yes. Nightly I'm plagued by a veritable bedlam of restless spirits—corpses swinging on the square, an ax woman stalking my backyard—"

"What?"

"And . . . well, I grew desperate and agreed to let Winnie and the others help me."

"My heavens!" He stepped closer, his expression eloquent with shock and pain. "But if you were so desperate, why didn't you come to me? We could have prayed about it."

"I tried to tell you once, remember?" she cried. "And you shut me out."

"I remember we discussed the occult in general terms—"

Agitated, she cut in, "Aubrey, what would you have said if I'd told you that my house has a ghost in its bathtub, a leg sprouting out of the ceiling, a werewolf howling in the garden—"

"My God, Viveca!" Expression horrified, he reached out to cover her mouth with his hand, curtailing her ramblings. "I would have said you needed help, my dear. Serious help. And I would have seen to it that you were provided it." Backing away, he held up the paper. "Now . . . I fear 'tis too late."

"Now that I'm facing social ruin?" she inquired bitterly.

He scowled. "Viveca, my place in this community is crucial, and you've placed me in quite a precarious position."

She turned, blinking away hot tears. "Your place, eh? Never mind my confusion, my torment, as long as we don't forget your hallowed station. Well, fine, Aubrey. You don't owe me anything."

She felt his hand on her shoulder and flinched. "Viveca, I'm not abandoning you."

"That's how it feels," she said thickly.

She heard him sigh. "Surely there may still be hope. Perhaps if you make a full statement before the church, a public repentance, and of course discharge the Jamaican woman—"

Viveca whirled. "I'm not firing Winnie."

He appeared incredulous. "Why ever not?"

"Didn't you listen to me? This is *my* fault, not hers. What she did, she did with my blessing."

"That still shouldn't stop you from sending her on her way. Why, the woman is little more than a witch, a practitioner of sorcery, along with her devious associates. Why wouldn't you be rid of her?"

"Because it wouldn't be fair!" Viveca burst out. "And as the ostensible champion of morality in this community, you should be the first one to point that out—that is, *if* you cared more about *souls* than you do about appearances. But perhaps I've misjudged your alleged Christian compassion. Perhaps you're just a pious prig."

At that, Aubrey flinched. He squared his jaw and clapped his hat on his head. "My dear, I think I'd best be going."

"Yes, I think you should. Forgive me if I don't see you out."

"Indeed, that will not be necessary."

After he turned and left the room, Viveca paced around

angrily until she heard the front door slam. "Hypocrite!" she yelled, slamming her fist down on the piano keys, then howling from the pain.

Max sat in his front parlor reading *The Savannah Daily*, thunderstruck as he stared at a picture of the woman he'd made love to last night, kneeling before a voodoo priest.

The article that followed thoroughly vilified Viveca. Oh, heavens, when he'd unleashed Beryl Bliss on her, he'd had no idea she would go to these lengths. The woman was evil, totally without conscience.

Nonetheless, he had to admit that Viveca had brought some of this on herself. Pictures didn't lie. Outlandish as it seemed, she had hosted a pagan ritual in her basement in an attempt to exorcise the demons from her home. It seemed ludicrous—but then, this criticism sprang from a man who had shot at trees in a frantic attempt to scare off phantoms. She'd clearly been desperate—as he'd also been on many an occasion—and his heart welled with sympathy for her, as well as self-loathing for inadvertently causing her this terrible embarrassment. Indeed, she might be ruined in the community.

Was that what he really wanted? To ruin her, so he could keep her for himself?

He frowned as he heard the sounds of a horse trotting down Lost Lane. Rising, he went to the window and peered outside to see Aubrey riding toward Viveca's gate. Jealousy welled within him. After Aubrey went inside, Max went out on the veranda, staring at her house and trying to restrain himself from storming over there.

He wasn't successful. Indeed, he was well on his way across his side yard when Aubrey came bolting back out her door, slamming it shut behind him. Features tense, he took no note of Max as he charged for his horse. Then Max heard Viveca yell "Hypocrite!" amid the jarring blast of her hand hitting the piano keys.

Hmmm . . . Now did seem a splendid time to go calling.

* * *

"Viveca, whatever possessed you?"

At the piano, Viveca gasped, then turned to see that Max had slipped into the room and was regarding her quizzically as he held up the newspaper she'd seen too many times today. Even though she was highly agitated, heated memories of their stirring passion swept her at the sight of him standing there, so handsome, with features so intense.

"Must *everyone* ask me that?" she managed.

He stepped closer, eyeing her with concern. "I heard you banging the keys. I hope you didn't break that lovely piano—or your hand."

"No, both are fine."

"Really?" Close to her now, he commanded, "Give me your hand, Viveca."

With a groan she extended it.

His fingers grasping her hand were gentle; nonetheless, she winced at his touch. He whistled, then tenderly kissed her tight fist. "My dear, you hurt yourself. You must take greater care. This could bruise."

She disengaged her hand and lifted her chin. "That's the least of my worries."

"Ah—so I take it Aubrey was no paragon of goodwill and supportiveness when he came calling?"

"You saw him come?"

"And I saw him leave."

She blinked rapidly. "Yes, I'd venture to say he could not wait to get out of here. Are you happy now?"

Max grimaced, his expression mirroring genuine concern and regret. "Am I happy that your association with him has apparently ended? Yes, I'm happy. Am I pleased that it has ended in this manner? Absolutely not. I don't relish seeing you humiliated—or watching him act like a self-righteous jackass."

Though his words left Viveca feeling torn, she had too much on her mind to deal with Max right now. "Thanks for the words of encouragement. Now tell me what you're doing here, and why you've intruded on me without knocking."

He raised an eyebrow. "This from the passionate wench who intruded in my bedroom last night—and got quite all the comeuppance she deserved."

Face hot, she turned away. "That is best forgotten."

"Can you forget it, Viveca?"

Not responding, she sat down, and gestured at a chair for him. "What do you want, Maxwell?"

Following suit, he flourished the paper. "Why, to hear your side of this fascinating story. I thought last night we drew about as close as two human beings can be. Funny you didn't mention you've joined some sort of voodoo cult."

Viveca slammed the upholstery with her uninjured fist. "Damn it, Max, if I hear the word 'voodoo' one more time, I shall scream. I've joined no such cult. And if I didn't tell you . . . well, about the ceremony in my basement . . . it's only because I knew you'd respond by jumping to these very conclusions, just like everyone else in this town."

Max whistled, leaning toward her with an expression of reproach. "Viveca, do you really think I'd judge you so harshly, considering all we've shared, all we've *both* been through? I bared my soul to you last night, told you all about my own hauntings, how the female ghost has—"

"I know—and I'm sorry, Max," she hastily apologized. "I've been knocked sideways by this, and I'm lashing out. I shouldn't lump you with everyone else. You're definitely one of a kind."

He grinned. "I'll take that as a compliment. And I'm sorry if you'll be made to suffer over this, my dear."

But Viveca had her doubts. "Are you really, Max? Sure, you may feel some regret, but prior to last night, all you've ever wanted was to chase me out of town—you and that horrible Bliss woman, who has targeted me for some reason I can't fathom."

He coughed. "Yes. Perhaps I should have a word with her."

"Don't bother. Hilda has already gotten her discharged from the newspaper."

He grinned. "Good for Hilda."

"She's also going to try to help me control the damage as best we can."

"Splendid. I have every confidence in the Queen, but let me know if I can help, anyway."

She nodded. "In that regard, I must say you're a better person than your cousin."

He flashed her a tight smile. "Was Aubrey a complete cad?"

"He was shocked, outraged, hurt that I hadn't shared this with him. He did suggest I try to make some sort of public repentance, and then . . ."

"He was out the door?"

"Yes."

"The sniveling little coward." Gravely Max winked. "Shall I shoot him for you, dear?"

Though she shook her head, she had to smile. "I think you should stick with weeds."

"I think I'll stick with you, my dear." He rose, crossed the room and sat down beside her, taking her hand and eyeing her with touching tenderness. "I'm relieved it's over between him and you, Viveca, though I do regret the circumstances."

"Do you?"

With surprising humility, he admitted, "I was really hoping you would give him up—for me."

Though Viveca felt warmed, she had to ask, "So I might languish as your mistress, and not his wife?"

"He doesn't deserve you."

"And you do?"

He pulled her into his arms and chuckled tenderly. "No, but it seems I must have you, nonetheless."

Gently, sweetly, he kissed her. All the yearnings she'd tried to suppress flooded her body and soul once again. She clung to him, needing, craving his comfort, but fearful she'd lose control of herself again.

She gazed up at him starkly. "Oh, Max. What are we going to do?"

He pressed his mouth to her hair. "I want you to come to me again tonight."

She winced helplessly. "Max, I can't."

"Of course you can."

"You're going to ruin me."

At that, he smiled and pressed his cheek to hers. "According to you, you're ruined already, so what have we to lose?"

Only my heart, she almost said aloud. "Max, please, I still need time to think."

He pulled back and ran a fingertip teasingly over her lip. "Later, then, love."

With aching eyes, she watched him stride out.

Only seconds after he left, Winnie stepped into the room. Her eyes were strangely moist.

"Winnie, what is it?" Viveca asked, standing.

Sniffing, Winnie pulled a handkerchief from her apron. "I heard you talkin' with Mr. Aubrey and Miss Hilda. You stood up for me when you din' have to."

Viveca was touched by this display of emotion coming from her housekeeper. "Winnie, I stood up for you because it was the right thing to do."

Winnie dabbed at her eyes, her mouth quivering with anger. "De fad'er with all his highfalutin 'Christian ways, he din' do that."

"You're right, he didn't. No matter what people may say, I think you're a better Christian than he is."

Winnie smiled, her expression near-ecstatic. "No one ever stood up for me before, mistress."

Viveca strode over to pat Winnie's hand. "Don't fret, Winnie. I was glad to do so."

Viveca was amazed when Winnie made a hoarse sound, then flung her arms around Viveca, hugging her tightly. She spoke in a voice stark with emotion. "Old Winnie neber forget. You got a fren' now, mistress. You got a fren' forever."

Watching her turn and leave, Viveca ironically reflected that the day may have brought a blessing, after all.

Chapter Thirty

For once, Viveca was relieved when evening came, even welcoming the miasma that crept up from the swamps and shrouded the landscape with its eerie haze. At least with the advent of nightfall, there was less chance she'd have more unexpected callers—earthbound ones, that is. The day had been draining, to say the least. She been publicly maligned as some sort of voodoo witch. She'd lost Aubrey—and strangely enough, she didn't care.

She should care. She knew she must somehow salvage her place in this community, for her livelihood depended on it. The fact that her afternoon piano students had failed to appear worried her greatly. Should she apologize in church as Aubrey had suggested? She had no more students scheduled until Monday, so at least she had the weekend to fashion a plan for controlling the damage. It could not, of course, involve discharging Winnie—indeed, she smiled each time she remembered her housekeeper's touching turnaround, her vowing, "You got a fren' forever." That might not be such a tragedy—she needed all the friends she could get right now.

Of course, Max had offered his support as well, in an ardent, touching manner. But she just wasn't prepared to pay the price an emotional commitment with him would bring.

Late that evening she again took a bath, needing the relaxation after her stressful day. Sitting in the tub with her hair pinned up and the essence of rose floating around her, she did not sense the presence of the phantom. Lulled by the warm water, she lay back, half in a trance.

She was stunned when the bathroom door creaked open and none other than Max strode brazenly inside, grinning. "Hello, my dear. My, don't you look fetching tonight."

Gasping, trembling with both shock and treacherous desires, Viveca thrust her arms over her breasts and shot upright. She couldn't believe Max was actually standing there, that he'd intruded on her bath Alex Fremont style.

But Alex was a ghost and Max was *real*, so earthy and virile, his hair askew, his jawline dark with stubble, shirt unbuttoned and black pants clinging sensuously to his wonderful hips and muscled thighs. Not to mention that delicious bulge at their joining.

Viveca could barely speak, her throat was suddenly so dry. "Max, what on earth are you doing here?"

He grinned and unabashedly perused her nude body. "I missed you, my love."

Totally flustered, not to mention aroused, she stammered, "B-but—my God, you've sneaked inside my house, invaded my bathroom—"

He strode to the tub and sank to his knees before her, impaling her with his ardent gaze, his fingers toying with a damp curl at her nape. "Yes, darling, but it's not nearly as dastardly as it sounds. You see, I tried to stay away, but I couldn't, I missed you so."

She groaned.

"So I stole over to your property—"

"Hoping to eavesdrop again?"

He caressed her bare shoulder with his fingers, raising quivers. "Well, perhaps just hoping to hear your voice at the window or catch a glimpse of you on the veranda. Then, when I heard the bathwater running, well, I couldn't resist, so I crept in your back door—"

"Heavenly days! Did anyone see you?"

With bold, assured moves, he pulled her arms away from her breasts, and proceeded to stare at them so hungrily that her nipples puckered painfully. "If they had, you would surely have heard an unholy ruckus, no?" He touched a taut-ened peak and she winced. "Ah, so lovely."

"My God, Max." To her shame, she nearly panted the words. "You still haven't explained why you would intrude on my—my bath."

He reached inside the tub to take a palmful of warm water, which he sluiced over her neck and shoulders in a wickedly sensual caress while she shivered with delight. "How long has it been since you've had someone bathe you, darling?"

The tender though titillating words drenched Viveca with longing—and she was already so hot she feared she might set the bathwater simmering. "Max! You're being a reprobate!"

"Well, of course I am," he teased. "I am a scoundrel, after all, but a lovable one, I do hope. Besides, I think it high time we exorcise the ghost from this bathtub."

"Exorcise the—er—what?" she cried, even more scandalized and shockingly stirred. "But I'm sure he's already gone. Tamos must have chased him away the other night."

"Then we must test that theory," Max continued solemnly, leaning over to tease her damp neck with his tongue. Amid her helpless sighs, he murmured, "Is the bawdy spirit truly expelled? Or does he still lurk in the shadows of your bath-room? You know I won't let him have you, darling."

"You—you won't?" Unwittingly she smiled.

He trailed that tantalizing tongue over her cheek, her mouth. "A battle to the death, my love. Me against your demons."

"Ummm . . . how sweet of you to take on my demons. But—but I really don't see Mr. Fremont as much of a threat now."

"You think not?" Ardently he stared into her eyes. "Will he let the two of us make love here?"

"Here! Make love?"

"Whatever do you think he was trying to do to you?"

"I—well—"

Max chuckled wickedly. "My love, you look gorgeous with your eyes so large and wide. And I plan to make them go wider still."

At that, Viveca knew she must be a harlot to her soul, for she could hardly wait.

Leaning toward her, Max slowly, sensuously licked her damp ear. "Will he let you be mine?"

She could only stare at him, lips trembling, parted.

"Perfect," he murmured, leaning over to kiss her, his tongue doing a carnal dance in her mouth. With a soft moan she looped her arms around his neck and mated her tongue with his. He was sinful, lurid, wonderful—and she loved it. It was all she could do not to tear off his clothes and haul him into the tub with her, she wanted him so badly.

After a moment he pulled back and with a deep sigh regarded her breathless face. "Well, well. That was some kiss."

"Yes." She grinned crookedly.

He traced that tormenting finger over her lips. "Think of it this way, my dear. Would you prefer I return home to be seduced by *her*?"

"No!" she declared shamelessly, drawing his lips down to hers again. She kissed him fervently, while he chuckled deep in his throat.

A moment later he pulled away and stood, tearing off his shirt. Viveca knew this was madness, that she should take charge of herself and stop him, but the words were frozen in her throat, so mesmerized was she by the sight of him undressing, the candlelight gleaming over hard muscles and smooth flesh.

In less than a minute, he climbed into the tub looking so

splendid, long and lean that he took her breath away. He grinned, caught her wrists and slowly, sensuously slid her body on top of his. "Oh, Viveca, darling. You feel wonderful."

So did he. Hot, slippery, sinewy and so hard.

He was trembling too now, and feeling the shudder that seized his body touched her to her soul. She slid upward and kissed him ravenously. Impatiently he tore at the pins in her hair, tumbled her heavy locks, then buried his face in the perfumed mass.

"Love me," he whispered in tortured tones. "Please, love me now."

Viveca responded at once, wildly kissing Max's mouth, his throat, running her tongue over his neck and chest, savoring the taste of him. Within minutes she was settled astride him, wantonly crying out as he penetrated her deeply, fully. He gripped her breasts and smiled up at her as they continued their torrid mating dance.

"No more ghosts, darling, eh? No more ghosts?" he whispered.

"No more ghosts," she choked back.

Indeed, tears burned Viveca's eyes as she realized Max was banishing the ghosts not just from her house but from her heart and soul as well.

"We're going to have to do something about this, you know," Max murmured.

Viveca glanced up at him, unable to believe they were still in the bathtub, bodies tightly locked, though the water had grown tepid.

"Do something about what?" she managed.

He arched upward provocatively, bringing a heavy sigh to her lips. "This."

She grinned impishly. "Like what?"

He regarded her soberly. "I don't know. Like marry, perhaps."

"Marry!"

His brows shot up. "Now you're irate because I'm broaching the subject of matrimony? Woman, is it impossible to please you?"

"When you do so in such a cavalier manner? Yes!"

He frowned. "How do you know I'm cavalier? I could be perfectly sincere."

She frowned back.

"Couldn't I, Viveca?"

Helplessly she waved a hand. "Max, I don't know. I know you enjoy this, but perhaps you're offering to wed me out of some . . . well, some latent sense of chivalry—"

"Ah, so now I want to make an honest woman out of you?"

"Well, something like that. Or, maybe it's just because you want me in your bed."

He glowered magnificently. "I couldn't just *want* you, eh, darling?"

Feeling stabbed by guilt, she flashed him a conciliatory smile. "Max, you must understand. It's not easy for me to trust—"

Quickly, soothingly, he kissed her brow. "I know—not after what that cad did to you."

"Before, when I gave myself in a relationship, it brought me only pain."

"And you expect similar treatment at my hands?"

Miserably she met his gaze. "Surely you can't blame me for having doubts about a man who's never known more than fleeting loyalties—"

"That's how you see me, Viveca?"

"The rogue? The man-about-town? The invader of ladies' boudoirs, their bathtubs—"

"*Your* boudoir, *your* bathtub."

"Perhaps so. But, Max, the sad truth is, I've never known you to be anything other than capricious so far."

"Then perhaps you don't know me well enough."

"Perhaps not."

Abruptly he clutched her close and spoke hoarsely, intensely. "Viveca, you *can* trust me. You *can* give yourself to me."

Tears stung her eyes at his tender words. Did she have a choice? She seemed to be giving herself to him—trusting him—whether she wanted to or not.

She didn't doubt his sincerity—at least, for the moment. But did anything really exist for Maxwell Beecher beyond the fleeting pleasures of the moment?

"Max, you need to go," she murmured at last. "The servants—"

"We need to discuss this."

"Perhaps we do, but not now. If you value my reputation at all, you must leave."

"Very well." He pulled her close for a last searing kiss, then slipped out of the tub. "This isn't settled, Viveca."

"No doubt," she whispered, but not until after he was gone.

Max was heading down the back steps when a shadow jumped out at him from the miasma, landing squarely in his path. A strong, wiry arm locked onto his neck, and a knife was pressed against his throat.

"What you doin' to Miss Viveca?" demanded a familiar husky voice.

At once Max was enraged, though also wise enough not to overreact and help commit his own murder. "Winnie! What in hell do you think you're doing, you miserable wench, accosting me this way!"

Her words came in an angry hiss. "You heard me, mon! What you doin' to Miss Viveca, sneaking in de back door like some tomcat on de prowl, joining her where no mon have a right to join her—"

"What we were doing is none of your business."

Winnie tensed angrily, nicking his neck with the knife in the process, ignoring his blistering curse. "Was you hurting her? 'Cause if you was, I'm gonna' slit your throat. I hear lots of moanin' comin' from de bat'room—"

"Why, you voyeur!" With a quick, skilled move, Max grabbed her wrist, seized the knife from her hand and shoved her away—and now it was Winnie who cringed before him.

Wielding the weapon at her, he snapped, "I should behead you like a chicken, you nervy little baggage! Damn you, you nicked my throat."

She tossed her head with bravado. "I ain't afraid of you, mon."

"You should be."

"I defend Miss Viveca to the death."

"Ah—so you're her champion now?"

"I her fren'," Winnie stated proudly. "And you been doin' what no mon have a right to do dat not her husband."

"If that makes sense," he scoffed.

Winnie shook a finger at him. "You know jes' what I mean, you low-down snake. She a proper lady."

"Now there, for once, we're in agreement," Max replied. "And although it's still *none of your damn business*, I'll have you know I just proposed to Miss Viveca."

"In de bat'room?" Winnie sneered. "What you been doin', mon? Smokin' ganja?"

"Of course not. And that's hardly the point."

"What de point, mon?"

"My intentions are perfectly honorable."

"Yeah, you and old Lucifer, too." Although Winnie appeared quite unimpressed by Max's declaration, she grudgingly asked, "So what Miss Viveca say?"

He groaned. "She sent me on my way."

"Humph! She know a rascal when she see one, just like me." Despite his having the knife, she stepped closer and tapped his chest with her forefinger. "You treat her right or I put de Obeah 'pon you. I curse you dead."

Max was far too much of a believer to scoff at *that*. Frowning, he watched Winnie turn and proudly retreat up the steps.

Chapter Thirty-one

"Oh, Viveca, darling! Rise and shine."

Viveca was awakened by a distant but oh so familiar male voice, coming from her garden. She hopped out of bed, pulled on her wrapper and went out to the veranda, laughing at the sight of Max standing below her in a shaft of soft morning light. He wore a white Panama suit and hat and held a breakfast tray embellished by yellow roses in a bud vase.

"What are you doing down there, you rascal?" she called.

"Why, I brought you breakfast, my love. Fresh scones and hot tea."

"You're jesting."

"Not in the least. And may I say you look especially lovely this morning? Such a bloom in your cheeks—"

"Oh, hush with the flattery, you varmint!"

"I will if you'll quash those unladylike protests and come down here—before I storm up there and fetch you, woman."

Chuckling, Viveca decided she'd best do Max's bidding before he did something scandalous. He could be such a charming rogue! She hastily changed into a day dress, and within moments she and Max were seated on her front steps, sipping tea from china cups and nibbling on delicious warm scones, while beyond them in the yard two squirrels battled over an acorn and vibrant flowers emitted their sweet perfume.

Max looked and smelled wonderful, too. In a departure from his sometimes-disheveled state, he was clean-shaven, and there was even a small nick on his neck. It charmed her to think he might have wounded himself while trying to look good for her.

Feeling almost coy, Viveca fluttered her eyelashes at him over the rim of her teacup. "To what do I owe this honor, sir?"

He feigned indignation. "Can't I bring my sweetheart her breakfast?"

"Hah! Usually you offer threats and ultimatums, brooding looks and slammed doors," she teased back. "Now you've brought me flowers twice—and breakfast. Why is the rogue playing the gentleman?"

He chuckled wryly. "Perhaps you're reforming me."

"Try again, Max."

He nodded sheepishly. "Well, for one thing, I have to convince Winnie I'm treating you right."

"You do?"

Max turned toward the front door, cupped a hand around his mouth and bellowed, "Oh, Winnie, dear! I'm treating her right!"

To Viveca's amazement, Winnie stuck her head out the front door, glared at Max, then ducked back inside, slamming the door shut.

Open-mouthed, Viveca turned to him. "What was *that* about?"

He rolled his eyes. "Your lovely housekeeper waylaid me at knifepoint last night as I left your house—"

"She what?" She gripped his arm. "My God, Max, are you all right? Did she put that nick on your throat?"

"She's the very one."

Viveca grimaced. "Knowing your temper, Winnie's lucky to be alive."

"She is, indeed."

"But why—"

Wiggling his eyebrows, he confided, "Evidently Winnie heard us . . . shall we say, in flagrante delicto in the bathtub, and subsequently threatened me with death and everlasting damnation if I should ever again try any such shenanigans with you."

Viveca shouted a laugh. "She *heard* us in the bathroom? Well, you were pretty naughty, Max."

"You were plenty wanton yourself."

"I can't believe she *heard* us—"

"Yes. Next time, I must stifle your screams with a towel."

She punched his arm. "After all that grunting and groaning you did?"

Both of them convulsed with mirth, and it occurred to Viveca how great it was just to have fun with Max. How long had it been since she'd enjoyed life this way?

She eyed him curiously. "So you're not angry at Winnie for threatening you?"

Suddenly turning solemn, he took her hand. "Actually, I'm not. I'm beginning to understand that protective instinct myself." He raised her hand, slowly kissing each fingers.

"Ah, that's sweet, Max." She cleared her throat. "Now tell me—is there some reason you've come calling, other than to bring me this delightful repast?"

"Actually, there is." Soberly he confessed, "I've come to tell you I must leave your fair presence and journey to Atlanta for a few days. Some legal matters concerning the family business."

"Oh."

He caressed her nape with his fingertips, raising shivers along her spine. "But I am rather concerned about your safety while I'm gone."

She inclined her head toward the door. "With Winnie hovering over me like a mother hen?"

"Well, that is a point. But even better"—he leaned over to whisper at her ear—"Viveca, love, come with me."

Though perversely thrilled, she had to protest. "Come

with you? And decimate the final shreds of my wrecked reputation?"

His eyes danced with mischief. "We could always elope."

"Elope?" She laughed. "And that would be *so* socially correct."

"You think I'm joking," he accused.

"Well—aren't you?"

He brooded for a moment, then gave a deep sigh. "Viveca, I need to get some things off my mind with you."

"Very well," she replied, frowning.

Staring her in the eye, he said, "First, I regret the way I've treated you, trying to strong-arm you into selling your home and leaving Savannah. You're right—at times I've behaved like an arrogant bully. I've been condescending, insulting—"

But by now Viveca was feigning vapors, a hand dramatically pressed to her brow. "Why, Maxwell Beecher, I'm stunned."

"Oh, hush, and let me grovel," he scolded. "I think I've behaved badly in part because you beat me to this property." He paused, gazing at her raptly. "But mostly, I think I tried to chase you away because I found you so very tempting and felt myself falling for you."

"You did?" she asked, both shocked and warmed by his honesty.

He clutched her hand and smiled tenderly. "Yes. In fighting you I was actually battling myself. So I can't blame you for remaining wary of my intentions. But . . ."

"But?"

"I'm really hoping we can put this matter behind us."

"Well, perhaps we can," she replied carefully. "Especially if you're contrite."

He placed his hand over his chest. "My dear Miss Stanhope, from the bottom of my heart, I apologize."

She grinned. "Apology accepted, sir."

Despite the moment of levity, his expression turned pensive again. "There's more, Viveca. You see, I think I grew up with a rather jaded view of family life—of marriage—"

"I know, you're not the marrying kind."

He wagged a finger at her. "Now wait a minute, don't say that. Haven't I already proposed to you twice?"

"Well, in a manner of speaking."

He glowered. "To get back to what I was saying, I was raised by a rather overbearing mother—"

"Yes, I've heard," she put in gently.

"Mother was, shall we say, a slave to the demons of her temperament. She could be giddy one moment, in tears or rage the next. She made my father's life a living hell."

Viveca's heart went out to him, and she squeezed his hand. "I'm so sorry, Max. How was she with you?"

"She loved me in her way. Sometimes she would rant, rave, call me names, even throw things at me—but she'd always be sorry afterward." He turned to Viveca with troubled eyes. "She'd be so shattered, so filled with self-loathing, that I couldn't help but forgive her, comfort her."

"Oh, Max." Viveca hugged him. "That must have been so difficult for you to live with. I had wonderful parents, and don't know what I would have done otherwise."

"But not everything in your life has been wonderful," Max put in meaningfully.

She raised her chin. "You're right. Not everything. What is it you're trying to say to me, Max?"

"My point is, I accepted Mother's limitations. I didn't allow her demons, her insanity, whatever it was, to make me hate all women."

"I'm glad to hear that." She frowned. "So you're saying I've allowed my experience with Erskine to poison *my* mind against men—particularly you?"

"Haven't you?"

"I suppose in a way I have." Mulling over his words, she slowly shook her head. "But, you know, Max, your mother loved you. He . . ."

"I know, darling." Even as her voice broke, Max clutched her close. "I'm so sorry."

She gazed up at him. "I'm sorry, too, that I've been slow to trust you. I'm beginning to see that some of it really hasn't been your fault."

He kissed her brow. "Well, I'll be honored to do all I can to help ease your doubts, to become a man worthy of your faith. I know it won't happen overnight."

"You're right." Bravely she smiled. "But I'm so glad we've had this talk. It helps me realize you have a sensitive side, you're more than just a naughty scamp intent on throwing me over your shoulder, taking me to bed and issuing orders."

"Indeed." He winked. "I'll save those particular pleasures for my return."

"Max!" She playfully shoved him.

He patted her knee. "May I hope you'll miss me?"

"Perhaps a little," she demurred.

"Please try to think about our relationship while I'm gone," he implored. "I know I certainly shall. And please behave yourself."

"*Me* behave myself!"

"No communal baths with naughty spirits," he teased.

"Max! I thought we exorcised that ghost. Besides, you're one to talk. What about your Lorelei?"

"Actually, she hasn't made an appearance since the night you came to me." With a wicked wink, he added, "Or if she has, I've been too tuckered out to notice."

Viveca chortled.

He touched the tip of her nose with his index finger. "So be good, will you? And promise me you'll steer clear of Aubrey."

Irate, she waved a hand. "Didn't you hear me yesterday? He broke things off with me."

Maxwell laughed. "No man can resist you for long, Viveca. If he doesn't pursue you, 'twill only be because he'd had himself gelded without informing the rest of us."

"Max, stop it," she chided. "We're never going to make it together if you insist on dictating to me like this. Don't make me regret calling you sensitive. Besides, it doesn't matter what Aubrey decides to do—"

"It doesn't?"

She clenched her jaw. "Because no matter what Aubrey says or does, I won't have him back."

Max grinned. "Well, bully for you. I'm proud of you, Viveca."

"Be proud if you wish, Max—but this is really all about me, not you. Aubrey abandoned me at the slightest sign of trouble, just like . . . well, I have too much self-respect to ever consider marriage with any man whose sense of honor bends with the whims of public opinion."

Max actually applauded. "Bravo, my dear. Well said. But do you promise? Is it really over between the two of you?"

She nodded. "That much I can definitely promise."

"Then I'll get back as quickly as I can." He clutched her close for a thorough kiss, then skipped off down the steps.

Viveca felt heartened after Max's visit. His honesty and humility had been both unexpected and quite touching. He had shared with her as never before; he actually seemed willing to make an effort to try to change, to make their relationship work. And it seemed they both had reasons to fear commitment, to hesitate to trust.

Could they overcome those barriers? More and more, she dearly hoped so. And she missed him more than words could express.

Otherwise, she had a markedly uneventful weekend. Indeed, the silence of the house put her on edge, especially as she endlessly agonized over whether she'd ruined her future here in Savannah. In Saturday's *Savannah Daily*, Herman Hargrove did print a brief retraction of Beryl Bliss's article. But he merely called the article "regrettable, ill-timed and distasteful," not commenting on its truth or lack thereof. She doubted this would change many minds; it was too little too late.

She considered going to see Hilda to plot additional strategies for achieving her own redemption, but could not bear the prospect of more histrionics and hand-wringing. Besides, much as it rankled, she already knew that Aubrey's suggestion was her only potential salvation. She would have to eat humble pie, make a public apology in church and hope she would be forgiven. That meant she would have to see the turncoat Aubrey again, face everyone; but there really was no other choice if she hoped to survive here. It wasn't just her piano lessons at stake—for as far as she knew, prayer meeting was still scheduled at her house for Wednesday evening. What would she do if everyone but Hilda snubbed her? This would be the final deathblow for her future in Savannah.

She took extra care with her appearance on Sunday morning, donning her best tailored navy blue suit and sedate feathered hat, and bucked up her confidence as she walked toward the front door of her home. That was when she heard soft footsteps behind her in the hallway. She turned, gasping, to see Alex Fremont standing just a few feet behind her, not far from the bathroom door. He hovered there in the sun-drenched dust motes, half man, half spirit. He was gazing back at her with infinitely sad eyes. She felt awestruck.

Do you think your shadow-catchers scare me?

She heard him ask the question, even though his voice never issued forth, his lips never moved. She struggled for something to say, to do . . . but before she could think of a reaction, he faded and was gone.

Damnation! She'd brought in an Obeah priest, complete with live chickens and snakes. She'd wrecked her own reputation. And still the ghost was back. No talisman, no charm, no witch doctor seemed to work in this hellish place.

Perhaps her only redemption could be found at church!

It was difficult for Viveca to walk down that aisle half an hour later, with everyone staring at her with bald curiosity. At least Beryl Bliss wasn't in attendance—evidently this woman who had no shame about maligning Viveca lacked the gall to present herself in church following publication of her hideous article.

Not that there weren't plenty of tense moments for Viveca.

A number of parishioners openly snubbed her; those few who did greet her, with the exception of Hilda, were curt and cool. En route to the altar, Aubrey barely acknowledged her presence with a nod.

Then after the prayer of confession, when Aubrey routinely inquired whether anyone in the congregation had anything to add, Viveca bravely stood. "Indeed, I have something to say," she calmly began. Turning to face the congregation, she spoke with as much humility as possible. "I know many of you are aware of some very strange goings-on at my home, and for that I wish to beg the forgiveness and understanding of this church and community. Last week, I foolishly allowed a pagan ritual to be performed in my basement, misguidedly thinking it might help me with . . . well, some pest-control issues I've been having of late." Viveca paused as shocked murmurs broke out. "At any rate, I should have realized that any solutions I might seek can only be found at this church, with this congregation. Therefore I humbly beg your forgiveness, and ask for your help. And I assure you that the—er—fiasco of the other night shall never be repeated."

The next few seconds, while the members whispered among themselves and stared at Viveca, were the most excruciating of her entire life. Then Hilda rose to her feet and began to clap. "Bravo! Bravo!"

Hilda continued pounding out her accolade until everyone else was compelled to follow suit, in an unexpected standing ovation. Soon the sanctuary was wreathed with smiles. Even Aubrey looked pleased as he held up a hand to quiet the throng. "Well, well, I'm sure everyone here appreciates Miss Stanhope's humility and repentance, and that in true Christian fashion you will forgive her, turn the other cheek and extend to her any assistance she needs."

As more positive comments were uttered, Hilda called out, "Beginning with you, Father. As a token of your Christian charity and kindness, I would like to suggest that you bless

Viveca's home after our prayer meeting there on Wednesday night."

The congregation grew hushed, all staring at Aubrey. Although at first he stammered and appeared flustered, soon he nodded. "Well—well, of course. I should be delighted to bless Miss Stanhope's house."

Hilda glanced about the sanctuary, shooting pointed stares toward a number of parents of Viveca's piano students. "That way, none of us need ever again fear a visit to her home."

"Indeed," Aubrey concurred, hastily flipping open his hymnal. "Well, shall we all now turn to 'Amazing Grace'?"

Viveca could have hugged Hilda. She was hardly out of the woods, but with the matriarch's help, she had made great strides toward repairing her tattered reputation.

That night, Viveca found herself desperately missing Max, tossing and turning, longing for his soothing arms to hold her, his heated lips to set her senses on fire. She couldn't wait for him to return from Atlanta. Oh, she knew she shouldn't count on his strength, but she was doing it anyway. More and more, she couldn't doubt she was losing her heart to him— and it was both scary and awe-inspiring.

Finally she succumbed to slumber and became immersed in a heated, erotic dream of the two of them making love, right here on her bed. But even as Max smiled down into her eyes and joined their trembling bodies as one, an angry, hissing sound intruded on her dream.

Viveca awoke with a start to see a mysterious woman cloaked in black, hovering over her bed with her knife blade raised. Oh, God, who was this? The enraged wraith of Lorelei? Or some other assassin, real or otherwise?

Stark terror clutched Viveca's throat. But just as she cringed at the harrowing thought of certain death, another black-clad figure leapt into view and charged the first with a howl of rage. The two fought and flailed, screeching like banshees, crashing through the French doors and out onto the veranda. As Viveca stumbled out of bed and watched in horror, the two threw punches at one another, then became locked in an ugly death clench, thrashing and shoving, then finally tumbling over the balustrade together like doppelgangers. Viveca rushed forward, staring down at the lawn in dread, only to watch the two scramble off into the night, both limping.

"Miss Viveca, what in God's name is going on here?"

Viveca turned to see Emmett in his long nightshirt approaching her with a lit candle. "I have no idea," she managed breathlessly.

He hurried to her side. "Are you all right?"

Tremulously she nodded. "I awakened to see a woman with a knife hovering over my bed—"

"Sweet Jesus! Was it that witch, Winnie?"

"I really don't know. Then another figure sprang into view, the two fought each other and fell over the veranda railing."

Emmett peered over the railing at the ground. "No sign of them now."

"I know. They ran off."

"Well, thank the sweet Lord they didn't kill you. Miss Viveca, you be all right while I go upstairs?"

"You mean to Winnie's room?"

"Yes 'um."

"Just be careful."

He left, returning within a minute or two, a dark scowl creasing his brow. "She not there. Which mean she's the one who attack you."

"Emmett, we can't know that—"

"Then where she be?"

Viveca sighed. "We'll speak to her in the morning."

"The morning? I go get the sheriff right now."

She touched his arm. "No, Emmett, we mustn't jump to conclusions this way. Besides, my reputation here is already so precarious. Heaven forbid I report any monsters lurking in the night."

"Miss Viveca, I think you being a fool. It better you be ruined than you be dead."

"Look, we'll decide this in the morning."

He set his jaw adamantly. "Then I stay right here, in your room."

"Very well. You can sleep on the daybed."

"No'um. That wouldn't be seemly. I sleep on the chair."

She waved a hand. "Don't be ridiculous. I've known you all my life and trust you completely. You need your rest just like me."

In the end, Emmett capitulated. He locked the doors while Viveca laid out a pillow and afghan for him on the daybed. Afterward as she lay in the darkness, sleep did not come easily to her. But the sounds of his snores were a comfort.

Who had attacked her in the night? Had the presence been otherworldly or human? And who was that figure who'd tried to rescue her?

Thank God Max wasn't here. Though she continued to long for his comfort, she knew that if he discovered what had happened here tonight, he'd insist she move in with him. Or he'd move in with her, society be damned.

As much as she cared for him, she wasn't ready for that drastic step.

The next morning when Winnie came limping in the back door to the kitchen, both Viveca and Emmett awaited her.

Emmett wasted no time, angrily surging to his feet. "Winnie, did you attack Miss Viveca last night?"

She appeared appalled, quickly crossing herself. "No. By the saints, no."

"Then why are you lame?" Viveca demanded.

"I—er—I stub my toe on a rock outside."

"Don't give me that inane excuse," Viveca scolded, also rising. "You were in my room last night, weren't you?"

"Mistress," she pleaded, "I didn't try to hurt you."

"Then were you the one who fought off my assailant?"

Winnie didn't answer directly, avoiding Viveca's accusatory

stare. "Mistress, please don't send me away. I got nowhere to go."

"Then tell us the truth!"

"I not try to hurt you," she repeated miserably.

"Then who did?"

The housekeeper shuddered. "Mayhap de duppies?"

"Nonsense. I haven't even seen any duppies—well, hardly any—since the exorcism. If you can't tell us the truth, then just leave us."

"Mistress, please, I—"

"I know. You didn't try to hurt me."

Viveca watched an exquisite struggle cross Winnie's face, then she dashed from the room.

Emmett glowered. "She hidin' somethin'."

"I know."

"I go send her packing."

She grasped his arm. "No, Emmett."

"But why? She the one, missy. She limping from the fall."

"Emmett, don't ask me why, but I don't think she tried to hurt me. If anything, I think Winnie's the one who tried to defend me last night."

"Then why won't she tell us who done it?"

"I don't know, but maybe she's protecting someone."

"The one with the knife?"

"Yes." Viveca sighed. "If she even knows."

Chapter Thirty-two

The blessing of Viveca's house was held on Wednesday evening following prayer meeting. Wearing a black robe, Aubrey led the attendees from room to room on a voyage of exorcism. At each port of call he sprinkled holy water with an aspergillum, while Hilda followed him with a bowl of consecrated water, Viveca with a candle, and Judge Endicott bearing a smelly bucket of incense. In each room Aubrey repeated the same litany: "The Lord sayeth, 'Get thee behind me, Satan,' thou art an offense unto me,'" followed by "I bless this house in the name of the Father, the Son, and the Holy Spirit. Banish all evil from its walls, and keep its inhabitants from all sin. In Christ's name, amen."

At each juncture, his entourage echoed "Amen!" and solemnly crossed themselves. Then as the tour finally concluded in the downstairs hallway, Aubrey turned and asked Viveca to kneel. She did so at once, the others coming to heel behind her while Aubrey delivered a scathing sermonette filled with brimstone.

"Viveca Stanhope, I supplicate you in the word of the Scriptures: 'Turn ye now from your evil ways and from your evil doings. . . . Resist the devil and he will flee from you. . . . Be sober, be vigilant; because your adversary the devil, as a roaring lion, walketh about seeking whom he may devour.' In God's name, hear my plea. Amen."

Mouthing an awed amen with the others, Viveca was then distracted as Aubrey sprinkled her with holy water, causing her candle to flicker but not die.

"Viveca Stanhope, do you renounce all sin?" he demanded.

"I do," she murmured.

"Do you humbly repent of your transgressions and beg for the Almighty's forgiveness?"

"I do."

Placing a hand on her head, he said, "We humbly entreat the Almighty to forgive you your sins, to shield you from all temptation, and to sanctify and cleanse this home. Amen."

"Amen," Viveca repeated.

Aubrey nodded to all those gathered and offered a hand to Viveca. "This concludes the ritual. Shall we have our refreshments?"

Viveca reflected that it seemed almost ludicrous to follow an exorcism with cookies and punch, but she might have expected such banality from Aubrey. As the others began chatting awkwardly, she thanked him, then rushed off to the kitchen to assist Winnie.

The attendees made quick work of blueberry wine and Scotch shortbread, then left—mostly shooed away by Hilda. Soon only Hilda, Viveca and Aubrey remained near the front door. Appearing smug as a well-fed cat, Hilda remarked, "Well, Aubrey, I must say you did a commendable job with the blessing. I was genuinely touched."

"Why, thank you, Hilda."

"Indeed, I'm certain Viveca's resident demons are quaking in their boots at your stirring oratory." Barely able to control her glee, Hilda winked at Viveca. "Now I'm sure you'd like a bit of time to—er—*personally* counsel her."

Glancing from her to Viveca, Aubrey blushed and stammered, "Well, I—er—"

"I'm sure that won't be necessary," Viveca said firmly.

But with a cheery "Good night, dears!" Hilda was already heading out the door, and Viveca could only grind her teeth.

Once Hilda departed, Viveca and Aubrey stared at one another for an awkward moment. Then she shook her head and offered him a strained smile. "Aubrey, I do thank you for the blessing, but you don't have to remain here as my captive audience—"

But he stepped closer and earnestly intervened. "Please, dear, you mustn't think I'm here under duress of any kind. The truth is, I—I'm glad to be here, and I think Hilda is right. Couldn't we talk for a moment?"

"About what?" she inquired coolly.

"About—er, our relationship." The words came out tortured.

"Forgive me, Aubrey, but I thought we didn't have one."

"Perhaps I was hasty," he offered lamely.

"Were you?"

He gestured toward the archway. "Please, sit with me in the parlor for a moment."

"Very well."

Once they were settled far apart on the settee, he cleared his throat and began. "My dear, when I saw the newspaper article, I didn't know what to believe—"

"Obviously," she cut in with some bitterness. "But why couldn't you have believed in *me*? Why couldn't you have given the matter more consideration? You could have asked me about it with an open mind, rather than—"

He nodded miserably, his pale eyes reflecting his guilt and anguish. "I know. Prejudging you. Perhaps you made a mistake, but I made a greater one in condemning you. Hilda has been scolding me about this all week. I was wrong, Viveca."

Proudly she lifted her chin. "I must say that's refreshing to hear."

Leaning toward her, he added, "Also, to be frank, I think I was offended because you didn't come to me first with your problems."

"Aubrey, you know I tried—"

"Yes, you did try. But when the news first broke in the newspaper—I suppose I was just too proud to see it."

"Well, I do appreciate your honesty, and humility."

Abruptly he slid closer and grasped her hand. "And I so appreciate yours. The truth is, Viveca, I've grown quite fond of you, and have missed you over the past days. However misguided you may have been in letting yourself become enticed by this kind of sorcery, what I saw on Sunday, and tonight, were acts of supplication—I must say, truly inspired ones."

"Thank you," she rejoined with dignity. "Though we really must thank Hilda for organizing this."

He smiled. "Indeed, she's been quite a champion for you. A tigress, even. And if she thinks so highly of you, who am I to disagree?"

Viveca almost winced aloud at his tepid endorsement, hardly a passionate outpouring of support, but rather new evidence of just how shallow his sense of "devotion" was. Still, she realized she couldn't afford to decline the olive branch he was extending, not entirely. Of course she didn't want to marry him, or to resume their courtship on any level, certainly not given her relationship with Max. But neither could she just thumb her nose at him and hope to regain her place in the community.

"Thank you, Aubrey," she pronounced smoothly. "I'm pleased to know that we can be friends after all."

He blanched. "Actually, my dear, I was hoping for more than just your friendship . . ."

She patted his hand. "Well, under the circumstances, we'll need to give that some time, won't we?"

Though he appeared disappointed, he acquiesced like a gentleman. "Yes, I suppose so. Just let me know when you're ready."

Never, she almost blurted aloud. Instead she asked pleasantly, "May I walk you to the door?"

"Yes, thank you." He stood and offered her his hand. " 'Tis such a lovely night. Won't you step outside with me?"

"Very well."

Outside, they stood in the wan light filtering out through the oval glass door panel. Glancing over Aubrey's head, Viveca thought she spotted a cigar glowing somewhere in the darkness between her and Max's house. Mercy, was he back from Atlanta, and watching her? A potent thrill swept her— Lord, she'd missed him so much!

Aubrey took her hand and spoke with exaggerated gallantry. "My dear, I so appreciate this second chance you've given me, and I assure you I shall not squander it."

Before she could respond, he leaned over and briefly kissed her on the lips. Then he left, whistling "Onward Christian Soldiers."

Her stomach thudding, Viveca glanced toward Max's house. The glow of the cheroot was gone now. She'd best get inside or she'd have the devil to pay.

The devil awaited her inside her parlor.

Viveca gasped at the sight of Max standing across from her, body tense, fire gleaming in his eyes. Her heart tripped with excitement.

"Max! How did you get in here—and so quickly?"

"Didn't you miss me, my darling?"

"Well, yes, but—"

"From your behavior, I'd say otherwise." He advanced angrily. "What was Aubrey doing here?"

"Attending prayer meeting with our group, and blessing this house."

"Blessing the house? But I thought you'd already hosted an exorcism."

"Yes, but the voodoo—I mean, the Obeah, whatever it was—wasn't fully effective."

"What do you mean?"

She was silent.

"Viveca?"

"I mean I sometimes still see Alex—"

"What?"

"Not in the bathtub, of course," she hastily added, "but hovering about like some sort of vapor. He's weaker now, far more nebulous—"

"Well, isn't that just splendid?" Max mocked.

"My point is, his hanging around seems to be proof that the—er—first ritual didn't completely work, which was why we needed the second."

He laughed bitterly. "Of course it had nothing to do with your trying to reestablish yourself in Aubrey's good graces. I'd say his exorcism worked quite well—on the two of you."

"I beg your pardon?"

His eyes blazed with outrage and jealousy. "Don't be coy, Viveca. He stayed after the others left, and I saw you kiss him good night."

"I didn't kiss him. He kissed me."

"Same difference."

"No, it's not. Tonight Aubrey apologized for having judged me so harshly. He . . . well, he wants to resume our courtship—"

"The son of a bitch!" Angrily Max kicked a footstool.

She grabbed his hand. "Stop it, Max. I've already informed Aubrey we can be only friends."

He pulled his hand free. "Hah! As if that will last."

Now Viveca was really becoming exasperated. "Why wouldn't it last, Max? Because I'm some helpless, fawning female, a slave to the whims of the male sex?"

"No, because you see Aubrey as a means to an end—a way to get the social esteem you crave."

"I can get that without marrying him."

"Then why didn't you just tell him to go to hell?"

Viveca made a sound of outrage, and took a long moment to regain her frayed patience. "Because I can't just snub him, Max. He's a part—an important part—of this community."

"So, for all your fine posturing, you really do care more about your place in the social register than you care about our relationship."

She waved a hand. "Damn it, Max, if we are to have a relationship, why can't I have both? Must we both be pariahs? Must I thumb my nose at polite society, as you do?"

Max paced for a long moment, muttering under his breath. At last he paused to hurl her a dark glance. "Well, you must at least stop kissing him."

Now Viveca laughed, for Max was almost comical in his outrage. "I didn't kiss him."

"Then kiss me."

Quickly he closed the distance between them, seized her in his arms and kissed her ardently, thoroughly. Viveca moaned and threw her arms around his neck. Yes, he was a maddening scamp, but she hadn't the will or the heart to fight him, she had missed him so much. It felt so wonderful to be in his arms again, drinking of his taste and scent.

He murmured in her ear. "I missed you like hell."

"Me, too. Um—how was Atlanta?"

"Fine. Now back to the subject at hand."

"Which is?"

He pulled back and grinned at her. "Your place or mine, darling?"

"Max!" Viveca was as scandalized as she was titillated.

His hand boldly kneaded her bottom, arching her toward his burgeoning hardness until she winced with desire. "Don't think for a moment you can assuage my jealousy with words alone. It's going to happen, Viveca, and we both know it. So make your choice."

"Well, we can't do it—I mean, not here," she pleaded. "Winnie will slit your throat."

He chuckled. "That would certainly nip this delightful relationship in the bud. Then we're off to my abode. Why not, as we still have Lorelei to exorcise, don't we?"

Viveca tensed. "She's back?"

Lecherously he wiggled his eyebrows. "No, but one never knows. You're not going to risk letting her have me, are you?"

"I—er—"

Before Viveca could frame a response, Max caught her hand and pulled her out of the room. Laughing, they ran together through the silvery, dew-drenched night. Once they were safely inside Max's house, his room, he lit a candle and rakishly grinned at her. "Take off your clothes. I want to watch."

But Viveca tossed her head. "No, I think I should be in charge this time."

"What?" He seemed half astonished, half delighted.

Proudly she lifted her chin. "Recently you told me you would try to become a man worthy of my trust. Well, Max, I want a partner, not a master. You've taken the reins so far concerning the—er—carnal aspect of our relationship. Now I want my turn."

He laughed. "You want a partner—but you want to be in charge?"

She flashed him a perverse smile. "Yes, Max, it's called shared responsibility."

"Shared pleasure?" he suggested wickedly.

She stepped forward, deliberately tickling his chin with her fingertip. "You intruded in my bathroom last time and made all the decisions, all the moves. Tonight I want to draw up the rules."

"How fascinating." He bowed. "Viveca, I'm shocked at you, but quite pleasantly so. Very well, my lady, I surrender. I'm yours." Solemnly he handed her his candle.

She stared at it eagerly. "You know, one of the times when I spied on you, I thought I saw Lorelei torturing you with hot wax. Did she really do it?"

He raised an eyebrow. "Yes, my darling voyeur, she dripped hot wax on me—at least in my nightmares. Is that what you want tonight—to see me suffer?"

She reached out and toyed with a button at his shirt. "I need to know I excite you more than she does."

"Oh, love, can you ever doubt that?" He leaned over and tenderly kissed her. "So, what is my lady's pleasure? What will you need to set the scene and master me? Scarves to tie me to the bed? Perhaps a whip to keep me in line, to secure my utter obedience and capitulation?"

Viveca laughed exultantly. "You know, what more thrilling thought than making *you* obey? Ummm, I think scarves sound very nice. And I think we should have some brandy, too."

"My heavens, quite a prim little sadist you are. However will I endure it?"

While she grinned and set down the candle, Max fetched brandy and snifters, putting the tray on the bedside table. Then he opened a dresser drawer and extracted two black scarflike silk cravats. Handing them to her with a naughty wink, he turned to another drawer, pulled out an antique dagger with a carved silver handle and carefully placed it in her hand.

"What's this for?" she asked, shocked but intrigued.

"For whenever you want to release me."

"Release you! Now, there's a decadent prospect. But for now, sir, I just want to release you from your clothing."

As he watched in fascination, Viveca used the tip of the dagger to cut buttons loose from his shirt; he whistled as she sent them popping to the floor. Then, insinuating the dagger blade between the waistband of his trousers and his flesh, she made several careful, strategic cuts.

He scowled. "Woman you're ripping my clothing to shreds."

"Ripping your clothes off—there's another sinful prospect." Setting down the knife, she began to tear at his clothes with her hands, laughing as she went. Afterward she ordered him to remove his boots.

"Viveca, I'm shocked at you. I've unleashed a monster," he declared a moment later, standing before her in just his drawers, with a hard bulge revealing his advanced state of excitement.

She licked her lips at the sight of him. "You have, indeed. Now to reveal all the delights you're hiding there." She retrieved her knife and cut the tie to his undergarment; as it fell off him, she feasted her eyes on his magnificent erection, the beautifully burnished planes and angles of his body. She reached out and stroked his hardness.

His eyes blazed in the candlelight. "Woman, if you don't do something soon—"

"Get on the bed," she ordered.

Chuckling, he did her bidding. She deposited the knife and scarves on the end table. Then as he lay back, watching her like a glorious reclining animal, she slowly removed all her clothing, keeping her gaze fixed on him all the while. The desire she glimpsed in his fierce eyes made her tremble with her own agonizing need.

When she climbed on the bed with him, his hand reached for her breast. But she grinned hoydenishly, slapped his hand away, then caught his wrists and pinned him down. Her bright red hair trailed teasingly over his chest, and her expression was petulant as she stared at him. "Now I want to tie you down."

"Perhaps that would be best," he growled. "Or I promise you, my lady, you won't be in charge for long."

Grabbing the cravats, Viveca straddled him. He groaned, staring brazenly at her most secret places, trying to thrust inside her. But she squirmed and dodged him, taunting him instead with the folds of her womanhood as she secured his wrists to the headboard.

"My God, Viveca, you're killing me."

"Hmmm . . . what shall I do next?" she murmured, staring impishly into his eyes.

"Hot candle wax torture?" he managed.

"Do you like it?"

"Hell, no!"

She chuckled. "Then perhaps I've a more appropriate torment in mind." She took the brandy snifter and placed it at his lips. "Drink."

Though he strained his neck to take a sip, he also grimaced. "Viveca, it will spill."

"That's the idea." She helped him take a sip and watched the excess brandy dribble down his chin, trickling along his strong neck to his muscled chest. Purring wickedly, she leaned over and licked the brew from his lips, his chin, then ran her tongue in tormenting circles on his furred chest, paying particular care to his taut nipples. He began to groan and pull at his ties. Chuckling, she gripped his penis with her hand, squeezing gently—and a low, feral roar escaped him as he arched his back.

"You know, it's really fun being in charge of you," she murmured. Taking a sip of brandy herself, she leaned over and dribbled the liquid all over his belly and loins.

"Viveca, my God—" he begged, yanking violently at the scarves.

But she was merciless, licking his belly, rubbing the drops into his erection, then flicking away the excess with her tongue.

"Viveca, *please*, release me," he pleaded, his words agonized.

"Release you? In what manner, my love?" She gazed up at him triumphantly, then latched her mouth onto his manhood. He uttered a strangled cry and went hard and warm as steel against her searching tongue. She continued to flick her tongue over him at her leisure while he groaned, cursed and struggled against his ties.

At last, just short of bringing him to climax, she glanced up at him and smiled. Never had she felt so gloriously empowered—and so intensely aroused.

"Are—you—done?" he panted, eyes glazed with tortured desire.

In answer, she straightened, retrieved the knife and cut him free.

In a matter of seconds, the dagger was yanked from her hand and she was tumbled beneath him, her legs pulled high and tight around his waist as he thrust into her with all the power in his being. Viveca sobbed, panting at the sweetness and the soul-deep, shattering ecstasy. Oh, she was falling for him, losing her heart, lost now.

The climax Max gave her was so exquisite, it left her drained, body and soul. When he spiraled into release soon after, she pulled his body down to hers and kissed him thoroughly, achingly.

Afterward he gripped her hands in his, and she could hear him breathing harshly at her ear. But the words he uttered were heartfelt. "Darling, you told me once you were afraid I'd devour your will. Perhaps at times I do. But in the end, I give you mine."

Those were the sweetest words Viveca had ever heard from him. Eyes burning with unshed tears, she clutched Max close to her heart.

Chapter Thirty-three

Something had definitely changed since the second exorcism.

Viveca no longer saw Murfa Divine, the Quaking Lady, the Street Sweeper or the Oleander Man. No specters leapt out from her armoire to attack her during the night.

Alex Fremont was still there, but he was an even more weakened presence. Sometimes she barely glimpsed his cloudy image as she walked up the stairs or down a hallway. Always he reproached her with his sad eyes, then vanished. He lacked the potent threat he'd exhibited before. He no longer haunted her bath, or her sleep.

Winnie had truly become Viveca's champion. She hovered over her mistress night and day. Frequently Viveca found salt on the window ledges, broken bottles or alligators' teeth hanging next to the doors outside—all powerful talismans to keep away evil spirits, she presumed. Viveca no longer questioned why or how things had changed; she was too grateful that the climate of terror had subsided.

Just as the atmosphere in the house improved, so her life in the outside world got better. Her students returned, and invitations to social events trickled in. She went calling on Miss

Lilac, taking her soup and fresh bread, but was dismayed when she didn't see Elvira Withersmith around the square. Perhaps, knowing that the Cunningham home would soon change hands, she had already departed. Although Viveca was disappointed that Elvira hadn't said good-bye, she could well understand the woman's pride; after all, she was all too proud herself.

She saw Aubrey at church and at Bible study, but tactfully declined his every offer of an escort. She saw Maxwell every night as the two continued their torrid affair. Sometimes they would take moonlit rides, stopping the buggy down by the Savannah River and talking for hours beneath the Spanish moss. They had their entire lives to catch up on and chatted endlessly—about their childhoods, their educations, their parents, their friends. She was amazed by their rapport. Weeks earlier, she'd assumed they had nothing in common; now they never seemed to stop talking to each other.

Max also began to stop by during the day, to bring her a volume of Walt Whitman's earthy poems or a sheaf of roses, to compliment her on a piano tune he'd heard from afar and beg for an encore.

One afternoon he was there, reclining on her couch, listening with an expression of sublime pleasure as she played Liszt's "Liebesträume," when Winnie ushered in Hilda Patertavish. "My stars," the matron greeted, eyeing the scene in rapt curiosity. "Don't you two look cozy. Have I interrupted a little tryst?"

As Maxwell stood, grinning, Viveca awkwardly popped to her feet. "Er—why, hello, Hilda. Of course you haven't interrupted anything. You're always welcome here."

"Tsk, tsk, my dear." Hilda was literally beaming. "Do sit down, Maxwell, darling, and continue ogling Viveca. I shan't stay for long."

Lips twitching, he nodded, but waited until both ladies had seated themselves before he followed suit.

"Well, well," Hilda began brightly. "As it happens, I just came from the Fitzpatricks' house. Cleo and Charles are hosting a reception for some old friend from out of town. At the DeSoto Hotel, no less. Unfortunately, I can't be there as Myron and I have a previous engagement on Tybee Island. However, I was helping Cleo make out her guest list—and of course both of you are to be invited. Indeed, Viveca, I've already suggested to Aubrey that he might escort you—"

Maxwell made a sound of strangled rage.

Hilda raised a hand to her breast in feigned shock. "Unless, of course, Maxwell here has other ideas."

"Maxwell, indeed, has other ideas," he snapped back. Staring straight at Viveca, he added, "I should be proud to escort Viveca."

"Would you, now?" Hilda appeared amazed and delighted. "What an intriguing turn of events. And is that your desire as well, my dear?"

Absorbing the heat in Max's gaze, Viveca nervously nodded. "Yes—er—that will be fine."

Hilda clapped her hands. "My, my—will wonders never cease? So the two of you are an item now?"

"We are indeed," Max replied testily.

Hilda stared open-mouthed at Viveca, then back at Max. "Tell me, Maxwell—does Aubrey know?"

Max glowered at her. "Hilda, aren't we keeping you from something?"

"Actually, you aren't, my dear. So why don't you shoo along now, Maxwell?"

"What?" he cried.

Hilda winked at Viveca. "Leave, darling, so I may grill Viveca about this most engaging development."

"Are you out of your mind? You want me to leave so you ladies can gossip about me?"

Hilda bobbed her feathers. "Absolutely."

"Women!" he cried.

"Max, please," Viveca pleaded, fearing a scene.

He stood, clapped on his hat and scowled at Viveca. "I'll be back."

"Oh, I'm sure you will be, darling," Hilda said with a tinkle of laughter. Watching him stride out, she turned back to Viveca with an awestruck expression. "My dear, my dear, I simply cannot believe it."

"Believe what?"

Hilda waved a hand. "Oh, don't be coy, Viveca. I can't believe the two of you have been hiding this little *affaire d'amour* from me. But most of all, I can't believe the love bug has finally bitten Maxwell Beecher."

"Love bug?" Viveca felt a surge of hope course through her. "Well, I'm not sure about that."

"I am. I've known Max all his life, and have never seen him display such passion over a woman. Not to mention protectiveness. Why, he was seething with jealousy that I wanted to interrogate you."

"I'm sure you exaggerate."

Looking utterly serious, Hilda crossed to Viveca's side, caught her hand and pulled her over to the settee. "Viveca, why haven't you told me about this most titillating turn of events? Why, Max is so much better a catch than Aubrey."

"He is? But I thought you were set on my marrying Aubrey."

Hilda sighed tragically. "Of course, I was prepared to sponsor a match between you and the good father, but given Aubrey's less than loyal conduct of late, his playing the weak sister instead of supporting you . . . well, under the circumstances, we must be practical. And I find Mr. Beecher to be an even more appealing candidate."

"Max? You do?"

"Why, he's rich as Midas—certainly richer than Aubrey. You'll never lack for any luxury, or have to hire yourself out teaching piano lessons." Hilda's eyes danced with mischief. "And from the fervency he just exhibited, I expect Max to sweep you off to the altar at any moment."

Viveca gulped. "You can't be serious."

"My dear, I've been around long enough to know what a bull looks like when he's about to choose his mate. Oh, he'll do right by you publicly, my dear. After all, you're a lady, so outwardly he must play the gentleman. Your place in society will be secure. Max'll never desert you at a whiff of controversy, like the pantywaist Aubrey did. Still, his soul will remain the devil's playground. He'll have his little peccadilloes, albeit discreetly, just like my George did."

Viveca clenched her jaw. "Then I feel sorry for the man."

"You do? Why ever for?"

"Because he wouldn't have long to live," Viveca said with murder in her voice.

Hilda howled with laughter. "You know, darling, you may just reform him, after all." She squeezed Viveca's hand. "Just promise me I may break the news of your engagement."

"Hilda, we aren't engaged!"

"Oh, you will be. I'll have a party at my home, and will make the announcement personally. I'll sponsor your wedding, of course, since you've no one else. And I shall serve as godmother to your children."

Viveca's jaw dropped open.

Hilda clapped her hands and hooted. "Oh, can't you just see Aubrey being compelled to eat bile as all of us stand before him and *he* is required to baptize darling little Maxwell Beecher the Third?"

At last Viveca smiled. ' "You know, that *is* a rather nice image."

Hilda chortled. "And after the poor man was compelled to expel the demons from your home."

"Well . . ." Viveca hedged with a grimace.

Hilda's eyebrows shot up. "You can't mean you're still—"

"I fear the ghost of my home's original owner still seems to be hovering about," Viveca confirmed with a discreet cough.

"Well, what a pity! And I was going to ask our good rector to exorcise the German parson from my sewing room."

Viveca playfully elbowed her friend. "You know, I've a feeling you don't really want to get rid of *him*."

Both women fell into gales of laughter.

* * *

"Don't you dare scold me for asking to escort you to the soiree."

Viveca was stunned when, only moments after Hilda left, Max stormed back into her parlor, features grimly set. Hastily she rose to face him. "Max, I didn't scold you. Indeed, I said yes—er, didn't I?"

"It was the most tepid acceptance I've ever received."

She couldn't resist needling him. "Used to ecstatic debutantes falling at your feet, eh?"

"Hah! You certainly didn't."

"But Hilda was here, and I just wasn't prepared—"

"Not prepared for what?" he cut in aggressively. "For society to know about our relationship? I must say you seem ready for just about anything in my bed."

She blushed to the roots of her hair. "I mean, to make this—"

"What? Public? Legal?" His eyes glittered with outrage. "Would you prefer it to remain secretive, sleazy?"

"It's not sleazy!"

"Finally we agree."

She eyed his stormy features in disbelief, then laughed.

"What?" he demanded.

She balled her hands on her hips. "If I didn't know better, I'd swear you were turning into a prig, Maxwell Beecher."

"A prig? Perish the thought!" Then he grinned. "Although I must admit that a certain wanton vixen, who tortured and ravished me recently, may have inspired in me a straitlaced streak."

"My goodness, a wanton vixen, eh? Who could that have been?"

Features rife with repressed laughter, he strode over and pulled her close. "Remember when, soon after we met, you called us saint and sinner. Well, how would you characterize us now?"

She wrinkled her nose at him. "I'd say we're both sinners and likely damned to hell."

"Amen." He drew back and regarded her solemnly.

"Viveca, all levity aside, you really do need to acknowledge what we have. You know the world is going to find out, whether you like it or not."

She sighed. "You're right, especially with Hilda already knowing—"

"And with me escorting you to the reception on Saturday night."

"Precisely."

He scowled at her. "So you're not going to try to back out of it?"

"Of course not."

"Good. But what about Aubrey?"

"What about him?"

"You need to tell him about our plans."

She mulled that over, then nodded. "You're right there, as well. I need to do so before Saturday night. Even though he treated me shabbily, I have no desire to embarrass him at the reception."

"He deserves it, but I applaud your high-mindedness nonetheless." He caressed her cheek. "My poor love. You know how it feels to be publicly humiliated, don't you?"

"Yes," she murmured, a little catch in her throat.

"Well, you're never going to have to feel that kind of devastation again. I promise you."

As he passionately kissed her, Viveca for once couldn't doubt him.

Viveca planned to break her news to Aubrey after prayer meeting on Wednesday night, and was actually relieved when he took her aside in the Thorps' dining room. Smiling at her earnestly, he said, "Viveca, I was wondering if I might escort you to the reception the Fitzpatricks are hosting on Saturday."

Viveca swallowed hard. "I'm sorry, Aubrey, but I've already accepted another invitation."

He paled. "From whom?"

"From your cousin."

"Maxwell?" Aubrey appeared shocked.

"He and I . . . well, being neighbors and all, we've chatted on occasion—"

"But I thought you detested the man."

She glanced away uneasily. "Not since I've gotten to know him better."

His brows shot up. "When did this happen?"

"Aubrey, he's my neighbor."

"As you've just stated twice now . . . although it sounds to me like Max is becoming a lot more than just your neighbor."

"Perhaps so," she replied proudly.

A stunned breath escaped him. "Then you must know Max is an irredeemable womanizer."

She stared him in the eye. "Aubrey, you of all people should know that no one is completely without sin—or beyond redemption."

Though he winced at her obvious reference to his earlier behavior, he forged on. "Viveca, Max is a faithless rascal, not the type to make any woman a proper—much less devoted— husband."

She gave a groan. "Heavenly days, Aubrey. Max and I are not getting married, only attending the party together."

"Which strikes me as playing with fire," he scolded. "Indeed, if you're approaching things in such a cavalier manner, I must question your own moral fortitude, Viveca."

Bitterly she shook her head. "So you will judge me again, Aubrey? And your cousin, as well?"

He appeared abashed. "No, I shan't judge you, Viveca. I won't risk losing your friendship again."

"Indeed, you shouldn't," she stated coldly and walked away.

On Saturday night, Viveca felt like a fairy-tale princess as she descended the staircase in her fabulous gold satin Worth gown, her hair upswept in curls and secured with a glittering tiara, pearls gleaming at her neck and earlobes.

Max stood below her, utterly splendid in his black tuxedo, his diamond studs and cufflinks gleaming, his hair impeccably groomed. His gaze was riveted to her as she approached and her heart tripped with excitement at the very thought that he was hers.

Handing her a luscious orchid corsage, he bowed before her, grasped her gloved hand and kissed its back. "My dear, you are a vision. I can't wait to get you out of that frock."

She blushed. "Maxwell, please, we're going out in proper society—"

He winked. "And I shall be having *improper* thoughts about you all evening long." Leaning close, he tenderly kissed her.

She smiled breathlessly and sniffed the fragrant orchids. "These are wonderful."

"Thank you, my darling. May I?"

"Of course."

She thrilled to his touch as he pinned the corsage to her bodice. She felt as if she were floating on air as he escorted her out to his stylish brougham, driven by a hatted coachman. In every way Max was playing the gentleman par excellence, and her heart welled with pride as they glided through the gaslit streets. When he squeezed her hand and smiled at her, her happiness was complete.

But was Aubrey right? Was she on the verge of losing her heart to a cad who could never be faithful to her? She refused to allow such doubts to spoil her wonderful evening ahead with Max. For now, she only wanted to live for this exquisite moment, for *him*.

Soon they joined a line of gleaming carriages at the facade of the Desoto Hotel, which glittered with a thousand lights illuminating its high turrets, chimneys, quaint dormers and dramatic Romanesque arches. Heads were turned as Maxwell escorted Viveca inside the sumptuous lobby. They followed the crowd into a grand salon filled with glittering chandeliers, where graceful couples danced or chatted amid the hum of Johann Strauss and the clink of punch cups. Heads turned at the sight of Viveca and Max together. She caught sight of Aubrey, standing near the string quartet and chatting with the Endicotts; when he smiled awkwardly and waved, she acknowledged him with a stiff nod.

Before Max could take note of Viveca's brief distraction, Cleo Fitzpatrick rushed up to greet them, looking stunning in a ruby satin gown. If she was shocked to see Viveca and Max there as a couple, she gave no hint. "Viveca, Maxwell—how wonderful to see you both. Come along now, I must introduce you to our guest of honor."

With their hostess leading them, Max and Viveca wended their way through the crowd toward a buffet table on the far side of the vast hall. "Ah, there he is now with Charles," Cleo murmured as their path finally cleared.

Viveca glanced toward the punch bowl and stopped in her tracks. Oh, heavenly days! Next to Charles Fitzpatrick stood none other than Erskine Pendergraf!

Chapter Thirty-four

For a moment, Viveca was certain her eyes must be deceiving her. That couldn't be Erskine standing across from her—it just couldn't be!

But it was. And that was none other than Beryl Bliss clutching his arm. Viveca's stomach thudded as Erskine turned his dark head and focused his predatory, though amused, gaze in her direction. He was certainly dressed for the occasion in his flawless black cutaway with pearl studs, his black hair slickly combed and gleaming with pomade. But, observing the rather sadistic smile pulling at his thin lips, she wondered how she could ever have thought this snake handsome. His thin, harsh features and bladelike nose could do justice to the devil himself; just the sight of him revolted her so, she feared she might become physically ill.

Why on earth was he here? And why was Beryl Bliss here with him? The possibilities that sprang to mind proved even more sickening.

She felt Max gripping her hand. "Darling, what's wrong?"

She turned to him helplessly. Even in her panicked state, she felt comforted by the tender concern in his voice, his eyes. Urgently she whispered, "It's Erskine Pendergraf, the man who—"

"Say no more, I'll take care of this," he cut in with restrained anger. Glancing in the same direction, he cursed. "Why, he's got that Bliss woman with him! Don't worry, darling, I'll get rid of them."

Fearing an altercation, Viveca grabbed his arm. "No, Max, please, let me—"

But her plea was cut short as Cleo, having lost them, doubled back wearing a puzzled expression. "Come along, you two. Don't you want to meet the honoree?"

Max glared at her. "First, Mrs. Fitzpatrick, kindly tell me what *that man* is doing here, along with Beryl Bliss."

Their hostess grew flustered, fluttering the red fan she held in one hand. "Well—er—the gentleman is Mr. Erskine Pendergraf, Charles's old friend from his California days. As for Miss Bliss—Viveca, I do apologize for her presence, but the creature just showed up with him."

"Miss Bliss has a habit of doing that," Viveca concurred ruefully. "Please, Cleo, you mustn't concern yourself."

Meanwhile, Viveca noted with a new surge of nausea, Charles, Erskine and Beryl had all started toward them. She could have slapped the cynical grin off Erskine's face—and clawed the smirk off Beryl's.

"Well, well, who have we here?" greeted Erskine, his sneer focused on Viveca.

Max started to advance, but Viveca grabbed his hand. Cleo awkwardly began introductions. "Miss Viveca Stanhope, may I introduce Mr. Erskine Pendergraf of San Francisco." Awkwardly she added, "I believe you know Miss Bliss—"

Before Viveca could frame a response, Max tersely interrupted. "Yes, and Miss Stanhope is also acquainted with Mr. Pendergraf from her San Francisco days. Quite regrettably so, I must add."

"Oh, is she?" Cleo stammered, obviously embarrassed. "Then—"

"Viveca, it's so good to see you, dear," Erskine drawled, ignoring Max's insult. "And looking so very ravishing, I must add. Please tell me you've room on your dance card for me tonight."

Before Viveca could frame a response, Max aggressively cut in. "Sir, tread lightly. I'll not hear you slighting Miss Stanhope."

"Slighting her?" Erskine inquired in feigned amazement. "By asking her to dance?"

Deliberately snubbing him, Max turned to Cleo. "If you'll excuse us, Mrs. Fitzpatrick . . ." and he summarily tugged Viveca away with him.

Miffed by his abruptness, Viveca glanced over her shoulder to see Erskine still grinning at her, while Beryl snickered at his side. "What do you think you're doing?" she demanded in a fierce whisper, trying to break free of Max's grip.

"Getting you away from that viper."

She whirled to face him. "How? By snubbing him, sneering innuendos and possibly creating a scene?"

Max's teeth were clenched, his eyes breathing fire. "Darling, I don't want that scoundrel within forty feet of you. It's only respect for your reputation that prevents me from throttling him on the spot. When I think of what he did to you . . ."

Though touched by his display of protectiveness, she admonished, "Max, stop it."

"Stop what?"

"Stop shielding me like I'm some sort of hothouse flower," she retorted. "The fact is, Erskine is here—along with that contemptible newspaperwoman—and I must find out why."

"Not by yourself, you're not."

She touched his arm. "Max, believe me, if I need your big guns, I'll call you in."

Though his eyes bore thunderclouds, a grudging smile pulled at his lips. "My big guns, eh? So you're trying to flatter me into getting your way?" As she would have spoken, he held up a hand. "Well, it won't work. Viveca, darling, I understand your feelings, but I refuse to allow that jackass to further insult or harass you. Let me speak to him first. I think I can pull out a trump card or two to send him on his way."

"No, Max, I must do this myself."

"Damn it, woman, I won't see you endangered—"

She gripped his arm. "Max, I'm not in danger, and I couldn't care less what that scamp says to me. I'll admit there was a time when Erskine frightened me, but that time is long gone. He's a coward, and the only way to deal with a coward is to face him down."

He gave a groan.

"It's important for *me*, Max," she went on passionately. "It's part of my proving myself as a person. Didn't you tell me that I'm much stronger than I think I am? Well, it's true. And it's high time for you to start trusting me, believing in my strength."

"Viveca, please, you can't—"

"I *mean* it, Max. There's no other way."

For a long moment he stood grinding his jaw, then acquiesced with a heavy sigh. "Very well. Speak with him on the terrace. But I'll be watching every minute."

"From a distance."

"Yes. And if that scoundrel tries anything to hurt you—"

"He won't. Just promise me you won't intervene unless it's absolutely—"

"I promise."

She squeezed his hand and walked away, feeling the heat of his gaze on her back as she crossed the room. When she approached Erskine, he stepped away from the others and greeted her with that same sardonic grin. "Well, Viveca, having second thoughts?"

She raised her chin. "I'll have a word with you, Erskine."

"Of course. How can I resist such an eloquent proposal?"

Even as he offered her his arm, she turned and stalked away. She could hear him following her, chuckling softly.

Outside on the terrace, she turned and faced him. Funny, she thought, how six months ago, being alone with him would have made her shiver. Now if she shuddered at all, it was with revulsion. He was a rat—a beady-eyed, surly-featured rat.

She got straight to the point. "What are you doing here, Erskine—and with that awful Bliss person?"

He whistled. "My, my, such a cool greeting. Haven't you missed me, Viveca?"

"I generally don't miss poisonous snakes."

"Oh, ouch." He shook his head. "This is a frigid reception, indeed, especially considering our history, and our long separation. Won't you greet me with a kiss?" He turned to sneer in Maxwell's direction; he was standing about five feet inside the French doors. "Especially with your escort hovering so near. We wouldn't want to disappoint the poor fellow, now would we?"

Ignoring his sarcasm, Viveca smoothly warned, "If you want to live through the next five minutes, Erskine, I'd suggest you not even touch me. I've witnessed Maxwell Beecher's fury before—as well as his prowess with a gun."

Erskine laughed. "Now, thereby hangs a fascinating tale, I'm sure. I should love to hear it, though I might remind you that I'm considered something of an expert myself with a dueling pistol—"

"I said, what are you doing here?" she interrupted harshly.

He was shaking his head. "My, my, you've changed, haven't you. No more naïve little girl, eh?"

She actually took pleasure in that query. "Yes, I've changed. I've become toughened, a survivor. Your betrayal made me stronger."

"Oh, I wince at that characterization."

"Truth hurts, doesn't it?"

He broke into an amazed smile. "So you've steeled yourself in armor, have you, my dear? I would think that would make you so much more fun to chase and conquer."

"You're delusional."

"Am I?"

"Tell me why you're here."

He chuckled. "Well, actually, Viveca, I've come to Savannah to see you."

"Me?" She was appalled. "Why, that's the most laughable insult I've ever heard. After the way you deceived me, ruined me, abandoned me—"

"Yes. I've come to regret all that, dear heart," he put in with mock humility.

She laughed bitterly. "You expect me to believe that, coming from a scalawag like you? Anyway, if you've had a change of heart, too bad. I've gone on with my life."

"So I've noticed." He reached out and touched the sleeve of her gown. "I've missed you, Viveca."

She recoiled. "What?"

With a dull sigh, he admitted, "Estelle died."

"She did?"

"Yes, in childbirth. She and the baby both."

Dismay swept Viveca. She might detest Erskine, but she took no pleasure at the prospect of his family suffering. "Erskine, I . . . I'm so sorry. For their sakes."

"Don't be. It wasn't my child."

With a cry of outrage, Viveca slapped him full across the face. While he gripped his cheek and glowered at her, she turned to see Max about to charge toward them, and violently shook her head. She was relieved when he slowly retreated.

"I see you haven't lost your spirit, my dear," Erskine snarled, rubbing his cheek.

"Get to the point, Erskine."

"Very well." Surprising her, he bowed. "Miss Stanhope, I have indeed been pining away for you during the unfortunate months of our separation. Accordingly, would you do me the honor of returning with me to San Francisco and becoming my wife?"

Viveca fell back a step, so shocked was she. "What? Your wife? You *are* insane!"

"Not in the least. With Estelle out of the picture, I'd actually enjoy having you, shall we say, at my mercy?" He smiled nastily and looked her over. "You were a rather passionate creature . . ." He inclined his head toward Max. "And, judging from the glower on your lover's face, I'd say your skills have likely only improved since our last assignation—and I'd relish having you back in my bed again."

Trembling with anger, Viveca almost slapped him again, but feared Max's response. However, she couldn't help but mock back, "Obviously, you enjoyed our little indiscretions a great deal more than I did."

He chuckled. "Viveca, you mustn't say such things to a man, especially one who knows you're lying. It tempts him to—er—prove you wrong."

"Go to hell."

"I take it that's a no?"

She smiled.

"Hmmm." Moving away, he began casually strolling about the veranda, admiring the potted plants, pausing to sniff a rose blossom here, to touch the curling leaf of a camellia there. Peering up at the moon, he mused, "Then won't it be a shame, darling, when word gets out to the community here that I'm the man you committed adultery with back in San Francisco? Should dry up all those piano lessons of yours, eh?"

Viveca gasped as reality fully hit her. "Now it's all making sense. I always wondered how Beryl Bliss got her background information on me. So you're the bastard who plotted with her! And that's why she's here with you tonight!"

He gave a shrug. "Miss Bliss is acquainted with a friend of mine at the *Courier*, and he put the two of us in touch."

"My God! So I'm right. You spoon-fed her the information that almost ruined me. You contemptible cad!"

He turned to her with a look of forbearance. "Now, Viveca, don't be hasty. Why would you want to settle in this backwater, anyway? You can have a good life with me back in San Francisco. Society will be willing to forgive you as my wife, especially considering my generosity in taking you back. As for Savannah . . . a lady with a past, a soiled dove trying to find her place among Georgia's hallowed nabobs..." He paused, clucking softly. "Doesn't sound promising to me, my dear."

Viveca was too furious to speak.

He stepped closer to her, eyes gleaming cagily. "What can you really have here, Viveca? Especially when your gentleman love finds out what we have shared?"

She tossed her curls. "He already knows—and he doesn't care."

"Then he must hold you in about as high esteem as I do."

Now Viveca did slap him again, hard. She turned with a gasp to see Maxwell storming toward them with bloodlust in his eyes.

Though he'd been scared to death for Viveca, Maxwell could barely contain his pride as he'd watched her stand up to the scoundrel who had used and betrayed her. In that moment he'd known as never before that he loved this woman. She was magnificent, so full of fire and righteous anger. Never would he allow any man to abuse her as this miscreant had!

He'd almost jumped out of his skin when he saw her slap the rogue. The man had insulted her terribly—he could tell from her expression. But he'd promised not to intervene, unless...

The second time she struck Erskine, he could abide no more. He tore outside and marched up to the couple, to see Erskine sneering like a snake. "Ah, my good sir. So has rescue arrived?"

Max was only human; he could only take so much. Muttering a blistering blasphemy, he struck Erskine across the jaw, knocking him to his heels. As the man lay moaning at his feet, he quickly turned to Viveca, who was staring at him in horror. "Viveca, go inside."

"Max, I—"

"I said, *go inside.*"

Waving a hand in frustration, she fled.

Meanwhile, Erskine had struggled to his feet and was dusting himself off. Rubbing a surely smarting chin, he glared at Max. "Well, Mr. Beecher, first Viveca assaults me, now you. And after all I've heard about Southern hospitality—"

"Shut up, you son of a bitch," Max snapped back. "And just to educate you a bit, here in the South we're known to become rather *testy* at the presence of vipers in our midst, especially those who have abused our ladies. So why don't you be kind enough to take your sorry presence straight to hell?"

Erskine whistled. "My heaven, Viveca just offered me much the same invitation. So let me respond to both of you. I should be happy to leave, but I shall be taking Viveca with me. I quite relish the prospect of bedding her again."

Max seized Erskine by the collar. "Over my dead body, you will."

"My, my, such gallantry," Erskine mocked. "Having heard from Beryl what a philanderer you are, I should think you'd be delighted to meet a man willing to relieve you of your obligations with Viveca."

Max shoved him away. "Then Beryl's as much of an idiot as you are."

Erskine clucked softly. "Such male outrage. And here I'm willing to wed the woman."

"You won't, but I shall," Max asserted.

"Really?" Erskine appeared incredulous. "So it seems we've reached an impasse, sir. Will you challenge me to a duel, then? Viveca was raving over your expertise with firearms—"

Max raised a fist. "Mention her name again, you slimy bastard, and I'm going to slam your teeth down your throat. You hurt the woman I love. For that you deserve to die. However—"

"Yes?" Erskine prompted.

Max broke into a sneering grin. "Rather than kill you, which I could happily do, I prefer discussing with you . . . shall we say, the wonders of the industrial revolution."

"What?" Erskine's flabbergasted expression was almost comical.

Max continued with deliberate relish. "Indeed, how rail-roads, trains, telegraphs, even the Pony Express, have so quickly connected this continent, making communication so very effortless compared with before."

Erskine's canny gaze narrowed. "Go on."

Maxwell took out a cheroot, slowly, deliberately lit it and blew smoke in Erskine's face. "You know, I recently attended to some business in Atlanta. While there, I met with a Pinkerton field agent."

"So what does that have to do with the price of cotton?"

"As convenience would have it, my contact in Atlanta is only a telegraph away from their offices in San Francisco."

Erskine was tensely silent.

"At my behest, a fine young detective there has thoroughly investigated your finances and background, sir. And he has submitted to me proof that you embezzled almost seventy-five thousand dollars from the business you partnered with Viveca's father."

Erskine blanched. "That's a lie."

"You're the liar, sir. We'll see what the state attorney general thinks. From what my operatives tell me, you've fallen out of favor with the majority party in California these days, eh?"

Now Erskine was clearly distressed, blinking rapidly, his jaw clenched. "What do you want, sir?"

Max chuckled, deliciously savoring his victory. "I want you to leave town tonight—and take Nelly Bly with you."

"Nelly Bly?"

"Beryl Bliss."

Erskine made a sound of contempt. "You're joking. That pathetic ugly ducking?"

"Sir, I assure you, I'm quite serious. The two of you have been conspiring together for some time now against Miss Stanhope, so I figure you must make good bedfellows."

Erskine shook his head in disbelief. "How can you know we've been conspiring?"

"I have my sources."

"Even if what you claim is true, why ever would I abandon

Viveca and leave town with that—creature? She has the jaw structure of a horse!"

Max grinned and said wickedly, "Ah, but there are benefits to a generous mouth, eh?"

Erskine gasped. "You want me to—"

"Seduce her, ruin her, strangle her, I don't care," Max continued with a flourish of his cheroot. "Just get rid of her. Oh, and before you and the darling Miss Bliss leave town, write Viveca a draft to cover her father's estate. With interest, let's call it an even eighty thousand dollars."

A vein popped out in Erskine's temple. "Eighty thousand dollars! Why, that's highway robbery—blackmail!"

"It's hardly highway robbery. But blackmail? Yes, of course it is."

"You could go to jail for that."

Max gave a shrug. "Maybe. But you surely would if I reveal everything I know to the California authorities."

"You son of a bitch!"

"I've been called worse."

Erskine began to pace like a trapped tiger, muttering angrily to himself. At last he turned. "And if I do as you ask?"

"As long as you—and Miss Bliss—stay out of our lives, the proof of your thievery shall remain sealed in a safe deposit box at . . . let's say, a bank of my choosing."

"Why should I trust you?" Erskine demanded.

Max dropped his cheroot and snubbed it out beneath his shiny dress boot. "Sir, you remind me of a fox up a tree, seemingly oblivious to the fact that he's pinned down by three bird dogs. To wit, *you have no choice.* But think of this from my point of view. Why wouldn't I want you out of Viveca's life—as quickly, cleanly and permanently as possible?"

After a long moment spent brooding, Erskine released a furious sigh. "Very well, you win, sir. For now."

He turned and angrily strode away. Maxwell hooted a laugh and hurried off to find Viveca.

* * *

Viveca stood by the punch bowl breathing hard, struggling to calm her frayed nerves after her wrenching encounter with Erskine. She couldn't believe he had showed up here tonight, out of the blue—with the despicable Beryl Bliss. She had seen Max and Erskine arguing outside—they'd seemed about to tear into each other. She'd known that Max would be furious if she intervened. Oh, where was Hilda when she needed her? Why did she have to choose this weekend to go to Tybee Island with her brother?

"Well, Miss Stanhope."

Viveca tensed at the sight of Beryl Bliss sidling up, wearing a silly-looking frock of mustard yellow with enormous puffed sleeves, and a huge, atrocious feather headdress. Her smirk was equally nauseating. As if things couldn't get worse!

Viveca's response was frigid. "Miss Bliss, for the record, Cleo Fitzpatrick is a friend of mine, which is why, so far, I haven't made a scene. However, I have my limits. So if you don't want to be showered with the contents of my punch cup, I'd suggest you leave."

Beryl chortled. "My, my, such a temper you have, Miss Stanhope. But then, Erskine told me you can be a feisty thing—'all hot air' is how I believe he characterized you."

Viveca glared. "I'm well aware of how the two of you have plotted together. As for his 'all hot air' theory, would you care to test it out between the two of us?"

"Tsk, tsk, my dear, try to control yourself," Beryl chided. "Besides, who are you to act so huffy, so high and mighty? Erskine Pendergraf may be a cad, but you've really gone slumming with that scamp Maxwell Beecher—"

"How dare you!" Viveca ranted. "Max is a thousand times better man—"

"Than Erskine?" Beryl laughed. "Really? Well, who do you think suggested I try to ruin you in the first place?"

Viveca was stunned. "You—you can't mean Max."

"Oh, but I do."

"You're a liar."

"Am I?" Beryl's eyes gleamed with sadistic pleasure.

"Yes."

Beryl chuckled softly. "As much as I hate to disillusion you, Miss Stanhope, Max Beecher is the very one who gave me the idea of exposing you as the charlatan you really are. If you don't believe me, just go ask lover boy yourself."

Before Viveca could hurl her cup of punch, Beryl flipped her skirts and sashayed away.

Viveca stood reeling. *Max* had set these horrible events into motion? It was he who had betrayed her, tried to ruin her life? It simply couldn't be true! Oh, God, let it not be true!

A moment later, with anguished eyes she watched Max rush up, all excited. Regarding her wan face, he gripped her hand. "Darling, are you all right? You look as if you've seen a ghost, and surely this hotel is far too new to be haunted."

She flashed him a weak smile. "I'm all right."

"Good, because I have wonderful news. It's over."

She frowned. "What's over?"

"Erskine is going to leave you alone—leave town, with Beryl Bliss."

"I see. How did you arrange that?"

"Do you remember when I went to Atlanta?"

"Yes."

"Well, I did have family business to attend to, but I also engaged the services of a detective agency. Their branch in San Francisco investigated Erskine, and—"

"Yes?" she cut in tensely.

"Viveca, not only did he betray you, he also embezzled seventy-five thousand dollars from your father."

"What?" Viveca felt as if she'd been punched in the stomach.

Max beamed with pride. "He'll be returning the money to you. I insisted."

Viveca was still struggling to absorb the shock of everything he'd said. "My God. So Erskine actually did steal from my father?"

"He did indeed, like the filthy, lying miscreant he is. If you like, I can show you the proof."

She shook her head in disbelief. "How could I have been such a fool?"

"You mustn't blame yourself."

She stared up at his triumphant face and felt disillusionment and doubt creeping in. "But—but why didn't you tell me you were investigating him?"

"I was going to, darling, as soon as I had the goods on him. But actually, he made it easy for me by showing up tonight."

"You couldn't have trusted me and let me handle it, right?" she asked bitterly.

"Viveca, please." He frowned. "What's wrong? You can't be that upset just because I was investigating Erskine without telling you."

Turning away, she muttered thickly, "Ah—but perhaps there's much you haven't told me."

"Such as?"

She gave a rueful laugh. "Now that I think of it, your secretiveness regarding Erskine makes sense. You investigated him out of guilt, didn't you?"

"What do you mean, guilt?"

She whirled to face him, drawing an angry, seething breath. "Guilt because you're the one who unleashed Beryl Bliss on me in the first place."

He groaned. "Did she tell you that?"

"My God. So it's true!"

"Viveca, please—"

"Well, I don't hear you denying it!"

He waved a hand in misery. "Viveca, darling, try to understand. That was ages ago, soon after we first met, when I was so exasperated because you wouldn't sell me your house, when we were still on tenterhooks—"

"As if that excuses your conduct! You mean you actually did it? You set Beryl Bliss loose on me?"

"I only dangled a suggestion before her—"

"A suggestion that almost ruined my life!"

He clutched her arm and spoke earnestly. "I know, darling, and I've regretted it every day since."

"Then why didn't you tell me?"

"Would you have given me a chance if I had?"

She was silent, pinning him with her accusatory stare.

"Viveca, I've done everything I can to fix things," he continued passionately. "I was wrong. Dead wrong. And I humbly apologize."

Again she did not speak.

He appeared nearly desperate. "Darling, please—"

As he would have advanced, she held up a hand. "I don't know, Max. I don't know what to believe anymore, whom I can trust. There are just too many things you haven't told me."

"Viveca, that's all of it, I swear. There's nothing else."

"Really?" she asked bitterly, fighting the rise of hot tears. "Why do I doubt that, Max? Perhaps because you're like a puppet master, trying to make me dance on your string. After Erskine betrayed me, I promised myself that never again would I allow any man to use me, control me that way. But, fool that I am, here I am doing it all over again."

"Viveca, please, that just isn't the case—"

"You wanted my trust, Max. But after what you've done, how can I ever give it?"

Now he was silent.

"I've heard enough. Please, just take me home."

"Viveca—"

"Do it or I'll ask Judge Endicott to fetch me."

"Very well." With a groan, he escorted her toward the door.

Chapter Thirty-five

After dropping off Viveca, Maxwell circled back to town, stopping at his club to have a drink. Sipping bourbon at the bar, he winced at the memory of the anger and reproach in Viveca's eyes as he'd left her, and wondered why he couldn't seem to get through to her. Yes, soon after they'd first met, he'd foolishly incited Beryl Bliss against her—but couldn't she see how much he regretted it, how heartsick he was over having hurt her?

Why did she distrust his every motive? Instead of realizing he wanted to protect her, she kept accusing him of wanting to control her life. Instead of acknowledging that he had acted in her best interests, she bristled because he had hidden things from her.

Now she'd insisted on time for herself, to sort things out. That sounded ominous. They needed to work things out together, not apart.

How could he convince her that he wanted only the best for her, for them? That she had changed him irrevocably? That he loved her.

He had to try. Moreover, he couldn't honor her request for

a separation, or leave her alone too long. Especially not with that snake Erskine Pendergraf still in town.

Back at home, Viveca continued to reel in the aftermath of the evening's shocking events and appalling disclosures. She could scarcely believe that Erskine had shown up, and tried to blackmail her into marrying him. Or that Maxwell had investigated Erskine without telling her. Or that Erskine had stolen from her father, from *her!*

Worst of all, it was Max who had set many of those horrible events into motion, by betraying her with Beryl Bliss. It was all almost too much to comprehend, and painful beyond belief. She paced the parlor, on the verge of tears.

She hadn't really learned her lesson, had she? she asked herself bitterly. Again and again, she had trusted people—trusted *men*. And all of them had let her down. Erskine, Aubrey, Max. With Max it was worst of all, she realized. For she loved him. Really, *really* loved him, as she'd never loved anyone before. For nothing else could bring such intense pain as she felt now.

Even as she was struggling against sobs, a familiar voice drawled, "Why, hello, dear. Having a difficult night of it?"

She whirled to see her adversary lounging in the archway. Revulsion swept her. "Erskine! What are you doing here?"

Features harsh and sweaty, he stepped forward and extended a bank draft. "I'm on my way out of town with Miss Bliss—"

"Miss Bliss!"

"Indeed, the darling creature is waiting outside in my carriage," he sneered. "But first, your lover insisted I give you this."

Viveca took the bank draft and stared at the sum—eighty thousand dollars! She felt almost numb. Strange how, at the moment, the money meant everything and it meant nothing. "So there it is—everything you stole from my father."

He gave a bitter laugh. "I could take issue with that, but why bother? Your lover has contrived a case against me, and threatened me with the authorities if I don't pay you off."

Viveca shook her head in disgust. "Still making excuses for yourself, aren't you, Erskine? Well, I know the truth now—the full truth. You are a liar, a thief and a cad."

He grasped her arms. "Does your lover know the truth about you?"

She shoved him away. "What do you mean?"

"How you shamelessly threw yourself at me—how *you*, in fact, seduced *me*? And that when my conscience got the better of me, when I tried to break it off and confessed my transgressions to my dear wife, how you begged me to stay, clinging to me like a pitiful—"

His words were cut short as she slapped him, hard. This time he slapped her back, all but setting her head spinning. Even as she cried out in anger and pain, he grabbed her wrists.

"Not so brave now, are you, my dear? Now that he's not here to protect you—"

"But I here," uttered a high-pitched voice.

It all happened in the blink of an eye. Viveca heard the words, then Winnie vaulted into the room, caught Erskine around the neck with a clenched elbow and pressed a knife to his throat. Eyes gleaming with malice, she hissed, "You touch Miss Viveca again, you miserable viper, and I slit your t'roat."

Staring horrified at Winnie, Erskine was reduced to pleading. "Viveca, please, get this awful creature off me!"

Viveca could only smile. "You brought this on yourself, Erskine."

"Viveca, for God's sake—"

Even as he struggled and beseeched her, Miguel limped into the room, his dark face gripped with tension. "Miss Viveca, you all right?"

She nodded. "Yes, Miguel. Why don't you help Winnie escort my guest to the train station?"

"Yeah," seconded Winnie. "You help, Miguel. Get Ruvi, too. He cut dis snake to mincemeat if he give us de bodderation."

"He'll *what?*" cried Erskine.

Viveca couldn't contain a laugh; Winnie was so fierce.

"*Sí*, Winnie. I get Ruvi," agreed Miguel, hurrying out.

Wild-eyed, Erskine continued to implore Viveca. "Viveca, I beg you—"

"Good-bye, Erskine. I'd say you've made your bed and you can lie in it." As Winnie dragged him toward the door, the knife still at his neck, Viveca quickly added, "Winnie, just promise me you won't hurt him with that knife."

"I promise." To Erskine, she snarled, "Now git out de door."

Viveca heard the front door slam, followed by the carriage rattling off. She collapsed onto the couch and stared in awe at Erskine's bank draft.

A few moments later she heard the front door bang open, and Max dashed into the room. "Darling, are you all right?"

She stood. He appeared so gravely concerned, she was hard-pressed not to rush into his arms, but her pain was still too great. "Yes, I'm fine."

"Have I lost my mind, or did I just pass a carriage conveying Erskine, Nelly Bly and three of your servants?"

"Yes. Erskine just paid me a little visit, and I asked Winnie and the others to see him and Miss Bliss to the train station."

Stepping closer, he stared horrified at her face. "My God."

Viveca held up the bank draft. "He gave me the money he stole from my father."

"Damn the money!" Max grasped her arms and eyed her frantically. "That son of a bitch hit you!"

She grinned crookedly. "You should see him."

Max was not amused. "I'll go kill him."

She grasped his hand. "Max, please, don't. He's gone, and it's over. Don't do something foolish that could send you to prison and prevent us . . ."

Now he snapped to attention. "Prevent us from what, Viveca?"

Realizing she'd said too much, she turned away.

Firmly she was turned. "From what, darling?" Max asked, his heart in his eyes.

Fighting tears, she said, "Prevent us from being together."

"Oh, darling!" He pulled her into his arms, and the bank draft fluttered to the floor. He kissed her wildly, hungrily, his lips devouring her cheeks, her mouth, her throat. "Does that mean you've forgiven me?"

"I . . ." Even as he would have kissed her again, she pushed him away. "Not so fast, Max."

He gave a groan, his features taut with guilt. "I know. I still owe you the world's most heartfelt apology for unleashing Miss Bliss on you. I don't know how, darling, but somehow, I swear, I'll make that up to you and regain your trust. What if I kiss your feet every day for the rest of our lives?"

"That might be an apt beginning," she conceded, fighting a smile. But as he would have grabbed her again, she braced a hand on his chest. "Otherwise, Max, I'm placing you on probation."

"Probation?"

"You're going to have to regain my trust—"

"I understand, darling. Believe me, I will."

"And you're going to have to stop trying to control me, stop keeping things from me."

"My life is an open book to you from this day forward," he vowed fiercely.

"And if we're going to make it, you're going to have to start trusting me, treating me as an equal—"

"I will, darling. But don't ever ask me not to protect you. Keeping you safe will always be my first priority."

She ran her fingers down his sinewy chest. "Well, I don't mind a show of masculine muscle every now and again. Which is another reason I think I love you so much."

"You love me?" His eyes were alive with joy. "Oh, darling, I love you too, with all my heart. And speaking of which"— he grinned—"come here, you ravishing creature."

Viveca laughed as he scooped her into his arms and bore her off up the stairs.

Chapter Thirty-six

Toward dawn, Viveca and Max were dozing in her bed when Winnie burst in. Shoving her arms akimbo, she stared daggers at Max. "Mr. Beecher, what you doin' in Miss Viveca bed? After I done told you neber come round here—"

By now Viveca had sat up and was glaring at her housekeeper. "Winnie, what is the meaning of this intrusion?"

Winnie angrily waved a hand. "I told you, I'm your fren' now, Miss Viveca, and I swears to protect you from bad mons like him."

Although fighting a smile, Viveca retorted, "He isn't bad, and I can protect myself."

"He a devil wit de ladies. Ever'body know."

Max, looking deliciously disheveled, sat up and grinned.

Viveca grinned back at him. "Well, he isn't a devil with me—er, except in the nicest way. And not that it's any of your business, Winnie, but Mr. Beecher has repeatedly offered to marry me."

Winnie harrumphed. "Then why you not do it?"

"Indeed, Miss Viveca, why not?" Max teased.

Wrinkling her nose at him, Viveca turned back to Winnie.

"That's between Mr. Beecher and myself. Now I think you've invaded our privacy quite long enough, Winnie. I want you to leave."

But Winnie held her ground, tapping her toe and sneering at Max. "He still a snake in de grass, jes' like dat bad mon and his ginnygog me and de boys take 'way last night. And he deserve his sufferation, jes' like 'dem other two."

"What on earth is she saying?" Max inquired.

Viveca grimaced, getting an uneasy feeling from Winnie's last words. "I'm not sure, but . . . Winnie, what is this about 'sufferation'?"

"Ease up, mistress, everyt'ing fit 'n' frock, you see." But Winnie's smile was perverse as she skittered out the door.

"Winnie, wait up!" Viveca called, but she was too late. She glanced at Max. "Heavenly days, Max, what do you suppose she—er, they—"

"We'd best get dressed, go downstairs and find out," came his grim response.

When they entered the kitchen moments later, Viveca was shocked to see Winnie, Miguel and Ruvi all seated at the table wearing matching guilty expressions. "What is going on here?" she demanded.

Ruvi popped up, hastily offering her his seat.

"Mistress, please, sit down," beseeched Winnie. "We gots somet'in' to tell you."

"Oh, brother," Viveca muttered, slipping into the vacant chair.

Max was lounging against a wall. Placing his arms akimbo, he scowled at Winnie. "Let's hear it."

Winnie nodded and turned to Viveca. "Mistress, it all begin with Miguel here."

"Miguel?" Viveca stared at him, and he averted his gaze.

"Yes, din' I tell you de poor boy misguided? Well, you see, mistress, dat devil woman what done you wrong—"

"You mean Beryl Bliss?" Viveca interjected.

"Yes'um. Dat bad chile have de evil eye on you, mistress.

An' she pay Miguel here to put de crosses and sufferations on you."

"She what?" Even as Miguel began to cringe, Viveca cried, "You mean she bribed him to target me?"

"Yes'um. She bribe de poor boy. So Miguel, he put on de black frock and veil and give you de bodderation in de night."

"He did what?"

"Till dat midnight in your room when I save you and stop his mischief for good."

But Viveca was beyond hearing her. Outraged, she shot to her feet and whirled on Miguel. "You mean you're the one who attacked me in my room with a knife?"

"Someone attacked you with a knife?" Max exclaimed.

"And you had the gall to disguise yourself as a woman!" Viveca cried.

"What woman?" Max demanded.

Miguel was cowering and nodding rapidly. "*Sí* senorita. I the one. *Lo siento mucho.*"

Max sprang forward, grabbing the small man by his arms and yanking him to his feet. "You little scamp! So Nelly Bly bribed you to hurt Miss Stanhope?"

Miguel trembled and violently shook his head. "No, senor. Not hurt. She only pay me to scare her, make her flee *esta casa.* She want Senorita Stanhope's man, the *hombre de Dios.*"

"You mean Father Parish?"

"*Sí*, senor."

"She paid you to scare Viveca away so she could have my cousin?"

"*Sí.*"

Max waved a fist. "I'll kill her! As for you—".

But even as Max would have punched Miguel, Winnie sprang between the two. "Please, sir, don't hurt Miguel. He no high-steppa, not no more. Ole' Winnie make him see de light. He help me last night and redeem himself, along wit' Ruvi."

Max glared at Winnie.

Viveca glanced skeptically at Ruvi, who grinned at her. "And just what has Ruvi been doing? Why should he need redemption?"

Winnie smiled sheepishly. " 'Cause he play de werewolf to taunt you, mistress. But he not do dat no more."

Viveca stared hard at Ruvi. "Was he pretending?"

He merely continued grinning.

"Don't be vex, mistress," Winnie beseeched. "We all confess sins and get salvation dis mornin' outside de A.M.E. church."

Viveca was puzzled as well as perturbed. "And what sins did you have to atone for, Winnie?"

Winnie lowered her gaze. "I a bad cook an' housekeeper."

Viveca hooted a laugh. "Amen. But besides that." Drawing a deep breath, she ordered, "Tell me what the three of you did last night."

Winnie hesitated a moment, then sheepishly confessed, "Well, we take dem two away to the train station just like you ast', dat bad mon and his nasty girl—"

"You mean Mr. Pendergraf and Miss Bliss?"

"Yes'um. Dein—"

"Then?" Viveca prompted.

Winnie's face lit up with vindictive pleasure. "Dein we tie dem up real good, sneak dem on de train and put dem in bed together in de Pullman car."

"You did what?" Viveca gasped, choking on a laugh.

"Saints preserve us," Max muttered with a groan that ended in a grin.

Winnie was preening proudly. "Oh, yes'um, we left dem two dere all a'flailin' and a'groanin', like de sinners dey be. De conductor mon, he should be finding dem two vipers right about now."

"All fit to be tied, I presume," Viveca quipped, and everyone chuckled.

"At least we din' dose dem wit zombie powder and bury dem alive," Winnie continued matter-of-factly.

"You mean you actually *considered* that?" Viveca inquired, wide-eyed.

Winnie's guilty grin confirmed that they had, indeed.

"Why, Winnie, I'm shocked at you," Viveca chided, although with a shameful lack of conviction.

Max stepped forward and wrapped an arm around Viveca's waist. "Actually, my love, I'm disappointed."

"You are?" Viveca asked.

Max solemnly winked at the housekeeper. "Were it not for Winnie's Christian generosity, we might all have gotten to go dig up zombies this morning."

At that image, everyone convulsed into laughter.

That evening, Max took Viveca out for a scrumptious dinner at the DeSoto. As they dined on lobster and sipped champagne, he reached across their small, candlelit table and clutched her hand. "Don't you feel relieved to have things resolved now?"

She smiled at him, noting how wonderfully handsome he looked in his dark suit with the candleglow highlighting his striking features and gleaming in his dark hair. "Oh, yes. Erskine and that abominable Bliss woman have left town. My house is no longer infested with ghosts—"

"Although we still have Alex and Lorelei to contend with."

She glanced up sharply. "You still see her?"

"Yes, though only faintly."

"Me, too. I mean, I still see a shadow of Alex. Much as we've tried, we're never been able to fully exorcise those two." Taking a sip of champagne, she mused, "What do you suppose they want?"

He appeared intrigued by her question. "Well, maybe they want what we want, darling—to be together."

Her heart was warmed by his eloquent declaration. "How sweet, Max, and you may be right. But it seems to me that they already are together. I mean, they've never hesitated to—er—well, you know . . ."

"Yes, dear?"

She leaned forward, and despite her blooming cheeks, asked, "Haven't you ever seen them making love?"

He feigned horror. "Viveca, my darling voyeur, whatever have you been doing? I'm getting jealous."

"But you haven't answered my question."

"Perhaps because I think your question is best saved for later—later tonight, that is."

"Max!"

"Indeed, I expect you to supply us with lots of depraved ideas."

"You rogue!"

He chuckled. "At least things have calmed down overall, and I no longer have to fear you're in mortal danger." He wagged a finger at her. "Though I could have roasted your delicate hide for not telling me you'd been attacked in your bedroom at knifepoint—twice."

"Max, settle down, it's over," she soothed.

He feigned a growl.

Struggling not to laugh, she continued, "I am so relieved now that the mysteries of Ruvi and the woman with the knife—also known as Miguel—have been solved. But was it really necessary to send the two of them packing to the River Street Boardinghouse?"

"Absolutely," he countered vehemently. "I don't want those two rascals anywhere near the woman I love—so if I have to board them up like a couple of mad dogs, so be it."

She had to grin. "Well, it looks like everything has been settled quite nicely."

"Not quite. One other issue remains."

"Oh?"

"Us." Clutching her hand, he asked, "Viveca, will you marry me?"

Though deeply touched by his proposal, she could only sigh. "Max, I just don't know."

"Don't you love me?"

"Yes, of course I do."

"And surely you must realize how much I love you?"

"I do. But I feel like I'm just now realizing my dreams, becoming my own person—"

"As well as financially independent," he pointed out with a touch of bitterness. "You don't really need me now, do you?"

"Max!" she scolded. "Of course I need you. And you're the one who saw to it that I became financially independent. So of course I'm grateful—"

"Viveca, I don't want you to marry me out of gratitude."

"I wouldn't."

"But?" he challenged.

She sighed heavily. "Max, I know you want to do the right thing. But I'm not sure you're really prepared for all the sacrifices marriage involves."

A grudging smile pulled at his mouth. "You mean like giving up wine, women and song?"

"Yes. Something like that. I'm just afraid your heart's not in it."

"There you are wrong, Viveca," he whispered intensely. "My heart is entirely with you."

"And mine with you."

"Then why can't we be together?" he cried in frustration. "You still can't completely trust me, can you? Damn it, I'm not Erskine, I'm not even Aubrey—"

She touched his arm. "I know, Max, and I'm supremely grateful you're not either of them. But take some time. Be very certain about this—"

"I am."

"Take a few days at least. For my sake."

He sighed. "Very well, darling. But you'll see—nothing will change."

"I'll hope so, Max. I'll hope so."

On the way back to her house, Viveca thought over Max's words. Yes, she felt he still had a ways to go in their relationship—but didn't she, as well? Couldn't she make a leap of faith and try to trust him? Though he was a rascal, though they'd been to hell and back together, ever since they'd come together as a couple, she'd had his undying loyalty. She could see that now. And she loved him so. Could she contemplate life without him? She'd certainly be miserable if they parted now. Wasn't it worth another spin of the dice, when the prize might well be eternal happiness for them both? Staring at him beside her, his striking features outlined in moonlight, watching him turn and wickedly wink at her, she suspected her resistance would not last long . . .

Moments later when he escorted her into her parlor, she was astonished to find Hilda Patertavish awaiting them on the settee. The woman popped up and asked petulantly, "Where on earth have you two been?"

"Out to dinner," Viveca explained. "Forgive me, Hilda; did we have an appointment I forgot about?"

"No. But I've been waiting here for over an hour with only the company of that evil-eyed, skulking Jamaican woman of yours."

Viveca chuckled. "She's appointed herself my protector."

"Well, pity you."

"Hilda, what are you doing here?" Max inquired.

She thrust her head high. "Well, first of all, I'll have you both know I'm prostrate with disappointment over missing all the high drama at the DeSoto last night. Tell me, Viveca, did that awful scoundrel from California actually appear there, along with Beryl Bliss?"

"He did, indeed," Viveca grimly confirmed.

Viveca and Max quickly filled in Hilda on the evening's shenanigans, including how they'd forced Erskine Pendergraf to cough up the money he owed Viveca, then leave town with Beryl Bliss.

"Well, good riddance to them both!" Hilda declared. "Such poetic justice."

"We agree," Max concurred rather irritably. "And now that you've assuaged your craving for gossip, Hilda, may I suggest—"

"Oh, hush, Maxwell, I know you're dying to get Viveca

alone, and I shan't take long." Hilda waved an elegant hand toward the card table. "I've decided it's high time we dispense with the remaining ghosts in this house, so they may no longer ruin Viveca's prospects—and accordingly, I've brought along my Ouija board."

"Your Ouija board!" Viveca cried. "I just knew you practiced spirituality."

Hilda gave a shrug. "Along with about half of this town. We have our little meetings, our discreet societies. But tell anyone and I'll—"

"Don't worry, Hilda, you know you can trust me," Viveca hastily reassured her, laughing. "But as you're aware, we've already had two exorcisms of sorts here at the house, and neither has been fully effective. I'm not certain we can completely end the hauntings."

Hilda wagged a finger. "Ah, but sometimes it's best to ask the ghosts themselves what they want."

Viveca was intrigued. "You know, Winnie once told me something quite similar."

Hilda scowled at Max. "Of course, I had not thought to include you, Maxwell. Unbelievers can—"

"Oh, don't worry, he's a believer," Viveca cut in.

"Are you, now?" Hilda grinned at Max in fascination.

Max coughed. "Yes. As it happens, I've a ghost of my own."

"Do tell!" Hilda urged gleefully.

Max glowered. "Shouldn't we deal with Viveca's situation first?"

Hilda rolled her eyes. "Very well, Maxwell, we'll exorcise your ghost another time. Come along now, children, sit at the table."

Exchanging grins, Max and Viveca did as bid. Hilda blew out all the lamps and candles in the room except for one taper, which she placed on the card table. As Hilda took her seat, Viveca noted that the atmosphere in the room had turned downright spooky—shadows were climbing the walls, sinister shapes seeming to lurk in the corners. The perfect ambience for ghosts and Ouija boards.

Hilda directed Max and Viveca to place their fingers on the planchette. "Now, no moving your fingers, children," she scolded solemnly. "Let the spirits speak through you. Very well, Viveca, we're ready. Ask your question."

"My question?" Viveca repeated, her stomach doing a thud. "Er—you mean about what the ghosts really want?"

"Precisely."

Though she felt ridiculous, Viveca glanced at the shimmery walls of the room, then back at the board. Urgently she whispered, "Alex, Lorelei, I summon you to, er . . . please, just tell us why you haunt us. Tell us what you want."

For several charged moments nothing happened—nothing could be seen but the kaleidoscopic reflections of the taper, nothing heard but the ticking of the clock on the mantel, the slight creaking and moaning of the house itself. Then Viveca went wide-eyed as the planchette began to quiver on the board. A moment later it squeaked into motion, slowly sliding about the board—pausing first on the letter "g," then on the letter "o."

Max and Viveca glanced at one another in astonishment. "Did you move it?" she demanded.

"Hell, no," he answered. "Did you?"

She vehemently shook her head.

Hilda clapped her hands. "Well, well, there we have it! Our answer. 'Go.' The ghosts want you to leave, don't you think?"

Again, Viveca and Max could only gaze at one another in wonder. "Well, I suppose so," she muttered.

Suddenly he shouted a laugh. "Well, I'll be damned."

"What?" she asked.

"You know, Viveca, I think our two perverse little ghosts were being matchmakers."

"What?" she cried. "After the way they treated us, torturing us and trying to . . ." Realizing she was about to say too much, she clamped her mouth shut.

"Don't you see?" Max went on excitedly. "They were driving us toward each other—and away from here. 'Go.' It was the simplest, most basic message in the world—but we couldn't see it."

Viveca thought it over, and laughed. "They wanted us to leave so they can be together. You're right, Max."

"What about me?" Hilda interjected, pouting. "Aren't I right, too?"

"Of course you are," Viveca assured her, patting her hand. "You're the soul of good friendship, the one who has helped us solve this final riddle."

"Good," Hilda replied smugly. "Well, that decides it. Obviously, the two of you should marry and move elsewhere, don't you think?"

"A splendid idea," Maxwell concurred. "Right, darling?"

At first Viveca hesitated, then she grinned at Max with all the love in her heart. "Yes, of course, we should do just that. After all, who would dare to defy Queen Hilda?"

Epilogue

In a vast, light-flooded bedroom in a house on Bull Street, Viveca Beecher sat on the magnificent rosewood bed she shared with her husband, a photograph album on her lap, her tiny baby daughter asleep at her breast. Although little Daphne Anne Beecher possessed her mother's dainty feminine features, she'd also been blessed with her daddy's wonderful thick, shiny dark hair and midnight-blue eyes. Every time Viveca looked at her child, her heart welled with a love that was soul-deep.

While the infant made soft sucking sounds, her little pink mouth still latched to her mother's nipple, Viveca leafed through memories of the past year. Max had chronicled their journey with his marvelous new Kodak Pocket Camera. There were shots of her and Max's wedding, of their honeymoon in Paris, the two of them embracing amid the blooms of the Tuileries. Other shots pictured them breaking ground on their huge Victorian home—where they now lived in blissfully spook-free fashion. There was also an image of a very pregnant Viveca strolling through Forsyth Park, and many portraits of their tiny daughter, Daphne, who'd been born only three months ago. She'd been conceived on their wedding night, both Viveca and Max believed . . . and what a night that had been!

Viveca especially loved the picture of Daphne's christening day. There they were, Daphne in her fabulous handmade linen gown, with Max and Viveca beaming as the proud parents, and Hilda serving as the equally delighted godmother. And just as Hilda had predicted, the image of the four of them gathered around a stiffly smiling Aubrey Parish was sweet revenge personified.

There was a rap at her door, and Winnie poked her head in. "Mr. Max, he back from de market and heading up dis way."

"Thanks, Winnie."

Winnie stepped inside, grinning at the sight of the baby, whom she doted on and protected as did Viveca. Pausing next to the bed, she stroked little Daphne's soft cheek. "How my little angel doin' today?"

"Just wonderful."

"You want me take her?"

"Do it and you'll be fighting with her daddy over her," Viveca teased.

Winnie cackled. "Mr. Max, he needs to learn to mind old Winnie."

"Don't hold your breath."

"Later, den." With a wink, Winnie retreated.

Soon Max slipped inside the room with a broad grin on his face and a corsage of red roses in his hand. "Happy Fourth of July, darlings," he murmured, crossing over to the bed and kissing Viveca, then the sleeping baby. Placing the corsage on the bedside table, he sighed. "What an amazing sight—my beautiful wife nursing my adorable daughter."

"You've seen it every day for three months now."

"And it will never stop filling me with awe," he replied hoarsely. "Well, hadn't you two best get ready for the picnic?"

She nodded. "I was just taking a moment to look at the album."

He sat down beside her. "Memories of our first year together?"

"Oh, yes. It's hard to believe we've been married that long, and already have Daphne."

"Indeed, in a few days' time we'll have an anniversary to celebrate."

"So we will." She shook her head wonderingly. "The time has been so joyous, it has just flown past."

"I agree, my love."

With a catch in her voice, she murmured, "You've been a wonderful husband, Max. Living up to your promises in every way."

He clutched her hand and kissed it. "And you've been the wife, the lover, of my dreams. Dreams that came true, this time." He carefully scooped up the baby, and she made tiny sighing sounds as he nestled her against his shoulder. Nuzzling the baby's cheek, he whispered, "Well, darling, cover up that delectable breast and put on your fanciest frock. We're off to Stanhope Park."

Viveca shook her head. "I still can't believe you renamed our old square after me—this after you bought all the houses and turned them over to the city as a public park."

"But there's surely plenty hereabouts with the Beecher name attached to it, not the least of which are you, my pet, and our precious child," Max replied tenderly. "I wanted to do homage to the woman who has brought such a remarkable change to my life."

"Oh, Max," she said dreamily. "Formidable as you can be, you really are a lamb at heart."

He feigned a fierce scowl. "But I can be a lion, too—you mustn't forget."

"Believe me, I won't."

He tweaked her nose. "Come along now and powder your pretty face. I want to show off my girls."

* * *

Viveca's favorite part of the revitalized "Stanhope Park" had to be the handsome brass plaque that stood on its ornate post before the square. She knew the inscription by heart; after all, she had written it herself:

> *Stanhope Park*
> *Dedicated to the citizens of Savannah*
> *And to the passionate memory of the star-crossed lovers,*
> *Alex and Lorelei.*
> *May the living walk the light.*
> *May their spirits rule the night.*

Approaching the plaque with Max by her side and Daphne in her arms, Viveca happily reflected that the living did, indeed, "walk the light" here. Gaily dressed families were gathered about recently installed picnic tables beneath the magnificent oak. Children romped on playground equipment where the old Tupper house used to be. Sunshine, flowers and birds drenched the scene.

In a stroke of pure genius, Max had decided that they should convert Viveca's old home into a living tribute to the square's "undead" occupants. Thus the "Hangman's House Museum" stood proudly on Lost Lane, its front door draped with cobwebs. Viveca's former abode had been transformed into a major Savannah tourist attraction, where visitors were greeted by black-gowned docents who presented memorabilia of the old Hangman's Square, who wove the tragic tale of Alex and Lorelei and told spine-chilling yarns of Murfa Divine and the Oleander Man.

Beyond the museum in the bunting-wreathed gazebo, a small band played "Dixie," the jaunty tune filling the arbor beyond, with several families listening on the steps of Max's old house, now a public library branch. Across the square, the Cunningham house, renamed Stanhope House, stood well kept as always.

"Quite a change, eh, dear?" Max murmured.

"I can't believe the magic you wove with this square," she

murmured. "Especially Hangman's House Museum. What better homage for Alex and Lorelei."

He chuckled wickedly. "Indeed, and we even retained the old bathtub. After all, I couldn't evict the infamous lovers' favorite trysting spot."

"Not to mention ours," she teased back. "Yes, I'm glad the bathtub has been retained—although I must say the lady's negligee draped over it has raised a few eyebrows—"

"Along with the bottle of champagne on the washstand," he finished wryly.

"You thought of everything, Max. You were especially generous to provide Miss Lilac an apartment in town. Emmett is devoted to her, and she almost never mentions her dead servants anymore."

"I think we've all had a more than adequate acquaintance with the dead," Max commented wryly.

"And you reshaped the Cunningham house into a public gathering place."

"With all the clubs and committees meeting locally, a facility was sorely needed."

"I agree. Hilda is over here all the time, and keeps telling me I must get out more." Ruefully she added, "She also reports that Miguel and Ruvi are 'quite' behaving themselves. It was so clever of you to sponsor them as permanent city employees, as caretakers for the square—"

"And allow them to continue to live in the Hangman's House Museum basement. Let's face it, dear, they belong here, with the creatures of the night."

"Amen." She laughed.

"God knows we couldn't employ them in our home; tolerating Winnie is bad enough."

Viveca eyed him with reproach. "Max, I think she's starting to mellow."

"No comment."

Gazing about, she murmured poignantly, "I do have a feeling the spirits are at peace now, that they got what they wanted."

"Especially in the case of Alex Fremont and his Lorelei."
Wiggling his eyebrows lecherously, he added, "They drove
us out so they might reclaim the night—and ravish their salacious souls through all eternity."

"Max!"

His grin was unabashed. "We know a bit about that, eh,
love?"

Both were laughing as Hilda Patertavish marched up,
beaming. Dressed in true Independence Day fashion, in a
blue and white striped gown and matching hat topped by a
flowing red plume, she greeted them with typical aplomb.
"Why, Viveca Beecher, you hand me that baby right now."

Grinning, Viveca handed Hilda little Daphne.

"Oh, you little doll, you!" Hilda gushed, kissing the baby.
"I'll swear your cheeks grow pinker every time I see you. Now
come along, Max and Viveca. I want you to meet some folks."

As she led them away, Max touched Viveca's arm, then gestured toward a middle-aged couple just ahead; he was tall and
slender, with a top hat and a goatee; she was short and plump,
wearing a black silk gown and matching bonnet. "Why, I
think they're the Cunninghams," Max said.

"You mean the former owners of Stanhope House?"

"Yes. It's been years since I've seen them, but I'm sure
that's them."

"Well, will wonders never cease."

The threesome paused before the couple, who regarded
them with polite curiosity. "Mr. and Mrs. Cunningham,"
Hilda announced, "may I present Mr. and Mrs. Beecher and
their darling daughter, Daphne Anne."

After a round of handshakes and "How do you do's," Mr.
Cunningham grinned at Max. "Well, Maxwell, it's been
some time since we've seen you. Congratulations on your
marriage—and your child."

"Thank you, Jon."

"And thank you for purchasing our house." He turned to
stare at it. "Looks like you've put it to good use."

"Oh, yes, Stanhope House is the social center for Savannah now," Hilda assured him. "Competing ably with the DeSoto Hotel and Tybee Island."

Viveca smiled at the bland-complexioned Mrs. Cunningham, who seemed much more reserved than her husband. "Mrs. Cunningham, after your house sold, I did wonder about your sister."

"My sister?" she asked, clearly taken aback. "You mean Elvira?"

"Well, yes." Gently Viveca continued, "I realize the two of you are estranged, but she has taken such wonderful care of your house during your absences. Last year, I saw her out gardening, and she told me about the house being up for sale. I was worried about her, and made her promise to stay in touch. But that was the last time I saw her."

Both Cunninghams were now gaping at Viveca. At last Mrs. Cunningham stammered, "I—I'm sure you must be mistaken."

"No, it was your sister, Elvira Withersmith. She and I visited a number of times, until she just disappeared—"

"Well, no wonder—she's been dead for over ten years!" Mrs. Cunningham cut in shrilly. "She's buried yonder in Colonial Cemetery."

Viveca gulped, and she and Max exchanged a stunned look. "You're jesting," she said at last.

"Why would I jest about my sister being dead?" the woman all but shouted. "Why, the awful creature went insane. She broke into our home one night and tried to murder us both in our beds!"

"She *what*?" Viveca cried.

"Have you some hearing impediment, young woman?" Mrs. Cunningham shrieked.

"Oh, my God!" Viveca declared, her eyes growing huge as realization dawned . . . and Elvira Withersmith's haunting words crept back to her. In an awed voice, Viveca whispered, "And instead of being caught, she turned the dagger on herself?"

A strangled sound escaped Mrs. Cunningham.

Viveca shot the woman a look of bitter recrimination. "And who could blame her for taking her own life, after you refused to speak to her for all those years?"

"H-how did you know all this?" the matron stammered, a hand on her fluttering bosom. "Why, Jon paid a king's ransom to keep Elvira's suicide out of the newspapers, so—er, we could bury her on consecrated grounds—"

"And hide your own culpability?" Viveca cut in harshly.

"Why, I never!" Mrs. Cunningham declared.

Viveca slowly shook her head. "You know, Mrs. Cunningham, if your sister is buried at the cemetery, I think you owe her a visit."

"*I beg your pardon?*" The woman had gone slack-jawed.

Hilda, who had been listening with fascination, spoke up excitedly. "Viveca, are you speaking of the pale, slender lady with the parasol?"

"Yes, that's her!"

Hilda waved a hand. "Why, we see her ghost all the time here, at meetings of the Ladies Beneficent Society. Sometimes she's seated on the square, sometimes out tending the flowers—"

"Yes, yes!" Viveca encouraged.

"And a few of the ladies have even run into her upstairs at Stanhope House. Always gives them quite a fright, especially when she walks through walls and such."

At this, Mrs. Cunningham uttered a horrified cry, and her husband gripped her arm to steady her.

"So Elvira's still around, and she did find her place," Viveca remarked wonderingly.

"So it seems." Raising an eyebrow, Hilda turned to the still-reeling Mrs. Cunningham. "Yes, Virginia, I think you definitely have unresolved business to attend to with your sister. I can't believe you actually drove the poor creature to her death. You should go over to the cemetery and apologize, give her some peace, for heaven's sake."

"Why, I never!" Mrs. Cunningham retorted, gasping. She turned to her husband. "Jon, we must circulate."

"Er—as you wish, dear," he replied awkwardly, leading her away.

Watching the two stride off, Viveca shook her head in awe. "Well, I'll be damned. So I actually met the Poor Relation."

"So it appears," agreed Max.

"Of course she told me her story herself—I just didn't connect it up at the time." Viveca snapped her fingers. "No wonder Elvira disappeared right after the second exorcism. Bless her soul, I do hope she's at peace now."

"I'm sure she is, and what a fascinating turn," Hilda concurred. "I can't wait to share this tidbit with the other ladies. Not to mention, my dear Viveca, I think you've stolen twenty years off Virginia Cunningham—a fate she doubtless deserves after the way she treated her sister." Hilda paused ecstatically as little Daphne gurgled, and cooed back at the infant. "Well, darlings, I'm off to gloat over my godchild."

As she strolled away, Viveca gazed about them. "Max, I'm so happy."

He squeezed her hand. "Me, too, darling."

"Although sometimes I do miss our little square. There's much we shared here, and left behind."

"Indeed—our houses, and the gazebo where we met."

"Yes, you and that silly gun!" Her gaze paused on the gazebo, which the band had left moments earlier. Suddenly she gasped at a hazy image she saw forming there. "Max, look!"

He craned his neck to see. "Well, I'll be damned. Looks like it's Alex and Lorelei, out in broad daylight together, embracing. Can you see—"

"Yes!" Viveca cut in ecstatically. "They're as wispy as a cloud, but they're definitely there. And they're happy, too—so happy now."

"I do agree."

"I can't believe they actually emerged in the light for once." She squeezed his hand as the image began to fade. "Oh, no, Max, now they're gone!"

"I think perhaps they just wanted to tell us thank you—and good-bye," he murmured poignantly.

"I'm glad you ascribe to them such noble motives," she rejoined. "But I do think you're right that they're at peace now." She beamed at him. "Well, shall we join the others?"

He offered his arm. "Of course, my love."

As they started off arm in arm, a slight prickling sensation at the back of her neck made Viveca glance back, frowning, at Stanhope House. As she did so she could have sworn she spotted Elvira Withersmith's nebulous hand waving at her from an upstairs window. . . .

EUGENIA RILEY
Bushwhacked
Groom

When Cole Reklaw offers a prime parcel of ranchland to the first of his five children to marry and produce a grandchild, his daughter Molly vows to win. She heads for Reklaw Gorge—where her pa had once "bushwhacked" his future bride off a stagecoach—only to watch that very vehicle comes crashing into the gorge, bringing with it Molly's own "hero" from across time, Lucky Lamont.

All Lucky ever wanted was to get even with his girlfriend for betraying him. Instead he finds himself in the clutches of a hellcat who declares she will marry him, or else. Then Molly Reklaw goads Lucky into a reckless kiss that soon results in a shotgun wedding! With the bride set on gaining the prize and the groom burning for revenge, can love find a way for *both* of them to win?

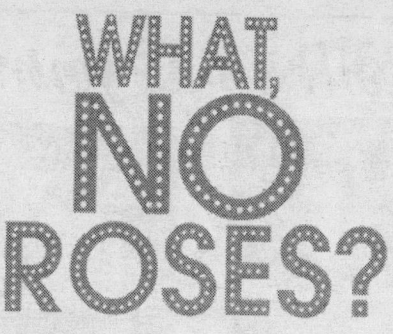

WHAT, NO ROSES?

MARIANNE MANCUSI

Unless Dora Duncan can stop it, it's going to be another St. Valentine's Day Massacre. A year ago, her (now ex) boyfriend Nick stood her up at the worst possible moment. That was when she gave up important TV reporting. And things have been a whole lot quieter. *Too* quiet. Until now. Now she's gotta go back in time and stop that very same Nick from messing up the time-space continuum. She has to travel back to a place where everybody speaks easy and cuts a rug—and this Chicago ain't no musical. Here, there are tommy guns and torpedoes, guys and dolls, gin joints, flappers, stoolies, rats and a whole lot more; and prohibition means anything but no.

The Reluctant Miss Van Helsing
Minda Webber

Having lived long amongst London's *ton*, Ethel Jane Van Helsing is an astute female who well knows her faults. She has a face unremarkable in its plainness. And yet…at a masquerade ball, anything can happen. There, even an ugly duckling can become a swan.

But tonight is not for fowl play. You see, plain or not, Jane comes from distinguished stock: Van Helsings. And Van Helsings are slayers. Her father, the Major, showed her very early on how to use the sharp end of a stick. Tonight, everything is at stake. Something is going to get driven very deep into a heart, or she isn't…

The Reluctant Miss Van Helsing